Scholar's Plot

Scholar's Plot

A Knight AND Rogue NOVEL

HILARI BELL

 Wild Writers Books http://www.thewildwriters.com/

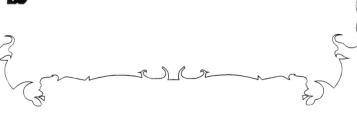

DEDICATION

This story revolves around a university, places that,
for all their faults, have been a source of reason
and enlightenment from...well, pretty much the
dawn of reason and enlightenment.
But universities rest on a broad foundation
of early education,
so I dedicate this book to the
enlighteners—to teachers, everywhere.
Because education really is "the silver bullet."

Scholar's Plot

CHAPTER 1

Fisk

I must have gone mad. Or been corrupted, horribly corrupted, all my values—not to mention simple common sense—driven right out of my head. Which was probably why I'd gone mad.

I was doing a good deed.

It was still fairly early in the evening when I rode Tipple into Slowbend. The sun was low enough to reflect in the diamond panes of the west-facing windows, casting fragments of sunlight over the cobbles and sometimes, curse it, into my eyes.

I'd spent most of the several months after I'd left Michael in Tallowsport trying to find a scam that tempted me...and failing. Curse him.

From sheer habit—never attract attention by studying a crib you plan to crack—I glanced casually at the tall gray towers of the university. They were the only tall buildings in town and dominated the view, just as coats in the university colors, black with red shoulder patches, dominated the garb of the crowd as I drew nearer to the campus.

I found a street going west, rode till I reached the river docks that formed the edge of the small city, and selected an inn there. It took a few minutes to find one that had stabling for my horse, since most of the people who visited that part of town had come down on the riverboats from Crown City. And after I found one, the stable boy made the usual joke about, "Where was rest of the show?"

I'd like to think it was Tipple's spotted hide—remarkable enough to make her owner memorable—that had kept me from finding a juicy target, settling in, and figuring out a way to siphon off a bit of that juice. I could have ditched Tipple in some nearby town and gone back for her after the scam, or even sold her outright. She was far too distinctive a mount for a con man to own.

But she'd always been my horse, as Chanticleer had always been Michael's.

I warned the stable boy about how she'd earned her name, and left him snickering. But he'd also promised to keep her away from any place liquor was stored or served, and he was old enough to be reliable.

It was easy to book a room, since the house was less than half full. We were four months from Appleon, which was when most university admissions took place. I'd lived in several university towns in my childhood, and I knew their rhythms.

When I came down the taproom was full, and if the locals ate here that promised well for the ham, cooked greens, and onion tart I ordered. I managed to fall into conversation with a couple of people as I ate and bought ale for several more, hitting my own mug sparingly. Some of their gossip was about the campus, but it usually concerned their own doings instead of the project I'd come to...research, shall we say.

I ended up talking to the tapster, which is probably where I should have started. He was plump, too young for his hair to be that thin, and his apron wasn't too badly stained. He didn't look particularly sharp, but when I came up to the bar his eyes narrowed shrewdly.

"Thinking of enrolling, sir? You're a bit older than most. Not that Pendarian don't take older students, 'deed they do."

I gave up on pretending not to be interested in the university.

"Not me, my friend. I mean, do I look like a scholar?"

"Actually, you do," he said. "Or maybe a clerk."

"Well, I'm not." I smothered my annoyance. Looking like a clerk instead of a criminal was something I used to appreciate. Only lately had it begun to annoy me. "But I've got a young brother who is a scholar, and since I was up this way my father asked me to check out Pendarian."

"Best university in the Realm, if you ask me," the tapster said. "The third that High Liege Pendarian founded, which means he had time to get it right."

I refrained from pointing out that since he'd probably only seen this university his opinion wasn't well-informed. And also that by that logic, all the universities that had been founded since Pendarian's day should be *better* than it was.

"It's not the scholarship I'm concerned about," I said, preparing to slander my nonexistent brother. "It's more what kind of rein they keep on their students. Not that Rob's a bad kid, but he's got too much brain for his own good, if you ask me..."

It was a useful gambit, as it turned out. I learned that although older students could take rooms in town if they chose, for the first two years they had to live on campus, under supervision. The campus was surrounded by a high wall and they had a gatekeeper, a "very reliable man."

I invented an interest in studying the nature of magic for my mythical brother, and got an earful about the "important project, funded by the crown itself," which was going on right now, as well as a number of other projects. Doing research all the time they were, at Pendarian.

A perfectly natural question about the dangers of messing with magic netted the information that the project was housed in an old tower, separate from the dorms and classrooms, and with tight security. No danger of some student getting involved with magica at all. And indeed, they weren't really dealing with magic, only with Gifts, so all the students were perfectly safe, as they always were, at Pendarian.

To change the subject I asked, but hadn't there been some scandal lately...?

It was a safe bet, for I've never heard of a university—or any institution with more than six people in it— that didn't have some sort of scandal going on.

Sure enough, his eyes fell. I bought another ale, and sipped on it as he assured me that scholars plagiarizing their theses were very rare at Pendarian, and that the man in question had only been a junior professor, and he'd been fired the moment he was found out.

If that was the worst scandal the place had, then it must be almost as clean as the tapster claimed. But most of my mind was considering the "tight security" around the project, and I almost missed it when he said there was a big lecture going on tonight.

Skinday is the day most guild workers have off, and universities don't hold regular classes then, either. This makes it the most common night to put on big lectures that the whole university is supposed to attend. I asked if a lot of people from the town went to those lectures, and learned that quite a few did. And if half the students lived off campus, there would be a lot of people moving past the gatekeeper all at the same time; and very shortly after that, the grounds would be almost deserted as everyone swarmed into the lecture hall.

I asked about getting a pass at this late date, and learned that since the lecture would start in just over an hour it probably wouldn't be possible.

I said I'd try and departed...not in search of a pass, but of something more easily come by.

In a university town, garb in university colors makes up most of the work in any laundry, and their drying yards have no security at all. It took me longer to locate a laundry than it did to climb the fence into the yard. Half the garments there seemed to be black coats with red shoulders, and there were even a few long cloaks with two red stripes flowing from neck to the hem. The cloaks' concealing hoods were tempting, but this early summer night was too warm. I took the time to pick a coat in my size—medium, to go with my medium brown hair and medium looks, all quite useful to a con man.

It was still a bit damp, but you can't have everything.

If I had time after I finished my errand, I might even return the... Curse it! That thought would never have crossed my mind before I'd met Michael.

By the time I emerged from the alley behind the laundry, I was near enough to the university and the hour was late enough that a number of people were flowing toward the gates. I fell into step with them. At almost twenty-one I was much of an age with the older students, though listening to them chatter about exams, and the size of the tavern maid's bosom at the Wicked Grape, I felt a thousand years older.

I didn't look forward to seeing the jeweler again. We'd first met him in Atherton Roseman's attic, where he'd helped his master keep us prisoner by creating magica collars, one of which I still sometimes felt around my neck in nightmares. His eerie madness was less disturbing to me than it had been to Michael—probably because Michael was afraid of going mad, too, though I thought if he were going to he'd have shown some sign of it before now. Instead, Michael had driven *me* mad.

When the Liege Guard had hauled the jeweler off, cringing at the bright sunlight, terrified, weeping for the loss of his pet rats, it had been perfectly natural to assure him he'd be all right. Anyone would have.

But only someone who'd been corrupted by Michael's lunacy for almost four years would have found themselves being haunted by that promise.

It wasn't all the time. I'd see a fine stone flash as a lady climbed into a carriage, and remember, not the collars that had bound Michael and me to do Tony Rose's bidding, but my promise to the jeweler who'd made them. I'd be reminded by a mouse in a trap, or a groom stitching a bit of leather...and after a few months, I'd started dreaming about the cursed fellow. Not every night, but often enough, and when I woke up, a voice in my head would whisper, "You promised he'd be all right. You don't know if 'tis so or not."

The worst thing about it was that my overactive con-science spoke with Michael's accent.

The real problem, I'd decided over the long weeks of wandering, was that I hadn't had much practice at setting my own direction in life. After I left my family, at my new and respectable brother-in-law's insistence, I'd soon been picked up by Jack—and since I was only his apprentice con man, he'd chosen our course. When Jack dumped me, I stayed on that course from sheer inertia till I met Michael...and immediately let *him* set my course.

This made it all the more ironic, and maybe fitting, that the quarrel that finally drove Michael and me apart was about my refusal to see Jack hang. I didn't think I was as spineless as my past suggested, but it was time for me to leave Michael and I was usually glad I had.

I was done with being a squire.

But I must admit, I wondered from time to time how he was doing. And it seemed to me that if I checked on the jeweler, and made sure he was well cared for, that curst annoying voice would stop whispering in my ear. Then I could finally move on, setting my own course...

It's hard to set a course, when you have no destina-tion in mind.

The Liege's guardsmen had told me where they were taking the jeweler, and that was as good a destination as any. Of course, if the poor madman wasn't being treated decently there was nothing I could do about it, but I refused to borrow the future's troubles. Getting in to see him would be trouble enough, if security on the project was as tight as the tapster had claimed.

He was right about the campus—the stone wall around it had to be twenty feet high, and the fancy wrought iron gates had no gap beneath them. There was a keeper at the gatehouse, too, and for all I knew he might be a reliable man. But now, all he did was nod and smile as a hoard of scholars and townsfolk poured past him.

I attached myself to the back of a group of students about my age, and since the best way to make it look like you're listening is to listen, I learned that Professor Darple had lost ten silver roundels on "that worthless nag" he favored, and was bound to be in a rotten mood when he graded their essays. But Connell was worse than Darple, because he was never in a good mood. I passed through the gates and into the campus without a hitch.

I considered shedding my damp coat then, but it was probably the least conspicuous garment I could wear here. In the gathering darkness those red shoulders would be less visible, even though the magica phosphor moss lamps that lined the lanes had begun to brighten. If they had those lamps all over the campus, Pendarian wasn't short of cash.

I followed the crowd down a wide avenue between two tall buildings, four and five stories tall and larger than most palaces. The avenue ended in an open square of neatly mowed grass, with yet more huge stone buildings around it, and still more beyond—a big campus, which I should have expected but somehow hadn't.

The lecture hall on the opposite side of the square was only two stories tall, but it made up for it by being almost as large as the open space I was crossing. At the top of the low steps, in front of open doors through which light streamed out and people streamed in, half a dozen students were checking lecture passes—though I noticed they didn't take them.

One of them was a girl, and the fact that they had female scholars here gave me a plausible excuse for wandering the campus in disguise. It would help if I knew one of the girls' names, but if worse came to worst, I could always claim I'd seen her in the street and fallen madly in love without knowing her name. It was silly, but I've sold stupider tales in my day.

I drifted to the edge of the crowd, then turned and walked briskly down the lane between two more buildings, like a student hurrying back to his room for the pass he'd forgotten.

If the project was housed in an "old tower" then it was probably in an older part of the campus. I took a thorough tour of the campus architecture over the next half hour. There were four main squares, and three smaller ones just to make the place more confusing. The lanes were paved with flat stones, and gravel paths marked the lesser walkways—smooth, but noisy. There were also sections that seemed older than the others, but when I finally found the tower it was surrounded by much newer structures—its original neighbors having been torn down and replaced.

Only the tower had survived. It was an old, square-style tower, not the more modern round kind, with its back against the great outer wall and a courtyard off to one side—though the yard's fence was a mere ten feet tall. I knew it was the tower I was looking for, because a bored-looking guard sat on a camp stool at the top of the steps that led up to the front door. His gaze was on something in his lap, that he worked on with small, deft motions.

He was so absorbed in his task that I walked clear across the square in front of the tower without him even noticing me. There were still a few scholars

wandering about, so lecture attendance wasn't manda-
tory, and if he had looked up it wouldn't have mattered.
I avoided the light from the scattered magica lamps,
and with only a sliver of the Creature Moon setting and
the Green Moon not yet risen, it was pretty dark.

Not your most alert guard, but no one could get
through that door without being noticed. The odds
of getting a twenty foot ladder up the outside of the
campus wall without being noticed by someone in the
street were pretty bad too.

On the other hand, there was a tree growing right up
beside the lower wall that surrounded the tower's yard,
out of sight of the door. And there might be more acces-
sible windows on the other side of the tower.

I made my way around the back of the neighboring
buildings, and walked along the campus's western wall
toward the place where the tower butted up against it.
My footsteps made no sound on grass, but it was so dark
that I barely avoided several thorny bushes. After I'd
been away from the lamps for a while my vision adapt-
ed, and it was worth it—there were three first floor windows on this side of the tower. All of them were dark,
like the windows I'd seen on the tower's upper floors in
front, but that didn't mean the jeweler wasn't there. He
preferred darkness.

Even the first floor windows were too high for me
to reach—the ground floor of the tower looked to start
about four feet above ground level—but with a bit of
searching I found a half empty rain barrel, tipped it
over, and rolled it back to the tower, as soundless as my
steps on the well-cut lawn.

I had little fear of being caught—a student prank can
explain almost anything—but my heart still beat a bit
faster as I tipped the barrel bottom up under the first
window and climbed up to inspect it.

Latched, from the inside. As was so often the case, the lock picks in my pocket were useless. Peering through the thick, bubbled glass in the dark was no help. I pulled out my pen knife and worked it into the seam between the window's edge and the frame, trying to push the latch up. It didn't budge, which probably meant it was the kind of latch that slid across instead of lifting, making that trick as useless as my picks.

I jumped down, and rolled the barrel over to the next window anyway. I hadn't much hope, but there was always a chance that someone had been careless.

No one had.

I wasn't worried about running out of time. Most university lectures last at least two hours, and that's before they start taking questions. My father would leave for a lecture after dinner and sometimes not be home till midnight. If I wanted to scramble up that tree, drop into the courtyard, and try my picks on the side door, I'd have time.

What would happen if I walked up to the front door, said I was a friend of the jeweler, and asked to see him? In the morning, in my own clothes.

I considered this as I rolled the rain barrel back to its place and tipped it upright. The Green Moon, which was almost full, was beginning to rise—not that there was moonlight on the grass, but the sky was bright enough to keep me from running into bushes.

If the jeweler was being well-treated, they might simply let me in to see him. He was sort of a prisoner—no one could let a man that mad run loose, particularly one who could work magic. Even if he'd do no harm himself, which wasn't guaranteed, he'd be prey to any villain who sought to use him—just as Tony Rose had.

There was no reason he couldn't have a visitor. If they weren't treating him well they'd refuse to let me see him, and I'd have alerted them that someone was interested, which might mean...what? Two guards? I couldn't get past one.

The alternative was to climb the tree—and returning to try my luck openly sounded more practical.

I was turning to make my way back to the lecture hall, to depart with the crowd as I'd come in, when I saw Michael walking calmly into a circle of lamplight.

Michael. *Here.*

He paused to examine the buildings around him, looking much as he had when we'd parted company. Taller and thinner than I was, with straight, light brown hair brushing his collar in a nobleman's longer cut.

He too wore a scholar's coat, and he walked from one circle of light into the next as if he belonged here, as if he had nothing to hide.

I had taught him that.

I could hear his footsteps on the gravel, drawing nearer to the shadowy corner where I stood. Rage and excitement and pain swept over me, in waves that left me shaking.

But mostly it was rage.

How dare he turn up, just when I was beginning to be able to forget about our quarrel? At least I didn't have to worry about how he was getting along without me—he was fine!

That was a good thing, because it meant that all I had to do was to see the jeweler, and when he turned out to be fine too, I could ride out of this town in the morning. And this time I'd take off for the far north, instead of dithering around on the Erran river plain as I'd been doing for the last three months.

The tree into the courtyard it was.

Michael was walking away from the tower, but even after he'd passed out of sight I kept an eye out for him as I made my way around the buildings once more, then walked down the outer wall to approach the tower on the yard side.

There was a slight breeze, enough to disguise some of the sounds I'd make, but I'd still have to keep as quiet as I could. And climbing a fully leafed tree wasn't going to be quiet.

I couldn't see the guard at his post by the front door—which was the point, because he couldn't see me, either—but if he decided to make a round of the property he was supposed to be guarding, he'd probably catch me. However, the security didn't seem to be all that tight. If they really cared about someone breaking in, they'd have cut down a tree that abutted the yard's wall. I could go in, chat with the jeweler...and then get out of town before Michael ever learned I'd been here.

I reached the courtyard's wall without incident, and there was now enough moonlight to inspect it as I walked toward the tree. Like the buildings, the wall was made of smooth river stones mortared into place. Because the stones were rounder, the mortared crevices between them were larger but, being round, all the stones sloped down and were completely smooth. River stone is worse to climb than stucco or brick, in my experience, which was considerable, as burglar had been my second criminal career. After picking pockets and before con artist, if you're curious.

But if the wall was unclimbable, that tree might have been grown with burglars in mind. Either Pendarian's groundskeepers didn't know much about security, or the university didn't really care. The tree had even been pruned so that, unlike wild elms, only the big branches remained. One was low enough that I only needed to put my hands on it and leap to be able to straddle it.

The branches' slender tips shook like rattles, no matter how carefully I climbed, but you can't have everything. And it grew so close to the wall that the branch I crawled out on only dipped a bit before it came to rest on the stone, creating a reasonable bridge.

I took a moment to examine my landing place, sitting on top of that high wall—and if you don't think ten feet is high, you've never contemplated jumping down from it. The Green Moon had risen enough to illuminate the interior of the yard and shone clearly on the door in the tower wall. There were four steps leading up to a small stoop, and only two windows. Even in the bright moonlight, I couldn't tell from this distance— about thirty yards—whether or not there was a keyhole in that door.

If there wasn't, I could still get out of the courtyard. Stacked against the taller, outer wall was a rack of woven wicker boxes, like chicken cages in a livestock market, and much of the rest of the yard was taken up with a mazelike series of pens and runs made of plank fencing or stretched canvas on stakes. A table with some benches sat near the door, and there was a privy tucked discretely into one corner. So even if my lock picks failed to get me in, a bench piled onto the table should get me back to the top of the wall.

Of course the *plan* was still to go in and chat with my mad friend, go out one of the windows on the far side of the tower, and then depart with the crowd leaving the lecture. But I've learned, over the years, that plans are usually overrated.

I rolled over and squirmed down till I hung from my hands, then pushed off the wall and dropped. The nearly silent landing jarred me from head to heels.

I walked briskly across the yard, and had just reached the bottom of the steps when the door at the top swung open. A middle-aged woman in a dark gown took two steps onto the stoop and then froze, staring at me. She drew in a deep breath.

"Please, don't scream." I offered her my most disarming smile—which is pretty disarming, if I say so myself. "I mean you no harm. I don't mean anyone harm. I just want to talk with the crazy man who's kept here. It's...it's a dare. And then you can let me out and I'll leave. Please, Professor." It was a guess, but she was too old to be a scholar, and the dark gown, with its narrow skirt and archaic ruffled collar, looked like the female version of an academic uniform. "Please, don't scream. And don't tell my dorm master?"

She eyed me consideringly for a moment before she spoke. "How stupid do you think I am?" She opened her mouth and screamed.

She went on screaming, and moments later a guard's whistle joined in.

There wasn't enough time to move the furniture, and in an enclosed courtyard with an unclimbable fence there was no point in running. I backed away from her, politely, and sat down on one of the benches to await arrest. Judging by the shouts it would be soon, and there would be lots of people to do the arresting. If I didn't alarm the professor any further—and judging by that cool speech, she wasn't very alarmable—maybe I'd get off lightly, even if my story about a dare failed.

I briefly considered telling the truth. It had worked for me last time, mostly due to the extremely peculiar fact that Michael and I were now regarded as heroes by all the Liege's guardsmen.

I discovered this when a bit of card sharping went twisty on me several weeks ago in Easton Township. It wasn't really sharping—I was too badly out of practice for that—but a mathematical trick I induced folk to bet on. And since I never encouraged them to bet more than they could afford to lose, it was usually safe.

But I'd been trying not to remember Michael's appalled amusement the first time he saw me do it, and I missed the fact that some half-drunk young idiots in the back of the crowd were betting too high.

So when half of them lost, of course they called the guard to arrest *me*.

The professor had stopped screaming now. And what had she been doing in the tower, without a single candle to warn a burglar she was in there? It hardly seemed fair. The shouts were suddenly muffled, which meant the forces of law were now inside the tower and my life was about to get complicated. But at least the whistling had stopped, and if he had any sense Michael would use that disturbance as a distraction from whatever nefarious purpose he'd come for, instead of rushing toward the commotion.

On the other hand, this was Michael.

And Michael's proclivity for getting us into trouble had paid off with the Liege Guard in Easton, as soon as they learned I was *Michael Sevenson's* comrade, who had summoned the guard to take down the Rose Conspiracy. And busted Tallowsport wide open, and saved the Realm from rebellion, maybe even an all-out war.

Myself, I remembered it more as a desperate scramble to save all our lives. The endgame had gotten ugly, too. Not to mention the quarrel after.

But when Easton's guardsmen learned that I was that Fisk, they were perfectly willing to listen to my side of the story, and also to the witnesses who confirmed I was telling the truth.

The guard who now came rushing through the door behind the professor would have knocked her off the stoop if she hadn't skipped aside, and a mob of burly students followed him.

After one look at their eager faces and muscular shoulders, I decided to be very meek about being arrested. I was considering whether to tell the Liege's men that I was *that* Fisk, one of the heroes of etc., etc., and that the man I wanted to see used to be the Rose's jeweler. And either that I just wanted to assure myself he was all right, or maybe that I was on an errand for the High Liege, which was far too secret for me disclose.

But as they pulled me to my feet to hustle me off, it occurred to me that my only crime was trespassing in a restricted area of the university. If I refused to pay my debt with coin, I'd probably be asked to redeem myself by working for the university, maybe even for the department I'd disturbed. I might be able to learn enough about the jeweler's situation that I could leave without having to see him. Or maybe talk my way into his presence.

And the more quietly I went with my captors, the greater the chance that I could avoid meeting Michael.

What *was* he doing here, anyway?

CHAPTER 2

Michael

What under two moons was *Fisk* doing here?

It had taken some time to find my way to the source of the commotion. Once I had, I barely had time to step into the shadow of a flowery shrub, and then watch as a band of young ruffians, and an older man in rough sturdy garb, hustled Fisk out of an old building and down the walkway.

He went meekly, and like me he wore a scholar's black and red. But something about the relaxed assurance with which he endured his captors' eager clutch made him look older and more confident than even the man who seemed to be in charge.

I let them pass me by, for trying to effect some escape would only have given away my own illicit presence.

Once they were out of sight, I even began to doubt what I'd seen. Not that I wouldn't recognize Fisk's walk and his curly crop, even by moonlight. But I'd been fantasizing quite often about finding Fisk in need of my rescue. If I'd seen a student who looked a bit like him, it wasn't impossible that my idle daydreams might have tricked my eyes.

It was only in the nightmares that I arrived too late, and found him maimed, flogged, and, in one particularly hideous dream, hanged from a beam that creaked under his slowly swinging weight. I'd awakened from that one gasping, and shaking so hard that True came and licked my face.

When I actually thought about our quarrel, I knew that Fisk didn't want to be found, much less rescued. So after I left Tallowsport, I'd dithered about the river plain for months, giving him time to get well ahead of me, whatever direction he'd gone in.

And now, when I wanted him, he was getting too far ahead, while I stood wrapped in bafflement.

I hurried off toward the main gate, taking one of the shortcuts I'd discovered while exploring the campus these last few hours. I'd found my target, the great library, quite easily, for my brother Benton's directions had been precise. 'Twas only as I stared up at its looming bulk that I'd stuck on the question of what to do next. My plan was to burgle the chief librarian's office. 'Twas what Fisk would have done, and I could think of no better scheme to find the evidence Benton needed. But when it came to doing such a thing without Fisk's assistance, I found myself at a loss.

So I'd wandered the campus for a time, figuring out escape routes—as an amateur burglar, I was likely to need them. I was about to start trying to open the library windows when I heard a woman screaming and a whistle blowing repeatedly—clearly an alarm.

'Twas also a good excuse to leave a task I was almost certain to fail.

Now my roaming stood me in good stead, and I managed to reach the corner of a building near the gates in time to watch the small party of law keepers approach. They stopped to exchange a word with the gatekeeper, and between the magica lamps and the moonlight I could see their captive's face clearly. 'Twas Fisk, no doubt about it. And despite his calm, somewhat depressed expression, he clearly needed a rescue!

I wasn't fool enough to imagine he'd fall at my feet, weeping with gratitude. But if I got him out of whatever scrape this was, mayhap he'd relent enough that we could talk calmly, and mend this break between us.

The mob of them went on through the gates. I'd stepped out of the shadows to follow when I realized that I was in disguise, and here without permission. Benton had said the old gatekeeper was nearly blind with cataracts, but that he knew men's voices well. And the scholar's guard, whom he could summon with his whistle, weren't handicapped in any way.

I took a breath and made myself think. I would be able to find Fisk any time in the next day or two, in the Liege Guard's lockup. This close to Crown City, in the High Liege's fief, there were no local guards except in the smallest villages. This might prove inconvenient, for the guardsmen who served the High Liege were generally better trained than local troops.

I'd probably only need to pay whatever fine Fisk had earned...and what had he been doing to raise such a ruckus?

If I tried to rush after him now I might end up under arrest with him, instead of being able to bail him out. All I had to do was wait till the lecture Benton was attending ended and I could depart with him, shielded by the crowd, as I'd come in. So I went back to the lecture hall. I paced up and down before the doors for several minutes before I realized that might look suspicious and set out to roam the campus once more.

I was too distracted to attempt burglary now. And if I could get Fisk's help, I'd be less likely to get caught, anyway. I knew what I was doing on a university campus, in disguise, but what was he doing here?

In some sense, if it hadn't been for Fisk, I wouldn't have been here.

When I was finally ready to leave Tallowsport, having had several matters to tend to before I departed, I abandoned some minor scruples and wrote to my sister, Kathy. I'd left that task to Fisk before, as it seemed to me that a man who is unredeemed—not to mention disowned by his family—shouldn't correspond with them. Not to mention that Father would be furious with Kathy if he caught her writing to me.

Over the next several years, as Fisk and Kathy's correspondence took on a life of its own, there was no need for me to contact her. Fisk shared her news with me, and passed my news on to her. But after Fisk had been gone for three weeks, I abandoned any hope he might return and wrote to Kathy myself, asking if she'd heard from him.

She hadn't, and she'd been frantically worried when his letters stopped coming so suddenly. After he'd written to tell her we were taking on the most powerful crime lord in the Realm, too. She'd begun to believe we'd both perished, and she expended quite a lot of ink describing exactly how inconsiderate that had been—of *both* of us.

I thought that unfair, since 'twas Fisk who was her correspondent. But he clearly wasn't now, so I told her of our quarrel—putting all the blame for her worry on Fisk, where it belonged.

Her next letter came from Slowbend, not Crown City, telling me that Benton was in trouble and I must come at once. When the letter carrier found me, I was only three days' ride away. In fact, I'd gotten into town just this morning, and Benton came down to the stable attached to his rooming house to make his case before I even got Chant unsaddled.

"I didn't do it," he said. "I was framed."

Benton was much of a height with Fisk, and also had brown hair. But where Fisk was solid, Benton's stocky frame ran to plump. And Fisk's sharp eyes never held the dreamy abstraction that so often filled Benton's.

When we were younger, I'd sometimes come across my brother standing with a book in one hand, and a single sock or half-eaten apple forgotten in the other.

Even Father hadn't thought to do anything with Benton except send him to University, pay his fees, and then (according to Kathy) boast to all the neighbors when he graduated last fall, with honors.

If this scandal destroyed his academic career, that would all change. They planned to hire someone to replace Benton for the fall term, he told me gloomily, which meant they'd start interviewing other scholars in just a few weeks. Once they'd given his job away...well, no university needed two professors of ancient history. Most didn't even need one, and Father wouldn't tolerate an idle son hanging about. Indeed, Benton might find himself forced into the job of steward that I'd taken up knight errantry to avoid—and 'twould suit him even worse than it would have suited me.

But after he graduated, the university had promptly hired Benton as a junior professor specializing in the history of the ancients. I thought 'twould feel strange, to go straight from sitting in a classroom to standing before one and teaching, but clearly no one at the university found anything odd in it. And, as I soon learned, he hadn't gone straight from learning to teaching. He'd had to write a dissertation, first.

"I know how it looks," Benton said. "But I didn't plagiarize it. Not one word!"

He was petting True's ears, and True leaned against him consolingly, his ropy tail beating the packed earth of the stable floor. True is mostly hound, with dashes of other breeds, and a short brindled coat in which the ears are the softest part. Benton not only shares my Gift for animal handling, he loves them even more than I do. He was distressed when I explained the dog was mute—though as far as I can see, it doesn't seem to bother True.

I had unsaddled Chant, filled the feed trough with hay and the big bucket with water, and was now brushing his dappled hide with long, soothing strokes. A relaxed setting for asking difficult questions.

"Who says you did? And why is that important?"

"Why...why is it *important?* A dissertation is a scholar's masterwork, Michael! Mine is the reason I got this job, instead of being packed home to Father when I finished my courses. And it must be *original* work. To copy your dissertation from someone else, 'tis...'tis the worst thing you can do!"

I thought there were things far worse, but maybe for a scholar 'twas true. If it was, this university must be a safe and kindly world. Which made it a place Benton would do well in. Clearly 'twas both my brotherly and knightly duty to restore him to it.

And besides that, Benton and Kathy were the only members of my family who hadn't scoffed at my desire to be a knight errant, even though 'tis a profession two centuries out of date. I didn't owe him much for that—I've become accustomed to being laughed at—but it did incline me kindly toward him.

"I'll take your word for the importance," I said. "So who accused you?"

"'Twas Master Hotchkiss, the head librarian," Benton said. "Not his fault. He's creating a catalog of all the books, giving them numbers and filing them in order. And he's working in the ancient literature room now, and he found this old thesis and read it and...Michael, it was mine!"

"'Tis not impossible for people working in the same craft to have the same idea," I pointed out. "Sometimes at near the same time, in villages at opposite ends of the Realm."

"It wasn't just the same idea," said Benton. "Someone else might have thought of it, too. Though I thought I was the only one who cared enough about the ancients, and their relics, to bother. If we were able to learn more about their lives, people might be more interested. I've found that—"

"So this other paper was much like yours. But why do they claim you copied it?"

When Benton started talking about the ancients, 'twas best to interrupt him quickly.

"It wasn't just that he had similar ideas," Benton said. "There were paragraphs, whole passages sometimes, that used the same words, the same phrasing I did. Not quite word for word, but with only a few things changed. Which made it worse, because it looked like I'd copied it, then deliberately tried to make mine look different."

I came out of Chant's stall and found the oat bin. 'Twas a good thing Benton's rooming house reserved space for its tenants in a nearby stable, or 'twould be expensive to house him. After setting up a tribe of orphan children in their own chandlery, I was a bit short of coin. In fact, if I stayed in the city for more than a day or two, I was going to have to ask Kathy to pick up Chant's tab.

"I didn't copy any part of my dissertation." Benton's voice was firm now. Bitter and proud. "I'd never seen that other paper before. And I'd have sworn I read every book on the ancient history shelves, in the years I studied here. Though it might have always been in another section—or even in another room, as disordered as things are in the areas Master Hotchkiss hasn't cataloged. He found it in a stack of ancient poetry, and it might have been there for years. If I had copied my thesis, that would have been a good place for me to hide it after I copied the parts I wanted. But I didn't."

The passion had left his voice now, only defeat remaining. I knew what 'twas like, to stand before a tribunal and be condemned, so I gave him an encouraging slap on the shoulder on my way into Chant's stall. I dumped a measure of oats into the feed bin, checked to be sure he still had enough water, and then departed, giving my horse a farewell slap on the rump. Much the same gesture I'd used on Benton, now that I thought on it.

"If that other paper was so much like yours, and you didn't copy it, then whoever created it must have copied you," I said. "How long is this dissertation of yours? Twenty pages? Forty?"

Benton cast me a wry look. "Two hundred and fifty-two. Though some of that is diagrams, and examples of how you might show the relationship of objects buried at different depths. You see, the deeper an object is buried the older it will be. So if you can determine the age of any item on that level, you can—"

"So creating this new dissertation, which mimics yours, would be no small task. Who hates you, Benny?"

The childhood nickname made him grimace, but he made no protest as he led True and me up a creaking side stair to the rooms he leased on the second floor.

"No one. And the dissertation Master Hotchkiss found wasn't new. It was dated from the reign of Liege Harold, almost ninety years ago, and the paper was yellowed, the leather cracked and—"

"There are ways to fake that." I knew someone who would have known how. But he wasn't with me, anymore.

Except now, as I restlessly paced the dark campus, it seemed he was. Or if not with me, at least in the same town, and in need of my rescue! When was this lecture going to end? I was circling the back of the buildings that ringed the square, so when people poured into it I could swiftly return. But every time I peered down the lane between buildings, 'twas still empty.

I wondered what Fisk would make of Benton's tale, when he heard it. As my brother had led me up the side stair to his rooms, he'd assured me that no one hated him, or sought his job as a junior professor of history specializing in the ancients.

But I paid this almost no attention, because when he opened the door to a pleasant sunny room, with padded benches and chairs, there was a young woman sitting at the table reading one of the stacked papers.

I hadn't seen Benton for almost six years, but I'd recognized him instantly. I had seen Kathy only a little over three years past, but even as she rose and came to hug me, I scarce knew her.

"You've grown up!" I broke her embrace and held her off a little, so I could look her over.

She snorted, and pushed up the spectacles that had slipped down her nose. "It would be peculiar if I hadn't. I wrote you—well, I wrote for Fisk to tell you—that Father had packed me off to court for the Liege's marriage fair. Did you think I was still fourteen? Although me going to court may turn out to be a good thing, because I know about something that might have given someone a motive to do this."

I was still staring, even as True frolicked up and introduced himself, and Kathy bent to give him a pat. She was thin, as always, with mouse brown hair and mouse gray eyes. But the child's gawky awkwardness had given way to the grace of a stalking marsh heron.

"Michael." She waved a hand in front of my eyes. "Pay attention. The Liege's only son, Rupert, is in love with a Giftless woman."

My brows flew up. "That's unfortunate. For everyone involved."

Magic doesn't exist in normal humans, under normal circumstances, but Gifts, which pass only through the female line, are much prized. All who are Gifted have the ability to sense magic, in plants or animals that have it. This enables them to avoid the catastrophes that occur when such plants or animals are harvested without proper sacrifice. But the ability to sense magic is often accompanied by a host of lesser talents and quirks. I'd once met a man who could instantly tell if something he touched was a forgery, and I wondered what he'd make of the dissertation that had brought my brother down so neatly. Still...

"What does the Liege Heir falling for some Giftless girl have to do with Benton? 'Tis tragic for them, since the High Liege will never let them wed. A simple baron would object to such a wife for his heir. But that's nothing to do with us."

Kathy looked glum. "You're not one of the sacrificial maidens the High Liege has hauled into court to induce Rupert to pick someone else. But as for this... Rupert's trying to find a way out of the trap. He's offered funding, and a huge reward for success, to anyone who can find a way to make a Giftless person Gifted. Or to have Gifted children, since that's the part that matters."

I sank down on one of Benton's comfortably padded chairs, though the statement wasn't so very shocking. People had been speculating about doing that for ages— from the time of Benton's ancients, probably—and no one had even come close.

Except for one terrible woman, and she hadn't been trying to Gift the Giftless, but to turn Gifts to full-out magic. The memory of her attempts, of rope chaffing my wrists as I fought, and potions cramping my stomach, and that terrible thrumming in my blood...

"Then the gods had best make an exception and look out for that poor woman, because... Wait a moment. If he loves her, surely the Heir won't allow anyone to experiment upon her."

"Of course not." Kathy gave me an odd look. "He's funding universities to do the experiments, to figure out what might work and test it. 'Tis only if they come up with something safe...and if they did, it's not just Rupert and Meg who'd benefit. Think of it, Michael— anyone might have Gifts! Gifted healers would be common, instead of rare. With so many herb talkers making it, magica medicine would become cheap. No hunter losing limbs because he happens to bring down some beast with magic, or house burning down because 'twas made with a magica wood."

"No lords or barons," said Benton, "since it was the ability to sense magic and avoid it that enabled our ancestors to rise to power. Though I think they started as tribal chieftains, which was a much more fluid position than—"

"Yes, Benton," Kathy said. "But the important part now is how you got caught up in the project."

"Oh, that." Sometimes my brilliant brother could be rather dim. "They wanted to know if the ancients had ever tried such a thing. And some of them had—there are songs and such that hint at the formulas they used. I compiled them."

I readied myself to interrupt a spate of information about ancient songs, but Benton said nothing more.

"And...?" Kathy demanded.

"Hang it, Kathy, it was nothing! I don't have a Gift for reading people, not that that would tell you much. It seemed like they were beginning to get results off some of the formulas I gave them, but that's all I really saw."

"And...?"

Benton rolled his eyes in a brotherly way, and turned to me. "I mentioned, once, that something felt a bit off about the project."

"What do you mean, 'off?'"

"Just... I don't know. It felt..." His hands waved vaguely, trying to shape something he couldn't describe. "I didn't see anyone do anything, or say anything wrong. I was mostly helping them with the rabbits, so even if there was something off I wouldn't know about it."

"Rabbits?" I asked. "Wait, they're not trying these formulas on people?"

"Of course not." Benton sounded shocked at the very idea. "First they have to find something that works on one species, then they have to try it on many others, to be as certain as they can that it's safe before they even start testing it on humans. They're a long way from that. Although they did seem to be getting some results from the formulas based on my notes. That's why they wanted me around. Or at least, Professor Stint did. He's the one who's actually creating the formulas. Once I turned over my research, I wasn't much use."

"But," said Kathy, "'tis a project that's bringing the university a lot of money, and if it succeeded would bring them even more. I've been talking to Benton for three days now, and there's nothing else in his life that gives anyone even a shadow of a motive to do this."

So she'd written to me even before she'd spoken much with Benton? That was sufficiently flattering that I wished I had some brilliant idea for what to do next.

"Kathy, have *you* spoken to this librarian? Asked him about finding this faked dissertation? Or about who knew where he was working, and could have planted it for him to find?"

Like our father, Kathy does have the Gift for reading people, and she cast me an exasperated glance. "You know it doesn't work like that. Even if I could tell something about him, 'twould more likely be that he's allergic to parsnips or hates pink, rather than anything useful. And I tried to see him day before yesterday. He refused to see me, just as he's refused to talk to Benton."

"He sent a message, that he'd said all he had to say at my hearing," Benton put in. "He doesn't believe me. I can understand that. I'm just glad the two of you..."

His voice husked into silence.

"Of course we believe you," I said. "You care about your ancients too much to cheat on them. You'd feel as if you'd dishonored them."

Which probably made him as crazy as most of my relatives think me.

"And you're the worst liar in the family," Kathy added. "If you were lying, 'twould show."

"Thanks," said Benton. "I think."

But there were tears of gratitude in his eyes. I could see this, because both he and Kathy were looking at me now.

"Well..." I cast desperately for another idea. And then it occurred to me: What would Fisk do? "If this Master Hotchkiss won't speak to us, mayhap a look around his office would prove enlightening."

So that was how I found myself roving the campus in the dark, trying to figure out how to break into a locked building without getting caught. And failing miserably. Despite his claims to hate burglary, such enterprises were always Fisk's idea.

Well, usually.

Soon I would be able to tap his expertise once more. I was eager to speak with him...so of course, the lecture went on interminably. When it finally came to an end, and the crowd poured out into the square, Benton was surprised at the speed with which I swept him out the gates. But once I'd explained, he not only told me where to find the town lockup, and reminded me to give him the student's coat I'd borrowed, he also handed over his purse to add its contents to mine.

He wasn't carrying much. I carried all the coin I owned, and the total was still rather small—but it should be enough to buy Fisk out of his cell until some final reckoning of his debt was pronounced.

Assuming the charge against him wasn't more serious than it appeared.

Between that unsettling thought, and my uncertainty as to what I might say to bridge the gap between us, I was somewhat agitated as I approached the lockup. 'Twas near the town hall, in the cellar of the guard barracks, though it had a separate entrance and offices above it. 'Twas also conveniently near both the university and Benton's lodging...where Kathy had been given the only bedroom, and Benton was to sleep on the padded bench in his front room, while I spread my bedroll on the floor.

Mayhap I should take Fisk to a tavern, so we could talk privately before returning to Benton's rooms. Though what to say...

I was in such a dither that the guardsman in charge of the lockup was reluctant to let me in to see his prisoner, even after I offered to bail Fisk out. He donned his sword, and insisted on accompanying me down the narrow stair, mayhap fearing I planned a gaolbreak, or some such idiocy.

So there was an audience to our first meeting after that terrible fight. Not, as it turned out, that it mattered.

The first thing I noticed, as a resigned expression spread over Fisk's face, was that he wasn't surprised to see me.

The lockup consisted of three iron-barred cages, so I could see him clearly. Little moonlight fell through the barred slit high in the wall—on the far side of the room from the cells, so no slipping in a note or weapon. But some kindly soul had left a lamp burning, to keep prisoners from finding themselves alone in the dark.

Not that Fisk looked ill at ease. He sat on the narrow cot, but he'd pulled the thin straw tick off the boards to pad the wall he leaned against. His relaxed hands were clasped about one knee, in a manner that suggested he felt quite at home. An attitude even the guard's glower didn't change.

"Fisk." For some reason my voice was hoarse. I cleared my throat and went on. "I've come to buy you out. I'm told the only charge against you is trespass, so I...that is, Kathy, will be able to pay your debt."

His resigned expression became more sardonic at this—though he knew how I'd spent my share of the reward, curse him.

"I shall pay your bail tonight," I finished more firmly. "Then we can talk."

Fisk contemplated me for a long moment, and then said, "No."

"What? What do you mean, 'No?'"

"Does that mean the prisoner refuses bail?" the guard asked precisely.

"Of course he doesn't."

"Yes, I do," said Fisk. "I'll stay here till the judicars total up my debt, then work it off."

"You'd sit here, in gaol, rather than accept my help?" I wasn't sure if I was more incredulous, or more angry.

"You'd be more comfortable in your own lodging, sir." The guard eyed us both with suspicion now. He'd probably never had a prisoner refuse to leave these cells, given the choice. And who'd have thought Fisk, of all people, would be so absurdly stubborn.

"Don't be ridiculous." I tried not to snap at him, but I fear I failed. "I'll get you out. Then we'll go to a tavern and discuss this trouble you're in, and—"

"You no longer have a right to say what I will and won't do. Noble Sir."

Those words had always stung, but never as they did now.

Fisk sat up, lowering both feet to the floor. If there was pain under the determination on his face, the dim light concealed it. He turned to the guard.

"I refuse bail. And if I refuse, you can't accept it."

Of all the lunatic, stubborn, asinine...

"No, he doesn't," I told the guard.

"Yes, I do," said Fisk.

"No, you don—"

"Well, sirs." The guard's gaze was now very sharp. "In fact, he can refuse bail. No one 'cept a judicar can saddle a man with a debt, if he don't choose it. May I ask who you are, and why it's so important to you this man goes free? And what was he doing, sneaking around the university in restricted areas?"

"I don't know why he was there." I had to force the words from my suddenly dry mouth. He suspected me of being Fisk's accomplice, as well he might. In a moment he would ask to see my wrists, and find the tattoos that mark a man as unredeemed. Those broken circles signify a legal debt that can't be paid in labor or coin, and men who bear them have usually bribed themselves out of being hanged or maimed. I hadn't killed anyone, and Father hadn't bribed anyone, either. But since I'd refused to return a criminal to justice (she turned out to be innocent, at least of the crime she was charged with), I'd failed to pay my debt to the law. And an unredeemed man is beyond the law's protection. If he saw those tattoos, I would probably end this night in the cell next to Fisk's.

Which wasn't a bad idea.

Unfortunately, Fisk's wit is quicker than mine.

"He's Michael Sevenson," Fisk said. "*The* Michael Sevenson. Of Tallowsport."

I was so startled my jaw dropped. I wasn't *the* Michael Sevenson of anywhere. And from my perspective, Tallowsport was at best a...mixed success. Yes, we'd brought down a great criminal, who'd held a whole town in his power and plotted rebellion against the High Liege. But to do it, I'd allowed things to happen that a true knight would never have permitted. And I hadn't been able to find another way.

But the guard's face lit with interest and delight. For a moment, I thought he was going to wiggle like a happy puppy.

"You are? Really?" His eyes came to rest on the small scars on my cheek and jaw, which confirm my description for most folk. "Sir! May I say how honored I am to meet you? And may I ask, how did you come to suspect that Roseman...?"

And so it went. I eventually extracted myself from his questions, but I had to flee the lockup to do it.

Without Fisk.

The guard was very sorry to disoblige me, but he couldn't force a debt on someone who didn't accept it.

And clearly Fisk wouldn't agree to be indebted to me, ever again. He'd rather stay in *gaol* than be my squire.

I should have gone back to Benton's rooms, but I was in no mood to answer questions—much less sleep on the floor, in a bed not much more comfortable than the one Fisk faced. So I went to the stable, saddled Chant, and rode out of town—cursing my recalcitrant ex-squire with every breath.

A long gallop cleared only some of the anger from my heart, but I refused to run my horse to exhaustion just because Fisk was the most miserable, stubborn, selfish villain in the United Realm.

As Chant clopped down the moonlit roads, beside fields of half-grown crops, I had time to realize that the reason Fisk hadn't been surprised to see me was that he'd seen me earlier, most probably when I was wandering about the campus. Even when he could have approached me without incurring any debt between us, he hadn't done so.

Dawn was bringing color into the red earth and green shoots by the time I was tired enough to accept that—as he'd said when we parted—Fisk wanted no more of my company.

He was, in truth, no longer my squire, and I had to accept that too. And if that realization made me want to keep on riding, to the farthest reaches of the Realm where there'd be no chance of ever setting eyes on my ex-squire...I couldn't.

None of this personal turmoil was Benton's fault, and his life had been devastated. If I was ever to call myself a knight errant again, I couldn't turn my back on anyone in such need, much less a brother.

Not to mention the fact that if I fled, Kathy would never speak to me again.

So I turned my tired horse and rode back to Slowbend...

Where a half a dozen men, in the blue and silver coats of the Liege Guard, promptly arrested me for Master Hotchkiss' murder.

CHAPTER 3

Painful as it had been, I thought I'd convinced Michael that I didn't need his rescue. So after a restless night in a lumpy bed, I was surprised to see him coming down the stairs again, with that absurd guard still asking for details about Tallowsport. Though the Liege Guard in Easton had reacted much the same, when they'd had me in their clutches.

"But how did you *know* Captain Dalton wouldn't betray you? Seems to me if he'd been working for the Rose that long, he might have gone over."

"If he'd 'gone over,' his wife wouldn't have been a prisoner still."

Michael's voice sounded stiffer than the question warranted. And if he was here to talk me into taking on another debt to him, why was he trying so hard to look anywhere but at me?

Even after I'd observed that, I was surprised when the guard opened the door of the cell next to mine, and politely gestured for Michael to go in.

Though the way my luck was running, I shouldn't have been.

"Captain Chaldon will be back in a few hours," the guard said, locking the door on my former employer. "He's still on the campus, checking out the scene. After that he wanted to see if the healer could tell anything about his death from Master Hotchkiss' body. But as soon as he's back, we'll get this settled. Because I don't believe for one minute that *Michael Sevenson* did this."

Master Hotchkiss' *body?*

Michael nodded absently, and went to sit on the far end of his own cot, putting as much distance between us as he could—which was about twelve feet. The sun cast small squares of light through the barred slit at the top of the opposite wall. In the time I'd been watching, they'd moved from halfway up the wall above my bed down to the floor. With only bars making up the cell wall between us, we might as well have been locked in the same small room.

Alone in that room, once the guard had departed, I waited, somewhat apprehensively, for Michael to break the silence. After a while, it became clear he wasn't going to. After an even longer time, the silence began to get on my nerves. A while after that, I gave up.

"So, what are you in for, stranger? Nothing too violent, I hope."

He could have refused to reply, but he must have been as weary of sulking as I was of watching him sulk.

"Murder. I'd tell them you were sneaking about the campus last night too, except they already caught you. You're probably a suspect as well."

"Along with everyone else on campus last night," I pointed out. "Which is only...what, eight hundred people? Maybe over a thousand, with that lecture going on."

"Probably," said Michael glumly. "It seems we weren't the only ones to realize that lecture would be a perfect time for villainy."

"Who's this Hotchkiss, and why do they think you killed him?" I'd become so interested—villainy and murder, after all—that the question came out quite naturally. But Michael gave me a sour look.

"What do you care? As you pointed out, you're no longer my squire. Are you going to tell me what *you* were doing, slinking around in the dark? No. So why should I—"

"I was trying to see the jeweler." I think my easy answer surprised me as much as Michael. But if I wanted his information, I was clearly going to have to trade. And if someone had committed murder on a campus where I'd just been arrested, I needed to know about it.

I really didn't want to have to tell them I was *the* Fisk.

"The jeweler?" Michael's stony expression relaxed in simple surprise. "Roseman's madman? Whatever for?"

I could think of no reason, except the truth.

"When the guards hauled him off... You understand, he was terrified. I told him he'd be all right. And I didn't know if he was. So I thought I'd check."

He was looking at me now, and I found that more uncomfortable than I'd expected.

"I see."

The silence lengthened until I couldn't take it anymore.

"So why do they think you killed this guy? In fact, how did they know you were on the campus at all? I didn't tell them."

For some reason his mouth tightened again, but at least he answered.

"They'd no notion to suspect me at first. Or so the guards told me. But my brother Benton is the only one they know of who has reason to hate the man. Fortunately, Benton had the sense to find some friends to sit with in the lecture hall, so he couldn't have done it. But when they went to ask the gatekeeper if Benton had arrived early, or departed late, the gatekeeper told them that someone he didn't know had accompanied Benton through the gates. The friends at the lecture had already said that they'd taken pity on Benton because he was alone. So they went to see Benton and Kathy, and the truth came out."

"What, they couldn't have lied?"

"Kathy might have," Michael said, though I'd have thought her a bit young to stand up to a High Liege investigator. "But Benton...he's a worse liar than I am, Fisk. Or than I was, before I met you."

Despite his glower, I wasn't offended by the implication that I'd taught him to lie. He'd needed those lessons. A lot.

"But why do they think your brother would want to kill this Hotchkiss person? Or have you kill him? Who was he, anyway?"

Michael hesitated again, but we'd nothing better to do. So I learned that Hotchkiss had been the university's head librarian, and how Michael's brother had been framed.

Unlike Michael, who was somewhat skeptical about the importance of an original dissertation, I had no trouble understanding why it was something a man might cheat, or even kill for. Though it didn't sound like Benton was the type.

Michael went on to tell me young Kathy's theory, about the project providing a motive to bring Benton down. I wondered if the jeweler might have been part of that project, though as Michael told me about it, I didn't see how. The jeweler didn't have Gifts—unless you counted the ability to infuse bits of glass with real magic. Most people wouldn't consider that a Gift, though I wasn't so sure.

I could see how a research project, particularly a well-funded and important one, might give someone a motive for murder. But not to murder a librarian who'd had nothing to do with it.

I was making that point, when the door at the top of the stairs opened and a stranger in a guard captain's uniform escorted a young woman down the steps.

It took me a moment to recognize Kathy, though she was still thin, and brown as a sparrow. Maybe the difference lay in the ease with which she handled her full green skirt, though she didn't sport as many petticoats as most noblewomen wore. More likely it was the tailored fit of the leather bodice, but she looked all grown up—astonishingly grown up—until her spectacles slipped, and she pushed them back up in a gesture I remembered from all those years ago.

"What, money and power aren't motive enough to kill for?" Her voice was deeper than it had been at fourteen, a woman's voice. Which I suppose was also to be expected.

"It would be," I said. "If Master Hotchkiss had been involved with the project in any way. As it is..."

No one had any motive to kill him, except brother Benton.

This realization struck everyone at the same moment, and Michael and Kathy stiffened.

"We haven't yet made a case against anyone, for Master Hotchkiss' death," said the captain pleasantly. "The only thing we know is that Profess—Master Benton Sevenson was almost certainly attending the lecture at the time of his death."

"How do you know that?" Michael asked. "The time he died, I mean?"

"We can't be certain," the captain said. "But it looks like he was leaving for the lecture when he was killed. After dinner, in his front hall, dressed to go out. And he was killed by a blow to the front of the head, as if he surprised someone coming in. I don't suppose either of you noticed anyone *else* lurking around the campus?"

"A few students," I said. "Walking on the paths."

"No one suspicious," Michael agreed.

"So it seems you two are my best suspects," the captain said.

We probably were. For a wonder, Michael said nothing.

"You shouldn't tease them," Kathy said. "They're scared enough as it is."

"We are not," said Michael. "We're innocent—well, I'm fairly sure Fisk is innocent—so if you're an honest man, we should have nothing to fear."

Actually, an unredeemed man should be afraid of any guardsman, anytime, anywhere. And despite his bold words, Michael's face was paler than it had been a few minutes ago.

"Ahem." Kathy cleared her throat, looking sternly at the captain. Who relented, clearly the victim of feminine wiles. From young Mistress Katherine, no less.

"But I'm inclined to believe Master Benton's telling the truth," the captain said. "And since I can't see any reason for Master Fisk here—yes, I figured out who you must be. But I see no reason for Fisk to have murdered Master Hotchkiss, and I have a hard time believing a man who'd just committed murder would go rushing into a guard station immediately afterward to bail someone out...though come to think of it, the man who brought down the Rose Conspiracy might have that kind of nerve."

"Captain." There was a distinct note of reproof in Katherine's voice.

"Oh, all right. Since I'm not prepared to charge anyone with this murder, yet, and since the charge against Master Fisk is minor, I've decided to release you on Lady Katherine's bail. She'll be legally responsible for your conduct, and your debt is to her. Once these matters are settled, assuming you're not guilty, her money will be returned and your debt to her ended. But until that happens, you're to remain in town and make yourselves available to the High Liege's authorities on request. Clear to everyone?"

It was perfectly clear to me. And if murder had been committed in a place I'd been burgling, I'd have been delighted to get out of gaol while they figured out I hadn't done it...and make plans to flee, if they didn't figure it out.

So I wasn't surprised to hear Michael object.

"You're letting us go? Without even..."

He started to lift his wrists and then thought better of the gesture, but the captain had seen it.

"Yes, Master Sevenson, we know you're unredeemed. But after Tallowsport, some of the guard decided to look into the circumstances. And I have to say... Well, maybe I shouldn't say that, about a justice system I serve. But I'm not inclined to hold it against you."

Kathy beamed at the man. He was fairly young, in his early thirties, and not bad looking, either. He also had no evidence we'd done anything worse than

trespassing, on Benton's behalf, and the Rose conspiracy's defeat had created a towering impression, almost
a legend, in the mind of guardsmen all over the river
plain—all over the Realm, for all I knew.

But Michael still looked like a stunned ox as we re-
trieved our knives from the guard's clerk and followed
Mistress Katherine out into the street.

It was Hornday, and most of the scholars should have
been in class, but there were dozens of them scattered
through the crowded street, like red and black punctua-
tion marks. We were only a block from the town square
and the streets were lined with high end shops: an
apothecary, a boot maker, and a stationer selling paper
and ink, which attracted most of the scholars.

"Mistress Katherine," I said. "Thank you. And now, if
you'll permit, I—"

"Don't thank me yet," she said. "Michael, go on ahead
please. I want a word with my...correspondent."

Michael suppressed a grin and started off to the west,
presumably toward his brother's rooms. Since my inn
was in the same general direction, it would have been
silly to turn and walk east. Even though, when Kathy
started after him, Michael was only ten feet ahead
of us.

I'm not sure I've mentioned it, but Michael has very
sharp ears.

"You know," I said, "Michael has very sharp—"

"How. Could. You? How could you just stop writing?
In the middle of trying to bring down Atherton Rose-
man? Fisk, I was beginning to think you were dead.
Both of you!"

I hadn't told Kathy the name of the monster we'd
set out to slay, but I should have known she'd figure it
out. She'd always been bookish. She knew how to do
research.

"Ah. Well, Michael and I were prisoners. After that first one, Roseman was reading my letters."

"Michael says you were held prisoner for about three weeks. And after that?"

After that, I'd been afraid that if I wrote to her, Michael would try to track me down. And she wasn't *my* sister.

I hadn't written to my sisters for about five months, come to think of it. I should probably pen up a letter to Judith, next time I settled in one place long enough for a reply to reach me. But Judith didn't know I was in trouble (though she doubtless assumed I always was) and she wasn't used to hearing from me regularly.

Ahead of us, Michael was walking more and more slowly.

"I'm sorry," I said. "I was...I didn't...well, I'm sorry."

"You should be. Fortunately, you now have a chance to make it up to me. Michael, you can come back now."

She hadn't raised her voice to say it, but Michael turned immediately, and I regarded this assured young woman with some alarm. Kathy-at-fourteen hadn't thrown orders about like this. But then, Kathy-at-fourteen hadn't been given a reason to be angry with me.

Michael rejoined us, smirking in a way that told me she'd scolded him, too. I tried again.

"My thanks to you, Mistress, but I need to get back to my own affairs. I'll stay in town till this murder matter is—"

"You're not going anywhere," Kathy said. "Either of you. You owe me a legal debt till they give my bond back, and I'm claiming it. I want the two of you to figure out who framed Benton, and get his job back for him."

I'd already seen this coming, but that was no reason to go down without a fight.

"I'm not Michael's squire anymore—"

"Which is fine with me," Michael put in.

"—and I won't work for him."

"Then work together," said Katherine. "Or pretend you've never met before. I don't care about either of your sensitive feelings. Once this murder is settled, Fisk will pay his fine and you can both get on with your lives. I think you're both crazy, but at least you can go where you wish and do whatever you want. Benton can't. This is the only life he wants, and he's lost it—permanently, if they hire someone else to take his place. You two are going to clear him before that happens. After that, I don't care what you do. But no more whining about it. We're here."

She turned into an alley between a couple of buildings, one of them presumably Benton's lodging. The walls were whitewashed plaster so the alley was reasonably bright, which let me see it was also surprisingly clean, and a stairway angled down the taller building's wall. Kathy's hips twitched with annoyance in a very feminine fashion as she climbed to the second floor landing.

Michael stood at the bottom, looking at me. His expression was mostly unreadable, but there was bitterness there, and maybe anger. He followed his sister up the stairs.

I could have walked away. Michael wouldn't chase me down, I knew that now. And in skirts, Mistress Katherine wasn't likely to catch me. On the other hand, she might get mad enough to send the guard after me. The cells hadn't been that bad, but I'd now been identified as *the* Fisk.

I probably should have whipped off a note before I left Tallowsport, but I'd just finished fighting with Michael and writing to his sister hadn't seemed necessary. So now, I was stuck.

I followed them up the stairs, and was almost knocked off the landing by a bouncing whirlwind of dog. It seemed Trouble had missed me, and nothing else could happen till I'd assured him that I'd missed him too—whether I had or not. Besides, watching his dog fawn over me made Michael scowl, so the time wasn't completely wasted.

Once Trouble settled down, I followed the others into a front room with two sunny windows and shelves crowded with papers and books, interspersed with bits of pottery and stone. It looked like a pretty fair collection of ancient artifacts, which hardly anyone collects, except for the few people who can't accept that the gods have no interest in man.

There was a fine carving of the Creature Moon, in its aspect of bear, the avenger: a full fat circle embedded in the stomach of a grizzly that was not only upright, but snarling in a way that made you want to avoid pissing off both the bear and the god.

This piece transcended artifact and became art. I was surprised to see it in the cluttered rooms of a junior professor.

Cluttered, and crowded. Looking through the only door, to the single bed in the room beyond, I could see that this was a fine space for one man. For two it would be tight. With the four of us, not to mention the dog, it would get downright claustrophobic.

Particularly with two of the four being Michael and me.

"I have a room at an inn," I suggested. "I can stay there."

Michael, to my annoyance, looked happy about that.

"Don't worry," Katherine said. "I've rented more rooms from Benton's landlady. You and Michael are in the attic, and I'm on the ground floor."

Hang it.

"Isn't that awfully expensive?" I asked hopefully. "You've already paid our bond, and as for Benton here..." I gestured to the plump, hapless looking man who appeared to be almost as disturbed by this news as Michael and I. "What's the difference between a bandit and a scholar?"

Michael grimaced and Kathy snorted. It was Benton who said, "I don't know. What?"

"A bandit has money, even if he just took it from you. Scholars don't have any money. Ever."

Benton grinned. "You're not wrong. But Father's giving Kathy an allowance for court, and as you can see—" he gestured to the fine linen skirt and glove-soft leather "—she doesn't spend much."

I'd have priced her outfit at a silver roundel for the skirt, and at least three for the bodice. But if her father was giving her money for damask, silk and gems, she probably did have a fair bit left over.

"Fisk and Michael are going to help you get your job back," Kathy told Benton.

I noticed that this news didn't make Benton look particularly cheerful, but she went on, "I've been thinking, and I think it's probably all tied together. Master Hotchkiss' murder, you being framed, whatever's wrong with the project. So many odd things, happening all at the same time, they have to be connected."

"Actually, they don't," I said. "It's inevitable that coincidences will occur, through the normal operation of random chance."

"Marman's law of coincidence," Benton supplied the attribution. I made a mental note not to quote philosophers in his presence.

Having established that we were still best friends, Trouble abandoned me and went to sit on Benton's feet, wagging confidently. Of course the man bent to pet him—Trouble knew a sucker when he saw one.

"Well, I think 'tis tied to the project," Michael said. "You were working on that, and even if you don't have a Gift for reading people, you sensed something wrong there."

"But it was Master Hotchkiss who accused him," I pointed out. "And then was murdered. Surely that's the sensible place to start."

And as soon as we figured out who killed the man... Who'd want to murder a librarian? But whoever it was, and whyever they'd done it, as soon as we found them my debt to Mistress Katherine would end.

"I can't believe anyone would kill him," Benton echoed my thoughts. "That brilliant mind... What a terrible waste."

"I still think we start with the project," Michael persisted. "Our task is to clear Benton, after all. So that's where we begin."

I started to shrug—in truth, I didn't think it mattered where we started since we'd get to the murder in the end. Then I remembered. I was setting my own direction, now.

"I say we start with the librarian's murder. You're not in charge anymore. Noble Sir."

Angry red stained Michael's cheekbones. "Is that what you wanted? To be in charge? To take us robbing, and scam—"

"I'm in charge," Kathy interrupted firmly. "And if you're both going to be so childish about it, you can take turns. First one investigation, then the other. Michael in charge while you investigate the project, Fisk in charge when you investigate Master Hotchkiss' death. Is that all right with you boys?"

"'Tis well with me," Michael said huffily. "I don't have to be in charge all the time. 'Tis Fisk who suddenly—"

"What about you, Fisk?" Kathy asked hastily.

It wasn't all right but Michael had agreed, and objecting would make me look childish and petty. And even if I felt that way, I didn't want to show it.

"That works for me. But once it becomes clear that the project's nothing, and it's the murder that matters, do I get to be in charge all the time?"

"And if 'tis the project that got Benton framed, then I was right, and I take charge!" Michael said swiftly. "Done?"

"Done!"

"Men," Kathy muttered.

"I'll even let Michael go first," I added magnanimously. Which not only made me look more mature, it gave me time to figure out something to investigate. Because right now, I had no idea where to start.

Michael realized it, of course. He was crazy, but he wasn't a fool. He just played one. And for almost four years—had I actually been mad?—he'd sucked me into the farce with him.

"That's all right," he said. "Unlike Fisk, I know what to do next."

CHAPTER 4

Michael

I claimed a few hours' sleep, having got none the night before, but the tavern across the street from Benton's lodging was still serving luncheon by the time we were ready to set out—so I insisted on a meal, as well. The turkey was cold, left over from yesterday, but the rolls were fresh from the oven and piping hot.

Conversation was stiff, for I declined to share my plans. In part because they were still a bit vague. Though Fisk had some questions for Benton I'd not thought to ask.

"When you had your hearing, did you think the university board or the headman might be in on it? Because if the fix starts at the top they're going to hire the first person who shows up, and we won't stand a chance of getting your job back."

Benton looked startled. "Oh, surely not. At least, I don't think so. They all seemed sincerely angry and distressed. Mostly angry," he finished glumly. "The board I mean. They went on and on about how a university's reputation is its most important treasure, and all it took was one cheating professor to defile it."

"What of the headman?" I asked. "He's the one who recommended that you be hired, wasn't he?"

Benton nodded. "He was both angry *and* upset. Headman Portner would never cheat on anything to do with the university, or anyone involved with it. The scholars make jokes about his title, the headman is coming for you, that kind of thing. But he's very tolerant of student idiocy. The only thing he's strict about is academic honesty, which is why he was so furious with me. He cares deeply about the university's integrity—he doesn't even tolerate academic sloppiness, much less cheating. So 'tis no wonder he said..."

His voice trailed off in misery, and Kathy put in a swift suggestion that before we went to the university we should go to Fisk's inn, and fetch back Tipple and his traps. By the time we got back, she added, our attic rooms should be clean. I noted Fisk's grimace as he realized the rooms weren't in use at the moment, and instantly resolved not to complain no matter how hot our lodging got, or even if the roof leaked.

Heat was the more likely problem. We had to hike across half the town to reach the inn, and the day was already growing hot.

Fisk went in to argue that since he hadn't slept in his room last night, he shouldn't have to pay full price for it, while I went to the stable to greet a dear old friend. Tipple isn't the companion to me that Chant is, but I can't deny that giving her to Fisk had wrenched my heart.

Though not as much as losing Fisk had.

What else could I have done? He'd freed a criminal, a man who'd probably earned hanging. A man who'd continue preying on others—and didn't that make all his future victims Fisk's, as well? And he'd done it without consulting me, because he knew I'd forbid it, because I'd have stopped him. He should have been stopped! 'Twas an outrageous, wicked, criminal...

'Twas mayhap as well that Fisk came out of the inn shortly, wearing a hangdog face that told me he'd not won his point. We strapped his luggage onto Tipple's saddle and set off for Benton's lodging.

By the time he'd stowed his gear the day was so warm we shed our coats before setting off for the university, but the distance was short enough that the silence hadn't grown too uncomfortable by the time we approached the gates.

They looked different in the daylight, tall enough to admit a man on horseback, with the great blank wall rising around it, both smaller and more formidable, despite the intricate wrought iron. Mayhap because this time there was no crowd to shield me.

I reflected once more on the utter uselessness of the magic Lady Ceciel's potions had given me. I could see magic, as a living glow around the animals and plants that had it, instead of feeling it as a tingling warmth against my skin. And sometimes it welled up within me, and performed prodigies of...well, magic.

But it seemed to answer to its own will, and never to mine.

I had lately come to believe that Fisk had been right about this, at least, and been trying to learn to make it answer to me. I had yet to succeed in any way.

'Twas quite exasperating. Last night, for instance. The magic that had once built a pillow of air beneath me as I fell from a high cliff wouldn't boost me over a twenty foot wall. Which left me no choice now but to approach the gates, whose nearly blind keeper had tipped the guards off to my last excursion here.

He looked up as the sound of our footsteps reached him.

"Good day, sirs. You've business at the university?"

Up close I could see the white film over his eyes. His expression was pleasant and helpful, so I answered readily.

"I'm Benton Sevenson's brother, here about his business. This is my...associate."

As soon as I spoke the murky eyes widened. "You're the one who came in with Scholar Benton last night! The guard, they came asking about you."

"Yes," I said. "I've spoken to them, and answered all their questions. So if we might pass?"

"Of course, of course. I'm not surprised he left some things behind, poor lad, hauled straight up before those old...ah, fired so sudden, like he was. Your associate, he has a name?"

His dim gaze turned to Fisk, clearly wanting to hear his voice, so I said nothing.

"I'm Fisk," my erstwhile squire said. "Did you know Master Sevenson well?"

"Since he was a student here. I was just getting used to calling him Professor when he lost the job, poor lad."

"Were you surprised," Fisk asked, "that he plagiarized his thesis?"

"I wasn't just surprised," the gatekeeper said. "I don't believe it, not for a minute, no matter what papers that Hotchkiss found."

Then he remembered "that Hotchkiss" was dead, and his mouth tightened. But he didn't take the words back.

"Professor Sevenson, he was in the scholar's guard when he was a student." The man lifted the copper whistle that hung around his neck on an embossed strap. "I work with everyone who volunteers for the guard, so's I'll know their voices and can't be fooled. And I'm not fooled, for all my eyes have gone, not easily. Professor Sevenson would never cheat."

He used the title deliberately, defiantly.

"Thank you," I said. "I'll tell my brother you believe in him."

"You do that, sir."

And the gatekeeper passed us through.

"So, we're going with your usual plan," Fisk said, as soon as we were away from the man's keen ears. "We're going to walk up to people and tell them everything."

"'Twill likely get us farther than your usual plan, of skulking about and trying to burgle things. Which got you caught. By the *scholar's* guard."

Fisk, who'd already opened his mouth to reply, closed it with a snap and I went on.

"Benton said the project was housed in a tower, at the west end of the campus, against the—"

"I know where it is." Fisk stepped out in front of me. "What building do you think I was trying to burgle? And it wasn't the scholar's guard who caught me—a lady professor was working late and we surprised each other."

"You think your jeweler's housed there?"

Fisk was leading me between the buildings, on neat graveled paths that bustled with scholars, professors, and even groundskeepers doing something with potted mums. The campus was more pleasant by day, with the sun glowing on windows that had been opened to vent the summer heat. Snatches of voices came from them as we passed, talking about quadratic equations, the essential nature of the gall bladder, and ballad cycles in the reign of High Liege Cormorigan.

I would go mad in such classrooms in a week, but Fisk looked wistful.

"Where else would someone who can work magic be, except part of a research project trying to give people magic?" Fisk asked.

"'Tis not about magic." A subject I find uncomfortable to discuss. "'Tis about giving Gifts to those born without them."

Fisk shrugged, also uncomfortably. His great grandmother had been from a Gifted line, but she had no Gifts, and passed none on to her descendants. This sometimes happens, and by Fisk's generation the family had fallen on such hard times that he'd been forced to take to theft to keep a roof over their heads. 'Twas after that he met Jack Bannister, who'd taught him far too much, and given him a taste for criminality that I, for one, refused to believe he'd been born with. Whatever he might say.

But Jack Bannister was high on the list of subjects we weren't going to discuss, and I was relieved when Fisk stopped at the intersection of several paths and gestured to one that ended at the foot of an ancient tower.

"There it is. And when we're finished with your part of the investigation, I'd like to stop by the library and take a look at this thesis Benton's supposed to have copied."

"You think you can prove 'twas forged?"

"Depends on how they did it. Or if it *was* forged. We have only Benton's word for that."

Even Fisk wasn't so cynical as to suspect Benton... which meant he only said it to provoke, so I ignored him.

Like many old buildings, the tower's door was several yards above the level of the ground. The windows held the thick glass rounds that let in light, but distort the view. There was a walled bailey off to one side, and I guessed there was a cellar with four stories atop. 'Twas probably there long before the university had been built up around it, and the guard at the front door would have looked quite at home had he been standing up with a halberd or a pike, instead of sitting on a camp stool and... "Is he knitting?"

"Looks like it," Fisk said. "I couldn't tell what he was doing last night."

"Is he the one who hauled you off?"

"Unless they've got two knitting guards."

I stared at the building, only a few hundred yards away, and tried to think of another way to do this. I couldn't think of anything, and 'twas unworthy of a knight errant to stand dithering.

"Come," I said. "We only want to ask a few questions." I matched the deed to the word, starting briskly off toward the guard with Fisk trailing reluctantly behind me.

The guard put down his knitting as I approached. It appeared to be a sock, which I was once told takes some skill in the turning of the heel.

"Good morning, sir, may I ask your..." His gaze went past me and found Fisk. "You!"

He leapt to his feet, started to turn for the sword that leaned against the wall behind him, and then realized he shouldn't take his eyes off us. I sympathized with his dilemma. My sword was currently where it usually is, rolled into the bedroll in my pack. This is by far the most practical place to carry it, but means I never have it to hand.

"What are you doing here?" the guard asked Fisk.

"I'm with him," Fisk said, unhelpfully.

"The guard released him this morning," I said. "And I'm here to talk to someone about the project. Perhaps you could bring a professor to speak with us?"

"Access to the project is restricted." But the guard's hand stopped twitching toward his sword.

"I know that," I said. "Which is why my friend and I will wait here, while you go fetch someone."

His hand went instead to his copper whistle, but as I made no move except to stand patiently, and Fisk did the same, he finally released it.

"I'll see if someone will come," he said. "Stay here."

Even then he backed into the tower without taking his eyes off us, and I heard the lock click after the door closed behind him.

"They should have put the lady professor on guard," Fisk said critically. "She had twice his nerve."

"I heard a woman screaming last night. Wasn't that her?"

"Yes, but it was *deliberate*. In fact, it was the smartest weapon she could have chosen."

People whose brains and nerve impress Fisk are rare, and I hoped someone less formidable would come to meet us. So of course the guard returned with a straight-spined dame in a professor's long gown.

There aren't many lady professors. The odds of two being assigned to this project were vanishing small, and I swiftly decided that trying to lie my way in would be ill-advised, as well as unworthy.

"Madam Professor, I'm Benton Sevenson's brother. I believe he didn't forge his thesis, that he's being framed because of something to do with your project. I'd like to discuss it with you and your colleagues."

"Access to the project is restricted." Her gaze drifted past me. "As your friend here could tell you."

"I know," I said. I didn't have to look back—I could feel Fisk exuding harmlessness and innocence. 'Tis an act he performs well, having had so much practice. "But doesn't it trouble you that someone went to such lengths to frame one of your colleagues? Aren't you curious as to why?"

"*If* someone framed him." Her gaze returned to me. "You haven't tested the foundation of your argument, young man. Can you prove he was framed?"

"'Tis why I'm here," I pointed out. "To find proof, and we'll be taking a hard look at that forged thesis shortly. But if my theory is right, don't you want to know the truth?"

"Sevenson's brother..." A frown gathered on her brow as she took in my rough, sturdy clothing, hard worn by miles in the saddle. "*Michael* Sevenson? The one who thinks he's..."

"I'm a knight errant," I said calmly. "In search of adventure and good deeds."

I've had almost as much practice saying that calmly as Fisk has at pretending innocence, and the guard's guffaw didn't ruffle me.

The professor snorted, as one accustomed to student follies. But her gaze lingered on my face and the frown deepened.

"I'm sorry for Professor Sevenson," she said. "But the evidence is clear. He forged his thesis. In any case, access to this project is restricted."

"Benton already knows all about it," I pointed out.

"Then you should talk to him." She turned toward the door.

"Wait," said Fisk. "I was here last night on another matter. I want to see the madman who used to work for Atherton Roseman. I know the Liege Guard brought him here."

"That poor crazy man? Whatever for?" But she'd turned back to listen.

"I'm...an acquaintance of his," Fisk said. "I want to see that he's well-treated. I know better than to hope he's happy."

"Acquaintance," she repeated. "Not a friend?"

"I don't think he has friends," said Fisk. "But it was Michael and I who got him taken from Roseman...and no gods look after man. No insult intended, but it's our duty to see he's being cared for."

She didn't appear to be offended, which I took as a mark in her favor, but she shook her head. "He's not really involved with the project. In fact, I don't know what they thought we'd do with someone who has magic, when our project only involves Gifts. But he's housed in the tower, and I can't—"

"Captain Chaldon would agree 'tis our duty to check on him," I said. "Since the guard brought him to you, 'tis a charge on their honor as well."

Mention of the captain made her hesitate.

"I don't suppose it does any harm," she said. "It might please him to see someone he knows. But if I let you in—" her stern gaze turned to Fisk "—no more trying to break into the tower. Agreed?"

"Agreed." Fisk could have been lying, but I didn't think he was. Which put something of a crimp in my backup plan.

"Very well," the professor said. "You can come in."

CHAPTER 5

Fisk

I brushed past Michael and made my way up the steps. The guard looked nervous about letting me past, and even more uncertain about whether his job was to follow me or keep watch on Michael—who wasn't coming in, but looks a lot tougher than I do. He was still looking back and forth when I followed the lady into the tower, and shut the door behind us.

"Thank you, Professor...?"

"Dayless. And I'm in charge of the project's operations, so don't think you can go over my head."

"I have no doubt that you're in charge."

It made her stern lips twitch, in a way that reminded me of my sister Judith. As Judith would be in thirty years, if she'd been given authority. I had *no* doubt this woman was in charge. But...

"He won't give up." I gestured to the door, where Michael waited. "He thinks his brother is innocent, and he's going to find the truth one way or another."

Michael fought for what he believed in.

"If Professor Sevenson was framed, I hope he does," she said. "In fact, I hope the truth is revealed even if he wasn't. But he can't have access to the project."

Inside the tower, one hallway ran along the front of the building, and another down the center, in a T shape. The bottom of a narrow staircase rose at the far end of the central hallway. They built them that way in the bad old days, to force an attacking army to march down the hall before they could start up. The professor led me down the central hall, and I counted three doors on one side and two on the side that held the staircase.

"Benton told us about his brother," she said. "How he'd gone off to do the craziest thing he could think of, mostly to annoy his father, but then...Benton said it sounds like he's actually *become* a knight errant. He said it was the best example he's ever seen, of illusion becoming truth."

It seemed that Kathy shared my letters, too.

"'Illusion becomes truth, when men believe it,'" I quoted Phisterian. "I suppose it depends on your position on the nature of truth."

The professor looked at me with new interest, which was what I'd intended. "You don't believe there's only one reality, unchanging, except in our perception of it?"

"Not even close." I could tell which room was the jeweler's—it was the only door with a lock.

She must have seen my expression change. "What else can we do? He can't go wandering about, not with the abilities he has." She was pulling out keys as she spoke. "He gave one of the maids a stone, a simple bit of quartz. It made every man she saw fall in love with her. Not just the lad she was courting, all of them. Fortunately the effect vanished when we smashed the stone, but... I asked one of them later, a happily married man in his fifties, what it was like. He said that it was as if everything he'd ever wanted, ever yearned for throughout his life, had been made real in the person of one, rather ordinary servant girl."

I sighed. "No, he can't roam loose."

"I'll send someone to open the door when you knock," she said. "All the staff have keys." After I went through she locked it shut behind me.

The curtains were closed, keeping out the light he hated, but a dim glow leaked around their edges. The musty scent was the same as in his old room—I'd attributed it to the rats he'd kept, but it must be him, quite distinct, even though I felt a draft from one of the windows.

It took some time for my eyes to adjust to the darkness, and there was no sound in the room. But once I could see I spotted him immediately, sitting frozen at a big table covered with tools, and scraps of wood and wire. The moment my gaze found him he relaxed. His clothing rustled as he reached for a mug that sat beside a tray, which held the remains of a decent luncheon.

"So you've stepped through the world once more." His voice was the same too, harsh and breathless. But his hair, once so wild, was pulled into a ragged queue. "Stepping on toes again, I'll warrant, cracking snails, cracking nails. Always the way, with you."

"I came to see how you are," I said, without any hope of a sensible answer.

But I got one.

"Not too bad, for being mad. They want me to perform sometimes, but I can pick my trick. The girls are kind, and the furry ones."

As my eyes continued to adapt, I could see more of the room. It wasn't the cluttered magpie nest of his previous quarters, but he'd only been here a few months. Already a handful of bright scarves had been nailed to the rafters, along with a mass of cut vines that dropped leaves onto the floor as they dried. But mostly there were cages, almost a dozen, made of scraps of wood and wire. Some hung from the ceiling, with the vines, still others were stacked on chairs, the desk, a bureau, and four or five were piled in a corner. All of them were empty, their doors open.

"The furry ones. Do they let you work with their rabbits?"

Could they be that stupid? Unless they wanted him to work magic *on* the rabbits, in which case I pitied the Heir's mistress.

"Rabbits! Never touch 'em. I don't have what they want, that's why they leave me alone, a stone, a bone. It's those cheating rabbits have what they want. But they lie, they lie. Rats, now, rats will tell you the truth. But they won't let me catch any."

So what were the cages for? I was about to ask, but the answer came through the window, brightening the dim light briefly as a squirrel's body pushed the curtain aside.

The jeweler, usually so voluble, fell silent instantly, watching the squirrel scamper along a chest to a plate with half a dozen nutmeats on it. Instead of snatching one and running off, it sat on its haunches, staring back at us as it ate and whipping its curly tail.

"Do you get a lot of such company?" I asked softly, though it was clear he did. The chest had been dragged over to the window to provide them with easy access, and the shells removed to encourage them. The squirrel chose another nut, nibbling busily.

"The sun and snow, they come and go. Some will eat out of my hand, if I hold like water. Been bitten too, but I don't mind."

The squirrel grabbed a third nut and whisked away. There was no cage anywhere near the plate...and all their doors were open.

"Thank you," I said. "I've seen all I need."

His eyes turned back to me, unexpectedly shrewd. "I don't have what you want either, but that don't mean you should trust those lying rabbits."

"I won't." I went to the door and knocked. I hadn't been there long, so I was pleasantly surprised when the lock clicked open immediately.

The man who let me out was middle-aged, and dressed more like a gardener than a scholar.

"Thank you for waiting." It helps to be polite to people you want to pump for information. "Are you one of the ones who look after him?"

"No, they mostly leave that to the maids. But they don't seem to mind. If you'd like to go now..."

He'd already locked the door, and was turning toward the big door at the end of the hall.

"I'd like to talk to Professor Dayless first. She's in charge of him, isn't she?"

"Well, yes. But she said I was to show you out."

What I really wanted was to get a look at the rest of the building, in case Michael was right about the project and I had to burgle it someday. Though I genuinely believed Master Hotchkiss' murder was a more likely thread to pull.

"How about you show me up to Professor Dayless' office, and then you can take me out. Master, is it? You don't look like a professor."

The man snorted, but he led me to the far end of the hall, where the stairs began. "I'm the gamekeeper who trapped those rabbits they're using. I help handle them, feed them, clean the cages. Unless they're running the tests, I've not much to do in the middle of the day."

"Professor Sevenson told us about the rabbits." I followed him up the stairs. "You must have known him."

"We talked some," the man admitted. "He didn't have much more to do around here than I did. Though they didn't make him hang around all the time."

As we walked down the second story hallway to the next flight of stairs, I noticed a strong scent of herbs and chemicals coming from an open door. Looking in as we passed, I saw glowing tabletop braziers, and flasks and jugs and mortars, and shelves of still more glassware against the walls. But the man who sat at the big table, in his shirtsleeves even though the windows were open to relieve the heat, was writing in a notebook. He was in his late fifties or early sixties, with a fringe of salt and pepper hair around a bald head shiny with perspiration. He didn't look up as we passed.

Professor Dayless' office was on the third floor, above the lab, but a lot smaller—there were six doors off this corridor. Like the chemist's, her door was open. Unlike him, she looked up immediately.

"What are you doing here? I let you see him. And frankly, sir, he's in my charge, not yours."

"He's being well-treated," I said honestly. "And probably as happy as he can be. I only wanted to ask... He said the squirrels bit him, but he doesn't seem to be trying to trap them."

"We think he meant to, at first," she said. "But they have sharp teeth, and are willing to visit if he sets out nuts. I suppose they've reached an agreement."

"It looks like it," I said. "Too bad the rabbits are such liars, or he could make pets of them."

She cast me a somewhat startled look.

"Just something he said. But thank you, professor. I'm satisfied."

CHAPTER 6

Michael

"Why did you tell her you were satisfied?" I asked Fisk. "You could have said you wanted to see him again, and gone back. And taken me in with you!"

He'd already told me about the number of doors on the first floor, the lab on the second, and that Professor Dayless' office was above the lab. Still...

"I didn't have to do this much," Fisk said. "The project is your investigation."

And what small progress we'd made was due to him, yes, I knew that.

"Very well. We can go to the library next, and you can take a look at that thesis Benton is said to have copied. It must be a forgery, and if you can prove it we might be able to establish his innocence before other applicants for his job even start..."

We'd been walking down the path, away from the tower, but now Fisk stopped.

"What? You were the one who said you wanted to see that thesis."

"So I may. Eventually. But it's my turn to investigate Hotchkiss' murder now, and *I* want to start by checking out the scene of the crime."

"He was killed in his home," I said. "As he was leaving to go to the lecture, according to Captain Chaldon. Why do you want to look at the place he died?"

"If I knew that, I wouldn't have to look. That's why they call it investigating. And you agreed that after you talked to the professor at the tower, it would be my turn."

"I didn't even get *in* to the tower." But that wasn't his fault. And I had agreed. "All right, 'tis your turn. What next, my...associate? You won't be able to simply walk into Hotchkiss' house, you know. 'Twill be locked. You'll have to get permission from Headman Portner, and maybe Captain Chaldon too. Whereas at the library, they might just let us in."

Fisk chose to ignore this sensible suggestion. "I don't need permission, I just need a key. And we will need it—if we burgled Hotchkiss' house in the middle of the night and wandered around lighting candles, someone would call the scholar's guard. This is a search we need to do by day."

"Where are you going to get a key to—"

I was interrupted by a pealing bell, and then doors in all the buildings around us burst open and scholars flooded out and down the paths like...I was about to say, like a flock of blackbirds, but the students where noisier, and most of them shed their black coats as soon as the sunlight heated them. Fisk had to grab one of them, to stop him long enough to ask directions to the office of the university's chief clerk.

"What makes you think the clerk will have a key? Much less give it to you?" I had to raise my voice to be heard over the clatter.

"The clerk always has spare keys," said Fisk. "You think the headman wants to be bothered every time someone locks himself out? As for giving me the key... I'll start out slow, a few questions, a bit of flattery... What man wouldn't want to help catch a murderer?"

"A man who doesn't want to lose his job," I said. "For passing out his keys to strangers."

"You'd do it," Fisk said. "If I pitched it right."

"I did fall for your pitch," I said. "Once. But this clerk may be a smarter man than I."

However, when we reached the clerk's office that proved impossible on the face of it...for the clerk was a woman.

"Are there many women working here?" Fisk asked pleasantly, after we'd introduced ourselves. "We've just come from talking to Professor Dayless and, well, it's unusual to see so many women in positions of authority."

Nancy Peebles was a plump, middle-aged woman with smooth dark hair and a comfortably worn face. Her office was small, but her desk all but filled it, and a clutter of papers covered the desk. Between that and the file cabinets, there was barely room for Fisk and me. I leaned against the wall, put my hands in my pockets, and prepared to watch the show. Fisk had done little to help with my investigation, after all. I saw no reason to intervene in his.

"There aren't that many of us," the clerk said. "Though if I had a sister I'd not hesitate to send her here, Master Fisk. Do you have a sister to enroll?"

"No," said Fisk. "My associate here is Benton Sevenson's brother, and since we were accused of Master Hotchkiss' murder, we'd like to look into the matter."

The woman's jaw dropped, small blame to her. I was almost as startled, by the rare spectacle of Fisk telling the simple truth. Though he doubtless had some sneaky reason for doing so.

"Accused...? But I thought... I didn't know Professor Sevenson had... Wait. If you're accused of the murder, why aren't the guards holding you? I thought they decided a burglar did it!"

"They did think that, at first," said Fisk. "Then they discovered that Professor Sevenson had good reason to hate Master Hotchkiss. And when he had an alibi, their suspicion fell on us. They have no evidence," he went on, a bit more mendaciously, "so they had to let us go. But you can understand how worrying it is, being suspected of murder. We have to find out who really did it, and clear ourselves."

I had to admit, 'twas a masterful ploy—surprise, to shake her off balance, followed by subtle flattery, along with seeming candor and genuine need.

But Professor Dayless wasn't the only one accustomed to seeing through student tales. The clerk regarded Fisk steadily.

"Isn't that the Liege Guards' job?"

"Maybe," said Fisk. "But if they're focusing on us, they might miss the real killer. For instance, did they talk to you?" Peebles only blinked, but Fisk is better at reading faces than I. "I thought not. And I'll bet you know more about this university than anyone."

She picked up a pen, turning it in her hands. The sharpened end was black with ink and the other ragged, as if someone had nibbled on it. Benton did that with his pens.

"How very flattering. You think that will convince me to spill secrets?"

"So there are secrets to be spilled?" Fisk countered.

"If there were, which there aren't, why should I tell them to you?"

"If they were actual secrets, you shouldn't." Fisk smiled, charmingly. First pull the line, then release the tension—it often hooked more answers than continued pressure would. Fisk seated himself on one of the stools before her desk, and after a moment of hesitation I quietly did the same. I was still somewhat miffed, but watching Fisk work a person was more educational than any class a professor might teach.

"But an innocent man's been murdered," Fisk went on. "And others are accused of the crime. Surely you can answer some ordinary questions. For instance, do you know if Master Hotchkiss had any enemies?"

"Besides Benton, you mean? No, you needn't protest. I knew Scholar Benton, as well as Professor Sevenson, and I don't believe he'd ever forge a thesis—much less murder anyone. I don't know that about either of you," she added.

It might have been Fisk's investigation, but 'twas for Benton's good. I couldn't resist stepping in.

"You don't know us. But if we'd done it, we'd not be so foolish as to hang about asking questions. We'd have run into the next fiefdom, and then two more. By the time they worked through the legal maze of three fiefdoms, we'd be long gone."

"There is that." She put the quill down again. "But Hotchkiss didn't have any enemies. He wasn't liked, not by most, but I know of no one except Professor Sevenson who had reason to hate him."

"Did you know him well?" I asked. Fisk had fallen silent, ceding me the conversation with the ease of years of practice. As if we were still a team. The thought hurt, but I pressed on, "Were you and Hotchkiss scholars here, mayhap?"

"I was never a scholar anywhere," the clerk said. "My son Seymour had the brains in the family."

Looking at the tidy filing cabinets, I doubted that—but the soft way she'd said his name told me her son was dead, so denying her statement wouldn't be taken as a compliment. Fisk had caught it, too.

"What did your son think of Master Hotchkiss, then?"

"I don't think he knew him," the clerk said. "Hotchkiss was several years behind him, and Seymour... He wasn't good at making friends."

Some rich and painful irony lay under those words, but Fisk was doing math.

"If Hotchkiss was younger than your son, he'd be in his...late thirties? That's very young, to be head librarian in a place like this. I thought he'd be around your age, maybe older."

"He was young," she said. "But he invented the alphanumeric system. He could have been head librarian anywhere in the Realm, these last twenty years."

I had no knowledge of this system, but Fisk clearly did. "The alphanumeric...*he* invented it? What a terrible waste. Now I want to catch the killer even more."

Her mouth tightened. "You, and all the others who didn't actually know... Well, a brilliant mind doesn't have much to do with a pleasant personality, and that's a fact."

"Working around here, you'd know that better than anyone," Fisk agreed.

"Hotchkiss wasn't always brilliant, either," she said. "He was originally a history scholar, like your brother, but he struggled to find a thesis. There was even doubt he'd graduate, but then..."

"People often come up with interesting ideas in a field adjacent to their own," Fisk said. "I remember my father saying..."

Fisk, who almost never speaks of his father stopped, but she picked up the thread for him.

"Professor Dayless, whose study is the mind, she says that not knowing anything about a subject lets you come at it from a fresh direction. But Hotchkiss... He also came up with the notion of getting third and fourth year scholars to write up summaries of books as part of their coursework—at least ten books per scholar per year, and credit if they did more. It let him catalog most of one of the largest libraries in the Realm in less than fifteen years, and other libraries are copying that, too. He'd finished with most of the collection, and was working on the stuff no one's really interested in, like unpublished dissertations. That's how he found...ah..."

"This document my brother is said to have copied," I supplied. "But Benton says he did no such thing. And if he didn't, someone must have planted it for the librarian to find."

"And now he's dead," Fisk said. "Mistress Peebles, we'd like to take a look around Hotchkiss' house. Do you have a second key, by any chance?"

"Yes," she said. "And no, I'm not giving it to you."

"Not even for Benton's sake?" I said. "This university, 'tis my brother's life. If he loses it, he has nothing."

"My Seymour was the same. But if I lose this job, then *I* have nothing."

"But what difference does it make if we look around the house?" Fisk persisted. "Captain Chaldon said the law already searched the place. And the servants will have to go in soon and clean up...everything."

"I should be so lucky. The maids are all saying they won't go near the place, much less be scrubbing up anyone's life blood. It'll be days, maybe weeks...but that doesn't mean I'm going to let you in."

"Cheer up," I said as I led Fisk down the hall. "'Twas not likely anyone would give up those keys. Besides, if there was something to be found in Hotchkiss' house the law would have found it already."

And besides that, there was nothing left to do now except examine the forged thesis. Which should count as part of Fisk's investigation, instead of mine.

"I am cheerful," Fisk said. "I learned what I wanted to know."

Before our quarrel, I'd have obliged and asked him what that was. As things stood I simply waited, and soon his need to boast won out.

"Mistress Peebles has the keys we need." He spoke softly, as we were still in the hallway surrounded by offices. "And a three-year-old could pick the lock on her door. All we have to do is wait till she goes home, pick up the keys, and we can let ourselves into Hotchkiss's house while it's still light enough to see. If we walk in openly, acting like we've got permission, there's a good chance no one will question us. And if they do we've got the key. We'd probably have time to skin off before they find out we don't actually have permission."

I've been involved with too many of Fisk's plans to think things would go as smoothly as he assumed.

But on these summer days the light lingered late, and besides...

"If we've nothing to do for the rest of the afternoon, then you won't have any objection to checking out that thesis, in the library."

CHAPTER 7

Fisk

When he really wants something, Michael doesn't give up on it. But I like libraries, and I now had a deep curiosity to see this one. "The alphanumeric system. And he was only a *scholar* when he came up with it."

We emerged from the building that held the clerk's office as we spoke. It was getting late in the afternoon, but with luck we'd have time to look at this forged thesis and maybe get some dinner, before returning to filch Nancy Peebles' keys.

"His brilliance didn't make Mistress Peebles like him any better," Michael said. "What is this system he created? You seem to know of it."

"Everybody knows about it," I said. "Well, everyone who cares about books. My father went to a lecture about it once, and raved about its wonders for the rest of the week."

I hadn't recognized it at the time, but I now wondered if some of his obsessive reaction had sprung from jealousy. It was always someone else who came up with the brilliant ideas. He'd died only a few months later. I pushed those memories away and went on.

"It really was important, for scholars. What he did was to create numbers for everything there is."

Michael's brows rose. "What, a number for horses? And flowers and clouds and spinning wheels and turtles and toothpicks and—"

"Yes." He was joking, but it was an enormous, incredible undertaking. "He created a number for toothpicks. A number for hoof picks for those horses, and for every disease those hooves can get. A number for everything there is, Michael."

He'd stopped joking, but now he was puzzled. "I can see 'twould be an enormous task, but why is it important?"

"Because before he came up with these numbers, that he painted onto the spines of books about those subjects, there was no way to put books about the same topic in the same place. Oh, great libraries like this one, they'd have rooms for particular subjects, with shelves labeled for books about this and that. But all it took was one scholar putting a book down in the wrong room, or stack, and it could be lost for years. For decades, maybe. Even if it was in the right room, you still had to sort through stacks and stacks of books to find the one you needed. My father said the alphanumeric system would make tasks that scholars spent days and weeks on take minutes and hours instead. It revolutionized research, in every library and school in the Realm. That its inventor came up with it here, that he put his system to work in this library first, was a huge academic score for Pendarian. They won't take his murder lightly."

"The more reason for them to forgive Benton, if you can prove who did it. Though I still think 'twill be the project that... We're here."

Michael, who'd planned to burgle it himself, was the one who knew where the library was, but I'd noticed the building last night. An old, three story manor house, that like the tower, had been captured when the university walls went up. It stood out among the drab rectangles of the university buildings like a grand dame among laundry maids.

We passed through the front doors into a lofty, marble-tiled entry hall. It had three arched doorways on the ground floor, with a split staircase winding up between them that came together at the center of the second story gallery. But the manor's furniture had vanished, replaced by a battered table holding flyers, and a large map of the house with a numbered list beside it.

I was stepping up to read it when a young man said, "Can I help you find something?"

A familiar copper whistle hung from a cord around his neck.

"Yes," Michael said. "We're looking for unpublished dissertations on ancient history. Particularly on excavation techniques."

"And do you have a pass to use the library?" It was clear he already knew the answer, but he was going to be polite about kicking us out. And there was only one person who could have told him we were coming.

"Has Professor Dayless had you standing here, waiting for us, all afternoon?" I asked.

"Most of it," he admitted. "But you really can't use the library without a pass. It's restricted to scholars, and guests who've been granted permission."

"Why would Professor Dayless keep us from using the library?" There was a suggestion of gritted teeth in Michael's voice. "We don't even need to use the library. We just want to see one dissertation."

She might have done it because she'd had years of practice anticipating scholars' attempts to evade the rules. Or she might have had some other reason—either way, I resolved not to underestimate the good professor in the future.

"You mean the dissertation Professor Sevenson copied." The officious twerp actually sounded sympathetic. "If it's any consolation, I don't think it's back on the shelves yet. Master Hotchkiss was still working on those dissertations when...ah, before last night. And today everyone's so rattled... I'm not sure anyone could find it for you. Even if access to the library wasn't restricted, which it is."

And he stood there, stubbornly staring at Michael, who stubbornly stared back at him, till I grabbed Michael's arm and dragged my erstwhile employer off to dinner.

The good news was that the burgling of Peebles' office went off without a hitch. We waited outside till we saw her leave the building, then Michael stood watch at the landing to make sure no one came by while I picked the lock...which took almost as little time as I'd optimistically suggested. It took only a few minutes to find Peebles' keys, which she kept in a desk drawer that wasn't even locked.

The bad news was that, as Michael pointed out, we'd probably have to burgle the library after all. But that could be put off till later, and I wanted a look at Hotchkiss' house before Peebles found someone willing to clean it.

A few questions posed to students in the tavern where we'd eaten told us Hotchkiss lived in a cottage that had once housed the old manor's groundskeeper. There was an open commons between it and the library, dotted with trees, flowerbeds, and big stone benches. The benches and grass were covered with students, who'd come out into the lowering sun to study and argue... and flirt, when there was a girl-scholar to flirt with.

We walked right through them, as if we had every right to be there. They paid us no attention at all.

The house was in the same style as the manor, and small only in comparison—two stories, with plenty of windows and two chimneys. The low wall that surrounded it wouldn't keep a rabbit out, much less a burglar. Though their "tight" campus security should have kept most criminals out...and I wondered why it hadn't.

"Must be nice, to be a groundskeeper here." The path to the cottage was well-laid brick, with flowerbeds tended by the university gardeners—who probably lived in town, in hovels.

"I expect 'twas called that when the university took it over," Michael said, pushing open the gate. A latch, but no lock. "Though 'twas likely built to house a dowager, when the new baron came to power."

"Or a mistress."

"'Tis in sight of the manor's windows, Fisk."

"You're right. Not a mistress."

Michael started up the path to the door, but I wanted to scope it out as a burglar would have. After a few curious glances when we went through the gate, the students went right back to ignoring us.

"Where are you going?" Michael demanded, as I set off around the house.

"I want to see how he got in."

"You mean the murderer? What makes you think he didn't go through the front door? Like we should be doing, if you don't want to attract attention."

"Whose attention? The ones who aren't deep in their books are arguing about the nature of lightning. They wouldn't notice if we...ah. I can see why the guards decided it wasn't a burglary."

We'd just come around the back of the house, and there it was—half a dozen dark streaks under a window, plainly visible on the stone wall, where muddy shoes had scrabbled for purchase.

Michael sighed. "All right, I'll humor you. Why do marks below a window, where someone has clearly tried to climb in, make it *not* a burglary?"

"Because burglars aren't stupid. At least, no more than anyone else. Why climb through a window over a muddy flowerbed, when there's a window two down that's over a brick path?"

"Mayhap the one over the path was locked," Michael said. "And the other open."

"And why scramble to get up, through either of them, when there's a crate next to the back door that would lift you high enough to climb in easily?" I thought he'd missed that.

Michael returned to the back door. The crate beside it held three pots of growing herbs, as if some cook had taken them off a kitchen windowsill and set them outside, for whatever reason one sets plants outside. Michael might have been able to tell me, but as I was currently up on points I decided not to ask.

"He might not have thought of it." But Michael's voice was slower now, less certain. "Particularly if he wasn't much practiced in his craft."

"A beginner wouldn't start on a campus swarming with scholars, or with the house of a librarian, who wasn't likely to be rich. No, if anyone went through that window it wasn't a burglar. Not even a beginner."

"But an amateur murderer might have," Michael murmured. "Most in that situation wouldn't be thinking clearly enough to notice the crate."

"Or think about finding a pail, or something else to stand on in that shed between the compost heap and the privy?"

Michael said nothing, so I led the way to the front door and tried the key. It took a bit of jiggling, as if it hadn't often been used in that lock, but it turned and I swung the door wide.

In this house the stairs started up from the front hall, in the usual way. Off to the left, through an open door, I saw the legs of an overturned chair and a corner of the hearth. Farther down the hall were two more doors, closed—kitchen and dining room, probably. The window with the muddy streaks would open into the dining room.

The hall itself held a coat rack laden with coats, cloaks and professorial robes, all in the university colors, and a bench where you could put on or remove boots in bad weather. And lastly, a rug that would have been quite nice, if not for the huge red-brown stain that marred one corner.

Michael, who for all his softness is less squeamish than I, knelt and lifted the edge. The blood beneath it was still wet and red. I didn't blame the maids.

"He bled a lot," Michael said.

"Head wounds do."

"That's how it seems, when 'tis bleeding into your eyes in a fight. But most scalp wounds clot, eventually. This blow must have broken the skull, as well as the scalp."

"I wonder what he hit him with."

"Whatever 'twas, the guards will have taken it for evidence. What *are* you looking for, Fisk? Captain Chaldon told us how he died."

"I know. I'm looking for *why* he died."

And there might be no evidence of that, but I saw no need to admit it, yet.

The front room, to the left of the hall, held formal furniture, much of it overturned, and a number of expensively bound books. Whether they belonged to the university and came with the house, or belonged to the librarian I couldn't say. But they'd been thrown off the shelves and were lying on the floor, some face down with their pages crumpled beneath. My father had taught me to care for books, and I suppressed an urge to pick them up and rescue them.

Someone had ransacked this room.

"If he knew about the lecture, and everyone in town seemed to, why didn't the killer wait till Hotchkiss was gone?" I asked. "When murders happen during a burglary, it's usually because you've made too much noise, and the homeowner wakes up and confronts you. If he'd waited a while Hotchkiss would have been gone, and he could have taken the place apart in peace."

"You're right," said Michael. "I understand, now, why Captain Chaldon thinks murder was intended from the start."

"Then why take time to wreck the place, after he'd accomplished his goal?" This violent search couldn't have taken place before the murder. It had been done while Hotchkiss' blood was seeping into that carpet, and the thought made me shudder.

"Mayhap 'twas a robbery after all, but Hotchkiss was running late? The killer thought he'd gone to the lecture, but Hotchkiss then came down and surprised him?"

It wasn't impossible. Figuring out what had happened by looking around a room was harder than the ballads made it seem.

"Was he looking for valuables?" Michael went on. "Or something else?"

"Hard to be sure. Something else would be better for us."

There were few signs of search in the kitchen, though several cupboard doors had been pulled open. Neither valuables or secrets are stored in a room where the maids might be looking for something at the back of a drawer or shelf.

"He'd not only finished dinner, he had time to wash his dishes." Michael gestured to a basin of cold, dirty water. A clean plate, cup, and assorted silverware sat on a towel beside it, along with an empty tea strainer.

"But he didn't get around to throwing the water out. Or putting the dishes away." There was a kettle sitting on the hearthstone, with a thick pad beside it. "Did he make himself tea while he washed up?"

"No tea pot," Michael said.

"Not here."

The killer hadn't disturbed much in the pantry, and the search in the dining room looked perfunctory.

Michael pulled open a drawer full of silverware and met my eyes. "So, 'twas a search for secrets after all."

I picked up a spoon, judging the weight. "It's plate over tin, and thin too. But if it was a burglar, he's pretty fussy."

"And Master Hotchkiss was well paid," Michael said.

Even silver plating is expensive. "I told you, any university in the Realm would want him. He was probably the best paid librarian, ever."

And he'd cared enough about possessions to spend money on them. The dining room rug was almost as good as the one in the front hall had been.

It was in the upstairs rooms that the search had gotten serious. The bed had been torn apart with absurd thoroughness. It's only in ballads that people hide things under their mattresses—paper crackles, and anything else is too lumpy to sleep on. All Hotchkiss' clothing had been pulled out of the big wardrobe and thrown on the floor. The linen was rather fine for a librarian, and while there was no lace on his cuffs— anyone who works with quill and ink knows better— the lace on his collars made up for it. It wasn't overlarge, but intricate, and soft as spider silk.

"A burglar would have cut this off. It would fetch a copper roundel a foot from a fence."

There was no point in going through the bureau—the killer had already done it.

The back bedroom had been simply furnished, for a guest or a valet. It was full of boxes of papers, most of which had also been dumped on the floor. But it was in Hotchkiss' office that the storm had really struck.

You could tell this was the room he'd lived in, the chairs not only padded, but comfortably worn. A candelabra, now lying on the floor with its candles snapped, was coated with the drippings of long evenings of reading.

The desk was sturdier than the rest of the furniture and older, not only well made, but stained and scratched. The bare shelves behind it told me where the clutter on the floor had come from.

"He didn't find what he was looking for," I said.

"How can you know that?" Michael bent to pick up a teacup that had fallen from a small table, which had once held the candelabra near the reading chair. Its saucer had broken in half, but the cup was intact.

"Because we've been in every room, and they've all been tossed. If he'd found what he was looking for he'd have stopped. There'd be at least part of some room untouched."

"And nowhere is. Here's the teapot, what's left of it."

Unlike the thin cup, its thick ceramic had shattered into a dozen pieces.

"Someone smashed this," Michael said. "Deliberately."

"Maybe he was frustrated, and wanted to smash something."

"Mayhap." He picked up a fragment of the bottom and sniffed it. Then he went and sniffed the teacup. "Spice tea."

"He died from a blow to the head," I said. "Not poison."

"Then why smash the pot?"

"Because it would be pretty frustrating to kill a man, and then not be able to find what you came for. In fact..." I reached down and pulled a paper from under a tumbled book. "Look what I found."

It was a pass to last night's lecture, a bit sloppily printed. Understandable, in something that only had to last a few weeks. I watched Michael's face change as comprehension dawned.

"If he was leaving for the lecture, as Captain Chaldon said, why was that not in his pocket? He must have been killed earlier," Michael said. "After dinner, but before 'twas time to depart."

"Then why was he dressed to go out when he was killed? Did he plan to go somewhere else first?"

"Either that or the killer dressed him, to make it look as if he was on his way to the lecture. But why?"

We stared at each other in bafflement.

"We don't know enough," Michael said.

"Then let's see if we can learn more." I went to the desk, righted the chair, and began running my hands over the frame and under the belly drawer. "People who are frustrated, they miss things."

It wasn't that well-hidden, once you started pulling out the drawers, though the lower drawer was deeper than the others, making the fact that it didn't slide out as far less obvious. I had to do some searching to find the catch that released it from the desk, but once you removed the drawer, the narrow compartment at its back was visible. How to remove the lid fitted over the top wasn't so obvious, and the light was beginning to dim. I carried it over to the window, to see better.

"How did you know 'twould be in the desk?" Michael asked, as I felt and pried at the panel.

"I didn't. But there's no reason to build a secret compartment in a house meant for your mother-in-law, so it would probably be in the furniture."

"Why not the bed, or the bookshelves, or—"

"The desk doesn't match the rest of the furniture, which I'm guessing came with the house. Some past librarian might have moved it in, but it was a logical place to—" The lid came off in my hand.

The drawer was deep enough he'd only had to fold the papers once to fit them in, all four sheets, with symbols and letters on the outside. Once they were unfolded...

"Ledgers," said Michael. "They're not supposed to look like it, but those are the initials of all the months, Hollyon, Junipera, Crocusa, Grassan."

"The numbers after that are amounts paid," I said. "But it doesn't say by who, or for what."

"That's on the other side," Michael said. "'Tis a code."

I turned the pages over once more. "Not a code. Just a symbol and letter so he can tell which sheet is whose. Heart, 'PN.'"

Master Hotchkiss' writing was as neat as you'd expect from a man who spent his days painting numbers and letters onto book spines. The small heart drawing, and capital P and N were quite clear.

"Professor N?" I speculated. "There's a PB as well."

"Professors? Surely not."

"Why surely? Do you know the difference between a professor and a bandit? You usually forget what professors teach you. The lessons you learn from a bandit stick."

Michael grimaced—and I have to admit, I've done better.

"'D,'" he said. "And hammer, 'A.' But the D's crossed out."

"There's only one set of payments on this sheet," I said. "Looks like D refused to pay. Here's a quill pen, but the 'PS' has been crossed out too...and no payments at all. Professor Sevenson, by any chance?"

"Benton didn't say anything about...whatever this is. Scales, 'M,' 87? And 'PB'... S 20, that's a year, isn't it? The 20th year of Stephan's reign. Eight years ago. But what does the 87 mean?"

"No idea." I turned that sheet over and looked. "But you're right, two sets of entries, and they run for just nearly eight years. It's not the largest account, either. 'AH' has been paying for almost twelve years now. Though it looks like AH is just one person."

The A was a bit off too, with one longer leg and the cross stroke curling past the second leg. The string of numbers and letters after these initials was incomprehensible, but I didn't care. I couldn't hold back the words any longer.

"You do realize what this means, don't you?"

"Master Hotchkiss was blackmailing these people." Michael looked gloomy. "How sad for a brilliant man to stoop to such a thing. And why? You said yourself that any university would have hired him. This house is a fine one! He had no need to prey on other men's secrets."

"It doesn't have to be need," I said. "Though he certainly spent the money. None of these sums are huge—not even Professor N's, and he pays more than the others—but they'd add up nicely over time. At this point, I'm surprised the silverware was only plated. But blackmail is often as much about power as it is the money. And this demolishes your theory about the project being behind it. If Hotchkiss was a blackmailer, that's almost certainly why he was killed."

Which left me in charge!

Michael looked even gloomier, but he rallied bravely. "Then why did someone plant that fake thesis, to frame Benton? The 'PS' was crossed out."

"Probably because Benton didn't pay him," I said. "Which might explain why he brought the forged thesis forward... It would take some nerve, to fake that dissertation, and then try to blackmail someone with it."

It wasn't how blackmailers usually worked either. It was their victims' knowledge of their own guilt that kept the money flowing.

"If he tried to blackmail Benton, and revealed his secret when Benton wouldn't pay, then your brother really does have a motive."

"But he'd have told me... No, this is Benton. Besides, he has an alibi. He was sitting with friends waiting for the lecture to start."

"That alibi only works if you assume Hotchkiss was on his way to the lecture when he was killed. And since he didn't have the pass with him, we're assuming that someone killed him earlier, and then tried to make it look like he was killed when the lecture was about to start. So they'd have an alibi."

"Then that lets Benton out," Michael said firmly. "He was with me before the lecture started. We came onto the campus together, and he went into the lecture hall while I headed for the library. But even if he didn't, Benton would no more murder a man than...than I would. In fact, I'd be *more* likely to kill than Benton."

For all his faults—and he had them—Michael wouldn't kill anyone, even a blackmailer. On the other hand, one of those faults was to see the best in people, particularly people he cared about.

Look who he'd picked to be his squire.

"If he was with you, then he's got an alibi for the time before the lecture as well," I said. We didn't know how long before the lecture Hotchkiss had been killed, but it wasn't likely Benton could have sneaked away from Michael and Kathy long enough to commit a murder. And only a monster could have then gone back and pretended nothing had happened so well neither of them would suspect him. "But while I'm willing to take your word for it, Captain Chaldon won't be. This makes you both look a lot more guilty than you did this morning. Which means we can't tell the law what we found here."

"I realized that," said Michael, "from the moment we broke in. Without permission."

"It's a good thing we did," I pointed out. "If Chaldon had found this..." My gaze went to the lecture pass, sitting on one corner of the desk. "He must only have glanced at this room, or he'd have found the pass and asked the same questions we did. And how did Benton get a lecture pass? It's not as if he's welcome on the campus these days."

Michael frowned. "I don't know. He had it, and was planning to attend when I arrived. Mayhap he got it before he was dismissed, and decided to go anyway. 'Twas open to anyone with a pass, even the townsfolk."

"Maybe." But I tucked the lecture pass in with the blackmail notes, and was about to leave when I remembered something else I'd seen in a desk drawer. I opened it again, and pulled out Master Hotchkiss' keys.

"Fisk! You promised not to... Well, even if you didn't, 'twas implicit that we'd not rob the house!"

"I'm not 'robbing the house.' I'm making it possible for us to get into anyplace Hotchkiss could go without having to burgle it. Including the library you want to get into so badly. We still need to look at that thesis, and I want to search his office. If Hotchkiss was the kind of man who'd commit blackmail, it's likely he was in on framing your brother."

Michael sighed, but evidently brothers came before knightly principles. He said nothing as I refolded the papers, and tucked them inside my vest since neither of us wore coats on this warm day. I would have left then—it was almost dark—but Michael led me down to the kitchen, and went to the compost pail that sat below the basin. I could smell the contents when he removed the lid, fresh and rotting at the same time. He reached in and pulled out a mass of damp brown gunk, then looked around helplessly for something to carry it in.

I went into the dining room and pulled a clean napkin from one of the drawers. It might stain the linen, but Hotchkiss wouldn't care.

"Was the tea magica," I asked, as Michael folded damp grounds into the cloth. "Is that what's bothering you?"

"No." Michael could see magic, as well as feel it, so he'd know. "But there's a scent to it that's...off. I just... 'Tis not right, Fisk."

Whether they're related to magic or not—and I think they are, no matter what the scholars say—Gifts are quirky, vague, unpredictable...and they work. So I nodded, and was grateful that the slowly dampening napkin would end up in his pocket instead of mine.

"Come on," I said. "It's almost dark, and I want to return Peebles' keys before we tackle the library."

CHAPTER 8

Michael

There were fewer students in the commons behind the library when we left Master Hotchkiss' house, locking the door behind us and strolling off as insouciantly as we'd gone in. Since there was no longer enough light to read by only the debaters remained, almost invisible in their black coats, for 'twas finally turning cool. Their topic had shifted from natural science to whether Mistress Selina could be brought to notice Tommy's attempts to court her, and most didn't think the odds were in his favor.

Several windows in the library glowed faintly, proclaiming that a few scholars had lit lamps to finish up their work. So I made no objection when Fisk insisted that our next task was to return Mistress Peebles' keys. We'd have to wait till the library was deserted before we broke in, since...

"Why would Professor Dayless set a scholar to keep us out of the library? Has she some reason to dislike Benton? He said nothing of it."

"More likely she doesn't like us," Fisk said. "I did try to break into the tower last night, and you came back this morning, snooping around her precious project. Or it could be she's just following the rules. You told her we were going there next, and most universities restrict access to their libraries."

"If 'tis something to do with the project that got Benton framed," I said, "she might have reason to fear our questions, and to keep us from the thesis as well."

"Possibly. But then you have to explain why, as head of the project, she brought Benton into it in the first place. And why she went to the trouble and considerable risk of framing him. All she had to do to get rid of him was tell him his services were no longer needed—which seems to have been true, anyway—and let him go back to his history. Not to mention why she'd kill Hotchkiss."

Talking about our rival theories reminded Fisk of our quarrel, and his voice grew cooler as he spoke. Involved in the puzzle of Hotchkiss' death, we'd fallen into the familiar pattern of working together, playing off each other's ideas.

But by the terms of our agreement, 'twas my turn to lead the investigation now.

"I think we'll find that whoever killed Hotchkiss also bribed him to proclaim Benton a cheat, to take him from the project," I said. "A man who'd stoop to blackmail would also take a bribe."

"You really think a blackmailer is going to be murdered by someone who wasn't his victim?"

"We haven't established for certain that he was a blackmailer," I pointed out. Though 'twas hard to think what else that list of payments might represent.

"We haven't established for certain that old thesis is a forgery, either," Fisk retorted, then scowled when he found himself walking down the logical trail *I* wanted to follow.

"Then we'd best do that next, hadn't we?" I said. "I'm so glad you agree."

Returning Mistress Peebles' keys was even easier than taking them had been, since the key to her office was also on her key ring. Fisk hesitated a moment before putting it back in the drawer, and I could understand why—that ring held over a score of keys, which would probably admit us to most of the buildings on the campus, including the tower. But there was no way for us to keep it without her noticing it had gone missing, probably within a day. And we still had the half dozen keys we'd found in Hotchkiss' desk to let us into the library, at least.

By the time we left the building that held the university's offices there were even fewer people on the paths, and the shadows between the phosphor lamps were deepening.

'Twas now late enough that the library might be deserted, and 'twas still early enough that the lamp we'd have to light would be taken for that of a hard-working scholar. We even had keys, which would probably open the library door. In short, 'twas the perfect moment to set about my part of the investigation.

So I shouldn't have been surprised when I saw the pale light of a phosphor lamp on the path ahead of us turn lavender, and then bright orange. We were too far away to make out the features of the thin man gazing up at it, but he didn't seem alarmed. On the other hand, phosphor light doesn't change color. Fisk and I both stopped to stare.

"Mayhap some scholar's experiment?" I said.

The light turned blue and the thin man—who wasn't wearing a scholar's coat—began to dance an awkward, high-kneed jig.

Fisk swore under his breath and began to run.

I followed, and though I hadn't recognized him, I wasn't surprised when I reached the light and found Fisk clutching the mad jeweler's arm.

"How under two moons did you get out?" Fisk demanded.

"The night lifted her skirts to me, the wicked hussy. So I had to step up, didn't I? Up to the sill, not my will. Defenestrated, they call it. But I stepped up like a man. Pork the whole night, I will."

A feverish excitement shone in his face—but now that he was distracted from it, the phosphor light resumed its normal silver-green glow.

On the other hand, anyone who'd seen that rainbow display was bound to investigate.

"We shouldn't stay here," I said, taking the man's other arm. "Where do we...?"

I started to pull him down the path toward the library, and saw three young scholars pass through the light of another lamp, hurrying in our direction.

We weren't the only ones who'd seen.

"Hang it!" Fisk turned, dragging the jeweler in the opposite direction. "I don't want him caught—they'll lock him up even tighter."

We had reached the darkest part of the walk, between two lamps. I pulled Fisk and the jeweler off the path.

"You hide him," I said. "I'll draw them off."

I turned to check on the scholars—whom I couldn't see at the moment, for they too were between lamps. But if I couldn't see them, they probably couldn't see

Fisk and jeweler. Particularly if I gave them something else to look at, and in one way young men resemble cats—if something runs, they tend to chase it.

I sprinted under the next lamp and heard a shout go up behind me. I too am a young man, and my heart leapt with the thrill of the chase. I kept to the path for some time, letting them see me as the circles of light flowed toward me and fell away. I'd hoped to simply outrun them—Benton couldn't keep up with any of us in a footrace—but these scholars evidently kept themselves in better shape than my brother had. If anything they were gaining on me.

At least none of them were members of the scholar's guard, for no whistle sounded. I might be able to outlast them...but I also might not.

My first thought, when I saw another scholar walking through the light ahead of me, was fear that he might join the chase. I didn't want to lose them too swiftly, but when I saw him I almost swerved aside.

My second thought was that if my magic worked as well as the jeweler's I could have turned the light over his head pink, and set them after him—he was even in shirtsleeves like myself, with his coat thrown over his arm. But magic didn't answer my command.

On the other hand, did it have to?

I summoned up my reserves and put on a bit more speed, increasing the distance between me and the hunters on my heels. I heard one of them gasp for his friends to go on, and glancing back saw him stop and bend forward, catching his breath while his more fit companions ran on.

The man in front of me was walking while I ran. I gained ground on him quickly, marking the intervals when he passed in and out of the light.

I caught him in the deepest shadow, and offered a breathless apology as I yanked his coat away, sending books and notes flying. His curses followed me as I raced onward.

My pursuers encountered him—indeed, judging by the shouting one of them almost ran over him as he knelt to pick up his fallen books.

But unless they stopped to talk to him, in which case I'd escape easily, they had no way to know that I now possessed the means to change my appearance. All I needed was another scholar in his shirt sleeves—and surely few would wear a jacket on a night this warm.

There was no one in sight at the moment so I put my mind to running, turning corners occasionally, but establishing a pattern of keeping to the lighted paths. I only prayed that the next people I encountered wouldn't be a troop of that accursed scholar's guard.

I gained more distance as they began to tire, but they clung to my trail with dogged determination and I was beginning to run short of breath myself.

I came up on yet another cross path, and off to my left saw a scholar walking away from me...and he too carried his coat over his arm!

I turned onto the leftward path, right under a tall lamp, and then put on the best burst of speed my laboring lungs could supply while I dragged the dark coat over my betraying white sleeves. I passed just one building, then in the darkness between the lamps I swerved off the path, falling into a walk moments before I reckoned they'd come into view.

'Twas an absurdly simple trick—but even if they noticed me walking away from the path, they should at least be forced to split up, uncertain which of us to chase.

I heard one of them call out as they rounded the corner, but he was so breathless I couldn't understand what he said. Fisk has trained me well enough that I didn't look back, but every particle of my being focused on the sound of their footfalls on the gravel as they ran nearer, nearer...and right on down the path, after my decoy.

I took to my heels as soon as they were out of sight once more, for they'd soon catch up with a man who wasn't running and learn their mistake. Now, I only needed to gain a bit of distance before I found a place to hide.

In the yard between four buildings, an ornamental garden that centered on a small fountain looked wonderfully inviting—it had benches to hide behind, flowerbeds, and even some sculpted topiaries.

I immediately turned toward the far less notable junipers that clustered beside the buildings, diving into the thickest clump I could find and burrowing in like a rabbit escaping the fox. The tangled woody stems were a bruising maze, but the branches were thick—and prickly enough to discourage casual investigation.

To refrain from hiding in the obvious place is a good trick for eluding pursuit. An even better trick is to be willing to do something your pursuers won't.

I was near the center of the bush when they burst around the corner, and immediately went still. In my stolen black coat I must be all but invisible, and the branches had twisted my face away from them. I closed my eyes and breathed through my mouth, as quietly as I could—though they were puffing so loud they probably couldn't have heard anything softer than a shout.

"Do you see him? If he was the guy in the coat, he must have come this way."

"I don't see anyone. I didn't see anyone in a coat, either. Are you planning to run around tackling everyone on campus? Because the last one almost took a swing at me."

"We both saw him take that path," the other one said. "If he wasn't ahead of us then he must have turned off, and I did see someone walking this way. Look behind that fountain, will you? And make it quick. He may be getting away."

"I hate to be the one to break the news, but he's *gotten* away." The scholar was walking around the fountain as he spoke. "I don't know why I'm running after whoever it is, anyway. *I'm* not an alchemist."

"Well, I am, and I want to know what he was doing with that lamp! It had to be a chemical...but did he put it on the phosphor moss? Into the water? Or if it was some sort of smoke or gas, how did he direct and concentrate it so quickly?"

"If you can find him I'll be happy to help you ask, but he's probably halfway across campus by now. Or snug in his own room."

"Curse it, I have to find out what he was doing! If he's part of Mumphrey's team then their project will beat ours outright. The council offered a prize, you know. Fifty silver roundels..."

They'd already finished with the easily searched garden. Their voices were growing fainter as they walked away.

"...will buy a lot of beer, even split four ways."

"That's great—for you and your team. I've got a class first thing..."

I waited till they were long gone before I struggled out of the bushes, which made only a slight shushing noise.

Remembering Fisk's jest about the difference between a bandit and a scholar, I pulled out my purse and tucked a brass roundel deep into one of the coat's pockets. I then hung it over one of the garden benches, trusting it would make its way back to its owner—with all these identical coats they must put names in them somewhere, if only to get the right coat back from the laundry, and this was the only apology I could make to the man I'd robbed so roughly.

I still had work to do this night, but first I needed to find Fisk. We'd had no time to discuss the matter, but I thought he'd have taken the jeweler back to his tower. He'd already determined the man was being well-treated, and what else could be done with him? Besides, I hoped to catch up with them before the madman was returned to his rooms. That scholar wasn't the only one who was curious about how he'd changed the color of that phosphor light.

But what I wanted to know was how he controlled his magic.

CHAPTER 9

Fisk

We stood in the shadows, watching three scholars go chasing after Michael as mindlessly as Trouble chased rabbits. I wished I'd had time to come up with a lie for him to tell if they caught him...though how I could have explained what happened to that lamp, I had no idea.

"Why were you just standing there, making the lamp change color?" I asked my companion critically. "You might as well have put up a sign, 'Mad Mage on the Loose.' If they catch you running around out here, you may end up in a real cell."

"They wanted it," he said. "I had to oblige."

But he looked thoughtful, and turned to go back to the tower without resistance.

Aside from a few small distractions, such as waiting for a lad to climb out of some female scholar's window—we knew it was a girl, because she leaned out to give him a lingering farewell kiss—we made it back to the tower with no trouble.

I headed for the elm, assuming he'd escaped from the yard his windows looked out on. But to my surprise, he took my arm and led me around to the other side of the building. All those windows had been locked last night, but now one of them swung open.

"You got out that way?" I kept my voice down, since the guard was still at his post at the front of the building. "Wasn't your door locked?"

"What's a lock when a man has wings? Flew to my love, I did."

I took that for madness...but then I remembered the way that lamp changed color, and how Michael's unpredictable magic had saved him when he was thrown off a cliff. He might be telling the simple truth.

For a moment I considered asking him to fly us up to the window, and promptly rejected that idea for several good reasons—not least of them that I had no desire to sprout feathers.

"We could go around and climb the tree," I said aloud. "But I got caught trying that last time..."

He went with me to fetch the rain barrel, and then refused to help me roll it over to the window, so it took me as long as it had last night. But once I stood it up beneath the sill he climbed up willingly. I gave him a final boost into the room beyond, and he waited there while I followed him up and in.

It was evidently being used for storage, with trunks and boxes full of papers, though the moons shone on the other side of the building so it was too dark to see much.

The door to the hallway was closed, which he might have done himself. But how had he gotten out of his room in the first place?

"Was your door left unlocked?"

"The door? Not to me. I was free."

He crossed the room and opened the door as if to demonstrate, gesturing for me to precede him like a some baron's fancy butler. So I did. His room was right across the corridor, and even in the dark I could see bright new splinters where the latch had broken out of the frame.

The back of my neck prickled in primitive warning. Prying open a latched door is the clumsiest form of burglary. It makes a lot of noise, and it shouts to everyone who walks by, Hey, this house is being burgled!

Jonas Bish, who'd taught me house breaking, had once handed me a crowbar and made me do it, so I'd understand why it was so important to learn to pick locks. And that had been a relatively flimsy door.

Whatever had broken this door open had twisted the doorknob in its socket, and bent the iron latch before the frame cracked. And maybe you could somehow muffle the noise that had made with magic...but if you could do that, why not use magic to pick the lock? For that matter, why not go out the window, and simply escape through the courtyard?

The jeweler was mad...but that didn't mean he was stupid. And if magic had done this, he was definitely going to get locked up in a real cell.

I opened the broken door and stepped into the smashed room beyond. The curtains had been ripped aside and moonlight poured through the windows on this side of the building, displaying the wreckage in the square patches where it shone and obscuring the rest. The scarves and vines had been pulled down from the ceiling, some of them shredded as if with claws. The delicate cages were in splinters.

It looked as if a giant squirrel had rampaged through the room, smashing things in rage and panic.

I didn't know much about magic—and he was mad, after all. But I couldn't think of any reason he'd destroy his own work.

The jeweler made a sound of distress, but instead of going to the smashed cages he hurried to the over-turned bureau, checking to be sure no squirrels had been caught in the furious destruction. He heaved a re-lieved sigh when he found no furry bodies, then knelt on the floor, carefully searching for something small.

"Did he do *this?*"

I jumped half a foot, even as I recognized Michael's voice coming from the doorway behind me.

"What are you...?" But it was obvious what he was doing here, and he would have seen the rain barrel and followed us in.

"How did you lose them?" I asked instead.

"Borrowed a coat."

He wasn't wearing it now, which was too bad—it was late enough that we'd stand out among the few schol-ars who were still wandering the campus. But before I could ask what happened to it, Michael went on, "How could he do all this without the guard hearing him? It must have sounded like a bull was loose in here."

"Could he have used magic to muffle the noise as he did it?"

The jeweler had been picking up nutmeats, carefully brushing them free of pottery shards. Now he put them on the largest piece of the broken plate, and set it on the sill outside his window. Then he closed and latched it.

"Dinner time's done," he said. "Break the law if you come in here, you will."

"You're asking me?" Michael's voice was exasperated. "For all I know he could use magic to pick up the tower, and carry it over the plains. But...would he do this?"

I didn't see why. On the other hand...well, mad. And I could think of a number of reasons he might feel the kind of rage that could provoke this.

Still...

"If you have to do something noisy during a burglary—opening a money chest you can't pick, say—Jonas taught me you could wrap blankets or a feather tick around it to muffle the sound."

The jeweler's feather tick had been pulled half-off the bed. I went over to look at it and saw nothing... Of course, the light was pretty dim, and I didn't want to kindle a lamp.

With Michael watching curiously, I ran my hands over the surface. Nothing. I grabbed one corner and folded the thick pad to check the other side...and cursed as I cut my hand on something sharp, embedded in the cloth. I felt more carefully.

"It's full of splinters and sharp bits. Whoever did this used the mattress to muffle the noise.

I didn't think madness tried to conceal itself.

"Beds always tell the truth," said the jeweler, coming over to join us. "Give all the secrets away, beds do. And they know plenty. Life and death, it all ends and begins in beds."

Michael gestured to the demolished room. "Did you do this?"

"No," said the jeweler. "Why would I? But the jay birds shrieking it will. Unrestful, birds are, but they can't help it. It's the seeds."

"If he didn't do this, who did?" I asked. "And why?"

"I don't know," Michael said slowly. "But I can think of one thing he did today, that was different from all the days before it."

"He talked to me." I had already reached that grim conclusion. "He talked to me, and someone let him out, and tried to make it look like he trashed the place. Who let you out? Did you see them?"

He'd already answered his one direct question for the day.

"The night doesn't have a face. Went to go dancing, I did, and I did."

"He said earlier that he was defenestrated," Michael put in. "That means someone threw—"

"I know what it means. If they tell the student guard he's missing, tell them he's dangerous, powerful..."

"What, you think they'd kill him on sight? That's absurd. The mad are always judged innocent, for they can't control their actions. 'Tis more likely they thought he'd flee, mayhap to some other town. That would keep him from talking to us, or anyone else, just as surely."

"And if they caught him, after this, he'd be closely confined," I said. "Probably somewhere no one is likely to talk to him."

Somewhere away from windows where squirrels could come in, away from kindly maids who'd comb his hair.

"We can't leave him here," I said. "If they're trying to keep him from talking to us, we need to find out what he knows. But where...?"

"The attic, of course." Michael sounded absurdly cheerful. "We're the only ones lodged up there, and Benton can care for him during the day. He needs something to do, anyway. Do you know my brother Benton, Master...?"

"He's a rat," the jeweler said promptly. "A rat amongst rabbits."

"And you think someone's afraid *he* might tell us something?" I said. "We'll be lucky if we can get him off the campus and back to our rooms."

"Do we have a choice?" Michael asked.

I had come to this town to make sure the jeweler was all right. To have him locked up in a cell because I'd gone to see him...

"No. We don't."

CHAPTER 10

Michael

"But what am I supposed to do with him?" Benton demanded at breakfast the next morning. "He's a madman, and his magic is said to be dangerous. You can't just stuff him in the attic like...like a spare coat rack!"

"I don't see why not," I said. "He settled down nicely last night, and he didn't object when Fisk locked him in this morning. All you'll have to do is feed him, get him whatever he needs to amuse himself, and check in on him every now and then."

"I put him in the room next to mine," Fisk added. "You probably want to square that with the landlady."

He'd also found a few trunks—long abandoned, judging by the dust on them—and left the jeweler decorating his new rooms with moth-eaten stockings and old-fashioned hats. He'd seemed reasonably content—and even more content after we'd gone to the convenient tavern across the street and picked up some rolls, sausages, and a pot of butter. We'd taken some of it up to him, and then brought the rest down to share with Benton and Kathy, hoping to soften the blow.

I thought Benton was taking it well, all things considered.

"Did you ask your madman more about the project?" Kathy said. "If he knows something someone's trying to conceal..."

"Then 'someone' wasted their effort," Fisk said. "He said he could dance with the best of him, and that all the girls thought so, but he'd given his rubies to the moon and had none left for us. We were lucky he kept his mouth shut while we whisked him out the gate."

Fisk had spotted several scholar's coats, which had been pegged out on a windowsill to dry after some accident—involving beer, judging by the lingering scent. The man who watched the gate that night wasn't the blind porter, who might have recognized our voices, and Fisk distracted him with a few questions while I pulled our mad friend past him.

When I'd asked the jeweler how he controlled his magic, he'd said it was easy because his fingers were fish, but that after they'd taken a nibble or two you had to let them wiggle away.

"With any luck," I said, "we'll be able to figure out what's wrong with the project, and who framed you and why. Then he can be returned to his keepers none the worse. Once the truth is out there'll be no danger to him, or anyone else."

"After we've figured out how Hotchkiss' murder fits into it," Fisk said, absently patting the dog. True had settled under the table when the basket was unpacked, hoping someone would drop him a forbidden treat. This seldom happened, but dogs are ever optimistic.

Benton had been understandably shocked to learn that Master Hotchkiss was probably a blackmailer.

"I still can't believe it."

"He didn't try to blackmail you?" I asked. "I know you didn't pay—Professor S was crossed out, and there were never any payments. But we wondered if he tried to use that thesis against you?"

"Of course not!" Benton's indignation was sincere. "I never heard of that other thesis till Headman Portner called me to his office. In fact, Hotchkiss shared my opinion of cheating—which is why I find it hard to believe he'd do anything like this!"

Kathy frowned. "How do you know how he felt? You said you didn't know him well."

"I don't. But there was a faculty meeting about a month ago, and we walked out together and ended up talking about how important a thesis could be, and how some scholars might be tempted to copy someone else's..."

We were all staring at him, so incredulously he finally got it.

"You think he was talking about me? Trying to blackmail me? He didn't say anything of the kind!"

"He wouldn't," said Fisk. "If you'd been guilty, you'd have picked up on his hints and probably offered to pay. And he wouldn't have said 'Pay up or else,' either. He would have talked a lot about what would happen to someone who copied their thesis, and then casually mentioned that he'd taken up some expensive hobby, or had some medical needs."

"His sister," Benton said. "His sister had some back injury, and he had to pitch in to help pay for her care. Was that it? I have to admit, I wondered why he was telling me. We were never... That is to say, I really didn't know him well."

"You mean he was a rotter, and you didn't like him," Kathy put in. "And because you hadn't forged your thesis, all his hints went right over your thick head. That's why he turned your thesis over to the Headman, because you didn't pay. Benton, 'tis nothing short of a miracle you weren't accused of his murder. Stop being so nice. You need to be honest about him. About everyone."

"But he's dead!"

"Yes," said Fisk. "And Kathy's right about your alibi— it's downright miraculous, and I don't trust miracles. But let's stick with blackmail for now. Can you think of anyone who particularly disliked our brilliant librarian?"

"Well...I don't really know of anyone who liked him," Benton admitted. "He was the kind of person whose idea of friendship was to get together and badmouth someone you both disliked. Which can work for a while, but...I'm not really all that surprised. Master Hotchkiss could be pretty malicious. Anyone who hated him would be lost in the crowd of everyone who disliked him."

"That's not very helpful," I said.

"But not unexpected," Fisk pointed out. "Blackmailers don't usually have lots of friends. What about the initials? Do they mean anything to you?"

He pushed some dishes aside, and spread the ledger pages out on the table. Kathy abandoned her dinner to lean over and study them, while Benton's gaze shied away. He didn't want to think ill of his colleagues, to pry at their secrets. But the puzzle of it tugged at his intellect, and soon he was staring at the cryptic notes as avidly as the rest of us.

"Two single victims," Kathy said. "And two sets. Though since one of the second set, hammer D, isn't paying, five victims in all."

"What about A and H," Fisk asked. "Maybe a couple, paying together?"

"This looks like a man who sticks to his systems," Kathy said. "And I don't think that's an A. 'Tis a drafts-man's compass."

Once she'd said it, 'twas so clear that Fisk and I shared a look of dismay at being outwitted by a mere girl.

"All right, Benton," I said. "'Tis time. Do you know who any of these people might be?"

"It's blackmail." Benton sounded most uncomfort-able, kindly soul that he is. "If 'tis something they'd pay to keep secret, how would I know about it? Except..." He tweaked PN's page out of the pile. "There are ru-mors that Professor Nilcomb takes...takes an undue in-terest in some of the female students."

"You mean he seduces them," Fisk said. "And pays with better grades?"

"Or threatens them with poor grades if they refuse." Kathy's voice was tight with anger and disgust, but Ben-ton shook his head.

"'Tis not like that. Many of the girls aren't even in his classes, and those that are seem to get the grade their work deserves. There was a girl in one of my classes, when I was a first year—basic literary composition, a required course. She got a sixty-five, and the only rea-son anyone was surprised was because it was so low, with all the 'extra tutoring' she'd had. And they didn't make it obvious, not in class. But sometimes their eyes

would meet, and you'd look at their faces and it was...
obvious. I couldn't prove anything."

Fisk turned the sheet over. "He's paying higher than
the others. Five gold roundels a month. I didn't think
professors got paid that much."

"He's married," Benton said miserably. "To the daughter of a man who owns a paper mill here, and shares of
lumber mills in other towns. She's his only child, too.
And for what 'tis worth, I've never heard that any girl
he slept with was in the least unwilling. In fact, a few
years ago one of them made a fuss when he...when he
moved on. They kept it from the faculty, but when one
girl goes to another's room and calls her a scheming
slut at the top of her lungs...well."

Kathy, I was sorry to see, looked less distasteful at
that, and Fisk grinned.

"So who's Professor B?" I asked. "And what's his scandal with scales M. Scales might signify a merchant. Or
a judicar, for the scales of justice."

"Or a moneylender," said Fisk. "Or a banker."

"There's only one person on the staff whose last name
starts with B," Benton said. "And Professor Bollinger
can't be your killer, because he was at the lecture too.
The teachers sit to the left and right of the dais, and I
saw him there."

Looking up at the place where he'd once sat? Benton
was putting a brave face on it, but I know my brother.

"What about Professor Nilcomb?" I asked. "Was he
there?"

Benton frowned. "I don't think...I didn't notice him.
But teachers sometimes sit with the scholars. I might
have missed him. And I have no idea who 'scales M 87'
is, or why Stephan 20 is important. Assuming that's a
year, and not another name."

"Do you know Professor Bollinger well?" Kathy asked.

"Not really. He teaches law, so I never took a course from him, but I've never heard a whisper of—"

"So the scales probably do signify a judicar." 'Twas nice to be right about something.

"And eighty-seven," Fisk said slowly. "A test score, for some M who graduated that year? Final exams are graded one to a hundred, aren't they? And for law students, the score matters."

"Sixty five is a passing grade in most fields," Benton said. "Including law. But 'tis hard to get hired with a score lower than an eighty. But this is pure speculation! That 87 might be someone's age, or...or..."

There weren't that many possibilities.

"A book number," I suggested. "One of Master Hotchkiss' numbers for everything? What subject is 87?"

I'd been half-joking, though now that I thought on it, the man who'd invented that system might use his own numbers as a reference. But Benton was shaking his head.

"All the system numbers have at least three digits," he said. "Most often more, for subdivisions of a subject. For instance," he plucked out another sheet, "I'm pretty sure these are book numbers. And the numbers after the dashes refer to the page."

He gestured to the number strings after A...no, compass H's initial.

"284.629 – 42," Fisk read. "And 443.04272 – 297. What subjects are they?"

"The four hundreds are the sciences," Benton said. "Beyond that I'd have to look at the master tables to tell you."

"It's something we can check," Fisk said. "And speaking of checking..." He pulled out Hotchkiss' lecture pass and laid it on the table. "Benton, how did you get a pass for that lecture? Who gave it to you?"

"I don't know. Someone gave it to my landlord, with a note 'twas for me. I took it for a gesture of kindness from one of my friends, but no one told me they sent it. Why does it matter?"

Benton might have been puzzled, but Kathy stiffened alertly.

"You think someone gave him an alibi for the murder? Why? 'Twould make more sense for the killer to want someone else to take the blame."

"For an ordinary murderer that would be true," said Fisk. "But a blackmail victim might be a perfectly nice person—or at least, not want someone else, maybe even a friend, to hang for a crime they committed. And Benton's quarrel with Hotchkiss was fresh in everyone's mind."

"I didn't quarrel with him," Benton objected. "I knew he had no choice but to come forward with what he found."

Fisk brushed this aside. "The killer gave the most obvious suspect an alibi. Then he tried to make it look like the work of some anonymous burglar, who'd never be caught because no one would be fencing any loot. I think our killer has more of a conscience than his victim. Benton, do you still have the note that came with your pass?"

"I don't... I might." Benton went to his desk and fished among the papers there.

If Fisk was right about this, if Hotchkiss' murder led us to whoever had framed Benton, and the project had naught to do with it...but I didn't believe that. All that money, all that prestige, and Benton in the midst of it. The project had to be the source of the whole affair—

not some sordid blackmail scheme that had nothing to do with my brother!

"Ha!" Benton carried two bits of paper back to us, one half sheet, and one roughly a quarter. "Here's my pass and the note that came with it."

The note said: *Thought you might enjoy this.* There was no signature.

"Plain printing," said Kathy. "Schoolroom style. Do you recognize the writing?"

Benton shook his head.

"Or is this someone trying to disguise his usual hand, because Benton might recognize it?" I asked. "It looks a bit clumsy."

Fisk was still studying the note. "No clue to the identity of the writer. Even the paper is thin and cheap, though not as bad as..."

He frowned, and picked up the two passes. "The paper here is different."

Now that he'd pointed it out, I could see that the paper on which Hotchkiss' pass was printed was more yellow than the other.

"So they ran out of one batch of paper in the midst of the job, and opened a new bundle."

The print was smeared too, as if the printer had rolled his ink too often before he took the time to clean the gutters between the raised letters. But Fisk stared at the blurry letters as if they held the secrets of the universe.

"No," he said. "They weren't. But someone went to considerable trouble to get this one for Benton. Look here." He shoved Benton's pass toward us. "At the *y* on the end of 'the second Finday.' And here, in *anyone.* The tail is longer, and curlier. This was printed on a different press than Hotchkiss' was. Or more precisely, with type face cut by a different carver."

Now that he mentioned it, I could see a difference in the lowercase *q* as well. In the midst of such sloppy printing, 'twas not something most would notice, but once Fisk had pointed it out, I noticed that some of the other letters were subtly different as well.

"Is there any reason for a printer to change the typeface in the middle of a job?" I said.

"None I can think of." And Fisk would know. "How hard is it to get one of these passes? Are they assigned to people?"

"No," said Benton. "They're given to professors to pass out to their students, and any townsman who wants to attend a lecture can ask for one at the clerk's office."

"So does that mean the killer didn't have access to a pass?" Kathy asked. "Someone outside the university?"

"Either that, or the need arose after the regular passes had been given out," I said, but Fisk waved this quibble aside.

"Either way, someone wanted to get Benton off the hook so badly they went and had a single copy of this pass printed, all for him. Maybe using a different press. Which means," he finished, "that all we have to do is visit the local printers, find out who ordered just one copy of the lecture pass—or maybe just find this particular set of type—and we'll have our man."

CHAPTER 11

Fisk

All right, I might have been exaggerating. Though I didn't think my theory was as ridiculous as Michael and Benton made it out to be. And Mistress Katherine, a sensible girl, agreed with me.

"There are other possible explanations. But Fisk's explanation is possible too. I'll go to the printers with you, and help you check it out."

Which is how I found myself setting off to visit printers with Kathy, while Michael stayed home to introduce Benton to his new charge. He could have come with us, but Michael said he hadn't spent much time with Benton yet.

I translated that to mean that he was going to take Professor Dayless' advice and ask Benton for more details about the project. Though I was pretty sure it wouldn't do him any good. Since Master Hotchkiss had turned out to be a blackmailer, I was fairly certain his murder was at the bottom of everything. As soon as I found a bit more evidence—that one of the victims had given Benton that lecture pass, for instance—then *I'd* be in charge.

For now...

"Why did you want to come?" I asked Kathy. "Really."

We were making our way through the lighter crowds of midmorning. The early morning throng, as workers who lived in the outskirts of town came in to their jobs, had made it hard to cross the street to buy our breakfast. Now there were women with shopping baskets on their arms and delivery men with carts and wheelbarrows. The scholars, who'd been so prevalent before, weren't as visible at this hour.

"Honestly? I've been cooped up in Benton's rooms for almost a week. And he tries to hide it, but he's so depressed he's making me gloomy as well. This probably makes me a bad sister, but I think the dog did him more good yesterday than I did. Having to look after your mad friend will be a kindness for him."

"He's not my friend. I just went to check on him because, well... Is every place in this town only a few blocks apart?"

Benton hadn't known where any print shops were, though the history department used a shop called Demkin's Press and Ink. But he had known the people who'd have that information—there was a bookshop two streets from his lodging.

"'Tis all centered on Pendarian," Kathy pointed out. "Any business that services the university would likely be nearby."

"Everything centered on the university...including what happened to your brother. Do you still think the project is behind his troubles?"

"I'm trying to keep an open mind," said Kathy with dignity. "Which is more than I can say for some."

"I've never wanted an open mind," I said. "It's too easy for things to fly in."

That had been an old joke between Father, Judith, and me...and somehow, remembering those silly, scholarly jokes didn't hurt as it used to.

Kathy had a lovely giggle and she took my arm, in a friendly way, as we strolled on down the street. It had been a long time since I'd walked with a woman on my arm, and it felt...nice.

I *really* had to figure out something better to do with the rest of my life. It had been a pretty fair mess, to date.

The bookshop had a bell over the door, and shelf after shelf of books, with more lying open on stands, their sealed pages cut open so scholars could browse them more thoroughly. The scent of leather, glue, and ink brought the best part of my childhood back in one rolling wave. And that did hurt.

"Hey, the house! Anyone here?"

"A moment, sir." The man's voice came from an open door at the rear of the shop, and he hadn't had to shout to be heard. Anything Katherine and I said would be audible to him too, so she turned to one of the open books and began studying pages.

"Are you looking for the curly 'y'?" I murmured. "That cutter could have sold his type to shops all over the—"

"Sorry to keep you waiting." The man who emerged from the back of the shop had white hair, wrinkles to go with it, and was wiping his hands on an apron. "I'm repairing an old binding, and once you get the glue on you have to strap the leather tight before it cools. What can I do for you, Master and Mistress?"

"I'm looking for a printer," I said. "For a small project. If you could give me a list of all the shops in town, I'd be grateful."

I pulled a brass ha' from my purse and flipped it, to show exactly how grateful I'd be.

"Who you'd want depends on the nature of your project," the bookseller pointed out. "I can give you the full list, but if you're looking for anything larger than a bound pamphlet, you'll be happier taking it to the big presses in Crown City. I can give you their names too," he added. "And you can see samples of all their work, right here."

My gaze followed his to the well-stocked shelves. "What, there's no book making here? Right next to the university?"

"None now," the man said. "The scholars here are fussy about their proofing—as they should be—and with Crown City so near, I guess most book makers wanted a share of the city's market."

Most great universities support at least one press, sometimes several, and Crown City was a long day's ride. But that had nothing to do with murder. I told the man my project was small enough for a local shop, and he gave me directions to Demkin's and another press, Marleybone Printing. Two names weren't worth a brass ha', but with Mistress Kathy looking on I decided not to quibble.

The print shops weren't near the university, one being on the outskirts of town to the east and the other to the west—which still wasn't far enough to make it worthwhile to go back to the stables and saddle a horse. I'd already noted that Mistress Katherine's sensible skirt and bodice were paired with sensible low-heeled shoes, chosen for walking over cobblestones.

That bodice fit nicely enough to remind me she was no longer a little girl, but she was still Michael's sister. So I might as well pick her brains.

"Does it seem odd to you that a university this size only supports two printers, and no book binding at all?" I asked, as we took to the streets once more.

"As the man said, Crown City's not far. It probably makes sense for people to use the big presses there. How do you know so much about printing, Fisk?"

"My father was a tutor, who fancied himself a scholar as well," I said. "His family couldn't afford university tuition, and he couldn't come up with a thesis that would get him in on merit."

Though he'd beggared our family, and ultimately killed himself in trying. It had left me somewhat soured on the subject of scholarship. Which didn't mean those books hadn't tugged at me, too. The only reason I hadn't gone looking for that y myself is that once I start reading I have a hard time stopping. Between me and my luggage, Tipple has enough to carry. I can't start a library. And I didn't want to talk about my father.

"How's the Heir-hunt at court going? You wrote that you had a scheme to take yourself out of it, but you didn't tell me what it was."

Mistress Katherine had lifted her skirts to step around a patch of dung, so her grimace might have been for that...but I doubted it.

"Rupert's scheme is working better than mine," she said. "His tactic is to let the really determined girls corner him, and then he does nothing but talk about how wonderful Meg is."

"And is she?" I asked. I thought that instead of summoning eligible maidens from all over the Realm to try to win his son, the High Liege would have done better to let the affair run its course. The worst likely outcome was that she'd produce a few bastards before the Heir tired of her and went on to marry the nubile and Gifted young noblewoman he was supposed to wed. Opposition only makes lovers more determined. Though as Jack had taught me, there were ways around that.

"So what was your tactic? Did you invent some mythical lover of your own to babble about?"

"Nothing so silly," Kathy said, "though I might have been better off trying that. No, I decided to befriend Meg myself, thinking that would make it too awkward for me to chase after Rupert. And that wasn't hard— she's no brainless court ninny. She was studying law at Mortmain University when she and Rupert met. She was supposed to become an in-house lawyer for her family's textile business—they raise both flax and sheep, though most of their money comes from weaving. There's a good-sized town north of Crown City that does almost nothing but weaving for Merkle Cloth and Thread. Meg says that on a still day in summer, when the cottage doors are open, you can hear the clack of the looms half a mile away."

I'd been through some of the great weaving towns, and what struck me most about them wasn't the noise, but how much bolder women become when they're making a decent wage. Having tried to save three sisters from poverty, I liked that better than most men would.

"So Mistress Margaret was supposed to be checking over the family's contracts, but she fell in love with a prince instead. How very backward."

The Heir's romantic tangle was more interesting than I'd first thought.

"The irony didn't escape them," Kathy said. "Me, I think a queen with a thorough grounding in the Realm's law and history would be a good thing, but..."

No Gifts. Which meant none could be passed to her sons, either.

"Young Rupert can't be serious about dosing her with who-knows-what to try to give her Gifts. Not if he loves her the way you say he does."

"He isn't, really," Kathy admitted. "Neither of them has discussed it with me, but I think their plan is to stall till the Liege gives up, and all this research is just an excuse to wait. They talked the Liege into offering that big reward for a successful result—they had to do that to prove they were serious, and Rupert doesn't have that kind of money, not on his own. But part of the bargain was that they won't try anything till 'tis proven safe. And how can you prove that, really?"

"So what went wrong with your scheme? It sounds like all you have to do is enjoy the court till either Rupert or his father gives up."

But she wouldn't do that—like Michael, she was a fighter.

"You wouldn't say 'enjoy the court' if you had any idea how boring it is." Kathy's gaze swept over the street, where a baker was setting out fresh loaves and a delivery man tossed bundles of straw into a basket maker's shop. If she thought this was as interesting as her delighted expression implied, then court must be *very* boring.

"'Tis like being a little girl's doll, Fisk! You dress for breakfast, and then go right up afterward to dress for riding. You ride no more than half an hour, and then change clothing again for sewing, or some other proper lady's pursuit, till you have to change for luncheon, and after that... I once changed my clothing nine times, in just one day!"

I had to laugh. "That's exactly how Anna and Lissy played with their dolls—three hours' dressing, to half an hour's play. Even Judith did it, though she wasn't so bad. I thought girls liked that kind of thing."

"Not nine times a day," said Kathy fervently. "I want to go home, where I can help Mother run the house, and Father and Rupert—our Rupert—run the estate."

The current High Liege's father had been Rupert, and half the noblemen in the Realm gave their sons his name in the years after he died. A confusion that was increased by the High Liege naming his own son Rupert, too.

"I've ended up doing what Father wanted Michael to do," Kathy went on. "I spend half my days figuring out what to do about flooded fields, or crop blight, or fences that need mending. Court may look glittery and glamorous, but it's *dull!*"

And what would her home life be like, if Benton went home and took that job from her? Yet another reason to find Hotchkiss' killer, and clear Benton. Before someone else was hired for his job.

"It does sound like you're wasted at court," I told Kathy. "So what went wrong? You befriended Mistress Margaret, and then...pox. Really?"

"You're quick," said Kathy. "I didn't see it coming at all."

"To be fair, neither of us is the middle-aged ruler of a whole Realm. The High Liege is." I wasn't sure whether to be appalled, or to laugh.

"The perfect solution, the Liege called it," Kathy said grimly. "We could just share Rupert. He could go right on loving Meg, get me pregnant on a regular basis, and none of us would fight or fuss about it, because we're all such good *friends*. If you laugh, I'm going to kill you."

"I'm sorry," I said, through helpless huffs. "It's not the suggestion, which is appalling. It's just...plans! I sometimes think you should never make them."

Her lips were twitching too. "'Tis not funny. Poor Rupert sputtered out something about not thinking that would work. Meg and I said no, as loudly and firmly as we could without having screaming tantrums. Which we would have, only that would have convinced everyone we were silly hysterical girls, who'd settle down and go along with it eventually."

She was right, it really wasn't funny.

"What did your father say? You're seventeen, so it's his opinion that matters."

"Except it doesn't," said Kathy bitterly. "Another of the High Liege's oh so clever notions was to have the barons give him wardship over all the breeding stock, at least in terms of marriage, before they ever went to court. Thinking that the instant poor Rupert showed interest in any of us, he'd marry us off on the spot."

I frowned. "What about marriage contracts? For noble houses that's a big deal."

Jack and I had once run a scam based on a forged marriage contract, three generations old. And had been paid to burn the thing so promptly, I still wondered what was lurking in that family tree. The current baron was a nasty piece of work, and if his ancestors were like him...

"The marriage contract 'to be negotiated later, in good faith,'" Kathy told me. "Even Father admitted that when this High Liege said that, it would be in good faith. The Liege would be so relieved, he'd probably even be generous. Half those girls brought wedding gowns to court with them, just in case."

"And in trying to sneak off the hunting field, you suddenly found yourself leading the chase." I had no desire to laugh now. She could really be in trouble.

"Benton's letter couldn't have come at a better time," she said. "'My family needs me! I must go!' And I packed and fled before the Liege even had time to hear about it."

"And of course, you didn't happen to mention which family member it was."

"No point in being stupid about it. I also didn't admit that the only thing Benton had asked me was how to get in touch with Michael. Interesting, that when there's real trouble the person he goes to for help isn't Father, or even Rupert—our Rupert—but the family scandal."

"Sometimes you can be more effective outside the law," I agreed. "And he knew Michael wouldn't judge him."

Michael saved his moral judgments for me. But I was about to prove myself better at knight errantry, by clearing Benton's name. I refused to worry about what happened after, because the first print shop was before us.

I couldn't tell the clerk at Demkin's Press and Ink that I had a job for them, or I might end up paying for a bundle of pamphlets. I pulled out the two lecture passes, and asked about them.

"We printed these," he pointed to Master Hotchkiss' pass. "We print most of the lecture passes, unless we're too busy to handle it, and then they go to our competitor—so we try not to be too busy. This other one...I don't recognize that type offhand, and the paper doesn't look like any we've had in for a while. That yellowish tinge, that's due to different kinds of wood going into the pulp. Would you like to ask Master Hornby about it? You'd have to come into the back—he's keeping an eye on some new apprentices on the press."

Going into the back was no hardship for me. My father had considered the work of a common printer beneath a scholar. But at one point, when Mother had turned all the girl's dresses twice, he'd worked in a print shop for a whole summer and into the fall. I'd been five at the time, just old enough to take his luncheon to the shop when he left it behind. I still remembered my first sight of the place, being fascinated by the moving parts on the press, and reaching out to touch one of the wet rollers. My black, sticky palms had made wonderful prints all over my shirt and britches, till someone saw me and sent for my father.

My mother had made a sufficient impression on me that I hadn't played with the rollers again. But I'd loved that shop so much I used to distract Father with questions as he left in the morning, trying to trick him into forgetting his basket so I could take it to him.

The big sheets, eight pages on either side of them, hung on the drying lines like rustling paper laundry. The press used a lever, not the old-fashioned screw, and it folded up like a sitting frog. The ink made a sticky, tearing sound as the roller went over the type. I swear my palms felt that old familiar itch to play in it.

Katherine stared all around us, and behind the flashing spectacles her eyes were bright with the same fascination I'd felt when I was five.

Master Hornby, a middle-aged man in an ink-stained apron, proved his right to the title "master printer" by noticing the curly letters in his first glance at Benton's pass. "No, we don't have anything with those long descenders. I can't say as to the paper. We've used some like it, from time to time. But this doesn't look like a font from any of our cutters—and besides, I'd remember doing a second batch of those passes. We printed eight hundred in the first run, just like they usually order for a big lecture. I'm surprised the university needed more. And that they didn't come to us for them."

"We weren't thinking you'd printed a second batch," Kathy said. "But that someone might have asked for a single pass, this one, to be printed."

Master Hornby's brows rose. "I'd certainly remember that. It would have cost 'em high for just one—most of the cost of a small job lies in setting the type. It's only when you get into big jobs that the price of paper and ink starts to matter more. And why would anyone want to print one pass? All you have to do is ask for one at the clerk's office."

"'Tis a point," Kathy said, as we made our way out of the shop and turned toward Marleybone Printing. "Even if the killer works outside the university, why not just go ask for one?"

"Because I'll bet clerk Peebles has a very good idea who she gave those passes to—she's an efficient sort of woman. If he planned to use it as part of a murder, the killer might not want some professor or scholar remembering that he'd asked them for a pass. Which either means that he isn't a professor or a scholar, who could get one without being noticed, or that all the passes had already been given out when he made his plan. But whatever the reason, we know someone had it printed because of the different paper and type."

"He'd be afraid someone would remember him asking for a pass, but not think that a printer would remember being paid to print one?" Kathy asked.

"Well, he...um. That's a point. He's either the kind of noble who thinks people like printers are part of the furniture—"

"Not likely for a professor, who teaches merit scholars," Kathy put in.

"Or he's stupid," I finished. "Also not likely for a professor. And most of the people in that blackmail file have been paying Master Hotchkiss too long to be scholars."

"Young doesn't mean stupid," Kathy said. "Although thinking of some of the girls at court... No, we can't rule out stupidity."

"You never can," I said. "But Jack used to say that you can't rely on it either. And this...it doesn't feel stupid. He made a few mistakes about what a burglar would do, but that's just lack of knowledge."

"He or she," Kathy said. "And 'tis knowledge most blackmail victims wouldn't have. I wouldn't. Though it still might not have been someone Hotchkiss was blackmailing."

"Who else has motive? Besides your brother, of course."

She was thinking so hard she brushed my provocation aside. "What are the usual motives for murder? Greed, hatred, love, revenge."

"A blackmail victim could be operating on three of the four." I pointed out.

"What about love?"

"There's no sign that our librarian had a lady friend. Or a gentleman friend, either."

"There are other kinds of love," Kathy said mildly. "Parent and child. Or even friends, who can be closer than brothers."

"Or real brothers," I cut in, not liking the turn this had taken. "I love my sisters, crazy as they make me. But generally it's the romantic, man-woman love that people kill over."

She eyed me askance for a moment, but gave in. "From which I'm running like mad, though I haven't managed to escape it. Have you ever been in love?"

"Once," I said. "Lucy was a butcher's daughter, but even her dowry and an apprenticeship in her father's business wasn't enough to frighten me away."

"What was she like?" Kathy pushed up her spectacles, and waited while a woman herded a flock of geese across our path. "Aside from a butcher's shop for a dowry?"

"Glossy black curls, glowing dark eyes, and a figure that made the eyes and hair irrelevant," I said. "At the time I thought she was remarkably sweet and special and honest and pure and true and...well, all the things you think, when it's a fantasy you're in love with instead of a person."

"So what burst the fantasy? Did it just wear off? Or did you actually work a week in the butcher's shop?"

"Neither—though the first would have happened eventually, and a week in the shop would certainly have done it. No, Jack bribed her to dump me."

At this point I felt quite cheerful about it, though at the time...

"Heartbreak doesn't ache," I said. "Not like a broken bone does. It's more a burning pain. But since heartburn is actually indigestion, no one says that."

"So she broke your heart?" Kathy managed to look both sympathetic and skeptical. "Or was it Jack who did that?"

"Oh, they both did. Though Jack's 'betrayal' actually hurt more. The moment I saw that garnet necklace she was flaunting I began to suspect. She did her best to let me down gently, but she was a lousy liar. It became clearer and clearer, until she finally broke down and said that the money Jack had paid would buy her jewels, and red leather shoes, and a lace wedding dress when her pa finally chose someone."

"I'm sorry," Kathy said softly.

"Don't be. I shortly realized that Jack was right; he'd saved me from a horrible fate. And I'm not talking about the butcher shop, though that would have been horrible too."

"But if she was pressured..."

"Not pressured," I said. "Bribed. And though it took me a while to realize it, when I finally figured out that she was more interested in garnet necklaces than she was in me...I stopped loving her."

"Hmm. That's not very romantic," Kathy said. "But I have to say, 'tis practical."

"So was your plan to avoid marrying the Heir," I said. "And look where that got you."

We reached the far side of town more swiftly than I thought we would, or at least, it felt swift. Kathy and I had been corresponding for so many years, I'd come to know her better than I'd realized. Talking with her was much like writing, except that she could respond instantly, and I could watch expressions chase one another across her mobile face.

Now that Kathy had pointed out how stupid it would be for the killer to draw attention to himself by having a single pass printed, I wasn't surprised to learn that Marleybone Printing hadn't produced any passes for that lecture. They had no font with long curly descenders, either.

CHAPTER 12

Michael

It took some time to locate a suitable chicken. But if Fisk was wrong, and 'twas poison, I didn't want to kill some innocent animal. The animal's owners would have objected too.

First I had to introduce Benton to the jeweler, though the man had seen enough of my brother out his windows that he only nodded, and asked for a hammer and nails to tack a series of old-fashioned crimped ruffs around the attic windows.

Benton asked the landlady for tools, and paid her still more of Kathy's money to rent another attic room "to my kinsman's friends." We then delivered the tools, and the jeweler took them up with such interest that we felt no real need to stay and watch him work. Besides, I wanted to investigate the tea grounds I'd taken from Hotchkiss' compost...was it only last night? It felt like days had passed, but 'twas only night before last that the librarian had been struck down from behind, which is hard to do when a man coming down his own stairs surprises you in his home. Granted, as far as we knew the librarian's murder wasn't linked to the project, which was my investigation. But we knew so little yet, that hardly seemed relevant, and there was something about those tiny damp flecks that just felt... wrong.

Benton was as bored as I watching the jeweler exclaim over awls and pliers so he offered to assist with the investigation—but it turned out he had no idea who might have a chicken to spare. I asked at the tavern where we'd purchased breakfast, but they got their meat from a butcher. The butcher told us he bought his livestock on market day, which was four days hence.

In the end, we checked on the jeweler once more—he was building what looked like a tiny ladder—then I saddled the horses. Benton rode Tipple, and with True frisking at our heels—or sometimes under our patient horses' hooves—we rode out to the countryside and found a farm with a large chicken coop. For a tin quart, I talked them into parting with an elderly rooster who was soon for the pot—though if his meat was as tough as he was, they were fortunate to miss the meal.

They threw in the use of some dishware and hot water, and while Benton boiled up the tea grounds I'd taken from Master Hotchkiss' compost pail, I chased the rooster around the pen. True did his best to help, and when told his assistance wasn't required he sat and panted while Benton held his collar. I finally cornered the rooster, at the cost of a few pecks, and shoved him into the crate the farmwife offered me.

If he was as thirsty as the chase had made me, we should know soon enough. By this time 'twas midafternoon, and the sun beat down.

Benton poured the tea into a shallow pan to cool, and the rooster regarded us malevolently. His feathers were a deep red-brown, his stride arrogant as a lord's.

"So now what?" My brother's gaze was full of amusement. "You don't really think this mess is drugged, do you? Hotchkiss died of a blow to the head."

The brew looked like weak spice tea, and the sweet sickly scent of it still made a warning prickle down my nerves. Our mother's herb talking Gift has been known to crop up in all her offspring, from time to time.

"Remember when you told Rupert not to set his snare in that patch of brush by the spring, and he ignored you?"

"Oh. Well, I did warn him." Benton didn't look too distressed at the memory. Rupert had been inclined to claim an older brother's authority that neither Benton nor I had been willing to grant him. And it wasn't as if Mother's salves hadn't soothed the truly horrendous rash. But she'd had to use magica, and she'd been furious with him. As Benton said, he'd been warned.

We seated ourselves in the shade of the barn, with a clear view of the crate and the dog between us.

"Tell me more about the project while we wait," I said. "It might have been your Gift that made you uneasy, but you might also have seen or heard something without realizing it."

"I already told you," Benton said. "All I did was supply some ancient lore. I spent most of my time there helping Lat Quicken with the rabbits."

"Who's Lat Quicken? No, wait. I want the whole story, in order."

'Twas not as if we had anything else to do, but Benton eyed me askance.

"How did you first hear about it?" I prompted.

"Everyone learned about it at the same time. All the professors, I mean. Headman Portner called a meeting, and told us the Heir was offering a huge sum to any university who could figure out a way—a safe way—to give his lady friend Gifts. Or at least, let her bear Gifted children. I thought he was crazy," my brother went on, apparently oblivious to the fact that most of our relatives considered his obsession with the past a bit mad too. At least, until my misconduct cast his into the shade.

"Even if it wasn't madness, I still think a savant would be a better source for something like that than a university," Benton continued. "Only that wouldn't work, for obvious reasons."

Savants are half-feral hermits, who intercede between men and the gods they've offended when magica is harvested without the proper sacrifice. I've had dealings with several in my wanderings, and found them...well, a mixed lot. But they take nothing from those they've helped, except the goods and food they need to survive in the wilds. The Heir's reward would mean nothing to them. And they might have refused the task, anyway. Most believe that the savants' purpose is to keep the balance between man and nature. The Heir's request might be perceived as something that would upset that balance.

Or it might not. The savants never say what their purpose is.

"So Portner instructed his professors to come up with a way to earn the reward?"

Benton cast me the glance reserved for someone who really should know better.

"He told us that if we wished to launch such a project, the university and the Heir would fund it between them, and that a reasonable share of the reward would accrue to whoever succeeded. The prospect of having someone fund your experiments, without you having to beg for it, is enough to make anyone take notice. If he'd been offering to support research into the past, I'd have leapt at it. But no one ever does," he added. "Except sometimes some baron, who wants the true story of his ancestor's heroic deed. And when you find out that what really happened wasn't all that heroic, they—"

"Who leapt at this project?" I asked. "Professor Dayless, who studies the mind—I suppose that makes sense. Who else?"

"Professor Stint," Benton said. "He's a chemist, and an apothecary, so that made sense too. The thing is, they've got completely different theories about how Gifts work. Stint says that all your reactions to drugs— pain killers, sleeping draughts, hallucinogens, even alcohol—it's all the chemistry of the drug interacting with the chemistry of the body."

"Chemistry in our bodies?"

But the mention of drugs reminded me, and I checked the pan. The tea had cooled, so I poured it into a saucer and pushed it into the crate.

The rooster ignored it.

"This may take a while," Benton said.

True evidently thought so too. He lay down and closed his eyes.

"Chemistry of the body," I reminded him.

"On the other hand, Professor Dayless believes that Gifts exist in everyone's mind, but in some people they're locked behind some sort of mental door. And that if you could find a way to open that door, everyone would have Gifts."

I considered this. "It sounds more likely than that we've got an alchemical laboratory inside us. Has this Stint never gutted game?"

"Don't let Stint hear you talk about alchemy," Benton said. "'The difference between wishful superstition and science' is a ten minute lecture. And how do the kidneys or liver strip poison and waste from our blood, if not through chemistry? Anyway, as soon as Portner asked us to submit theories they both popped up and started arguing for their own theory about how Gifts work, right there in the meeting. Portner hauled them off for a private conference, and the rest of us departed thinking we were well out of it. Only I wasn't," he finished glumly.

"But if they succeeded, think of all the old trash you could dig up with your share of the Heir's money."

The rooster paced back and forth in the crate, still ignoring the tea. 'Twas three feet long and two wide, so he had room to go on doing this for some time.

"In fact, what do the ancients have to do with the mind or chemistry? Or how Gifts work, either?"

"Just because their tools were primitive, that doesn't mean they were stupid," Benton said. "It takes more skill, more knowledge and cleverness, to survive with primitive tools than with advanced ones! Just as the poor must use more wit and courage than the rich." He was so heated that True roused to lick his face, and he gave the dog an absent pat.

'Twas an old argument, and one that hadn't endeared Benton's studies to our parents. Though having lived by my wits for several years now, I was inclined to agree with him.

"Did your ancients know how to Gift the Giftless? I have a hard time believing that bit of knowledge would ever be lost."

"I doubt they did," said Benton. "Though I think they tried. There are no written records, of course."

'Twas the creation of writing that separates the primitive ancients from those ancestors who simply lived longer ago than the rest of us.

"But bits of their world still survive. Rock carvings, in incredible detail—some of which show herbs clearly enough you can make out the species. Then there are the people who still worship the gods. How ancient are the roots of that old religion?"

"I have no idea." Once philosophers had determined that the gods cared only for those plants and animals they Gift with magic, most folk had given up worshiping them. And that was almost at the dawn of written language. "How old is it?"

"I don't know," said Benton cheerfully. "No one does. But that's the point. It really could have started back in ancient times. And you know that old granny rhyme, 'Vervain, dittany, tansy, rue—'"

"'The fates will bring a gift to you,'" I finished. "Then the old beldame cuts the cards, or reads the leaves in your teacup, and... Wait, you think 'tis not 'gift' but Gift? That's ridiculous."

"Why? I've found older versions of that rhyme—a lot older. 'Twas once, 'The gods will bring a gift to you.' So why not Gift?"

"All right. So you supplied ancient herbal formulas to Professor Stint, and he made the potions?"

"Nothing so tidy. I gave him whatever bits of lore I could scavenge, from pictures on pots to talking to folk who deliberately destroy magica, and let the gods punish them in order to talk with them, or be more worthy, or some other mad thing."

I decided not to mention the time when I'd wanted to contact a savant, and endured ant bites, hornet stings, and a skunking to do so. The thought that I should warn Fisk not to tell him crossed my mind, and then I remembered I couldn't tell Fisk to do anything. He was no longer my squire, or even really my associate, though we'd taken to introducing each other that way.

And what was I doing, out in the countryside watching a rooster pass and ignore his water dish, as I helped investigate *Fisk's* theory of the crime?

But I knew the answer; a man had been murdered, and whether 'twas a Gift or instinct speaking—'tis often hard to tell the difference—I knew there was something wrong with this tea. To refuse to follow that clue, wherever it led, was not the act of a knight errant...or even a good man. I couldn't betray my nature, even to score a point in this odd contest with Fisk, and I...

Wait. When I asked him to turn Jack Bannister over to the law, had I been asking Fisk to betray *his* nature?

'Twas a thought so shocking my body jerked, and Benton glanced over at me. I turned my gaze to the rooster, peering as if I'd seen something, but in truth I was almost blind.

If Fisk's nature was to let criminals go free, then I was right to ask him to betray it!

Or was I? I'd long known that loyalty was a thing Fisk valued high, even when he gave it to those who might not deserve it, like the sisters who hadn't defended him when his brother-in-law drove him out of town. Or even a criminal confederate, who seemingly had betrayed Fisk in every way short of death.

Or a certain knight errant, who always insisted on following the voice of his own heart...but mayhap hadn't listened to the heart-voice of his squire?

"Rubbish," I said aloud. "There's no virtue in letting criminals go free. They'll keep right on harming others!"

Benton was staring at me in some alarm. "I never said there was. What are you talking about?"

"Nothing." I gave True's back a scratch. "A disagreement I once had with Fisk."

"The one that's got you two circling each other like fighting tomcats? What was that about, anyway? Kathy didn't know."

A few minutes ago, I'd have said I didn't know either, not really. Now...

"'Tis complicated," I said. "So you gave whatever bits of knowledge you found to Professor Stint, and he created a potion from it?"

"Potions," said Benton. "He's tried about eight variations so far, and he and Professor Dayless argue like fury every time he wants to make changes. She's the one who keeps all the rabbits' records, so I can see her point."

"'Tis these rabbits you dose with the potions, I take it." As I was trying to dose this stubborn rooster. "How can you tell if a rabbit has Gifts at all?"

"That part was Professor Dayless' contribution to the project. Most scholars agree that all animals have the Gift of sensing magic."

"How else could they avoid it, in the wild?"

"Yes, well, it was Professor Dayless who figured out that if human sensing Gifts varied, mayhap animals' do too. She hired Lat Quicken—he's a gamekeeper, who usually works for one of the university's trustees. But the trustee's at court now and Lat's daughter had broken her leg, so badly it needed magica medicine to mend it. You know how expensive that is. Dayless was kind enough to hire him to trap thirty wild rabbits for her. Then she bought a pot of magica lettuce—and she paid more for that than she paid Lat for the rabbits.

But when she put magica lettuce into the run with other rabbit food, some of the rabbits stayed farther from it and were more unwilling to approach, even when she put something they liked near it. Eventually she worked out a ranked scale of sensitivity to magic, and gave all the rabbits a score on that scale. She'd had Lat trap over a hundred for her by that... He's drinking."

I'd been so distracted, less by Benton's narrative than my own tangled thoughts, that I'd forgotten to watch the rooster. He was now dipping his beak into the saucer and lifting his head to let the water trickle down, in that curious way chickens drink. The chase must have made him thirsty after all, because he drank quite a lot, for a chicken.

"How soon would this drug take effect?"

Benton's voice was hushed, as if the rooster might overhear. And absurd as it was, my voice was lower when I replied.

"Soon, I think. Though 'tis probably weaker, brewed twice." Or it might not work on chickens, or might not be drugged at all.

The rooster resumed pacing, our eyes locked upon him. And nothing happened. And more nothing happened.

"Rabbits," I said, settling back. "The point of all this was to see if the rabbits who'd been dosed started staying farther away from the magica?"

"Exactly. 'Twas really boring watching them graze, and then writing down the nearest they'd approached, and averaging their distance and so on. Professor Dayless took reams of notes, Quicken handled the rabbits, and I'd assist either of them. It didn't even get—"

"Wait!" I sat up abruptly. "Did he just stumble?"

Between the slats of the crate and the shadows they cast 'twas difficult to be sure, but it looked to me as if the rooster's straight path had wavered.

"I can't tell."

I couldn't tell either. "What was it you were you saying?"

"Oh, just that it didn't get any more interesting when results started to show."

That wrenched my gaze from the rooster.

"Results? You mean one of your rabbits who'd gone close to the magica began to keep away?"

"Nothing so dramatic." Benton was still watching our experiment. "It just means that with some of them—the ones taking the potion based on that old granny rhyme, in fact—the average distance they kept away from the magica lettuce seemed to be increasing. But you could only tell if you were looking at the numbers over time, or at that graph Professor Dayless— There he goes!"

The rooster had definitely staggered that time, and even as he recovered, his strong gait looked less sure.

'Twas a quick acting a drug, as I'd supposed. A few minutes later, the bird was stumbling about the crate like a sailor on his first night ashore. In fact, he finally sat down in one corner, though his long neck kept weaving drunkenly.

"You wouldn't have to chase him around now," Benton commented.

"I think 'tis why the killer used this drug," I said. "So he'd not have to chase his victim down, or fight him."

Anyone planning to attack the rooster would have an easy time of it, and chickens could be savage. I suppose we could have returned then, but I was curious as to the drug's full effect—which might help a mediciner figure out what it was—so Benton, True, and I watched the rooster fall asleep, and then wake up and resume his pacing. When he seemed sufficiently alert I returned him to his pen, and bought a clean bottle with a cork stopper from the farmwife.

I told her the results of our experiment, warning her that traces of the drug might linger in the rooster's flesh, and she shrugged.

"He'd probably be a tough 'un, anyway."

Mayhap we'd won the bird a natural death, instead of the axe for which he'd been slated. Man eats meat, as do hawks, wolves, and all manner of other creatures, but treating them as kindly as we can is the sign of a good man, according to the philosophers. There is also some fear that the gods might punish those who badly mistreat creatures, even those that have no magic.

But no god looks after man, so when man's conscience fails, as it has been known to, there's nothing to stop one from murdering another except his fellow men. 'Twas no random burglar responsible for Master Hotchkiss' death. Someone had drugged his tea, so they could slay him with no danger to themselves, and tomorrow I had to report it, to both our comrades and the guard.

Even if 'twould make it look as if Fisk was right.

CHAPTER 13

Fisk

I had thought Benton was supposed to watch the jeweler. But when we returned from our tour of the print shops it was to find squirrels in the attic—literally—and the landlady banging on the jeweler's locked door demanding that he "take that contraption down and stop bringing flea-ridden vermin into my house!"

It took Kathy twenty minutes of tact—and an unknown amount of money—to soothe the woman's outrage.

While she was doing that, I went into the jeweler's room and persuaded him to take down the rather ingenious squirrel ladder he'd built from the attic window to a nearby tree. I tried to convince him it was rude to invite the squirrels in when he had no cages built to welcome them. I also took the ladder away with me... but he'd built this one in half a day, so it wouldn't take him long to build another.

Michael and Benton returned late that evening, Michael looking depressed that his hunch about the tea had been right. Which meant *I* was right that Hotchkiss' murder was premeditated, and probably involved in Benton's troubles, too.

But by the time we finished discussing the proper care of madmen it was late enough for Michael to claim he was ready for bed, taking away my chance to crow about it. Benton stayed up and told Kathy and me all about the rooster, and that Michael had bottled up the remains of the tea they'd brewed, as well as the much-used grounds, to turn over to the guard.

It wasn't till breakfast, which I fetched from the tavern back to Benton's rooms, that I had a chance to object to this.

"If you give the guard that tea, we'll have to admit we searched Hotchkiss' house. And took things."

"We'll have to tell Captain Chaldon about that, sooner or later," Michael pointed out. "You have to give him that forged pass, too. And tell him the results of your investigation...such as they are."

That kind of dig was unusual for Michael. Was our contest getting on his nerves? Or was it the fact that I was winning?

"All the more reason to wait till we can also tell him who the killer is. And we now know that the killer had, or has, access to his own printing press. There can't be many of them, even in a university town. All we have to do is find that press, find that type face with the long descenders, and we'll have our man."

"Just as you said...the day before yesterday," Michael murmured.

"It's still true. Since then we've also learned that the killer drugged Hotchkiss, so—"

"*We've* learned?"

"—so we can be certain it was deliberate murder, not burglary."

"Would not a burglar want to drug his victim?" Kathy asked. "To make sure he slept though the robbery?"

"Oh, if you could do it, a burglar would be delighted to slip his targets a sleeping draught," I said. "The problem is that you have to break into the house to put the drug in the household's tea, or whatever, and then break in again for the theft. The extra break-in increases your chance of getting caught more than the drug lessens it."

"Unless," said Kathy, "whoever drugged him also dined with him—or at least had tea."

"There was only one cup in the study," I pointed out. "So he was probably drinking tea alone. Whoever-it-was could have put whatever-it-was into his tea canister any time since the last time he brewed it. Though he must have known Hotchkiss well enough to be pretty sure he'd brew a pot after dinner."

"Or she," Kathy said. "Isn't poison supposed to be a woman's weapon?"

"Or a coward's," said Michael.

"Or a smart person's," I said. "If I was going to bash someone over the head, I'd certainly prefer to have them groggy. Or better yet, unconscious."

"Then since *Benton and I* proved 'tis murder," Michael said, "the more reason to hand our evidence over to the guard."

The stress on those words wasn't too hard, but Benton suppressed a grin and Kathy reached hastily for a biscuit. She'd come to breakfast in her dressing gown, with her brown hair rumpled, and she looked almost as young as the hobbledehoy schoolgirl I'd first met.

She didn't seem to mind that Trouble was leaning against her leg and shedding all over her, either.

"All right," I said. "You're the one who proved it. But it's still evidence that I was right, that Hotchkiss' death is the source of the trouble. Are you willing to concede—"

The way Michael's shoulders stiffened, it was probably just as well that a knock on the door interrupted me.

Benton's brows rose, confirming this wasn't a common event, but he went to answer it.

A man in the blue and silver of the Liege Guard stood on the threshold, and the silver bars on his shoulder announced a sergeant. A man in my profession makes a point of knowing guard uniforms, and their ranks, too.

"Master Benton Sevenson? Good. And these gentlemen would be Master Fisk and Master Michael Sevenson?"

It could sound threatening when a guardsman said things like that, but this man's eyes lit with enthusiasm when they fell on Michael. Once again, I congratulated myself on having made sure that, even though I'd sent for them, Michael was the one who'd dealt with the Liege Guard when they arrived in Tallowsport.

The dog, never fussy, pranced over to the stranger for a pat, and the man demolished his dignity even more by obliging.

"We are." The resignation in Michael's voice wouldn't have been audible to someone who didn't know him well.

I did know him well, and I wasn't sure I'd had enough time to convince him to keep what we'd learned to ourselves. I picked up a biscuit, split it, and began spreading butter, trying to think how I could shut him up if he started to confess, without looking too suspicious.

Nothing occurred to me.

"Captain Chaldon sent me," the guardsman went on, "to ask Master Benton Sevenson if he, and the rest of you, have an alibi for last night."

The biscuit crumbled in my fingers, leaving butter behind. "Last night? Has something *else* happened at the university?"

For once, we hadn't even been there.

"Well, night before last that madman they were keeping went and vanished," the guard said. "A friend of yours, wasn't he Master Fisk?"

"Not really. But he was taken with the rest of Roseman's men, and since no god looks after man...well, I felt it was my duty to make sure he was being well-treated. And he was."

I despised myself for playing the Rose Conspiracy card...but that was better than having the guard take it in his head to search the house. Or even talk to the landlady.

It had its effect too—the guard's voice was notably more polite as he went on.

"Aye, and since it looks like he went and broke himself out with magic... We're looking for him in the town, and the scholar's guard is searching the campus, too."

"I'm glad you told us," I said. "We'll keep an eye out for him. But you asked about our alibis for *last* night?"

"Last night someone broke into the old tower, and burned up all of Professors Dayless' and Stint's notes about that project of theirs," the sergeant said. "Both the formulas they'd created, and the records of the..." Incredulity crept into his voice, but he went on gamely. "...of the rabbits' progress. The professors are very upset about it."

"Of course they are." Benton looked pretty disturbed himself. "If the rabbit records are gone they'll have to start over from scratch! Six months' work. Who could have done such a thing?"

"And how?" I'd tried to break into that tower myself. I might have succeeded, if Professor Dayless hadn't been working late, but it wasn't an easy crib to crack. "I'd think their guard would have noticed a fire. Or did they take him out?"

"No," said the sergeant. "It looks like the intruder climbed over the courtyard wall, then entered the tower through the side door—either had a key, or picked the lock. That door was unlocked when Master Quicken went to feed the rabbits in the morning. He was the one who raised the alarm because he'd locked it the night before—with their pet madman vanishing they were all a bit twitchy, so he was certain. It was Professor Stint who found the ashes—they were burned in the hearth, in his lab...lab-o-ra-tory, and he hadn't had a fire there for months. There were a few bits of paper left in the ash, so once he looked close he knew what they were. And his formulas, and Professor Dayless' records, are missing of course."

"Horrible," said Benton. "Why would anyone do that?"

"Because they want to sabotage the project," I said. "Which is why suspicion falls on Master Benton. Right, Sergeant?"

It was also why Michael's expression had lit with excitement—because if someone was trying to destroy the project, that pushed the investigation back toward his theory. I had to admit that something strange was going on there. And Benton was more closely connected to the project than he was to Hotchkiss.

Curse it.

"Sergeant, I don't think my brother knows how to pick a lock." Kathy was keeping her eye on the target.

"I'm not sure he'd be able to climb a ten foot wall, either."

"Hey," said Benton. "I may have put on a few pounds, but I can...ah, I mean, if I ever wanted to..."

There was no way that sentence could end well for him, and the sergeant's lips twitched.

"That question was raised, sir. Where were you last night?"

"Here," said Benton. "Asleep in bed."

"That's the problem with crimes committed at night," I said. "Almost no one has an alibi. But he doesn't have a key, not anymore. And do you really think he knows how to pick a lock?"

"No sir, most don't. But he did have a key before, and he might have had a copy made."

"I might have," Benton said. "But I didn't. Why should I? I had no idea I was about to be fired till I was called to the headman's office. And I turned over all my keys to Peebles that afternoon."

"So Headman Portner said," the guard admitted. "But there's more than one way through a lock, and after your last encounter, well, Captain Chaldon did some checking. Given Master Fisk's criminal past..."

"No," said Michael firmly. "'Tis I who am unredeemed. Any debt Fisk owed, to man or the law, has been paid in full."

How very like him. But I didn't need any sacrifices. Noble Sir.

"A few points." I kept my voice mild. "First, Benton's wasn't the only key to that tower. Where does the university clerk keep her keys? Does she lock her office when she goes for lunch, or runs an errand? I thought not. Second, it was Hotchkiss who got Professor Sevenson fired, for reasons that had nothing to do with the project. He has no motive to hurt Professors Stint and Dayless, or their work."

Benton obliged me by looking indignant and distressed and innocent...probably because he was indignant, distressed, and innocent. And even Michael had figured out this was the wrong time to talk about our nighttime adventures on campus—he kept his mouth shut.

"But with so much money at stake in these projects, there's certainly motive for outsiders to sabotage them," I went on. "Have you checked with other universities that are working on the same puzzle, to see if they've had similar problems? Or checked to see if someone suddenly has more money than he should?"

I actually gave this about a thirty percent chance, but it could keep them busy for days, maybe weeks if schools far from Crown City had taken up the Heir's challenge.

"That's another thing the captain thought of," the sergeant said. "And he's sent to other universities to find out. But with Master Hotchkiss' murder, and Professor Sevenson being connected to both Hotchkiss and the project, you can see how it looks."

Benton appeared even more disturbed by this, but it wasn't him the captain suspected. Not really.

"Professor Sevenson has an alibi for the murder," I reminded everyone. "As for the project, he has no reason to disrupt it. In fact, if they succeed using the ancient formulas he supplied, he'll be due a considerable share of the reward. Sabotaging that project is the last thing he'd do."

Benton's jaw dropped, making it clear that this sensible thought had never crossed his mind. At least being that transparent probably weighed in his favor.

"Captain thought of that, too," the sergeant admitted. "But he said we needed to ask."

A squirrel scampered along the window sill. Not unheard of on the second story of a building with a tree nearby...but not common, either. The guard's brow rose.

"Pesky creatures," I said. "The landlady has a real problem with them. They've been nesting in the attic. As soon as she finds one hole and boards it over, they chew another."

"Ah," said the guard. "Did that in my cousin's barn. Got into the grain, they did. He had to fasten metal strips around the bin."

He took his leave soon after that, leaving us all staring at each other.

"Who would want to sabotage the project?" Michael asked. "Benton, think about this. You must have seen someone do something suspicious. 'Tis why they had to get you out of the way."

"I've been thinking," Benton said. "Hang it, I've been racking my brains to explain this mess, ever since it started. And there's *nothing*. It's hopeless."

There didn't seem to be much to say after that, and the silence stretched until Benton sighed.

"I'm sorry. I'm grateful for all you're trying to do. For everything my friends have done. I just hope no one figures out you borrowed Nancy Peebles' keys. I'd hate to get her in trouble."

"Is she a friend of yours?" I asked.

"She is, but she befriends most of the scholars who study here. They go to her when they get in a scrape, because she takes their side. Because her own son had so much trouble, I suppose. He was a scholar when he died."

That could certainly explain a mother going soft on other scholars—in fact, it was the kind of deep emotional hook Jack used to look for when he was setting up a scam. Which was why I would never become Jack.

"Died? So young?" Kathy asked. "Did some illness take him, or was it an accident?"

"Killed himself," Benton said. "And it may have been...well, not the university's fault, but he didn't have an easy time here."

Something Benton understood all too well.

"He was one of those odd geniuses, whose mind seems to work only on their chosen subject, with no room for anything else. A mathematician, admitted on merit. They say his scores on the admission tests were higher than most students' scores on the test to graduate. But the older Professors still talk about how hard he was to deal with. He'd go for weeks at a time, without saying a word to anyone about any subject except math—not even "hello" in passing. And he once tried to *eat* a bit of work his professor wanted to look at before he was ready to show it. The ink stained his tongue. Black for weeks."

"I see why he'd have trouble with the other scholars," Michael said. "Was that why...? Poor Clerk Peebles."

"He was always afraid someone would steal his work, his teachers say. One day he started ranting, really shouting, that someone had stolen his numbers. He scared them. Then he ran home, and threw himself out of a four story window."

"Poor lad," said Michael. "Sometimes a mind so sharp is also fragile. And in the end, he slipped into true madness."

"Or maybe somebody did steal his numbers," I said. "Like someone stole Benton's reputation, and Hotchkiss stole his victims' secrets. Universities may seem placid, but they're no better than any other group of people—often worse."

Kathy looked startled by this, but Benton shrugged.

"They're a little smarter, but no better in other ways. Though I didn't realize how vicious...that is, I didn't think anyone disliked me."

"We shall find out who did," Michael promised rashly. "And mayhap 'tis not you, but this project they hated. Could forging that thesis for Hotchkiss to find have been their first attempt to damage the project, and burning its records the second? Where does that leave us?"

It left us with Michael in charge of the investigation— he was being so careful not to look at me, he clearly knew it.

"I wasn't that important," Benton said. "The lore I passed on to Stint was useful at the start, but after I'd given him my notes I didn't matter."

"Whoever is sabotaging the project might not know that," Kathy said. "Say they heard the formula that was getting results was based on your work, so they got rid of you. Then, when the project went right on without you, they had to burn the records."

It wasn't a bad theory. Hang it.

"I thought you were on my side," I told Kathy. "'How fickle is woman, she blows with the wind, loves tall then short, loves fat then thin.'"

"'But coin is constant always,'" she added the refrain. "I'm blowing with the wind of logic. Who's to say Hotchkiss' murder and the sabotage of the project aren't connected? In fact, they are connected if whoever is sabotaging the project used Hotchkiss to frame Benton. 'Tis really one investigation—you're just pulling on different threads from the same garment. And I have to say, if I'd known you were going to take my sensible suggestion and turn it into a bone to scrap over, I'd never have—"

This time the knock made us all start and Benton hastened to the door. But instead of a Liege guardsman, a young man in a scholar's coat, with spectacles thicker than Kathy's, stood on the landing.

"Roger? What are you doing here?"

"I'm carrying a message from Professor Dayless," he said. "You won't have heard, Prof— that is, Master Sevenson, but someone broke into the tower last night and burned up all her records, and Professor Stint's too."

He saw that his condescending announcement had fallen flat, and peered at us more doubtfully.

"I did hear. The guard just paid us a visit." Benton's voice was cooler than I'd ever heard it. "Scholar Roger is one of Professor Dayless' assistants. And this is..." His gaze swept over us, but classification was too complicated. "These are my friends. What do you want, Roger?"

I wondered if Roger was someone Benton had always disliked or, more painfully, someone he'd once liked, who had abandoned him when the scandal broke. Even if we proved that the thesis Hotchkiss found was forged, going back to his old life would be awkward.

Michael had hold of the dog's collar, but Trouble didn't seem eager to approach this man. I never said the mutt was stupid.

"I don't want anything." Under our critical gazes, Roger was regretting his rudeness. "It's Professor Dayless. She can recreate most of her records from her finished copy—"

"Wait, she made a copy of all those statistics? Why?"

"Her notes were just the raw material," Roger said. "She was already working on a final report to the Heir, which will include not only our conclusions, and the graphs, but a clean copy of all the data for his scholars to examine."

The scrabbling of squirrel claws on wood sounded in the room overhead. I wondered how the jeweler had rebuilt his ladder so quickly. I also hoped Kathy had given the landlady *a lot* of money. Roger glanced up, his brows rising, but he went right on talking.

"Whoever made that nasty little bonfire didn't know about that, or he'd have burned the final report, too. But Professor Stint only had one draft of his formulas so he's going to have to recreate them, and for that he needs your notes. So if you'd please give them to me, I'll take them to him now."

I was beginning to see why Benton didn't like this twerp, but like Michael, Benton had been raised to be obliging.

"I don't have a copy either, so my notes probably burned with Stint's. I'll have to recreate them, and it's going to take at least a few days. I might have them by—"

Clearly, Benton's brain shut down the moment anyone asked him for help. Also like Michael.

"No, you won't." I rose to my feet, drawing all eyes. "Professor Sevenson is too busy trying to prove the accusation against him was nothing but a malicious lie. He has no reason to waste his time helping people who don't understand that."

"But..." Roger sputtered.

"But..." said Benton foolishly.

"But," I swept on, "he might be willing to generously offer you his time and expertise, if Professor Dayless will grant his investigators—" I gestured to Michael and Kathy, as well as myself "—access to every part of the university as her sponsored guests. That includes complete access to the project."

"The project is restricted," Roger said.

"Which is why we need Professor Dayless' permission. Because it's beginning to look like your project may be involved in what happened to Professor Sevenson."

Now it was my turn to avoid Michael's eyes. He didn't have enough proof to put him in charge of the investigation, not yet.

"If Professor Dayless wants Professor Sevenson's cooperation, then she's going to have to cooperate with us," I concluded.

Behind the thick lenses, Roger's eyes were wide. "I... I'd have to ask her about that. I was just sent to pick up Professor...I mean Master...um, the notes."

"Then you should go ask her, shouldn't you?"

He was still wiggling and objecting when I pushed him out the door and closed it in his face. Under three approving Sevenson gazes I went to the window, chased yet another squirrel off the sill, and peered out.

"He's almost to the bottom of the steps. And now he's off to the university. He's running." Well, it was a rapid jog. Professor Dayless must want Benton's notes, badly.

"You think she'll agree?" Kathy spread the question between Benton and me.

"Yes," I said. "She wouldn't have sent her beggar boy if she didn't have to. It actually costs her nothing but a bit of pride."

"There was a lot of detail in some of the formulas I complied," Benton added. "Lists of herbs and minerals, twenty or thirty long, with notes on how they may have been gathered or treated. If he has to recreate his work, Stint will need them."

"Then you'd better get started," I said. "Because I think we're going to hear from Professor Dayless shortly."

In fact, Kathy barely had time to dress and comb her hair before Roger returned, red-faced and breathless, to say that Professor Dayless would like to meet with *Professor* Sevenson's investigators.

CHAPTER 14

Michael

"Why are you helping with my investigation?"

Roger and Kathy were walking down the street ahead of us, and I pulled Fisk back to ask my question. If he was up to something, I needed to know it.

"Why? Do you think I'm up to something?"

There was an edge of anger under the irony. And with Fisk, anger is often a mask over hurt. I took a moment to reach past my own frustration to honesty.

"Naught that would harm Benton's cause, I'm certain of that. Nor anyone else. But the project is my part of the investigation, and you've no reason to help me win our wager, so... What are you up to, Fisk?"

"Nothing all that sinister." He now sounded amused at my suspicion. "I don't care what you investigate, because the problem will be solved by finding who-ever went to such lengths to give Benton an alibi for Hotchkiss' murder. Which is why I need access to the library...and hopefully, a chance to look around Hotchkiss' office and finally get a look at that forged thesis! I also want to see if we can match some names to those initials."

"Ah. Hence the bargain for all of Benton's 'investigators.' I must say, that was quick thinking. But did you need to include Kathy?"

"Why not? She thinks quickly too, in case you hadn't noticed."

I had, and 'twas the prospect of two quick wits, with me for their target, that made me wish she wasn't coming along. However, if we each took our own path they wouldn't be so likely to team up against me. And 'twas now time to catch up, for we were nearing the university's gate.

As usual in daytime the gates were open, but the gatekeeper greeted everyone who passed by. Watching closely, as he wished us well, I saw that he recognized both Fisk's and my voices. He was happy to meet Professor Sevenson's sister and tried to chat with her long enough to learn her voice too, but Roger was in a hurry to complete his task and he hustled us onward.

Classes were in session and only a handful of scholars wandered about, not the bustling tide the bell released. We reached the tower shortly, and Professor Dayless came to meet us on the steps. The guard hovered nervously behind her.

"So." She was accustomed to weighing young men, and her gaze didn't waver. "One of you isn't an idiot."

Fisk took this to himself. He was probably right.

"I don't see why Benton should help you, if you won't help him. In fact, I see several reasons he shouldn't."

Did a hint of color stain those thin cheeks? Her stern expression didn't change.

"It may seem ridiculous to you, to maintain such tight security on this project—though what happened last night demonstrates exactly why we need it. And with that madman..." She frowned at Fisk. "I should tell you, your mad friend used his magic to demolish his own room night before last, and then blasted his way through the door and escaped into the campus. I don't suppose he went to you?"

"He's not my friend," said Fisk. "And the Liege Guard told us about it this morning. Which makes what happened last night even more inexplicable, because you must have tightened your security."

"Why? The madman broke out, not in. We'd no reason to think..." She stopped, rubbing her head as if it ached. "Looking back on it, with the usual perfect hindsight, we probably should have increased our security *before* he escaped. You must understand, whoever succeeds in doing this can write his own ticket with the Heir. Possibly with the High Liege himself. Nearly unlimited funding for research, for more classrooms, staff to expand the curriculum... Do you know why your brother joined this project, Master Sevenson?"

I thought 'twas because Headman Portner told him to. But I was there to learn, so I gestured for her to go on.

"He wants to found a new department, for the study of the ancients. The first on that subject, drawing scholars and professors interested in prehistory from all over the Realm. And he'd be running it in the best university in the Realm, which we could become with the Heir's reward. Given that the stakes are that high, explain to me why I should give an unredeemed man and a criminal access to it."

There'd been a time when this formidable dame would have intimidated me, but an unredeemed man has to deal with snubs of all sorts.

"Because without Benton's notes, there's less chance your project will succeed," I said. "If his name isn't cleared, Benton will never be able to head that department, even if you can make the Heir's mistress shoot sparks out her ears. And from what Benton's told me, there's little about your project we don't know anyway."

"You don't know Stint's formulas," she said. "And they're at the heart of it. I'm just grateful the idiot— whoever he was, and whoever sent him—burned them instead of stealing them."

"Are you sure he didn't steal them?" Fisk asked. "Or make a copy, before he burned the originals?"

"Not completely," she admitted. "But Stint found fragments of his work in the ashes, and they'd take a long time to copy. Most of the night, he says. So odds are the formulas were destroyed, and all he has to do is recreate them."

"Which he'll have trouble doing, without Benton's help," I said. "And if we'd been your saboteurs, Fisk, at least, would have kept the formulas and only burned the bits he couldn't sell."

Fisk grinned in a way I'd have found unnerving, but the dragon only looked us over and sighed.

"What do you want?"

"Very little," I said. "I want to move freely about your tower, observe what I may, and ask what questions occur to me. Fisk wants access to the campus, so he can determine whether or not Master Hotchkiss' death fits into this."

"Hotchkiss? I thought a burglar killed him. And he had nothing to do with the project. One of the first things I did was have my scholars comb through all our books on the mind. A number of people have attempted to give people Gifts, but it's never come close to working. There's nothing in the library that helps."

"Then there's no harm in letting me look there," Fisk pointed out.

I could see her beginning to yield, but she turned to Kathy next. "And you, in your fine court clothes. What's your interest in this?"

Kathy wore a red linen bodice today, and a brown skirt without many petticoats. And though the lace at her cuffs and collar was rather nice, I'd not have taken her garb for "court clothes." But she smiled up at the black-gowned professor.

"I'm here to keep Fisk and Michael on task. Though I think I'll go with Fisk today. Benton told me all about your project, days ago."

'Twas a shrewd stroke, and after a brief stiffening as the thrust sank home, the professor's shoulders slumped.

"I suppose he has. I suppose he's telling every passing beggar and town drunk all about it, and we've no way to stop him. I told the headman... All right," she said. "Come in, and I'll write a note to the campus clerk, sponsoring all of you as my guests. That gives you access to all public rooms, including classes in session, though you are only to observe and not interrupt."

I guessed that "sponsored guest" was the status given to folk who were thinking of enrolling a child here, but it should suit Fisk's purposes. I had what I most wanted, when she told the guard I was permitted to come and go from the tower as I willed.

Fisk and Kathy set off for the clerk's office, with Professor Dayless' note, and Roger was dismissed to his own concerns. Then the professor turned to me.

"Master Sevenson. What do you want to know?"

"I'd prefer to start with Master Quicken, since Benton seems to have spent more time with him than anyone."

Her brows rose, in the surprised contempt of those who dismiss such folk as gamekeepers as unimportant. 'Twas the first foolish thing I'd seen her do. Those without power must use their wits to protect themselves from those who have it, and their observations of their "betters" are usually keen.

But she led me down the central hall Fisk had described, through a room that held vegetable bins, scraps of wood, and other materials and tools for making or repairing cages, then out the door in the far wall to the tower's courtyard.

I put Quicken's age in his early forties, but he rose from the crate he knelt beside with a muscular flexibility that spoke of days tramping through woods and over fields, instead of puttering about on this tame campus.

"Master Sevenson is Professor Sevenson's brother," she told him. "You may answer his questions, and help him find whatever he needs. And yes, that includes questions about the project." She turned, and went back into the tower with no further ado.

Lat Quicken eyed me in some surprise. He'd probably been told not to talk about the project to anyone, on pain of some dire penalty. 'Twas no wonder he was wary at this sudden reversal.

"Benton sends his regards." I had no qualms about saying this, for Benton had told me enough about the man that I knew he'd have done so. "And I'm to ask how your daughter fares."

'Twas the right approach; the man's wary expression faded into relieved joy.

"She's doing well, sir. The surgeon says she'll be off her crutches in another month, and likely walk without even a limp, someday."

"It must have been a terrible accident." Indeed, chatting as we rode home from the farm Benton had described a compound fracture, followed by an infection that might have carried the girl off, though she seemed to be recovering now.

"Twelve's the age they get into the most trouble, if you ask me. Even the girls. We told the youngsters to stay out of that old mill, that the floors were rotten. Maybe now they'll heed the next warning."

"Do you think so? My brothers and I never did."

He laughed, and turned back to the cage he'd been cleaning. "Well, maybe not. My brothers and I were the same. What do you want to ask me, sir? I only care for the rabbits, and trap more when they want to try another batch of potions."

'Twas too soon to ask anything that mattered, so I grasped at a random question. "Do these potions hurt the rabbits?"

"No sir," Quicken said. "Not that either of them would... Ah, they seem to be painless."

I doubt many would have cared—though I'd wager the Heir's mistress did. I remembered all too well how Mistress Ceciel's potions had hurt me.

"They might not care," I said. "But Benton would. Here, let me assist with that."

I helped lift the cleaned crate back onto the end of a row—one of several rows of solid-bottomed crates, that covered the end of the yard and must have held several hundred rabbits. Each rabbit wore a chain with a numbered tag about its neck, but they seemed none the worse for it. As we cleaned the cages, with me drawing buckets from the well and moving rabbits to and from the runs, Lat told me that he'd trapped almost three hundred rabbits for them.

"But I released about fifty that were too wary of magica to show any 'improvement.' And about five magica rabbits, caught in my snares." He shook his head in amazement. "You feel 'em wiggling in your hand, fur and bone, and even the beat of their hearts...but you can see your own hand right through 'em. A chancy business, letting 'em loose, but they go visible as they scamper off and none was harmed, so no ill luck to follow."

I could feel the heartbeat of the rabbit I held—more rapid than a man's, but not the racing beat of fear. These wild bunnies had settled into captivity remarkably well, and Master Quicken seemed to have settled too.

"When Benton was dismissed, how did folk around here react?"

Quicken cast me a sharp look. He knew what I wanted. The question was, would he answer, or retreat behind a servant's dutiful politeness?

He took some time making up his mind, and I waited for him. Which may have been what tipped the balance.

"None of 'em seemed relieved, or happy, or nothing like that. Scholar Roger smirked a bit, but then he would. If anything, they was angry at the Professor for getting hisself in trouble. And Dayless said they should keep him on, maybe doing some other job, so he couldn't go off and sell his old songs to the highest bidder. As if he would."

"He might," I said. "If some other university offered him a job that let him study his ancients. Why not help some other project along?"

"That sounds like sense to you and me," Quicken said. "But there's no other university would have him, not after he went and copied his paper. They put a powerful stake in papers around here."

"So they do. Benton told me about Professor Dayless and Stint, and you, of course. And I've met Scholar Roger. Who else works on the project?"

"As to working, I'd not say any but the professors. They have scholar assistants, who help 'em with this and that, but even that Roger, who's here more than most, isn't regular like."

"No one's been promoted to take Benton's place? I heard they were going hire someone to take his classes in the fall."

And unless we solved this matter before the applicants turned up to be interviewed, Benton might not have a job to return to even if he was proved innocent of all wrongdoing.

"Aye, but how much will they know about those ancients of his? When there was nothing for him to do Professor Benton used to sit, holding a rabbit just like you are now, and natter on and on about them."

I found myself smiling. That was the brother I remembered, far more than the sad, worried man he'd become.

"You've no assistant, Master Quicken? Now that Benton's gone."

Quicken snorted, his hands moving quickly to pull nails from a cracked slat. "I'd no need of his help. There's not more'n half a day's work here, unless they're running the rabbits, and I didn't need help then, either. It's mostly sitting around. That, and making sure you've got the right collar number when you take 'em out of the cage."

I pulled the chain on the rabbit I held around and looked at the number stamped into the tin plate—54.

"Who makes these? I saw no metal-working tools in your storage room."

"We order the tags and chain from a tinsmith in town. All I have to do is cut 'em to length and wire the links together."

I felt through soft fur and found the joint. He'd done a good job, bending the ends of the wire in so the rabbit wouldn't be scratched. And he'd relaxed into our conversation enough by now that I might get a candid answer.

"Can you think of any reason someone would wish to be rid of my brother?"

Quicken's hands and gaze remained on the slat he was marking to cut, but a sigh of regret filled his lungs before he replied.

"I can't, sir, and that's a fact. Nothing that has to do with what goes on here. But I'm just the gamekeeper. I don't know what's involved in the professors' formulas and graphs and all."

So I bade him farewell, and went in search of formulas.

Thanks to Fisk's description, I knew Professor Stint worked on the second floor, but I took the time to open a few doors on my way, and found nothing but unused offices, with dust upon desk and chair.

Professor Stint was in his laboratory, but today no braziers burned, no potions bubbled. He was staring at a sheet of paper with notes scribbled over it, and even I could see blank spaces where some item or procedure was missing.

"Who're you? This building is restricted." But he threw down his pen with an air of relief, oblivious to the splattering ink.

"I'm Benton Sevenson's brother. Here to—"

"You have his notes? Hand 'em over, sir!"

"I don't have them, yet. He says 'twill take several days to recreate them. And in exchange, Professor Dayless has granted me and my associates access to the campus and this project, so we can investigate the events that led to his dismissal."

"What's to investigate?" Stint said. "He copied his thesis. It's sad, but it happens, and Portner's right. We can't tolerate it. A thesis must be original work."

"You've dealt with my brother, and used his knowledge of ancient lore." 'Twas a struggle to keep my voice even, but I managed. "Why would he need to cheat on his thesis? He knows more about the ancients than anyone in the Realm."

"Not anyone. There's Golfew over in Camden, and another man at Harold and Benjamin University who studies them too." But my point must have struck him. He looked thoughtful for several whole seconds, before he shrugged and said, "If that's true I'm sorry. But what does it have to do with me?"

"It means that if you want to see his notes you have to answer my questions about the project," I said. Tact would be wasted on this man, but he wasn't a fool. I needed to frame my questions carefully. "Benton said you were beginning to get results from one of your formulas?"

"So Dayless says, and she's the one who runs the trials. One of my more complex formulas, too, and I made it several months ago. I need those notes, curse it! I want to try pulling some of the factors that failed in previous attempts, to see if we can isolate the element or elements that are affecting the rabbits' brain chemistry. Then I can work from evidence, instead of that 'comfrey for cunning, rue for sight' nonsense."

"You really think Gifts are just chemicals acting on the mind, like alcohol or drugs? Even though Gifts work no matter what one eats or drinks?"

I didn't care about his theories, but Fisk has taught me that folk want to talk about their passions. If you get them started, all manner of information may be washed out with the flood.

Then I wondered if Jack Bannister had taught Fisk that, but Stint was eyeing me critically.

"You have Gifts, don't you? Thought so, from the accent. It feels like they're as much a part of you as your emotions, right? As much as joy or rage or laughter."

He spoke as he would to a student, so I answered as one.

"Exactly like that. And emotions are feelings, not chemical reactions. So why should Gifts be?"

"Have you ever been drunk?" the professor asked bluntly.

"Not often. And not deeply. I don't much care for it."

"Why not?"

"Well, the alcohol makes me feel...oh."

"Precisely. Alcohol, a chemical, can produce a range of emotions from merriment to melancholy. If your emotions aren't chemical in nature, then how can chemicals affect them? It's not just alcohol, either. Think how valerian soothes nervousness, how poppy juice not only blocks pain, but gives you a sublime sense of well-being...as long as you keep your dosage low enough that you don't fall asleep or die."

I might not be much of a drinker, but I had once had potions forced upon me that had changed me profoundly. That was a tale I dared not share with anyone, least of all these ruthless professors, but... "All those things have other effects," I pointed out. "'Tis not only emotions they work upon."

"Of course they affect the chemistry of the rest of the body, too. That's why we need to isolate the elements that affect Gifts as much as we can, before we call for human volunteers to test them."

"But if all the chemistry in the body is involved, how do you know 'tis not the drug's effect on the body that will unlock or enhance Gifts? Those who are tired or in pain, which are changes in the body, are more likely to succumb to grief or despair than those who are rested and hale. That's the body's trouble affecting emotions. And sometimes emotions affect the body; 'tis well known that those who mourn a loss are more likely to fall ill than those who are content. So how can you separate body and mind?"

"You can't."

I'd become so involved in the chemist's discourse, for personal reasons, that Professor Dayless' voice made me jump.

"I've been trying to tell this fool all along that the body and mind are intricately linked, and what drugs really do is to unlock doors in the mind, doors that reveal emotions, memories, visions even. So why not Gifts or magic? But that's all his potions do."

"You say 'lock' like there was a mechanism of iron pins and keys. What you're talking about is a chemical process—"

Professor Dayless was already bristling and I broke in hastily. "So you think Gifts and magic work in much the same way?" Had Lady Ceciel's potions merely *unlocked* my strange magic, instead of creating it? I divided my question between them, but it was Dayless who answered first.

"Of course. It all springs from the mind. It must, when you think about it, for where else could either Gifts or magic come from? Unless you're one of those pathetic fools who think the old gods are real."

I looked to Professor Stint, who shrugged. "She's right about that, if nothing else. Though everything in the mind is chemical reactions, at the core. Even thought must be a chemical reaction of some sort, because chemicals can disrupt it."

"Most folk think that magic and Gifts are different. That Gifts are natural, if not common, and magic in normal humans is impossible. If there was ever a normal human with magic 'twould be a freak, like a man with two heads or a tail."

Or 'twould drive a normal man mad, which was the thing I'd feared most in all the world for the last four years. I awaited her answer with my heart pounding in dread and hope.

"If it's unnatural," said Professor Dayless, "then why do animals have it? Or why does it sometime crop up in the simple or the mad—which are entirely different mental troubles, and spring from different roots? Why do they sometimes have magic as naturally as animals do?"

"I...I don't know."

"That's because, like 'most folk,' you haven't bothered to think it through. When you do, you quickly see that the main difference between the humans who possess magic and those who don't is the ability to produce controlled and complex thought. So there must be something about that type of thinking that shuts the door in the mind behind which magic resides."

I felt as if the solid foundation of the world had shifted, and everything I knew resettled into a new and better place. "So if that door was opened by some chance, by a chemical formula say, and a man who wasn't mad or simple was given magic, he'd not be able to use it at will. But in moments of great emotion, when his thoughts stopped working clearly, 'twould spring up?"

"It might well work that way." Professor Dayless appeared pleased by my comprehension and Professor Stint looked sour. "The more the controlled, thinking mind shuts down, the wider the door to magic should open. But why do you ask? We're not working with magic, only Gifts. Which should be simpler, for that door opens easily for some, even when complex thought is present."

"'Twas only an example," I said. Complex thoughts were swooping through my mind like a scattered flock of sparrows. This explained why I could never make my magic perform when I tried to. And why the times that it broke out, to fight a fire, to save me from falling to my death, to help my horse leap an impossible chasm, were moments in which I had no thought but to fight or die.

"What of you, Professor Stint? Do you agree that Gifts and magic are so similar?"

"I've no idea," said Stint. "But it's all chemistry."

I managed a few more questions, then took my leave, for I'd a great deal to think about...and not much of it involved poor Benton. But my complex, controlled mind had observed one thing, even in the midst of my emotion—'twas Stint's formulas that would cause the change they hoped to create, but 'twas Dayless who was in charge. And for all it might be naught but a chemical reaction in his brain, Stint resented it.

Fisk had hinted that the saboteur was probably well-paid. I wondered if Professor Stint had need of money.

CHAPTER 15

Fisk

It felt odd to leave Michael behind once more—but walking off with his sister at my side was a lot more comfortable, now.

"Is Michael any good at extracting information?" she asked, as we strolled along the paths to the clerk's office. I was beginning to know my way around campus, to feel the peace that reigned while lectures were in session, with only a handful of scholars in sight. You could even hear a bird singing in one of the trees, though only country-raised Michael would know what it was. Come to think of it...

"What kind of bird is that?"

She listened only for a moment. "Barn sparrow. Is he that bad?"

"What? Oh, Michael. No, he's surprisingly good. He asks nothing but soft questions, and then sits there looking all sympathetic and honest and interested. After a while they start babbling. And he's not as bad at seeing the holes in a story as you'd expect. If the project is behind Benton's woes, he'll probably figure it out."

Kathy gave me her version of Michael's honest, interested stare, but hers was more penetrating than soft.

"Do you really think 'tis Hotchkiss' murder will solve his problems, and not the project? Or did you take up that theory to score on Michael?"

Her questions weren't soft, either.

"Honestly? At this point, I give it fifty-fifty odds either way. But Hotchkiss' murder is the crime they suspect Michael and *me* of."

"Ah."

Michael would have been disturbed by my cynicism. Katherine wore the pleased look of someone whose hunch has panned out. And if I was getting that predictable, Jack would say it was time to change my pattern.

"We're here."

I led the way up to Clerk Peebles' office. If anything, the stack of papers on her desk had grown in the last few days, but she set her pen in the inkpot and read Professor Dayless' note in silence.

"So, Master Fisk, what do you want to see?"

"Isn't that request for free access to the whole campus?" I knew it was; I'd read it as soon as we left the tower.

"Of course." Peebles pulled out a sheet of stiff paper as she spoke, and cut three slices off it with a set of shears. "One for you, one for Master Michael, and one for Mistress Sevenson here, correct? But all the passes do is give you permission to wander around and drop in on lectures. If I know what you're looking for, I might be able to help you find it."

"That's very...helpful."

Too cursed helpful, given her original resistance.

"I told you, I like Professor Benton," she said. "And I find it hard to believe he needed to plagiarize any part of his thesis. This is my school, as much as any scholar or professor's. So what are you looking for?"

"I want access to the library," I said. "I want to see this thesis Benton was supposed to have copied."

There was no reason to mention the blackmail notes we'd taken from the desk in Hotchkiss' study and some very good reasons not to, but I could still feel Kathy's critical gaze. I didn't look at her.

Clerk Peebles had a neat hand and she wrote quickly. "Give these a moment to dry before you pocket them." She handed over three slips of paper, introducing us as guests of Professor Monica Dayless, to be welcomed in all public spaces on this campus. "When you get to the library find a scholar-assistant there, Maddy Flynn. Tell her what you're looking for—and *why*—and she'll help you."

Kathy caught the stress as well, and her brows lifted. "Thank you, Mistress Peebles. I'll tell my brother of your kindness."

"Just clear his name," said the clerk briskly. "That's what matters."

The end-of-class bell tolled, like the shift bell in the town where I'd grown up. But even the end of the workday didn't produce the jostling mob that bubbled out of every doorway. I blew on our passes to make them dry more quickly.

"They look like a flock of blackbirds." Kathy eyed the growing crowds. "Only nosier. And that's saying a lot."

She had to raise her voice to be heard. I pocketed the passes and took her arm to keep us together. It felt slim, but not fragile, and warm to hold on a day this hot.

The library's marble entry hall was delightfully cool, but there was still a member of the scholar's guard, a bored young man with pimples, stationed by the big map at the foot of the divided staircase.

"Can I help you? Access to the library is restricted to scholars, unless you have permission to use it."

"We've passes." I pulled them out to show him. "We're looking for a scholar, Maddy Flynn, who works as an assistant here."

He looked at the passes long enough to be sure they were what I said they were, which surprised me. He saw it.

"The scholar's guard was told to keep an eye out for people who don't belong on campus, after Master Hotchkiss was...um. I don't know where Maddy is, but Master Hotchkiss' clerk manages the staff. His office is at the top of the stairs, right side of the balcony there."

Master Hotchkiss' clerk was in his office, and had probably taken over his boss's duties along with his own—there were five people waiting to see him. After a few minutes in line, I asked my fellows-in-waiting if any of them knew where Scholar Flynn was working today, and learned she was shelving books in history-the-seven-hundreds.

Seven centuries ago had been the midst of the Barony Wars, and I'd never heard them referred to in any other way. He saw my confusion.

"Downstairs, left door, long gallery on the left," he said. "She's the plump, pretty girl with a big basket of books."

We went downstairs, took the hallway to the left, and then went through an open arch into a long room, which had been three rooms before the dividing walls had been torn out. One wall was lined with windows, which cast rounds of sunlight onto the polished wood floor. The other wall, and a number of freestanding shelves in the middle of the room, were covered with books.

History is an interest of mine, and the bright leaf on their bindings exerted a pull as strong as a tray of glittering jewelry would...maybe stronger.

But Kathy was looking at the people in the room, and she soon strode off toward a girl with a long, honey-brown braid glowing against her black scholar's gown.

Maddy Flynn had plump pink cheeks and an even plumper bosom. She was pretty, too, but the moment Benton Sevenson's name was mentioned it was clear that no one else stood a chance with her.

"Is he all right?" Her pleasant face was dark with concern, and bright with caring. "I haven't... It didn't seem right to harass him. I mean, it might be painful for him, seeing scholars. But I, we, a lot of us have been worried about him."

"You were one of his students?" Kathy's gaze was full of sympathetic curiosity.

"History's my field," the girl said. "Though I'm more interested in the warring period and rise of the lieges than the ancients. But I... Well, never mind that. Is there anything I can do to help?"

She meant *anything*, and I saw why Clerk Peebles had directed us here. But we didn't need to break any rules, much less laws. At least, not yet.

"I'd like to see the thesis Professor Sevenson is said to have copied," I told her. "Then we've some book numbers to locate: 284.629 and 443.04272."

"The 200s are math," she said. "And the 440s engineering. I'll get you a master sheet, and you can probably find them yourselves. Just remember that a longer number isn't necessarily a larger number and you'll be fine. If you get confused, ask the room clerk."

"I know how decimals work," I told her. "But I don't have a number for that thesis."

"I'm not sure it's got one, yet," she said. "Master Hotchkiss was cataloging that section when he found it, and then it was taken away for evidence and then he died. I'm not sure where it went, but I'll find out." Determination gave her face a firmness it had lacked, and I wondered if Benton had seen this side of her. "You can look for your other books, while I do that."

She led us out of the long gallery, past another, and into a cluttered, book-strewn office where she lifted a sheet of paper from a stack on top of a cabinet.

"They give us these when we first start shelving."

One side showed a map of the library, both floors, like the map in the entry. The back held a long, numbered list...of everything.

The alphanumeric system. I was still looking at it when Maddy left, and Kathy had to pull me out of the office.

"A number for everything," I murmured. "It's not complete, of course."

"They're cataloging the Liege's library at court," Kathy told me. "I've already seen it."

"Zero hundreds: the human mind. Thought is the tool we use to understand the world, so I suppose that make sense. But he put emotions first, numerically. Maybe because we feel before we can think? One hundreds: the physical world, geology, geography, cosmology. Two hundreds: math, used to measure that physical world. Three hundreds: language... It tells you something about old Hotchkiss, about the way he thought, that he put math, with its precision, before language."

"Then he didn't think much of literature and the arts," Kathy said. "They're the nine hundreds."

If she knew that without looking at the sheet it must be a subject she was interested in. But I was more focused on Hotchkiss, how his mind was revealed through the numerical system he'd created. Four hundreds: science, physics, alchemy, magic. Five hundreds: ecology, plants, farming. Six hundreds: animals, animal and human anatomy, human and veterinary medicine.

"Interesting that he counted us as animals, at least in terms of our bodies."

"But not in terms of intellect," said Kathy. "He started his system with that. You're right, this tells us a lot about our blackmailer."

It felt like a dash of cold water in the face—and yes, I've experienced that. But blackmail, linked with this clear intricate structure giving numbers to all of reality, was as jarring as...as a mouthful of vinegar when you expected tea.

The four hundreds, which included engineering, were upstairs, divided between two rooms that hadn't had their walls knocked out.

Sorting through the book numbers was tricky, particularly when you got into the decimals. But it got easier with practice, and within minutes I pulled 443.04272 from its shelf.

"*Devices with Multiple Applications*," Kathy read aloud. "How could this have anything to do with blackmail?"

I turned to page 297 and found a diagram of a screw-like thing, with an X stuck on top of it. It was set into some sort of base, and surrounded by tables and formula to do with pressure and force.

"'Tis a screw," Kathy said.

"A screw that 'expresses exponential force in a downward direction based on...' well, a lot of math. I'll admit it's not up there with embezzlement, or an affair."

"But 'tis a screw 'from the thesis of Scholar Willet Halprin.' Could that be compass H, who paid four silver roundels a month?"

"Maybe. Let's take this with us, and go find the other."

Mathematics, the 200s, was on the other side of the second floor, in a single room that held fewer books than any of the others. Also fewer scholars—we were the only ones there.

"*Formulas for Determining or Measuring Pressure and Stress,*" I read. "*And a Surefire Cure for Insomnia, Which Works Even Sitting Upright in Broad Day.*"

I really did like Lady Katherine's giggle.

I turned to page 42.

"No pictures here," Kathy said.

"Then it's a good thing we can read."

We could even read boring mathematical theory... that became unexpectedly interesting about two-thirds down the page, when the writer described how the force of leverage might be applied to a twisting motion. If one attached levers to the top of a screw, that leverage would then be applied downward at a ratio of...

"'Tis the screw thing." Behind the spectacles, Kathy's eyes were bright with excitement. "He found it in this book and he built it."

The binding of the book in my hands looked older than the book she held, but I flipped to the printer's page to make sure.

"This was printed in Stephen nine, almost twenty years ago. What about yours?"

She was turning to the front of the book as I spoke. "Stephen twenty-five, just three years ago. And in the back here it talks about the contributors. It says Willet Halprin is now working for High Liege Stephen, in the Bureau of Projects and Works. This Halprin, he did what they say Benton did. He copied his thesis."

"He could have credited it," I said. "He could have mentioned in his thesis that he got the idea from what's-his-name, and modified it."

"If he did that, then why is he paying Master Hotchkiss?"

She was right.

"You've been at court for a while," I said. "Could Master Halprin be fired for having cheated to get his engineering credential?"

"I don't know. That's not what the sacrificial maidens usually gossip about. It might depend on how well he does his work, or how much his boss likes him. But even if it wouldn't cost his job, 'twould be worth paying a reasonable sum to keep it quiet."

Sobered, we replaced both books and went to find Scholar Flynn. She led us up to a very small office on the third floor, hardly more than a closet, with one narrow slit of a window. It held a table that all but filled the room, piled with books, chapbooks, pamphlets, and three great tomes, open on their own stands.

"This is Master Hotchkiss' cataloging room. I'm told they put the thesis back here about a week ago, so he probably hadn't time to work on it before he died. It should be in one of these stacks."

"Where does that door go?" I gestured to another door, off to one side.

"That's Master Hotchkiss' office. But you don't need to worry about being interrupted—it was locked up after his death. This room's left open, in case someone needs to consult the master lists. And your passes...

It's not exactly a public room, but it's not exactly not, either."

Even a chance to browse through the complete alphanumeric system didn't interest me now.

"Thank you," I said. "We'll try not to be caught here, and we'll tell Professor Sevenson how kind you've been."

"Don't you want me to help look for the thesis?"

She clearly imagined herself heroically risking all for love.

"We'll manage. I'm sure you have other tasks you need to get back to."

"Not really," she said. "I could—"

"Got it!" Kathy exclaimed. "It was right near the top."

"Oh. Then I'll leave you to it."

And she finally did, though she still cast a wistful glance back as I shut the door.

"Did you really find it?" I asked. "Though if you didn't, I'm not complaining."

If she hadn't, she'd been very quick-witted. Which she was.

"'Tis here. I wonder if Benton knows she's sweet on him."

"How could he miss it? My guess is that, unlike our friend PN, your brother doesn't sleep with scholars."

"Good for him," said Kathy firmly. "And it's not as if she'll be a scholar forever."

"Benton may not be a professor long enough for that to matter, unless we can prove this is forged," I said. "Hand it over."

It was a chapbook, stitched between two flat leather panels instead of bound up the spine. It certainly looked like a thesis, handwritten, and dated Rupert eighteen, nearly fifty years ago. There was dust on the ridges where the folded pages had been cut.

"Someone really wanted to nail your brother," I said. "If this is a forgery, it's perfect."

"*If?*" Kathy asked indignantly.

"Look how the paper is beginning to yellow, not splotchy, like someone was holding it over a flame, just that gradual color fade all round the edge, like you get when it fades from time, light, and air. And every page the same. The only way to do that is by keeping it in a sealed case with some sort of smoke or mist, for days on end, so it creeps into the paper at a uniform rate. And if you make it too damp, the whole thing..."

Kathy was staring at me.

"What? All kinds of scams require forged documents. Maps, deeds, diaries. I had to know this stuff."

"Can you prove it was forged?" Kathy asked hopefully.

"Prove it? Probably not." I picked the book up and sniffed it; if whatever they'd used to age the pages had a scent, it had faded. "I can tell you this was done by someone who knew what they were doing, and they spent a lot of time getting it right."

"How much time?"

"At least three days to write it up. No, more than that, because they'd have to do some research even with Benton's thesis to base it on. Say five or six days. Three or four more to bind and age it. And that's assuming their first try worked perfectly, which it usually doesn't."

"So if Benton saw or did something that alarmed someone, 'twas more than a week before he was dismissed," Kathy said. "Over a month ago now. No wonder he doesn't remember."

"More than that. It had to be planted for Hotchkiss to find, too."

"Unless they bribed him to find it, and bring it forward," said Katherine. "I'd not put it past the man."

"At this point there's not much I'd put past our genius librarian. Which brings us to the next part of today's program. Keep an eye on the hallway, would you, and make sure no one's about to pop in?"

Kathy went to the door and peeked out.

"No one there now. What are you going to do?"

"Ordinarily I'd be trying to pick the lock," I said. "Which is harder, and takes longer, than most people think. As it is..."

The fourth key on Hotchkiss' ring opened the side door to his office.

"Be quiet in here," I murmured, as Kathy whisked into the silent room. "And stay away from the windows. We're on the third floor so we don't have to risk closing the curtains, but if someone sees movement..."

"Of course. What are we looking for? Where do I start?"

"We're looking for whatever we can find." I closed the door and locked it behind us. "But I've got an idea for where to start."

Only a few days after the man's death, his office had already developed that "unused" smell, which isn't so much a matter of dust as of undisturbed air and emptiness. Like his office at home it was cluttered with books, and papers covered his desk. A large sturdy desk, that looked a lot like the one in his study.

"People are so unimaginative," I told Kathy. "It makes a burglar's life much easier."

The hidden panel was even behind the same drawer, but there were a lot more papers in this one.

"That looks like a page from a play script," Kathy said. "'CON: Taking down walls is a bigger job than it seems. You've got to disassemble them, careful like.' CON is a contractor?"

"Sounds like it." I ran my eye down the page. "And I'm guessing BRD is a member of the university board. Look here, where BRD says, 'Your bid for this job is one of the highest, Master D. I wish I could see a sample of your work. I've got a small job to be done at my home, but I'm afraid I couldn't pay your price.'"

"Oh dear," said Kathy. "The board member is hitting up the contractor for a bribe."

"Do some work at my house for free, and I'll approve your expensive bid for the job. Probably taking out walls right here in the library. Master Hotchkiss might have overheard this conversation himself."

"And he wrote it up in the form of a play, in case someone came across this page."

"And kept it, with all these documents, separate from his register of payments," I said. "So neither set screams blackmail to anyone who might find them. He was no fool. But then, his system told us that already."

"So hammer D, who was crossed out and hadn't paid anything, he's a contractor," Katherine said.

"And A. is a member of the university board," I added. "Who's been paying for years. We have our second suspect."

"Here's our screw again." Kathy picked up the next sheet in the pile. It was the same drawing we'd seen in the engineering book, but on cheap thin paper. It was also more roughly drawn and beneath it was a handwritten note: *from the thesis of Willet Halprin. In force multp. Or change dir.?*

284.629 was printed in the upper corner, in Hotchkiss' meticulous hand.

"This was probably written by whoever put the *Devices* book together," I said. "I don't know how Hotchkiss got hold of it, but when he did I bet he remembered that passage in the math book and checked it out."

"This next page looks like it was crumpled up and then smoothed out," Kathy said. "Do you think he pulled it out of the trash?"

"Looks like it."

Spread on the desk and smoothed a bit more, it proved to be a course report for one Franklin Mabry. Judging by the topics he was being graded on: *considerations, revocation, dissolution, misrepresentations, fraud*, he was taking contract law...and failing.

"Only a sixty-three," said Kathy. "Benton said sixty-five was passing."

"And that a lawyer needed higher than eighty to get a decent job," I reminded her. "The professor's name's not on this, but...let's say that PB scales, otherwise known as Professor Bollinger, has totted up Master Mabry's course score and finds he didn't pass. He decides to break the bad news in person, instead of however they do it, and tracks Master Mabry down in the library, or maybe in the garden outside this window."

It offered a good view of the garden, and if the windows were open we'd have heard the students' voices.

"Mabry learns that he's failing and loses his temper, rants, weeps—"

"You do know you're making this up, right?" Lady Katherine, critical. "He could have known full well he was likely to fail, and been plotting what to do about it for weeks. Professor Bollinger is quite surprised at how calmly he receives the news."

"Either way, Mabry makes Professor Bollinger some kind of offer, and the Professor accepts. He then gives Mabry this, the true report, and goes back to compose a fake one that raises Mabry's score to a respectable number. M 87, Hotchkiss' ledger said. High enough for him to get a job and then some. Mabry crumples this up and throws it away...and Hotchkiss, curious about what he's just seen, unfolds it and learns that Franklin Mabry has failed. Only then he doesn't, and his final score when he graduates is impossibly high. And Hotchkiss realizes that what he saw was Mabry offering Bollinger a bribe, and Bollinger taking it."

"How long have they been paying?" Kathy asked.

"Over ten years. They were his first victims."

The next four papers were all letters, written in a flowing, extravagant hand.

"'My dearest Moonbeam?'" I couldn't blame her for sounding incredulous.

"Why not? They're signed, 'Your devoted Mugglewump.'"

Kathy laughed aloud, then stopped with a guilty glance at the door.

"It's not a bad way for PN to avoid signing his name," I pointed out, running my eyes down the page. Which I then shifted quickly out of Kathy's sight.

"Hey!" But she said it softly.

"It's not so much the content." Although it was. "I'm afraid you'd laugh."

"I wouldn't. If this is a professor writing to one of his scholars 'tis not funny."

"Benton says there's no sign Nilcomb coerced any of them," I reminded her. "Or changed their grades."

"Still, ick. At the best, ick."

"I don't object to that as much as I do to his prose."

"Then you're a horrible person," Kathy said promptly. "This matters, Fisk."

"So does good prose. 'Your breasts are like the two moons, touching as they cross. Except yours are matched for color and for size.'"

Kathy made a choking sound, but at least it was quiet. "You're kidding. No one would write that."

"No, really. The rest is almost as bad."

"Let me see."

I turned to avoid her reaching hand. "No, fair maid, I don't think so. Oh, ick. You *definitely* don't need to see them."

Neither did I. I folded them and added them to the pile, which I tucked inside my vest, rather regretting that she didn't make another try for them.

Michael's sister, I reminded myself.

"Were any of them signed?" Kathy asked. "I wonder how Master Hotchkiss came by such...personal documents."

"No idea. And they may not be signed, but I'll bet Nilcomb's students could identify his writing."

We had both sobered.

"So," said Kathy. "Board member A, who asked the contractor to bribe him; Halprin, who plagiarized his thesis; Mabry and Bollinger, who changed the grades; and Professor Nilcomb. Five suspects, if you count blackmail a sufficient motive for murder."

"Which most do."

"But no connection to Benton, or the project he was working on."

"We've just started looking," I pointed out. "We need more information about all of these people. I wonder if the helpful Clerk Peebles would let us buy her luncheon."

"Dinner," said Kathy. "'Tis an hour past midday, so she's likely eaten by now. Besides, if she agrees to dinner we can bring Michael and Benton along and catch them up on what we've learned."

Clerk Peebles said she'd be happy to dine with us. Kathy and I snagged a hot pie from a street seller outside the campus gates, and spent the rest of the afternoon tracking down a sample of Professor Nilcomb's handwriting.

It matched.

CHAPTER 16

Michael

I wasn't averse to dining with Mistress Peebles, but Benton suffered an attack of...not shyness, so much, as a perfectly understandable desire to avoid her pity, and he declined to join us. Given the way he colored up at the mention of Maddy Flynn's name, I wondered how he'd have reacted had *she* been attending. But in order for Benton to have a love tangle with a scholar, he'd have to go back to being a professor.

Benton also pointed out, unhelpfully, that he could alibi professor Bollinger for the time of the lecture, and even if Hotchkiss was killed before that, he couldn't believe the man could come straight from committing bare-handed murder and then calmly listen to the speaker.

There were two board members whose names began with A, Amliss and Arnoll. And Benton had no idea which of them was involved with the library renovations.

We took Mistress Peebles to the same tavern we'd been dining at, but for this Fisk rented a private parlor and paid for a nice salad, cooked beets in a sauce of mustard and honey, mashed potatoes, a whole roast goose, and fruit tarts for dessert. It must have set him back two silver roundels, but then he still had most of his share of the reward from Tallowsport.

I recounted some of Fisk's and my more amusing adventures during the meal, Kathy supplied court gossip, and Fisk himself had the tact to speak only about neutral topics while we ate. 'Twas only as we finished up the sweetened cream that had topped our tarts that he expressed curiosity about one Scholar Franklin, whose name, he said, had "come up."

"Franklin Mabry?" Clerk Peebles blinked in surprise. "He can't have anything to do with what happened to Professor Sevenson. He was a law student here...what, ten, twelve years ago?"

"Ah." Fisk sometimes delights in being uninformative. "Do you know where he is now?"

"Not for certain. I heard he'd finally become a judicar, in some town near D'vorin up on the north coast. That's where his family's from, I think."

"What's the last time he was here?" Fisk pressed on.

"After he graduated? Never, that I know of. He'd have no reason to return, except to enroll a son or daughter with us someday. That's how I see most of the old scholars, if they ever come back."

'Twas spoken matter-of-factly, but what would it be like to lose a son, and then to lose the children you befriended in his place, year after year? If we succeeded in restoring Benton's reputation, I would tell him that we owed our triumph to this woman's help, and that he should make it a point to seek her out in the future.

She would have at least one youth in her life who wouldn't leave her.

Fisk went on to determine that some engineer in Crown City had also never come to visit the university, even though he was so near. Then Kathy took over, asking about the renovation of the library, what had been done there, who was the contractor, and how he'd been hired. If Peebles knew which board member A was involved, she didn't say.

I wished there'd been time for Fisk and Kathy to report more details of what they'd discovered, but I'd spent most of the afternoon perusing Professor Dayless' data on the project. She said if I insisted on seeing everything I might make myself useful, and set me to making a new copy of the trials of one of the formulas that had produced inconclusive results. In fact, inconclusive was a fair description of my whole day. I now understood, both how the experiment with the rabbits had been done, and why Benton found it so boring.

Fisk finished his interrogation by asking Mistress Peebles what she knew about Professor Nilcomb, and her lips tightened in distaste.

"I can guess what you're talking about, but I don't see how that...how any of this has anything to do with Scholar Benton."

She'd been willing to relay harmless information about past students and building renovations, but she clearly wasn't going to besmirch a man's reputation without knowing why.

Fisk eyed her over the gravy stained plates and half-full goblets, and made up his mind.

"Master Hotchkiss was blackmailing the people I've asked you about. Which makes them suspects in his murder."

"Blackmail?" Mistress Peebles' eyes widened. "You mean, for money? No, of course you do. I'm sorry, this is silly of me, but somehow I didn't think your investigation would involve anyone else."

"'Tis understandable you'd be shocked," I said gently, "that someone you knew would stoop so low."

"Hotchkiss... He helped me get my job." She picked up her goblet, but didn't drink, staring down at her hands. "That was after Seymour died, and I needed it badly."

"Then there must have been some good in him. I find people are seldom all one or the other. Benton told us of your son," I added. "He says the professors still speak of his intelligence."

"And how odd he was?" She looked up at me then. Her eyes were bright, but there were no tears. "They were the only ones besides me who saw it. How very smart he was. Most people took him for simple, but he had notebooks full of mathematical formulas, and even scribbled them on the walls of his room. A few years after he started studying here, he told me that numbers could define anything."

She smiled, so sadly a heart of stone would have cracked.

"I asked him, 'Even love? How big is love in numbers?' Teasing, because he was always so logical. Emotions confused him. Frightened him, I think. He told me, 'Nothing, nothing, nothing.' But then he kissed my cheek, because whatever he said, he knew it wasn't nothing."

Now her eyes had filled, but she shook her head sharply, defying grief.

I would definitely speak to Benton.

"Unlike Fisk, I'm looking into Professor Dayless' project," I said, giving her a chance to regain her composure. "Can you tell me anything about her and Professor Stint?"

"I don't know much about Stint," she said. "He's only been here for two years. We've had the usual dealings, about course schedules and paying his salary and such."

She was calmer by the time she finished speaking. For all her grief, her son had died long ago.

"What about Professor Dayless? Is she new to the university?"

"Oh, no. Monica was hired before I was, and I've been working for the university nearly twenty years. In fact, she was kind. There aren't many women working here, and we tend to know each other better than the men."

"We didn't find any evidence of it," Kathy said, "but could Master Hotchkiss have been blackmailing one of the professors who works on the project? You knew about Nilcomb's...problem. Is there anything like that about either of them?"

"No, there isn't. And if there was, I'm not sure I'd tell you. I don't mind giving you harmless information, but I won't repeat malicious gossip. Which might not even be true! There's one thing you should know, however. For Professor Sevenson's sake. The first of the scholars applying for his job was interviewed this morning."

This was probably something she shouldn't have shared with us, and her lips folded tightly over the words.

"How many candidates are there to interview?" Kathy asked. "How long before they make a decision?"

"Just two more interviews. One of them's not even in town yet, but they're talking to the other man day after tomorrow. So you may not have much more time, but I still hoped... Well." She rose to her feet, declaring her intention to depart.

"You hope to help Professor Sevenson?" Fisk said swiftly. "Then would you be willing to supply a bit more harmless information, such as where some of these people live? We have to talk to them, and it will be less likely to damage them if we can do so privately than if we have to track them down on campus."

That made her hesitate.

"I'll think about it," she said. "Come to my office tomorrow. I'd have to look up the directions to their homes, anyway."

She said I didn't need to escort her home, but I insisted. And as it turned out, her house was so nearby Fisk and Kathy were still at the table when I returned.

I thought Kathy looked a bit irritated, and Fisk can be annoying—though he usually wasn't, with her.

"I don't suppose you got any malicious gossip out of her," Kathy asked.

"Whatever it is, Benton should be able tell us," Fisk said. "Though it may be hard to sort gems from glass. Places like this are usually awash with gossip. I wonder why he hasn't enlightened us already."

"You don't know Benton," I said. "The only people he cares about have been dead for thousands of years. He only told us about Nilcomb when we pointed to the man's initials and asked directly."

"He probably tried to ignore all the gossip," Kathy added. "I suppose we ought to sit down tomorrow and pry it out of him."

"That's an excellent idea," said Fisk. "If you would. Tomorrow I want to find the homes of all the people on our list and ask their neighbors what they're like when they're not at work. Which means we probably ought to head home."

He rose from the table as he spoke, and Kathy followed him as she said, "We don't even know which board member A was being blackmailed. And if they've started the interviews for Benton's job, we're running out of time."

"We may not have his name." Fisk closed the parlor door behind us, and gestured to a maid that we were leaving. "But I'll bet we can find out who the contractor was, and he can tell us."

"Why would he?" I asked. "He paid that man a bribe to get the job."

"A solicited bribe." Fisk put on his sympathetic face, which is so good that Kathy looked startled. "That poor man, he must have been furious doing all that work for nothing, to get a job that he deserved, anyway." The kindly expression vanished, like a candle flame blown out. "When people are furious, they want to talk about it. I'm not worried about getting our board member's name."

"And assuming Halprin and Mabry are out of town, that leaves Professors Bollinger and Nilcomb," Kathy said. "Benton might know where they live."

"And I want directions to the homes of Professors Dayless and Stint," I added, as we stepped out into the dark street. It was cooler now, and both moons rode high in the sky. "Particularly Stint."

"Why particularly?" Kathy asked.

"Because he's new to the university, at least relatively, which leaves more room for secrets in his life. And he doesn't much like the fact that Dayless was placed over him."

"That sounds more interesting than trying to get Benton to remember gossip," Kathy said wistfully.

Had I been truly noble I'd have volunteered to do that myself, and let her go with Fisk. There might be some gossip Benton would hesitate to repeat to our young sister, too. But I'd no doubt Kathy would drag it out of him, and I really wanted to learn more about Stint and Dayless, not to mention Fisk's suspects.

Kathy wasn't all that noble either.

"All right, I'll do the dirty work. But you have to promise to tell me everything when you get home," she said. "And that you won't muck it up because of this stupid cock fight the two of you have—"

Four men emerged from the alley that led to Benton's door, three of them pulling another along with them.

"Pepper in the soup," he was saying. "The secret is moderation, not too much, not too little, or it sets the walls to sneezing."

"Hey!" Fisk shouted, but I had already broken into a run.

They reached the street and tried to dash off, hampered by the jeweler who not only refused to run, but seemed to be struggling. We'd have caught them easily... In fact, we did catch them easily, whereupon two of them turned and pulled out short but effective cudgels.

Fisk and I, unarmed, skidded to a stop. Kathy ran into Fisk's back and set him staggering.

"What do you think you're doing?" Fisk demanded. "That man is our guest."

"Yeah? Well, we been paid to un-guest him," one of the men who'd stopped us said.

The third man was hustling the jeweler on down the street. The poor man's struggles were more effective against just one captor, but the end was in no doubt— he would be carried away.

And unarmed, there was little Fisk and I could do to stop it. If we rushed the thugs their clubs would make short work of us. If we ran back to get our weapons, they'd be long gone by the time we—

An ear-shattering scream ripped the quiet night.

All of us jumped, including the thugs.

"Help!" Kathy shrieked. "Help, robbers, help, please, somebody get the guard, help, robbers, help!"

She darted around the startled thugs, still shrieking. The nearest one had the sense to swing at her, and Fisk—who never goes near armed thugs if he can avoid it—took advantage of his distraction and tackled the man. They went down on the cobbles in a welter of flying knees and elbows, and Kathy ran after the man who'd taken the jeweler, still screaming at the top of her lungs.

"Here now!" The thug who was guarding me stared wildly about, as windows and doors began to open. A man in his nightshirt, waving a poker, charged into the street looking for the source of the commotion.

"I'd run if I were you," I said pleasantly. "She's got a scream that could pierce plate armor. She always did, even as a toddler."

He was running before I finished speaking. His comrade released the jeweler and raced into the night. The last man had to fight free of Fisk before he could flee, and the outraged citizens nearly caught him.

Fisk rolled to his feet, cursing with a fluency that assured me of his well-being despite the blood flowing sluggishly from his lower lip. Kathy was explaining to half a dozen concerned men and a few sturdy women that we'd been dining in the tavern, and had just met up with our uncle when we'd been set upon.

She had our "uncle" by the arm, and I heard him mutter something about, "wicked rabbits, running off like that." But Fisk was headed in her direction, and I had faith in their ability to keep the jeweler under control, and also keep the citizens from summoning the guard. Our assailants were long gone so there was little a guardsman could do, and Kathy would no doubt promise to report the crime in the morning.

Besides, a more urgent matter pressed for my attention.

The only sign of disturbance in Benton's front room was an overturned chair, a dropped quill that had spotted the floor with ink, and half a dozen papers that had fallen from the desk. 'Twas the sound of thumping that led me to my brother, lying bound and gagged on his own bed with the blankets wrapped around his head to muffle shouts. Which was why, a smart man, he'd given up on shouting and was energetically kicking the wall. He was bruised and shaken, but aside from the shock of being overcome and bound he'd not been harmed.

I heard footsteps overhead as I was freeing him, and deduced that Fisk and Kathy were restoring the jeweler to his own room. But Benton had time to put his room to rights, and put a kettle on for tea, before Fisk and Kathy came down to join us.

"We'll have to set a guard," Kathy was saying as she came in. "If they tried for him once, there's nothing to stop them from trying again."

"We'll have to find somewhere else he can stay." Fisk's voice was unaccountably sharp. "We can't have you tangling with thugs—thugs with clubs!—every night, or people will start to notice."

I looked at Fisk closely, but his lip had already stopped bleeding and his movements were easy. 'Twas not injury that made him so testy.

"Phoo," said Kathy. "He missed me by a good foot. You're just miffed that I stopped them when you couldn't. Though you may be right about finding some other place for the jeweler to stay—we can't stand guard all night and investigate by day. Not for long."

"*You're* not standing guard," said Fisk. "Or investigating either, if this turns into a thugs-with-clubs affair."

"Which brings us to the real question," I murmured. "How did they know he was here in the first place?"

CHAPTER 17

Fisk

It took all three of us to convince Mistress Katherine she wasn't going to take a watch shift. Michael went and got his sword to take the first watch and Benton took the second. This left me to rouse the jeweler before dawn, to pack before he left for his new lodging.

Benton, after some thought, had come up with a friend he'd studied with, whose older brother owned a farm in the countryside.

"He was a merit scholar, and a good one, but his whole family could use the money," he said. "They're kindly people, and there are lots of animals for your mad friend to bring into the house. If he likes squirrels and rats, he should be delighted with goats."

He probably would be. But Michael was right; the real question was how they—whoever they were—had known he was here. The landlady might indeed have talked to someone about our guest. Or someone might have gotten suspicious and come looking for him. I was his only "friend" in town, after all, so it made sense they'd look for him here.

But somehow that didn't convince any of us. I was glad we were getting him out of town. Preferably at an hour we weren't likely to be followed, which was why I was going in to wake him before dawn.

I found the jeweler already awake—assuming he'd slept, which he might not have. He was working by lamplight on a tangle of gears and wires that lay on one of the tables, his mad eyes framed by tousled hair.

But the hair was clean, and so were his clothes. Benton had been taking good care of him, just as the university maids had. Hopefully Benton's farmer friends would do the same, but all this moving about had to be unsettling for him.

"What are you making?" I wanted to break the news that we were going to move him again gently, but taking a closer look at the intricate mess of springs and levers I became genuinely curious.

"A puzzle, a toy, a meal. Like the one you're playing at, but not for you, this one's for the others. Catnip to cats, your puzzle is, setting them rolling and playing with their bright teeth, biting, biting, biting."

"No." I sat down beside him. "I really want to know. What does it do?"

He peered at me, and saw that I meant it. He picked up a handful of nuts, which Benton must have provided, and dropped them into a hopper at the top of his contraption, which he then latched shut.

"Here," he pushed it across to me. "The bar's the star, though the comets jingle. Give it a press."

There were lots of dangling chains and gears, very bright and tempting, but I pressed down on the small bar hidden in the midst of the distractions. It moved easily, probably pulled by springs hidden in the mechanism. A series of wheels spun and flashed, and a single nut rolled out of a gap at the bottom of the mechanism.

"For your friends." I was smiling. "I think they'll like it very much."

"They'll play with it even after the nuts are gone, for they like moons and stars and buttons. Have to bolt it down, I will," he added. "Or they'll run off with it."

I seized this small, lucid moment.

"Remember last night, when those men tried to take you? We think they were sent by someone involved in the project the professors were working on, back at the tower. There's something wrong with that project, and we're afraid someone thinks you saw something." Come to think of it, he might have seen something. His windows looked onto that yard. "Do you know what's wrong with the project?"

"Oh, I know all kinds of wrongs and secrets. The rabbits keep 'em, so sly they are. Not like rats, rats are honest, and even clever squirrels aren't the liars rabbits are. But your friend, he's already finding the answers he needs."

"Michael? What do you mean? He's trying to find out about the project too, but he hasn't learned much."

"The project, the reject, a bunch of shiny spinning wheels, that is. I meant that he's finally falling into bed with that magic of his. Prickly, ickly, but he's beginning to figure it out."

"How did you know...?"

Michael, with his magic, could see a glow around magica. Who knew what this man, with his magic, could see or sense.

"You're about to fall too." He cackled suddenly, a sound that lifted the hair on the back of my neck. "But you'll like it, lad, they always do, the cockerels strutting off to the slaughter. Led by pretty pullets, they always are. But goats aren't rats, or even squirrels. He's a fool to think it."

The thread of this conversation was getting slippery.

"Then you know we're going to take you to a... Wait a minute. How do you know what Benton said about goats?"

"The birds sing it, the wind sighs it. How's a man not to learn what the voices in his own head tell him?"

But I was watching, and his eyes flicked aside as he spoke...to the empty hearth between the windows. A hearth with a chimney that would go straight down through the rooms below it.

I rose and went to kneel beside it—no fire, not in late Roseon, and in the predawn dark the whole world was quiet. I stuck my head inside to listen.

At first I heard nothing but a sort of windy emptiness. I stilled my breathing, closed my eyes, and focused on a faint scratching sound. Then I distinctly heard the clink of glass, and a muffled curse. The scratching sound resumed till I heard paper rustle, as a finished sheet was set aside to dry. Benton, up early despite taking a midnight shift, working on his notes.

How much louder would voices be?

I went back to the jeweler. "So you know we're going to take you to stay with Benton's friends in the countryside. And you know why. Are you willing to go? It may be dangerous for you here, and Benton wouldn't send you to anyone who wasn't kind."

"So were the tower folk but I don't care for humans, any more than the moon gods do. Fur is better, even the soft fur of liars. Though squirrels, they're soft too, and don't bite as much as rats. Want the nuts they do, and ready to pry, to lie, to cheat, to die. Or let others do it for 'em, more like."

"Do you mean Hotchkiss? Was he involved with the project somehow?"

"I never mean anything." The bright eyes met mine, for all the good it did. "I'd offer you a nut, but you've already got two that are speaking to you, and a number that don't. I miss the tower squirrels. Kindness, now, they had cheese in all their paws."

There were tears in his eyes. But however kind the squirrels might be, the humans back at that tower were the ones in charge. And one of them knew he was here.

"You need to pack," I said. "Benton will take you to the farm at first light, and you can bring anything that can be stowed in two horses' saddlebags. There lots of squirrels, out in the countryside."

His gaze went back to his mechanism, shutting me out, and I suspected Benton would have to pack for him. It was the only form of protest he had, and he knew why he had to go. I said goodbye and locked the door behind me, wondering just what he'd heard coming down the chimney back in the tower. Stint's lab had been right above his room, and I thought Day- less' office might be above that, as well.

"'Tis probably how he learned so much about Rose- man's organization," Michael said.

We'd seen the others off—somewhat later than we'd intended.

The jeweler had refused to pack for himself, and when Benton had gone up to pack for him he'd insist- ed on taking half the attic's contents. He had three horses' saddlebags to fill, however—Benton rode Chant, the madman mounted Tipple, and because he was being so recalcitrant, Kathy accompanied them on the placid mare she'd borrowed from the royal stables. Michael and I, on foot, trailed them to the outskirts of the city and made certain no one was following when they set out.

That matter seen to, we got ourselves an early breakfast and were waiting at Clerk Peebles' office door when she showed up for work. After a night's thought, concern for Benton had won out—she not only gave us directions to the homes and offices of the known blackmail victims, but to Professor Stint's home as well.

Michael was optimistic about his theory that Stint resented Dayless' control over the project enough to sabotage it, and he wanted to ask his neighbors if the professor needed money. Or had suddenly come into money, even if he didn't need it.

However, two of the three people we wanted to investigate today, board member A and Professor Nilcomb, were Hotchkiss' victims, which meant I was in charge. We were now on our way to the workshop of Master Dobbs, the contractor who'd worked on the library six years ago, and I hoped he'd be willing to name the board member who'd demanded a bribe. Whom Hotchkiss had blackmailed for it.

But Michael was still talking about the project. "Voices do travel up and down chimneys. You can't hear them if you're talking yourself, you have to really listen to make out words, and it doesn't work if the wind is blowing...but he had nothing to do but listen, in that quiet room. He probably knows everything that was said in Stint's lab. 'Tis too bad he can't relay it sensibly, or the case might end right now. And he'd be out of danger, free to go home to his friends."

There was only pity in his voice, not the fear that had been there before.

"Was he right? *Are* you falling into bed with your prickly magic?"

"I'd not say that, though I do have some new ideas. After we speak with Master Dobbs, shall we go on to Professor Stint's home?"

"Depends on what Dobbs tells us."

Michael was focused on Stint, but I've known him long enough to know when he's using one topic to distract me from another. "What new ideas? About magic, I mean."

He hesitated a moment before replying, confirming my suspicion.

"Professor Dayless was speaking about the project yesterday, and the subject drifted from Gifts to magic. She said... Well, the short version is that she thinks the use of rational thought blocks off our access to magic, but that if it didn't, 'twould be no more unnatural for us to possess magic than Gifts."

I'd been saying something like that to Michael for almost four years, but he'd ignored me. And the part about rational thought blocking it was interesting.

"That would explain why the simple and the mad sometimes have magic," I said. "And why you've only been able to use it when you're panicking about something."

"I wasn't panicking," said Michael. "Well, mayhap with the cliff, and that was justified. But if 'tis true, it means that magic doesn't drive you mad."

"I told you that," I said. "Years ago."

"Yes, but now I wonder... Ah, here's Dobbs' work yard. And after this, we go on to Professor Stint's. Agreed?"

He looked so relieved that it was clear he'd thought better of finishing that sentence. And it was no longer my job to find out what he was wondering about.

"We've got a lot of people we need to talk to today, and if they've started doing interviews for Benton's job we'd better get them done as fast as we can. We'll figure out the most sensible route once we know where board member A lives."

The contractor's shop was near the river, about half a mile from the university. Once he noticed Michael's noble accent, he ushered us into his office and asked us to sit with the good will of a man delighted by the prospect of new business.

"What can I do for you, young sirs? Renovating some rooms near the campus? Pigsties, most of those student apartments. I'm sure I can make the place more comfortable for you."

"We're not scholars," Michael said, in his absurdly honest way. "We've a few questions about the renovations you did in the campus library."

Dobbs looked a bit uneasy, but his gaze was steady. "Yes? I took out walls on several floors. Did a good job, if I say so myself, particularly with the decorative plaster that covers up the scars. Do you need walls removed?"

"No," I said. "We need to know the name of the board member who demanded you give him free labor before he'd hire you. And whether or not he paid Hotchkiss' blackmail. You refused, didn't you?" I let sympathy and admiration ooze into that last sentence, but the man still hunched his shoulders like an angry bull.

"Cursed straight I didn't pay him! Why should I? Yeah, I had to do a bit of extra work, show my skills to get the job. But I did good work in that library, for fair pay. You got any complaints about my brickwork? Is the plaster falling off? Then you got nothing. If I didn't pay him, I'll be hanged if I pay you!"

Dobbs' accent was more carpenter than contractor now. And I liked his attitude.

"We don't want anything," I said. "Except the board member's name. Because while you didn't pay Master Hotchkiss, I'm afraid he did."

The bunched shoulder muscles relaxed, but his eyes were wary. "I heard Hotchkiss was killed. They said a burglar did him."

"'Tis not likely," said Michael. "Given that the man was a blackmailer."

Dobbs sighed and sank back in his chair. "Can't say I'm surprised. Or very sorry, either. But I never paid a fract, so I've no motive to kill him. And the Liege Guard can check my accounts to confirm that."

"They don't need to," I said, trusting he wouldn't go to them and suggest it. "We found Hotchkiss' records. But the board member did pay, the one who demanded that you bribe him for the job. And Hotchkiss only wrote down his initial, A."

"Huh. There's a thing. I don't see why I should shield that cheap bastard, either," said Dobbs, making up his mind. "It didn't bother me much. It wasn't a big job, and he said it gave him a chance to see my work, see it was worth the price. I put in a brick walkway at board member Arnoll's house," he finished. "You should look at it when you're there. It's good work."

He had no problem with giving us directions.

Michael said Professor Stint's lodging was nearer, just on the other side of the university, and we should go there next. But Master Arnoll and the amorous Professor Nilcomb lived in the same area, no farther from where we were now than Stint's lodging.

Michael, who can be curst stubborn about getting what he wants, said that by the time we reached the other end of town we'd have a much longer walk back to Stint's place, and that he'd let me take us to Dobb's work yard first.

I pointed out that we'd have to walk the same distance from Stint's to the west end of town as we would from the west end of town to Stint's, and reminded him that this time *I* was in charge.

Michael shut up rather abruptly, but the walk to the richer neighborhood that lay between the river and the Crown City road was long enough that after a while we had to start discussing what to do next. The best houses in that neighborhood, Dobbs had told us, had gardens that backed down to the riverbank and often had their own docks—and professional boatmen to ferry them about, because despite the name, Slowbend, the current here was strong and swift. Master Arnoll's house, brick instead of the local stone, didn't back onto the river...but the houses across the street from him probably did.

As we'd discussed it, I'd made up my mind not to confront Master Arnoll with the evidence that he'd paid blackmail—he might be able to get us kicked off the campus for keeps. Instead, I'd tell him what we'd discovered among Hotchkiss' papers and give him the fake play script, which Michael was carrying. Then I could ask, sympathetically, how a nice man like him had come to be paying Hotchkiss, why he thought the killer might have done it, and any other questions I could work in before we asked, tactfully, where he'd been on the evening of the lecture.

Michael, rather stiffly, approved this approach...so it was a considerable letdown to be told by the housemaid who answered our knock that Master Arnoll had gone into the country for a hunting party, and wouldn't be back for several days. Though she'd be glad to give him a message, if we cared to leave one.

Jack used to say that the death of one plan hatched the next—a metaphor that made no sense, even knowing as little about birds as I did. But I knew how to bring it off.

"How long has he been at this hunting party?" I asked. "How far out of town is it?"

"He left yesterday." Her voice sounded a bit less polite. "And his friend's estate is half a day's journey. If you'd like to leave a message?"

That last was said in a way that made it clear the door was about to close.

"We're keeping you from your work." I offered her an apologetic smile. I also let the coins jingle as I dug into my purse. "Here's a tin ha' for your trouble. It's too bad Master Arnoll's not here, to answer my questions."

I handed her the ha' as I spoke. A silver roundel, likely a week's pay for a housemaid, remained in my hand, flashing as I turned it.

The door didn't close.

"I don't know if I can help you. Master Arnoll's an important man with the university. I couldn't talk about his business, even if I knew it. And I probably don't."

Ah, she suspected academic skullduggery, which meant she'd overheard some of it going on.

"It's nothing like that," I said, regretfully. Academic blackmail appeared to be profitable. "I just want to know where Master Arnoll was last Skinday evening. Do you know if he attended that big lecture?"

Nothing more harmless than a board member going to an open lecture at his own university, but her eyes fell to the silver coin and her lips compressed. A silver roundel was too much to pay for anything "harmless."

But it was enough to get results.

"No, he was home. He hosted a meeting of the staffing committee, over dinner. And I can't tell you what they decided. I wasn't paying attention," she added firmly.

Which meant she'd remember exactly what was said, if a few more roundels showed up.

"Did the meeting run through the time of the lecture?" I flipped the coin, casually. "It lasted pretty late, you know."

"The committee meeting ended before the lecture started. A couple of members were going to attend, and they were worried about missing the beginning. But Master Arnoll and three of the others, they went into his office and went on talking for several hours after that. I've no idea what they said," she finished regretfully. "They took the wine with them, and served themselves."

She could probably be persuaded to tell me what had been said at the staffing meeting, but I already knew they were interviewing people to take Benton's place. I tossed her the roundel, which she caught neatly, and I also declined a final offer to leave a message— making certain that even if she wanted to tell her boss she'd been bribed to reveal his whereabouts, which wasn't likely, she wouldn't be able to say who'd paid her. Not that it mattered.

"It seems Master Arnoll is even more thoroughly alibied than Professor Bollinger, whom Benton saw at the lecture," Michael remarked. "What will you do if all your suspects have alibis?"

"Either find new suspects or break the alibis," I said. "We're just assuming that Halprin and Mabry aren't in town. And Bollinger is only alibied for the lecture, and Hotchkiss was killed before that. Besides, there's still Professor Nilcomb, who was paying the most, anyway."

But I actually thought that if Halprin or Mabry were in town, the efficient Peebles would probably know about it. And if Bollinger was cold-blooded enough to murder a man, and then go and sit through a lecture without giving anything away, even Benton-the-oblivious should have wondered about him before now. Which meant my likely suspects were down to one man.

Professor Nilcomb's house didn't back onto the river either, but it was grander than Master Arnoll's. I approached his door ready to bribe whoever answered, because I figured this time of day he'd be teaching. So of course the manservant who answered the door said the professor was in his study, and he'd given instructions for his scholars to be admitted.

It was useful to be of student age, even though we weren't wearing the school colors. The man led us into a marble-tiled entry, down a corridor covered with fine rugs, and into a pleasantly masculine study, where a pleasantly handsome man in his late thirties looked up at us with a pleasant smile...which promptly vanished.

"You're not my scholars." He looked at his servant, who looked blank, then increasingly unhappy.

"We're not scholars," I said, before the conversation could disintegrate. "We're...associates of Master Hotchkiss."

He didn't gasp or turn white, but a distressed expression dawned on Professor Nilcomb's face.

"I'll see them, John. That will be all."

He waited till the door had closed and the servant's steps had retreated before he spoke. "Terrible, what happened to Master Hotchkiss. I was horrified when I heard. Horrified."

"I bet you were," I said, sinking into a chair. "We were investigating his death when we found these."

I nodded at Michael, who took out the love letters and laid them on the desk. Nilcomb stared as if they were a nest of writhing snakes.

"I'll pay you. I'll pay you the same amount I paid him, and I was regular, very regular with my payments. He can tell you..."

The professor then realized that Hotchkiss couldn't tell us, and stumbled to a stop.

"How did Hotchkiss get these letters?" I figured I'd better go for a softer tone, or the man might melt from fear right in front of us.

"I don't know, but I assume Jessalyn must have... She was angry when I...when we...that is..."

"She got mad when you dumped her," I supplied, trying not to sound judgmental.

Kathy was right about the ick. I remembered her laughter at the terrible metaphors, her indignation over the moral failing that lay beneath. But Nilcomb was talking again.

"I got more cautious after that. I read my letters, my poems, aloud to my inspirations. Then we burn them, together, so no other eyes will look upon the words."

From the man who'd written the letters I'd seen, that was actually credible.

"You must understand," he went on. "My wife's family didn't approve of our marriage."

And they'd been so right.

"They wouldn't understand. *She* wouldn't understand, but a writer, we need our inspirations."

"I don't care about that." In fact, I preferred to avoid hearing more. "I just want to know where you were on the evening of the lecture, four days ago."

Now he did turn pale, a sickly shade his current "moonbeam" probably wouldn't appreciate.

"I meant to attend. I really did. I may have sat toward the back. Yes, I came in late and sat in the back."

"No, you didn't," I said, confidently. "We talked to the pass checkers, and they hadn't seen you."

"They must have forgotten. Like I've forgotten who I sat beside. In the back."

"Professor." Michael's voice was more gentle than I could manage. "Where were you that evening? You *weren't* at the lecture."

Nilcomb searched for a bit of spine, and to my surprise he found it. "I won't tell you where I was. I've already said I'd pay, and I will, but the rest is none of your business."

"You mean, it's not our business who you were with," I said.

"I deny that. I completely deny that and you have no proof. And indeed, I might be able to pay just a bit more?"

Ick. I was out of even pretense-sympathy, so I gestured for Michael to take over.

"We don't want your money, Professor. In fact, you may keep these letters, and as far as I know there are no copies. But you should consider," he went on, "that if you go on sleeping with your scholars, sooner or later your wife and her family are bound to learn of it. It seems..." He waved a hand, to indicate the luxurious room. "...a high price to pay for 'inspiration.'"

It was some time after we left the house before I started feeling clean again.

"I swear, the jeweler's less creepy than that man."

"I think that's a fair comparison," Michael said soberly. "'Tis an illness with him, whatever he tells himself. For whatever pleasure he gains, he risks losing wife, wealth, reputation, and being blackmailed. He's pitiable."

"He's a creep," I said. "But not a murderer."

"I've never seen a worse liar," Michael agreed. "The thought that we might consider him guilty of murder never even crossed his mind."

"Which it would, if he'd done it," I agreed.

And unless Professor Bollinger could commit murder with his own hands, and then sit through a lecture chatting with his colleagues as if nothing had happened, or one of the others had crept into town without anyone seeing him just to commit this murder—neither of which was likely—then all my suspects had alibis. Which not only meant that I had no idea who'd killed Master Hotchkiss, it meant Michael was now in charge.

Curse it.

CHAPTER 18

Michael

"So, is there any difference between a bandit and a chemist?" I asked only to draw Fisk out of his silence. He'd been sullen ever since his last suspect turned out...not to be.

"Not that I've heard. The profession's probably too new. But I can tell you the difference between a bandit and an alchemist."

"What?"

"Even a bandit knows you can't turn lead into gold."

I snorted, and Fisk began to look more cheerful. 'Twas well past midday, and we'd not eaten since breakfast, so I added to his cheer by stepping into a nearby tavern for sandwiches, and ale cold from the cellar. 'Twas pleasant enough to walk about town in the morning but the afternoons were hot. Even fortified with food and drink, the walk back to the lodging house where Professor Stint had rooms proved as tedious as I'd said 'twould be.

"He's out now," the landlady told us. She was a stout dame, in that indeterminate age where women are no longer young but not yet old. Her cap and apron were clean, but there was no lace on cap or cuffs and her hands were rough. A woman who worked in the building she owned.

"I thought he might be teaching today," I said. "In fact, I hoped I might talk to you. What kind of tenant is he? Does he pay his rent regularly?"

What I really wanted to know was whether Stint was short of coin, and thus had reason to take a bribe to sabotage the project—particularly a project where he might well think that he should be in charge. But I don't care to lie, and unlike Fisk, I hadn't enough money for bribes.

When I planned my approach, Fisk had pointed out that Stint, above all others, knew that getting Benton fired would do the project no harm—at least, until the papers were burned. And he didn't see why Stint would choose to sabotage the project by destroying his own research.

I countered that Stint could easily have made a secret copy of his formulas before he burned them. Destroying his own work would keep anyone from suspecting him, and he could have assumed that Benton would be so bitter over being fired that he'd refuse to give them his research a second time...though 'twas hard to imagine anyone who knew Benton would believe that. Whatever the case might be, losing those formulas had set the project back by weeks, mayhap months. That might be all that was needed.

I had thought my questions harmless, but the landlady's eyes narrowed.

"Why do you ask? Is he looking to rent from you? He hasn't said a word about leaving!"

"No, nothing of the kind." And I dared not have her report this conversation to Stint, or we might find ourselves barred from the project. Again.

"No," I went on desperately. "I'm working for...for someone Stint asked to invest in...in a project of his. Chemical research. Secret chemical research. My employer wants to inquire into his habits and character, but quietly. I'd appreciate it if you wouldn't tell the professor about this. Very much."

I reached behind me and dragged Fisk forward. I could feel him laughing, even though his face showed nothing. He was already digging into his purse for a brass quart.

There was a time, before I met Fisk, I'd have refused to lie. But just as I'd sparked his conscience, it seemed that he'd rubbed off on me. And curse it, I needed to learn about Professor Stint's finances. His landlady was the best place I knew to start.

She looked at the coin, shrugged, and tucked it into a pocket.

"What do you want to know?"

"Does he pay his rent in full, and promptly? And has he always done so?"

"He has since he moved in, several years ago now. I know he gambles a bit, but he's never missed a payment."

"He gambles? He didn't tell my employer that."

Fisk stopped smirking. A gambling habit could leave a man with a serious need for money. "What's his game?"

"How often does he play?" I added.

"Moon's Bane. And he plays most Scaledays. But Moon's Bane isn't a bad game if you've a head for cards, and he seems to. He wins more than he loses, as far as I can tell."

She might not be able to tell. I could think of a number of reasons not to inform your landlady that you'd lost the rent. But 'twould not do to show the excitement coursing through me.

"Where does he play, do you know? Does he have a regular group, or pickup?"

She told us that Stint usually played at a tavern near the river, the Fighting Fish, and that while he had several partners he preferred, the others at the table were usually pickups.

"But he's good," she insisted. "At least half the time, when I see him come in, his purse is heavier than when he left." I asked a few more questions, thanked her, and departed, ignoring Fisk's sour expression. His investigation had been snuffed out, but mine was ablaze!

"He gambles! 'Tis a perfect reason for him to need money badly enough to sabotage the project!"

"You can win at Moon's Bane, if you're good." Fisk strolled beside me, hands in his pockets. He was beginning to look interested, despite himself. "In fact, if he racked up a big debt and Hotchkiss found out about it, that could have led to blackmail!"

"Then why wasn't he mentioned in Hotchkiss' records? Besides, the university might not approve of deep gambling, but as long as it didn't affect his teaching no one would care. None but those he owed, and if they pressed hard for payment..."

"Yes, and we might be able to find out who they are. I suppose we're going to that tavern, next?"

I took an unworthy pleasure in this tacit acknowledgement that 'twas I who was now in charge. But I had a better idea.

"Have you ever met Professor Stint, Fisk? When you visited the jeweler, mayhap?"

"No. I looked into his laboratory, but he didn't see me. You're not thinking what I think you're thinking. Are you?"

"Why not?" I said. "If you were to win a large sum of money from him, 'twould not only prove he was vulnerable, you could then demand information to settle the debt instead of coin. 'Tis a bribe he'd be hard put to resist and costs us nothing."

"That's silly. He's not going to confess to murder to clear a gambling debt. The worst a judicar would do is set up a payment schedule, and forbid him to gamble till he'd paid it off."

"Not the murder, of course. But if we pretend to want the name of his contact at court, the man who paid him for the sabotage, he might confess to burning the papers and framing Benton."

"Assuming he did frame Benton," Fisk said.

"Even if he only burned the papers, learning who paid him might be the loose thread that unravels the whole stocking!"

Fisk looked skeptical. But then, he was losing.

"If you're that certain I'm going to win, then you're proposing that I cheat. You do know that, Noble Sir?"

"'Tis for a worthy cause," I said. "And 'tis not as if we'll keep his money. We only want to persuade him to talk."

"What about his partner? If Stint loses, his table partner will too. And that's assuming a two couple game — what if there are six players?"

This stopped me. I could see my way to cheating Stint out of some information, particularly if he proved to be guilty. I couldn't cheat the other players.

"You can slip me the money after the game breaks up," I said. "I'll go after the losers and give back their stakes, in exchange for their promise not to tell Stint we did it."

"And they'll promptly return to the tavern, and beat the crap out of me for cheating," said Fisk. "Moon's Bane players take the game seriously."

"By then, you and Professor Stint will be gone," I said. "You can offer to set up a payment schedule, and discuss it as you walk him home. If he's played deep, he'll be interested. I'll catch up with you as soon as I've restored the other players' money."

"All right," said Fisk, who didn't really care about the other players anyway. "That takes care of Stint's partner. What about mine?"

CHAPTER 19

Fisk

"I'll partner you," Kathy said. "I've played at court enough to be pretty good."

Benton and Kathy had gotten back too late last night for much discussion, though they did report that the jeweler had settled in reasonably well. The farm family welcomed the money and Kathy, who'd shelled out that money, agreed with Benton that they'd be kind. Now we were eating breakfast together, while Michael told them how little we'd accomplished yesterday. Including the elimination of my best suspects.

The morning sun that was so warm on my back made Kathy's fair skin look almost translucent. Her innocence shone even brighter. Which might be a useful, in a con.

On the other hand, when things go wrong in a con they tend to go fast and bad. The memory of that club swinging toward her still made me cringe, whenever I thought of it.

"The question isn't 'can you play?'" I told her. "It's 'can you cheat?'"

The answer was plain on her disappointed face, but she wasn't a quitter. "Then teach me! We've got till tomorrow night—two full days. And you have to admit, I'd be less suspicious sending you signals than Michael would."

"It takes more than two days to teach someone to cheat at cards," I said. "A lot more."

"Two days is all we have," Michael said firmly. "Stint plays on Scaledays. With the final applicant on his way to town, we can't waste over a week before we strike."

"I've almost got my notes ready for Stint," Benton said hopefully. "Mayhap you could use those to bribe him, instead of—"

"Don't bother," I said. "You won't talk Michael out of it. I tried."

There are two ways to cheat at Moon's Bane. It's played with a partner, and most of the arguments afterward aren't between losers and winners, but between the two winners about who really carried the team. Even if Kathy was a good estimator, which she might be, or could count how many royal cards had fallen, which most couldn't, I had no doubt that I'd be carrying Kathy.

She'd been watching my face too. "Oh, good! Benton and Michael can make up a table so we can practice. Though we'd better keep Benton out of the tavern. Stint's bound to recognize him, even across the room with his hat pulled down."

"And what will I be doing in the tavern?" Michael sounded resigned. "Across the room with my hat pulled down. Which will look curst suspicious, indoors."

Mistress Katherine waved this quibble aside. "Fisk will disguise you. And you'll be sitting by the door, so when we get caught and have to run for it you can trip our pursuers."

"Hey! Have a little faith," I said, stung.

If it came to that, I could distract everyone into chasing me while Michael got her out. But if I was competent, it wouldn't come to that.

"I do have faith," said Kathy. "In backup plans. I've got four older brothers. There's no way this isn't going to fall apart."

Moon's Bane is a trick-taking game. If you're playing honestly, most of the game consists of correctly estimating your likely points. You bet the number of fracts you think you'll score that hand, and whoever's score is closest to his bet wins two-thirds of the pot, with the other third going to his partner.

Of course not everyone is playing honestly.

The simplest way to cheat is for one partner to send the other signals about what's in his hand. But it's also the easiest cheat to catch, as I explained to Kathy when she demanded I teach her signals.

"How can you be sure of winning if we don't cheat?"

"Watch. Closely." I said it with more confidence than I felt, for I was years out of practice. And the subtler forms of cheating *require* practice. But I'd learned them in a hard school, and over the next two days, as Kathy and I learned to judge each other's play—and Michael's and Benton's, too—I slowly, steadily, and with increasing frequency, won.

And not one of the Sevensons detected the slight roughness that thickened the edges of the royal cards.

At first I only marked the long side of the green cards, and the short side of gold. But as my fingers remembered the moves, I was able to mark all four suits in different places, and read the markings when I dealt. It was a slight advantage, but over a long night's play, it would be enough.

After luncheon on Scaleday I called a halt to give my hands a rest. Michael took the dog and promptly vanished to exercise the horses. Benton, who was a lousy player, went back to putting his research together for Professor Stint. He was almost finished, and claimed he'd be glad to be done with it.

But that was a lie. His face was alight with absorbed contentment, as he thumbed through books and notes with ink all over his fingers.

Michael and Kathy were right. If we couldn't restore him to some academic position... Well, saying he'd never be happy again was an exaggeration. But he'd go through the rest of his life knowing this was what he was meant to do, and that he wasn't doing it.

As my father had.

"You're awfully somber." Kathy had remained at the table with me, running the deck from hand to hand. And she still hadn't noticed those roughened sides. I'd marked six decks in the last day and a half, and though I'd seen all of them looking at the backs of the cards for marks, none of them had thought to feel the edges.

"You're really not going to tell me how you do it?"

"If I don't tell you, you're less likely to give the game away. And the problem with signals isn't just that it's easy to catch someone at it."

I left it there, curious to see if she'd figure it out.

"All right, I yield. I don't know what you're fishing for."

"What does Benton do when he has a good hand?" A child would have picked up on that one.

"He pinches his lower lip to keep from smiling. And

Michael's expression goes blank, which wouldn't be so bad expect that he only does it when his hand is good. I haven't seen any tells from you, though."

My tell had been to click the edge of a good card with my fingernail. Jack had brought a switch to the card table and put a welt on the back of my hand whenever I did it. I had no tells now, at least none Jack could see.

Kathy's was a rather adorable quirk of one brow, followed by pushing her spectacles up. I saw no need to warn her about it.

"But those are tells," she went on. "I still don't see... Oh. Dear. Really?"

"Tells only let you know if they've got a good hand, or a bad one. After a few hours watching someone signal, you'll know as much about their hand as their partner does. You have to let a fair number of hands play out, before you're sure that when they're strong in horns they tug an ear, or rounds is patting a pocket. But once you get their signals down, they're all yours."

"And they'd never have been that vulnerable if they hadn't tried to cheat," Kathy said. "I find that satisfying."

She was Michael's sister, after all.

"So that's why I won't teach you signals. But I can teach you what to look for."

Michael departed for the Fighting Fish half an hour ahead of us, to get a table near the door and establish his presence before we arrived.

I'd disguised him by the simple expedients of a few days stubble, pulling his hair into a short queue, and darkening the hollows under his eyes, which made him look not only tired, but several years older. Combined with rough, dirty clothes, and keeping his mouth shut so no one would hear his accent...well, it wouldn't confuse someone who knew him. But someone who'd only met him once, in a different setting and circumstance, wasn't likely to recognize him. People almost always see what they expect to see.

Lady Katherine, currently wearing what was probably a modest afternoon dress for court, had demanded a disguise too. Instead, I'd come up with the cover story of a wicked friend of her brother's, taking an innocent maid out for a *moderate* adventure on the rough side of town.

Kathy pointed out that that was true. But being true is what makes the best lies stick. The way her eyes widened as we stepped into the tavern, boisterous with deep male voices and a few shrill female ones, couldn't have been bettered. But I didn't want her to be too intimidated. Not even if it was good for our cover.

"What's the difference between a bandit and a gambler?"

"I don't know," she said automatically. "What?"

"A gambler gives you a good game while he takes your money."

She relaxed into laughter, and was still snickering as we passed Michael. I had to give her credit—her gaze swept over her brother as if he was part of the furniture.

He'd found a seat at a table by the door and was picking at his dinner. He looked sufficiently rough and surly to keep people from wanting to join him, but a long card game might tax his ability to drink slowly enough that he could stay sober. I hoped we wouldn't need him.

Kathy had tucked a hand in my arm and was crossing the room boldly...until she stepped onto the slightly sticky floor, and pulled her skirts aside to see why her soles made that popping sound.

I gave her a grin that felt as authentic as her reactions, and put a reassuring arm around her. The limber body under her stiffened bodice almost distracted me from scoping out the potential players.

One large round table was already set up, but people there were playing Fox Hunt—which was probably why Stint, and an older man with spectacles thicker than Kathy's, were sitting at a smaller table with a pot of tea between them. Not drinking as you play is the mark of a serious gambler. I made a mental note to order ale when I sat down...and then to drink it very slowly.

There was no point in dallying, and it would have been out of character, so I went straight up to the tapster.

"I've promised to show my young friend here how Moon's Bane is meant to be played, and I'm told this is a good place to pick up a game. Any chance of that tonight?"

"Why, yes sir, there's a pretty good chance. Master Stint and Master Carmichael were just hoping another pair of players would happen along. They're over at that table by the wall."

They both introduced themselves as "Master," and I noted that Stint wasn't a professor tonight and wondered if Carmichael might be one too. The thick spectacles gave him an otherworldly air, but the eyes behind them were keen.

We agreed to play for brass points—a modest stake, though it would add up as the play went on—and settled ourselves around the table with partners opposite each other. My ale and Kathy's tea pot arrived. Stint claimed he'd rather be drinking ale, but it troubled his digestion. Carmichael, with a dry twinkle, said that he simply preferred tea.

Then the tapster brought us a new deck...and another pair of players.

"Do you folk mind playing six?"

Most Moon's Bane players prefer six. It's the same number of points in a round, but with six cards in the trick you go through the deck faster, so over time more money changes hands. But looking at the couple who followed the tapster, I considered objecting—I've never seen a more obvious Pig and Squirrel.

The con is named after an old fable, where the pig chases off a boy who's gathering nuts, and the squirrel picks them up and then splits them with the pig when the boy is gone. It's only supposed to be used if a cheat gets caught, to recover as much of the stake as you can before you make a getaway—which not only assured me that these two intended to cheat, but that if worse came to worst they were likely to get away with it.

The man towered over the tapster, who was about my height, glowering in a way that made it clear 'terrifying' was his default expression.

"We'll play for silver," he decreed.

"But brother," the small woman beside him murmured. "Maybe these people would fear to play so—"

He spun on her with startling speed, and she flinched visibly as he barked, "Silver!"

Kathy was frowning at the pair, her expression shuffling between anger at the bully and sympathy for his target.

"We'd agreed to play for brass," she said, with a pleasant firmness she'd probably learned in court.

"But we don't mind upping the stakes," I said quickly. "Unless these gentlemen object."

It was a good thing we were prepared to play high.

The purses Kathy had provided to stake the game would cover silver points, as long as our luck wasn't too dismal—outside of court or a nobleman's party, no one played for gold.

Stint and his partner had come to gamble, and they cheerfully agreed to the raise in stakes.

"You." The big man gave his sister a shove. "Sit there."

She ducked her head and seated herself between Kathy and Stint, and Kathy's outrage deepened. Me, I'd have put money on her being the brains behind the team, and him being a first rate actor—though he was good enough that he might be the brains. They were both brilliant actors.

As he growled at her for losing a vital trick in the first round, and she tearfully protested that she didn't have any higher horns, they almost distracted even me from the fact that they were signaling each other like crazy.

Mind you, they were pretty deft at it. I spotted their signals, but only because I knew what I was looking for.

Kathy, who'd missed all the cues, gave me a "why don't you stand up for the poor thing" look, and I rubbed one eyebrow in the most obvious signal I could manage.

Her brows came together in puzzlement, then rose sharply, and her eyes darted from the woman to her brother and back again.

I decided never to partner her in a game that required bluffing, and scraped one side of the knave of leaves against the edge of the table. That's harder to do, without calling attention to yourself, than you might think, but part of the secret is not to try to mark all your cards—or even any, in the first few hands. The bickering between Pig and Squirrel let me do it faster than I normally could, and still left me with time to observe the marks we'd come for.

They weren't flashy about it, but the fact that they'd brought enough money to play for silver points told me they were good.

As hand followed hand, I saw that whenever Pig rubbed his belly, he was strong in rounds. Horns was a touch to his nose. Squirrel nervously nibbled her fingernails, only sometimes she bit the second finger, sometimes the third, sometimes the first. When her fist clenched, she had nothing in that suit.

Now that she was looking Kathy caught the signals fairly quickly, so we were able to hold our own against the cheaters. It was a lot harder to keep our coin out of Stint and Carmichael's hands...because, as I slowly realized, they were both counting cards.

Most people track the fall of royals and moons in the suits they have. Better players can track all the royals. But Stint, and particularly Carmichael, were counting a lot deeper than that, and they seemed to be tracking all four suits as well.

Despite all their cheating, the piles of coin in front of Pig and Squirrel slowly shrank and the piles in front of Stint and Carmichael stayed about the same. But we were cheating better, and as several hours passed, the piles in front of Kathy and me began to grow.

I had all the royals marked in the first forty minutes, but that only gave us an advantage when it was my turn to deal—one hand in six. Since I wasn't nearly practiced enough to pull the cards I wanted out of the deck as I dealt, it only let me know who held what high cards. It was enough that we were winning, but at this rate we'd be here all night. And while we'd take all of Squirrel and Pig's money, Stint and Carmichael were holding their own.

The death of one plan should hatch another, and

I was never going to win enough of Stint's money to matter. On the other hand, I might be able to earn his gratitude...and maybe a few answers with it? It might not work, but it was better than nothing, which was what we had now.

I gave up a couple of tricks I should have taken, throwing several pots into Stint's hands. We all agreed, amiably, that the luck seemed to be turning—except for Pig, who growled. Squirrel begged him not to let it upset him. Kathy assumed a sympathetic expression, but her misty eyes were sharp and bright.

When Stint rose, complaining about how fast tea went though you, I said that ale did the same and followed him out. The privy was in the yard behind the tavern, and while I've seen and smelled better, I've also seen worse. I waited till he'd come out, buttoning up the front of his britches, before I spoke.

"I think our friends are signaling."

"What, the bully and that poor little mouse? She's so fearful, she'd... Hm. But they're losing."

I shrugged. "What can I tell you? He pats his stomach, he has all the rounds in the deck, practically. If it's horns he rubs his nose. When she plays with her necklace, she's long on leaves."

Then I went into the privy, leaving him to do what he willed with this. When I came back into the warm, beery fug of the tavern, Stint was speaking to the tapster. And the fresh pot of tea that followed him back to our table could have accounted for it.

But it didn't surprise me that the tapster, and the two maids who passed through the room serving the other tables, were now paying more attention to our game.

Master Stint should be kindly inclined toward someone who'd exposed a cheat. Maybe even kindly enough to answer a few questions, though if he played like this all the time, it was no wonder his landlady said he won more than lost. If he needed money he could pick it up at the card table. He had no need to accept any bribe, or sabotage—

"Hey!" The tapster darted out from behind the bar. "I've seen that signal three times now, Master, and I want you to show your hand. If it's long on daggers, then you're cheating. The game will stop, and you and your partner's stakes will be...divided..."

His steps slowed in time with his words, for as he spoke Pig had risen to his considerable height.

Belatedly, I remembered what triggered the Pig and Squirrel con and how it ran. As Kathy would say, Oh. Dear.

"Who called me a cheat?" Pig rumbled, in a voice that turned heads all over the room. "Who told you I'm cheating?"

It would have taken a stupider man than the tapster to refuse. He pointed to Stint, who promptly pointed to me. Where was I supposed to point? At Carmichael, who was sixty if he was a day? At Kathy?

I sprang to my feet, leaping to put the table between us. Pig solved that problem by putting one hand under the edge and flipping it like a tin plate. It probably weighed fifty pounds. It fell with a loud crack, followed by the rattle of falling coins, but I was too busy running for my life to watch Squirrel at work.

I dodged first between two tables where diners and card players sat almost back against back, hoping he wouldn't fit between them. But the startled men saw him coming and leapt from their chairs to get out of his way.

Next I dove under one of the long rectangular dining

tables, hoping he'd have to go around it while I made for the door. He knocked it down and stepped over it. The plates that had been on the table crashed, and the people who'd been eating shouted protests.

I dodged left, hoping Kathy had fled and that Michael would be free to play his part. But Pig was faster than he looked and cut me off, backing me up till there was only one, large round table between me and the corner of the room where the wall met the bar.

Then a chair swung up from the floor and crashed into the man's back. It didn't break—rough taverns make a point of buying sturdy furniture, for just these occasions—but it bounced off his shoulders with a meaty thump.

It wasn't till he turned to face his attacker that I saw Kathy, still holding the chair and looking surprised that he hadn't fallen down yet.

Why hadn't she run? Michael wasn't the only Sevenson who was crazy.

Pig reached out and grabbed a chair leg, pulling it aside. Kathy swung with it, like a terrier hanging onto a rag, till she crashed into a table and had to let go.

I could have run then, but that would leave her at Pig's mercy and his back was toward me. I folded my hands into a big double fist, rushed forward, and brought them down on the back of his thick neck. It felt like hitting a bull's neck, and I'd struck hard enough that I stepped back yelping, and shaking sore hands.

Pig didn't fall under my blow either, but he staggered a step and dropped the chair before turning back to me with a roar of rage. The diversion allowed me to leap aside, as well as back, and put the round table between us.

Designed to seat eight to ten players, it was big enough that even this man's arms wouldn't reach across it, and heavy enough he couldn't toss it aside.

He started around it to the right, and I went right too. He changed direction, and I went left. I hoped Kathy would have the sense to run. I wondered what Michael, and the tapster whose place we were wrecking, were doing, but I didn't dare take my gaze off Pig.

"Your partner's probably out by now," I said. "You could just let this go."

Understanding flickered in his eyes, but the doughy face never changed. A very good actor. Which wasn't all that reassuring, since beating the crap out of me would only add realism to his performance.

"Why did you say we cheated? I don't cheat!" he bellowed.

"Yes, you do." And I could cheat too. I started drifting toward the left, not too obviously, swerving back every few steps, but generally left.

And as I'd followed his movements earlier, he now followed mine.

"You and your partner were signaling cards all night. You'd tell her what suits you were long in by touching your stomach, or your nose, or ear, and she'd tell you how strong she was in that suit by which fingernail she bit."

"If we were cheating so good, why were you winning?"

There was a sincerity underlying that question that made me realize this wasn't all an act... But I'd now moved far enough around the table that his back was to the corner and my back was toward the room.

I spun and ran for the door. Most of the tavern's customers had fled, but I met crazy Mistress Katherine coming toward me. Somewhere she'd found a stout walking stick, which would probably have broken the man's skull and killed him. I grabbed her arm and pulled her along, removing the stick from her hands and tossing it behind us, though I didn't take time to aim.

Michael gave us a wide grin as we passed him, his eyes bright with excitement. I had wished he'd come to my rescue, but now I was glad he'd stayed at his post. Kathy's court petticoats and high heels were going to be a hindrance to running.

We dashed out of the tavern and into the street, turned at random, and started toward the university. We'd gone no more than a few yards when I heard the crash of the giant's fall.

Still running, I looked back in time to see Michael leap over Pig, who was already getting to his hands and knees. He grinned at me once more, and as the fallen man shouted, "You're with them!" Michael turned and raced off in the opposite direction.

Kathy and I had gained some distance and the night was dark. I whirled her into a shadowy doorway, pressing her warm body tight against mine, just before Pig emerged into the street. He looked toward us and saw nothing. He looked the other way and saw Michael, running toward the river. He chased after the prey he could see.

Lady Katherine clung to me, so close I could feel her gasping and shaking...with laughter.

"You're even crazier than your brother," I murmured. "And I didn't think that was *possible*."

"I'm sorry, it's just...'twas so funny. You should have seen your face when Stint pointed at you."

She had the sense to laugh softly, so I almost forgave her.

"I'm glad you find the thought of me about to be pulverized so amusing, but it's not a laughing matter. He knows we played him. As soon as Michael loses him, Pig will come looking for us. And Squirrel's still around here somewhere. If she sees where we go, she'll tell him. We need to go to ground for an hour or so."

And I led Lady Katherine, fine court clothes and all, into the darkest, dirtiest alley I could find, looking for a hideout.

CHAPTER 20

Michael

I leapt the fallen man's body and darted into the street. One flashing glance told me the direction in which Fisk and Kathy fled, and I paused long enough to make sure the man I'd tripped could see me before I headed off in the other.

I was not as dismayed as mayhap I should have been. From my post at the door, I'd seen that Fisk and Kathy had the matter in hand. Now, hearing heavy footsteps racing after me, I was glad I hadn't been forced to go to their aid—for more than one reason.

Ever since I'd heard Professor Dayless' theories, I'd been wanting to test them—or rather to push them even further, by trying to shape the form my magic took.

Since the chance to do so would only arise if I was in dire danger, I'd chosen not to mention my plan to Fisk, who objects to that kind of thing. But now I was in danger, for the large angry man whose honor Fisk had impugned might well take his annoyance out on me.

The professor had said magic was in the mind, but to me it felt like a well of some glowing viscous substance, deep in my gut, with a stone slab atop it. That power now stirred uneasily, but the lid stayed firmly in place.

Clearly, I wasn't yet frightened enough. Would it be too reckless to let the fellow corner me, mayhap strike me a time or two?

Probably, but as I ran toward the river docks another idea took shape. Could I use magic—which had worked upon the air to save me once before—to form a bubble of air around my head? 'Twould not do to get too deep in the river, for in those currents even a strong swimmer might be swept away. But near the bank it should be safe to experiment, to see if I could carry down enough air to breathe for a short time, and remain under the surface till my pursuer departed.

The footsteps didn't seem to grow nearer or fall back. I risked a glance behind and saw him running steadily, a determined look on his coarse features. I'd seen the way he treated his poor sister—if Fisk's accusation was true, I'm sure he bullied her into cheating for him. 'Twould be a pleasure to trick this man, and I began to form the bubble in my mind. I could almost see a thin skin of magic, rising in a perfect sphere about my head and shoulders to allow me to go on breathing when the water closed over it...but the lid on my magic stayed shut.

I was thinking, not panicking, and according to the professor these calm thoughts were what latched that lid in place.

Mayhap I had to be closer to the threat? As I ran down the road that fronted the riverside docks, its barges and warehouses only half visible in the light of the rising Green Moon, I began looking for someplace that both gave access to the river and would allow the hunter to corner me. Then I saw it; a long covered pier, extending out into the river for some distance, and mayhap open to the water inside. The doors were closed, but it looked as if a simple lever would lift the latch.

Ordinarily, I'd never allow myself to be trapped in such a place...but when would I next have a chance to test my theory? I had to seize it.

I pressed the lever and swung one big door wide. Inside, the first section was more warehouse than dock, holding bundles of cut wood and pallets of brick, loads too heavy and bulky for anyone to steal. Only as I ran down the dock did I see that next came a section in which one side of the building had been opened to the water, so the flat riverboats could pull up and load under shelter. On the dry side of the pier, bundles of cut hay were stacked, likely awaiting transport to Crown City. They covered half the floor with no space between them, leaving me nowhere to hide.

This might not have been as good an idea as it once seemed. My stomach sinking, I turned back just in time to see the big man step inside and close the great doors. He took in the room, and my position in it with a swift glance, then picked up a loop of wire that hung on a nearby pillar. I hadn't long to wonder what he wanted with it, for he wrapped the latch closed, four loops of wire and the ends twisted. It could be easily undone, but 'twould take some time. Time I wasn't likely to get.

I expected him to rush forward when he finished, but he moved with deliberation, reaching out to sort through a tool pile and extract a boat hook.

I found myself backing down the dock without making a conscious choice to move, a chill running down my nerves. Boat hooks are neither heavy nor sharp, but they're sturdy, and it extended his already superior reach six feet. If I couldn't wrest it from his grasp, which was unlikely with a man that strong, he could beat me to a pulp without ever coming into my reach.

A very bad idea.

"I've no quarrel with you, sir," I said. "I'm not the one who accused you of cheating."

"No." The man drew nearer as his spoke. His voice was still deep, but no longer a furious roar. "But you're with them. How did he know enough about our operation to set us up?"

This calm purpose was more frightening than his anger had been—faked anger, it seemed. But fear might still work in my favor.

My heart pounding, I backed out from under the roof and onto the open pier...where I found I'd made a misjudgment. We were deeper into the river than I'd wanted to go, and the light of the Green Moon rippled on the surface in a way that told of swift currents beneath. If I let myself be swept away, 'twould be hard to get back to shore.

Trying to convince him I wasn't working with Fisk would be no use, but mayhap the truth would serve?

"He had no intention of setting you up. He'd no idea you'd be there. How could he? You came in after him, and added yourselves to the game, remember?"

"I do."

The boat hook flashed out, without warning, and I barely managed to jump back in time.

"That's why I need to know who betrayed us, and why."

This man might not be nearly as dull-witted as he'd appeared, but his mind had fixed on his own conclusions. 'Twould not change, until I'd been beaten so badly no one could have kept silent.

I had to get out of here, had to hide...

We were nearly at the end of the pier now, moonlight glowing on the braided ripples where the pilings cut the current—too much current, too hard, too fast. But the shadows beneath the planks were dark...and my magic, finally, flowed sluggishly over the lip of its deep well.

I shaped the air bubble with all my mind, will and terror, and leapt off the up-current side of the pier.

There was no bubble. Water flowed over my face, my lips, and ran cold fingers through my hair. I was so startled by my failure that I hit the first piling before I realized the current was sweeping me along. I tried to grab the next dim shape as it brushed past—and missed. A rough band scraped across my chest and neck, and I grabbed wildly for it instead, the rope coarse and frayed, but solid under my hands.

The pull of the current against it raised me straight to the surface, not six feet from the pier where my assailant stared over the river. With me in the water and him swinging that accursed boat hook, the result of any fight was a forgone conclusion. I was about to release the rope and let the current take me, preferring the risk of drowning to the certainty of being badly beaten, when his gaze swept over me without pausing.

I blinked the water out of my eyes, hardly able to believe it, but he kept on looking, even kneeling down to look beneath the pier...only a few arms' length from where I floated in plain sight. I kicked my feet to keep my head above the surface, taking care to make no sound, no splash to betray my presence. But how could he miss seeing me?

To my own sight, my magic now flowed strongly through my body, making my hands glow beneath the river's skin like candle lanterns. He couldn't see magic. Except mayhap the jeweler, I knew of none who could. But surely the moonlight showed me clearly!

Yet as I looked at the rippling water, around me there lay a patch of darkness several yards wide where far less light reflected off the waves.

I looked back at the Green Moon, two-thirds full and well-risen. If I saw it so clear, there was certainly nothing to shadow me. And yet that curious dark patch remained. As the big man rose to his feet he looked around again, and again right at me...and he saw nothing.

He shrugged and walked back to the covered warehouse, his heels thumping hollowly on the planks.

He cast one more look back before he went inside, though this time he looked less at the area near the pier and more at the river downstream.

I stayed where I was, clutching my blessed rope with hands that grew colder by the minute. 'Twas some time later, far longer than it would take him to replace the boat hook and untwist his wire from the latch, before he came out from behind the corner of the warehouse and set off toward the Fighting Fish.

His size made him recognizable, even by moonlight. He turned his head several times, looking back at the pier and down the river. 'Twas only when he passed out of sight that the glow around my hands faded, and moonlight began to glint on the water around me.

I pulled myself up the pilings with hands numb with cold, even on this summer night. I felt as if I'd been in the river for an hour, though it must have been far less than that, and I clambered onto the dock with limbs that trembled and scuttled into the shadowed warehouse.

Eventually, I set off down the nearly deserted streets to Benton's rooms. The socks inside my boots squished miserably with every step, though I'd poured them out twice. After some time passed, I finally stopped listening for footsteps behind me and was able to think about the results of my experiment.

The magic had come, in response to fear and need, just as I'd planned—though it had taken more fear and greater need than I cared for.

Why hadn't it formed the bubble of air I'd wanted? I had thought of it, willed it with all my strength. Instead, it had hidden me. Not that I was complaining about that. In fact...in my heart, what I'd wanted was to hide. Not to breathe underwater, but to be hidden, safe from my pursuer. The magic had obliged, not my will—it had ignored that, as it usually did. It had obeyed the deepest wishes of my heart. This was good in one way, as I was alive and unharmed. But in the other... Professor Dayless' theory was still intact, but it seemed to offer me little chance to turn this strange, unasked-for Gift into a useful tool.

As for the other experiment we'd attempted this night... I'd have to learn from Fisk why he'd revealed the other cheats, but it seemed that task had come to naught as well.

And my boots squished.

CHAPTER 21

Fisk

There were puddles in the alley, and given how long it had been since the last rain, I didn't want to know what was in them.

Despite the narrowness of this gap between the buildings, Kathy had hoisted her skirts high. It wasn't as if either of us could see where we were going, anyway. I bumped into two different barrels, probably set there to collect rain, and a sharp-edged crate that caught me on the shin. Kathy ran into something that clattered like a child's block tower as it fell, and one piece of it got under my foot and rolled, nearly bringing both of us down.

By the time we reached the end and looked out into a moonlit stable yard, I was almost ready to go back to the streets and risk bumping into Squirrel. But even pitch dark alleys were preferable to an encounter with Pig, who might have lost Michael by now, so I looked around carefully before we emerged.

There was a large pen off to one side, with half a dozen oxen in it, and a very big stable with a huge load of tightly bound hay hanging up by the open doors of its loft. We were close to the river, and this was probably where freight drivers on the river road stabled their beasts, while they slept at some nearby inn.

The wagons those beasts hauled would be in the stable, which explained the heavy padlock on the door. If I had my lock picks with me, it would have been a great place to get out of sight...except for the fact that we'd no way to relock the door behind us. That missing lock would be clear as a signpost to anyone paying attention, and at this point I wasn't about to underestimate either Pig or Squirrel's intelligence.

"We have to go on," Kathy said. "There's no place to hide here."

"Maybe there is," I said, seized with a sudden idea. "How much do you think that bundle of hay hanging up there weighs?"

"About twenty-four stone," country-girl Kathy said promptly. "Hay's heavier than you'd think, packed tight like that. Why?"

"How much do the two of us weigh?"

"Mayhap twenty... Oh. Would that work? And how would we get down?"

"I could climb down the rope, and then lower you."

"Without dropping me?"

"And there might be windows we could open from the inside."

Despite her skepticism, she followed me across the yard to the stable.

"That pulley up there, it's designed to let someone lift things heavier than they usually could. It should work in reverse, too. I bet that book we found had a formula for it."

Thinking the process through, I took the loose rope that trailed from the cleat that held the load suspended, and tied two loops in it.

"Step into this." I slid one loop under her foot. "And hold onto the rope above it."

"Are you sure about this?" But she did as I asked, and I stepped into the other loop.

"Not entirely. But why not try? The worst that's likely to happen is that the hay is too light to lift us, I refasten the rope, and we go on."

I was unwrapping the rope from the cleat as I spoke, and I could feel the tension increasing.

"Or it could be so heavy it flings us into the air," Kathy said. "Or against the wall, and we get knocked unconscious and fall and break our necks. Or end up hanging upside down from a broken leg, or—"

"Hang on," I said, and the last twist of rope came free.

There were only a few feet of slack from the wraps, but I had only one hand on the rope I was undoing. I'd intended to release it slowly, but the weight of the hay yanked it through my grip at rope burn-inducing speed. The jerk on our looped feet would have knocked us down, if we hadn't been holding the suddenly stiff rope above it. But once our weight started balancing the drop of the hay...

"'Tis like floating!"

I wasn't sure floating entailed this much spin, but we were rising slowly now.

"'Tis like being lifted in some gentle giant's ha—"

"Watch out!" The great mass of hay was descending toward our heads. "Push off! Push off! Take us around it!"

Since we had to keep one hand on the rope, we both had to push and pull our way around the huge, prickly bundle, but by dint of squirming, and a burst of panic on my part, we managed to keep from being crushed or knocked off the rope and slithered higher—quite high enough to kill us if we fell, by the time the ride ended.

Because of the extra rope twisted around the cleat and the height of the bundled hay, the bottom of the portal was closer to level with our ribs than with our feet. But since our counterweight had settled on the ground, the rope felt almost stable. A bit of swinging allowed us to half fall, bruisingly, over the threshold and wiggle into the loft. Which turns out to be hard to do if you're wearing layer on layer of fluffy petticoats.

Thank goodness she wasn't wearing hoops, or I don't think we'd have managed.

"I should have disguised you as a boy." I freed our feet, and hung the rope over a hook that was so handy it had probably been set there for that purpose. "Those skirts are a cursed nuisance."

"I'll admit, britches would be better for— Oh!"

Kathy wobbled on her feet, and then toppled into a pile of loose hay, but even her startled shriek had been sotto voce, so as not to attract attention.

"Did you turn an ankle?" I knelt and pulled off her shoes, preparing to check for swelling. It had better not be broken. We still had to get ourselves down and home, once I was reasonably certain Pig and Squirrel had moved on.

But it wasn't her ankle that was broken—the heel of one of those fancy court shoes came off in my hand.

"Curse it. You can't go home barefoot on the cobbles."

"They weren't designed for fighting and running in," Kathy pointed out. "I'm surprised the silly things lasted this long."

She'd turned herself over in the hay, and was picking straws out of her rumpled hair.

The great Green Moon cast its light into the loft, sparkling on her spectacles, revealing the rueful amusement in her expression. Despite her fine court clothes, she looked no older than she had when we first met.

But that had been more than three years ago. She wasn't fourteen, now.

The universe shifted beneath me, and began to revolve in a new direction. My heart was beating so hard my ears rang, and her slim feet were still in my hands so she felt me stiffen.

"Fisk? What's wrong?"

"Nothing. I'm just glad you're not hurt."

So glad she was unhurt, and alive in the same world I was, that my whole body sang with joy.

But if nothing was wrong, there wasn't much right, either. Even if I said something, and she reacted the way I so wanted her to—which she probably wouldn't— the moment her father heard about this he'd clap her up in a tower, or marry her off to Rupert-the-Heir, or someone even worse. And as for what he'd do to me...

The baron had already seen one of his children run off with me, though Michael had been disowned at the time. I was pretty sure I'd end up dead if I tried to abscond with another. Particularly a child as precious to him as she must be.

"Fisk?"

My face was in the shadow, but I'd been sitting motionless too long. I let go of her feet, and turned as if to stare out at the yard. I should have been watching for pursuers, but in truth I paid so little attention it was a wonder I didn't step over the edge. The only thing I was aware of was the soft rustling sounds Kathy made as she settled herself to wait. I wondered that she couldn't hear the thunderous beat of my heart...but there was no reason for her to be as aware of me as I suddenly was of her.

And I didn't dare try to change that. Her father would stop at nothing to separate us, the moment he found out. I couldn't support her, either. I had no life but that of a roving con artist—which even *I* wouldn't ask Kathy to share. Though with a bit of training, she might be quite good at... No. And I had no prospect of any other life.

"Fisk? What is it?"

"Nothing," I said. Because it was nothing, and that wasn't going to change. Even if she could be brought to feel something for me, her father... Be hanged to him, *Michael* might kill me for this.

"Are you sure 'tis nothing?" She came to stand beside me, but instead of looking out she was looking up at me. She smelled like sunlight on leaves... Why had I never noticed that before?

"Yes." I had to clear my throat to go on. "Nothing out there."

But what was here in the loft breathed and pulsed with life, growing stronger by the minute.

I had to get out of here. I had to give nothing away, get her home, and then run as fast and as far as I could.

Even though I was indebted to her, till Benton was proved innocent? Forget the legal debt—I really did owe her for getting me out of gaol.

And Michael? What did I owe him? And what about poor Benton, and even the jeweler...?

How had I ended up with so many people in my life who *mattered*? It might not have been Michael's fault, but I had no hesitation blaming him for it, anyway.

"We have to get out of here," I said aloud. "Let's go down to the stable and find a window we can climb out of. Then I'll take you home."

Back to her brothers. Because no matter what else might happen, this woman wasn't for me.

Chapter 22

Michael

When we finally came together 'twas long past time for breakfast. Fisk and Kathy hadn't returned by the time I got back to Benton's rooms, so True and I waited up for them, growing more and more concerned. Since he was sleeping on a cot in his front room, while Kathy took his bed, Benton waited with us.

When they finally came in, some of the delay was explained by the fact that Kathy was wearing her and Fisk's stockings, while he carried her broken shoes. And it made sense that they'd take some time to make sure that big man's sister hadn't followed them.

I was tense from the long wait and would have had the full tale then, but Benton was yawning and Fisk said, rather shortly, that Kathy was tired.

She didn't look tired to me. She was stepping a bit gingerly but her eyes sparkled, and under the leftover excitement of that wild night I thought I saw a sort of wonder.

Fisk was the one who looked tense and pale. But I acceded to his request and we agreed to meet and share our stories at breakfast...though by the time we'd all awakened and wandered down to Benton's rooms, 'twas near midday.

I told them...not quite the whole story, for my possession of magic was a thing I'd shared with no one but Fisk, and I'd no desire for my family to learn of it. I was eager to talk to Fisk about it as soon as we had some privacy. And how odd it was to still feel anger that, when he'd freed Jack, Fisk had lied to me and betrayed all the principles I held dear...and at the same time, to know without doubt that he would never betray my secret to anyone.

Loyalty was the core of Fisk's nature, and 'twas loyalty, felt toward another, that had made him betray me. If I was relying on that very trait, was it right to blame him for offering it to others? But how could I not condemn it, when it induced him to let criminals, quite vicious criminals, go free? I knew that Jack Banister would never reform...and so did Fisk, and he'd let him go anyway.

I still couldn't agree with that, but I found it increasingly hard to maintain my anger.

I told them, somewhat truthfully, that I'd been forced to take to the river to elude my pursuer. Benton repeated a comment he'd made when I dripped my way in last night, about how only idiots strayed far from the bank, because the currents farther out could sweep the strongest swimmer away. Fisk, uncharacteristically, made no comment at all. Kathy said, somewhat absently, that she was glad I'd escaped.

She kept stealing glances at Fisk, and Fisk seemed to be taking pains not to return them.

They both became more animated when they talked about the game. Kathy assured me that even she
had seen the strange couple cheating—and that she'd
almost tripped over the girl as she'd gathered up the
money that had fallen from the table.

"So how much did you lose?" Benton asked. "You paid
for the jeweler's housing as well—aren't you running
short?"

Kathy shook her head. "'Twas was only one hand's
bet, and I haven't spent half the dress allowance Mother gave me. If I do run short, I can write and ask for
more."

An odd expression swept over Fisk's face, but it
vanished so quickly I thought I'd imagined it.
He launched into the tale of how, after leaving the
tavern, they'd crept down a nearby alley and hidden
in a stable loft till they were sure they could make their
way home safely. But I was more interested in another
aspect of the game.

"From what you say, 'tis unlikely Stint has lost so
much he'd accept a bribe to sabotage the project. Which
means the whole affair was for naught."

"We only eliminated one suspect," Fisk said. "Anyone
who worked on the project might have some need for
money that we don't know about."

"Benton should know," Kathy put in. "Since he works
with them. But I expect he's been completely oblivious."

"I'm not oblivious," Benton protested. "I just don't
pry into other people's business."

"Oblivious," Kathy repeated.

"But others might not be," I said slowly. "If we want
to inquire into that, 'twould make sense to start with

the one man that we know doesn't need money. Besides, he owes Fisk a good turn. Benton, didn't you say you'd finished recreating your research?"

"'Tis Skinday," Benton protested. "He'll be at home."

"All the better," Fisk pointed out. "We won't have to catch him between lectures."

"I think I'll stay home," Kathy said. "My feet are a little tender from yesterday."

This might well be true, but 'twas so unlike the little sister who'd trailed after us with bleeding knees, and once a badly sprained wrist, that Benton and I both stared.

She lifted her chin and stared back.

"I'll take the dishes to the tavern," Fisk said, "and meet you outside after you've bundled up Benton's notes."

He scraped off the scraps for True, loaded the empty plates and bowls into the basket and departed. Benton had already picked up his notes—which sat all of three steps away, tied into a neat roll with a bit of string. I looked sharply at Kathy.

"Did you and Fisk quarrel last night?"

"No."

"Then why hasn't he spoken to you all morning?"

"He asked me to pass the butter. And he told me I was an idiot for taking on that great ox with nothing but a chair. And he said that next time he's going to make sure I'm wearing sensible shoes, even if we're only crossing the street for dinner."

"Yes, but..." I couldn't put the constraint I'd seen into words, but I knew 'twas there.

"Don't worry about it. We didn't quarrel."

Her eyes were bright with mischief, and I wondered if she'd done something to tease Fisk. But my squire... associate...partner? could certainly hold his own against Kathy, so I took the notes from Benton and went out to join him.

On our way to Stint's lodging, I shared the true tale of my adventures. After remarking that he'd known I was holding something back—which I didn't see how he could—and the expected diatribe on my foolishness, Fisk started looking more thoughtful.

"If it obeys your heart's desire, you'd better be careful what you want."

"I thought of that. But it doesn't work unless I'm in desperate straits, so I don't think I'm likely to see someone I'm angry with drop dead, or have gold spring out of the air or some such thing."

"Pity about the gold." Fisk dodged around a scholar, who was so intent on the paper he was reading he paid no attention where he walked. "For the rest of it... I wonder if that's how it works for the jeweler. If he has so little control over his thoughts that nothing gets in the way of his wishes."

"If that were true, then Roseman would be dead. We saw him abuse the man."

"Being abused doesn't always stop people from loving someone," Fisk said soberly. "It should, but I've seen it, and I'll bet you have too."

I thought I'd seen it in his own relationship with Jack Banister, even if he couldn't see it himself. Which made his point even more clearly.

"Here we are," Fisk said.

The landlady, who remembered our previous conversation, gave us a curious look. But she let us in and told us that the professor had the left side of the second floor. He opened the door at my knock.

"I've brought my brother's notes," I said, holding them up to show him. "May we come in?"

Since I was now in charge of the investigation, I'd decided to go with my usual policy of telling the truth. It had worked better, thus far, than duplicity had.

Stint looked tired, though he'd risen and dressed. But when he saw the tidy roll of papers his whole face lit.

"Yes, of course, come in. I owe Professor Sevenson for...this..." His gaze had fallen upon Fisk. "What are you doing here?"

"He's working with me," I said, as Fisk followed me into the room. 'Twas much like Benton's, though Stint's shelves held fewer books, and instead were crammed with vials of mysterious liquids, powders, and crystals, and chunks of dull-looking ore.

"We're trying to clear my brother's name," I went on. "And Fisk played cards with you last night to see if you might have gambling debts so large you'd be tempted to sabotage the project."

He stiffened indignantly, and Fisk added quickly, "But someone who counts cards like you do isn't going to lose. Not enough to matter."

"George is better than I am." Stint now sounded torn between outrage and curiosity, and I gave him Benton's notes hoping to tip the balance. It took his gaze off of Fisk, and he met my eyes straightly. "Even if I was in debt up to my eyeballs, I wouldn't sabotage the project. Not by destroying my own work, and particularly not now, when it's beginning to show results. The payoff from this project could surpass any bribe. I wouldn't sabotage someone else's work, either."

That last was the more convincing because 'twas said absently, as his gaze returned to Fisk.

"Were they really cheating? Or was accusing them part of your con?"

"Signaling like crazy," Fisk said. "I suspect they're just passing through, or they wouldn't have run a Pig and

Squirrel. That's not a game you can play twice. They probably left first thing this morning, before the rest of us were even awake."

The professor shrugged off the notion of pursuit. "We get card sharps here sometimes, on their way to Crown City. Were *you* cheating?"

"Yes," Fisk said, to my surprise. "But my partner wasn't, and she's the one who put up our stake. And lost some of it."

"I saw that girl, gathering up the pot." Stint's gaze was still on Fisk, and a grin was spreading across his face. "But I wasn't about to go back in, not with her brother smashing the place up. You're very good."

"So are you," said Fisk. "Good enough to make all the money you'd need, without cheating. Which brings us to the real question; does anyone else involved with the project need money?"

"No one who counts," said Stint. "As far as I know. Dayless has nothing but her salary, but if she lived beyond her means she'd have gone broke long ago. The scholars are always broke, but they don't care. Their parents pay their tuition and give them a stipend for room and board," he added. "If they gamble they do it with each other, for tin points, so even if they lost all the time it wouldn't matter. And speaking of mattering, I owe Professor Sevenson for this. So if you're really planning to...what was it, clear his name? I should tell you that you don't have a lot of time. I hear they've already interviewed a second applicant for his job."

This news was so disturbing it almost distracted me— but working with Fisk has taught me that 'tis the things folk *don't* say that you have to listen for.

"Who is it that needs money, but doesn't count?" I asked.

"What?" He had to think back over what he'd said. "Oh, I was talking about Quicken, and his daughter's leg. It took magica medicine to get it to heal."

Fisk, who knows the price of magica medicine, winced. Stint went on, as oblivious as Benton.

"He has relatives in another town, connections of his wife's, who have some money and they chipped in to help."

"Or so he told you," Fisk said. "It sounds like he needed money badly."

"Yes, but that was four or five months ago. And I doubt Quicken has any idea what this project is about, or why it matters. I suppose if someone approached him, he might have understood that burning the notes would set us back. Though since Dayless had a copy, and I can reconstruct my formulas—" He lifted the rolled notes in his hand, in demonstration. "—setting us back a week or so is all it would do. Though he probably wouldn't have realized that, either. The man's only a gamekeeper, after all."

CHAPTER 23

Fisk

We left Professor Stint to his notes, and had made our way out to the street before Michael spoke.

"My father has many faults. But he taught every one of us that just because someone is poor, or Giftless, that doesn't mean they might not be brave or intelligent or kind or wise or good."

"It's not low birth that makes him 'only a game-keeper,'" I said. "Stint's probably taught plenty of merit scholars, and given them his respect. It's Quicken's lack of education. Stint's probably assuming, and he may be right, that the man left school as soon as he'd learned to read, write, and figure. So of course he couldn't understand a complex professorial experiment. But despite your desire to leap to the defense of the down-trodden, it sounds like the man had a serious need for money several months ago. And he works at the heart of the project."

I shared Michael's distaste for Stint's snobbery. But while I knew that the poor and uneducated could be brave, intelligent, and true, I also knew they could be cowardly, stupid, and dishonest. As could noblemen. The difference was that nobles had power and the poor didn't...which made the poor more likely to be desperate.

And speaking of desperate, the sooner we found whoever had framed Benton the sooner I could leave, so I tried to fix my attention on the problem instead.

"What's the difference between a bandit and a gamekeeper?"

Michael looked resigned, but he too knew his place. "I don't know. What?"

"A gamekeeper usually likes his victims...and he kills them, anyway."

"All right, he needed money. But according to Stint, his daughter's injury, and that need, came upon him four or five months ago. If he was hired then to sabotage the project, why hasn't he done something before this?"

"I don't know, though it's worth trying to find out. I wonder how many of Master Quicken's neighbors we'll have to talk to, before we find one who knows where his wife's rich relative lives."

"We may not need to trouble them," said Michael. "'Tis not that Benton is oblivious. He just chooses what to care about."

Benton looked startled at the question, but he knew that Mistress Quicken's maiden name was Barrows. Her brother who'd helped with their medical bills lived in Trowbridge, two days' ride from here, and in another fiefdom.

Since the third applicant for Benton's job might arrive any day now Michael and I set off immediately—leaving Trouble behind because Kathy said someone had to help her look after Benton, and he was too gloomy for her to manage alone.

Little did she know that I was leaving *my* trouble behind, because she agreed to stay in Slowbend.

It felt painfully familiar to gather up our gear while Michael readied Tipple and Chant for travel—but that was nothing compared to the sweet and terrible pain of being in Kathy's presence.

I'd hoped that the waterfall of emotion that had overwhelmed me in the loft might drain away. By the time I woke up the next day, I'd almost convinced myself it had. Then she came out of Benton's bedroom, wearing a worn dressing gown and thick socks, yawning, and the waterfall flowed into a river with deep, dangerous currents, like Benton had been babbling about. It swept me up, and carried me so far from shore that the idea of being separated from her for four days felt like I'd be leaving an arm behind. Nothing as violent as an amputation, just something I'd keep reaching for, and being constantly startled when it wasn't there.

Surely this sudden love would fade, maybe as fast as it had arisen...though thinking back on it, it wasn't all that sudden. I had grown closer to her with every letter we'd written over the last three years, without even realizing it. Now I felt as if I knew her as well as my own hands.

But I'd be away from her for several days, which should let me get my unruly emotions under control. Though pushing thoughts of her aside only left another matter, one that still preyed on my heart, to rise to the surface.

It was awkward between Michael and me at first. The project was his investigation, so he was in charge of the journey. But he seemed self-conscious about it, asking me for agreement on things we'd settled years ago, like him caring for the horses while I set up camp.

By the second day of the ride some of the awkwardness had worn off. Michael was fretting about the potential arrival of the Benton's replacement, and my absurd yearning for Kathy…it didn't fade, but I was able to push it to the back of my attention, thinking about something besides her for as much as, oh, five minutes at a stretch.

We ended up sharing a lot of details about the separate parts of our investigations. From Michael, I learned more about what Dayless said about magic, and his adventures with Pig—which sounded crazier and more reckless the more he told me. I also learned more about the rabbits and how the project worked, and we agreed that Quicken could have sabotaged that part of the experiment more effectively, more easily, and without drawing attention to himself.

At that point, if I hadn't been avoiding Kathy, I might have suggested we turn around—the gamekeeper wasn't an idiot, and the more we discussed his other opportunities the less it looked like he'd have burned those papers. But he *had* needed money, the only one close to the project who had, so we rode on.

As the day passed, I told Michael more about our adventures in the library, the intricacy and solidity of Hotchkiss' system, and how strange it was that such a mind would resort to blackmail. I knew scholars could be as greedy and vicious as anyone, but it seemed there was still a part of me that was disappointed that was so.

It was a sentiment Jack would have mocked mercilessly, but Michael understood.

We made camp early that night, and rode into Trowbridge in the late morning. It was a thriving small town, the administrative center of the fiefdom, not the farming village I'd expected. But instead of rowdy, scholarly arguments about whether Liege Jorrian was really a usurper, or the density of air, here the topics that raised people's voices were a drop in the price of barley, or whether the Bittner's dairy or the Happert's made the best cheese.

We chose an inn, booked a room for the night, and asked the stout and ruddy innkeeper if he knew of a man called Barrows, said to live near there.

"Ah, that'd be the Barrows' farm," the man said. "But you don't look... Well, it's an hour's ride north. You'll pass the tree Tam Longner was climbing, and fell out of and broke his arm. Take the first lane to the left after that, and you're there in no time."

Despite the stone-paved streets it was a country village, after all—at least, as far as directions were concerned. I was about to ask for a better description of the tree Tam Longner fell out of, when Michael spoke.

"We don't look like the people who usually call on Master Barrows? How so?"

"No disrespect, sir. It's that you look like someone who travels a lot, and not in a fancy carriage, either. But I shouldn't be saying more."

And he didn't. We had to ask a number of townsfolk, before we finally found a shopkeeper who said that no matter what Master Barrows claimed her compote hadn't made anyone sick. And that a score of folk had bought jars from that same batch, and eaten it with no ill effect!

A long discussion ensued, and we learned that a well-dressed gentleman, who traveled in a very nice coach, had called on Master Barrows several times in the last four months, and it was after that he'd started throwing money about. Which had raised some eyebrows, and not just hers, let me tell you.

"What did Master Barrows say to account for this gentleman giving him money? For I'll wager he said something," Michael added, with the easy air of someone who was country raised himself, despite being the baron's son.

"He said his sister's husband had landed a soft job at the university over in Slowbend. But if you ask me, that's rubbish. What's a scholarly place like that need a gamekeeper for?"

That part we understood—it was why the gamekeeper had been allowed to wait so long before earning his bribe that was a mystery.

Armed with this incriminating information we went back to the inn, resaddled our horses, and rode out to the farm to ask Josh Barrows just that question. And we only made two wrong turns, at other trees, before we found Tam Longner's.

The Barrows' farm showed the sudden influx of money; a rain barrel made of bright new wood contrasted with the barn's weathered planks, and there was fresh paint on all the doors and shutters...except for one set, which was being replaced by an actual glass window as we approached.

Master Barrows was outside, supervising the glaziers, and when we rode up he came over to us, with the authoritative air of the man who owns the place.

"Master Barrows?" Michael asked.

"Aye, that's me. What can I do for you gents?"

He'd been doing more than supervise, for there were sweat stains on his shirt...but his vest was new too, and of better quality than the rest of his clothes.

"We need to ask you some questions." Michael, taking charge. "About the man who pays you to send money to your brother-in-law, in Slowbend."

Barrows didn't flinch, but his expression congealed into blankness. "I don't know what you're talking about. It's me as gets money from Lat. He's paying back a loan I made him when he and Judy first married. 'Cause now he's got a job at the university, and all."

"He has a job," Michael admitted. "But it doesn't pay enough for him to buy magica medicine to heal his daughter's leg, far less send money to others. He claims his money comes from you, that you're rich enough to help your niece when she needed it so badly. And I'm sure you would," he added, somewhat hypocritically. "But you couldn't have afforded to do so, without the aid of that well-off gentleman from court."

It was the way color faded from his tanned cheeks that told us the arrow had struck home.

"I don't know what you're talking about," Barrows said. "And you've no business here."

He went into the house, slamming the newly painted door behind him.

After a few friendly words we took Master Barrows' place, helping the crew install his new window. They wouldn't let us construct the frame, but we could saw boards to the length they marked, mix the plaster and caulk, and when they had the frame ready, we helped lift the heavy panel of glass rounds into place. I launched a discussion of the price of even old-style glass, but the master carpenter gave me a shrewd glance, and not only refused to comment, he didn't let his men gossip either.

As soon as their cart rolled out of the yard, Michael went up to the door and knocked. "Master Barrows? We're not going to leave till you talk with us, so you might as well do so. The glaziers have gone, so you can speak free—"

The door swung open, and a red-faced Master Barrows almost knocked Michael over as he burst into the farm yard. It must have been maddening to skulk in his own house, listening as we tried to pull gossip out of his neighbors. But that didn't, in my opinion, excuse the poker he was gripping so hard his knuckles were white.

"Do you know that what you're doing is illegal?" I asked sharply. "You could be brought before the judicars to answer for it."

I had no idea if he'd done anything illegal or not, but there was a good chance he thought he had. He lowered the poker, and spoke instead of swinging.

"You got no call to say that. All I did was pass some money along."

"You just told us 'twas Lat who sent money to you," Michael pointed out. "Come, Master Barrows, tell us the truth. We intend no harm to you. Or even to Master Quicken, though if he's committed some crime he may have a debt to pay."

"That's not my problem," said Barrows, recovering a bit of his composure. "Anything he did, he did it in Crown fief, and this is Baron Martolk's land. I haven't committed any crimes."

"If Lat's been sabotaging the Heir's project, I think you'll find that your baron's judicars will do whatever the Liege's warrant tells them to. And if you've helped him, you may end up paying part of that debt yourself."

"The *Heir*? I didn't...I don't... Look, all I wanted was to help Lat out! This was over four months ago, not long after Nan broke her leg. The healer said she wasn't going to mend right without magica—a long course of it, not just one dose. All I did, all Lat asked me to do, was to pass the letters back and forth and then send him the money. Because it would be harder to track, across a fiefdom border, you know? It was only a few times," he finished desperately. "And they both said I could take three gold roundels from each purse for my pains."

I looked at Michael in time to see his brows rise sharply. If three gold roundels was just a fraction of that purse, Master Quicken had been very well-paid.

"What did Lat agree to do for all that money?" I asked. "And who was paying him?"

"I don't know," Barrows said. "And the gent don't say. He'd even had the crest that was on the door of his fancy coach scratched off, so I knew he wasn't about to give his name."

"What did he look like?" I asked.

Barrows shrugged. "Nothing much. Slim, brown hair. Older than you, not too tall, and an accent like your friend's here. But I don't have any idea who he was, much less who he worked for."

"He worked for someone?" Michael asked. "'Twas not himself who wanted Lat's service?"

"No. He said..." The man swallowed hard. "He said his employer was rich enough to pay for this, and more besides if Lat did well. And he must have, 'cause two more purses came after that."

"Do you know what your brother-in-law was sup-posed to do for this money?" Michael asked.

"He said it wasn't killing." The desperate eyes flashed back and forth between us. "He said it'd do real harm to no one. Just some scholarly stuff, with papers and experiments and all. Said that when folk put more stock in papers than in people, it served 'em right. But I didn't do anything but pass their letters and the money. And I don't know any more about it."

"Well, we know a bit more now," Michael said.

We'd returned to the inn, and cancelled the room we'd booked so early that we'd gotten our money back. Now we were on our way back to Slowbend.

"We have proof Master Quicken was bribed," he went on. "So it seems certain 'twas he who sabotaged the project. And we'll return as quickly as we can to report it."

He was right about the need for speed, but... "Why did he wait so many months before he did it?" I demanded. "From what Stint said, his daughter broke her leg four or five months ago, and Quicken gets paid three times before he does anything? And why burn papers instead of tampering with the rabbits, who were in his charge? It doesn't make sense. We can't just ask him about it, either. Unlike Master Barrows, he really has done something illegal, something that will cost him his job at the least. He isn't going to babble at us, in the hope that we'll go away again."

"I know," said Michael sadly. "But he'll talk to the judicars."

This was Michael's answer to every problem—he'd have sent Jack to the judicars, even knowing he'd hang. I felt a lingering flash of resentment, though I had to admit, it was softened by having come to know Benton. Knowing just how much Quicken's schemes had cost the scholar.

But it didn't matter what I wanted, anyway. Michael was in charge when it came to the project, but even if he hadn't been he'd have fought for this. Michael always fought for what he thought was right.

And I didn't.

Not when it came to people, at least. And when it came to the people he cared about, that was when Michael fought hardest. Like he was fighting now, for Benton. Like he was fighting for me, still trying to reconcile us despite everything I threw in his way.

And I had run from him. I hadn't been wrong, to let Jack go, but I could have stayed and fought it out with Michael. Instead I'd taken to my heels, just as I had all my life when caring about people got too hard. I ran from my family, instead of fighting the respectable Max. I'd run from Lucy when Jack challenged me—though that was probably smart, since someone who'd give you up for a bribe wasn't worth much of a fight. But worst of all, I'd run from Michael instead of trying to stand up for myself, for my own beliefs. Because running had always been easier, even with Michael. But not now.

I now knew why they called it "enlightenment"—the sudden burst of knowledge burned in my heart, like staring into the sun burns the eyes.

My first impulse had been to run, as it always was. And maybe it was impossible for someone like me to marry Kathy—but I hadn't been hanging around a knight errant for three years without learning that impossible things can happen, if you're willing to throw common sense in the air and *try*.

Kathy, more than anything in my life, was worth fighting for...assuming she wanted me to fight for her? That was the tough question. Did she love me at all?

I knew she liked me, but could she be brought to love me? And not just a little, but enough to marry me?

Even assuming she could, and would, I was going to need all kinds of help to bring this off. In fact, I'd need Michael's help, and lately I hadn't been doing much to earn it. He actually might not want me to marry his sister, and then there were her parents...not to mention the fact that I had a criminal past, no money, and no prospects.

Desperation isn't the only thing that hatches mad plans. Hope can be almost as bad.

Professor Dayless had said that whoever solved the Heir's problem could write their own ticket, not only with him, but with the High Liege as well. And the project had begun to get results.

If someone protected that successful project from saboteurs—and it could succeed, couldn't it?—then surely the hand of one maiden, who was technically in the Liege's wardship, wouldn't be too much to ask. And maybe a small estate to support her?

Hang it, if I had the estate and agreed to forgo her dowry, Michael's father might actually consent! He wouldn't be happy about it, but he wasn't some idiot tyrant. If what Kathy wanted was reasonable, he'd probably agree.

"What Kathy wanted" was still the biggest *if* of the bunch, and that was saying something. Even with Michael's help—and I no longer gave a rat's ass who was in charge—it would be hard to find the saboteur. Then the project had to succeed... And all of that paled beside how hard it might be to persuade Kathy to love me.

It was a chancy proposition in every way, but I'd made my living off chancy propositions since I was eleven. And like Professor Stint, I'd won more than I'd lost.

I wasn't running. Not this time.

If I could stop the saboteur, if the project worked, and if the Liege Heir was suitably grateful... If I could bring all that off, I might be able to ask Kathy to marry me.

CHAPTER 24

Michael

I had thought Fisk would argue about my decision to turn Quicken over to the guard, but he seemed a bit distracted on the long ride back to Slowbend. And whatever he said, this was my part of the investigation so the decision was mine. I wasn't about to see another criminal escape justice on Fisk's say so. Not with Benton's future at stake.

My worst fear was that Josh Barrows, or some messenger he sent, would beat us back to town and warn Quicken to flee, and the unpredictable arrival of the third applicant for Benton's job made our need for haste still greater. By pressing our horses we managed to reach Slowbend some hours after dark on the next day...and found Benton and Kathy waiting up to tell us that yesterday the Liege Guard had ridden out to the farm, and returned the jeweler to the university's custody.

"What were they supposed to do?" Benton asked. "The jeweler told the guards he wanted to go home, and went with them willingly. And he does want to stay there. Kathy went to see him yesterday evening, and she says he was fine...or at least, as good as he ever is."

"More to the point," Fisk murmured. "Is Captain Chaldon about to come and arrest us for kidnapping him in the first place?"

"No," said Kathy. "Because when he came to "talk" to Benton about it, I told him the jeweler had gotten off the campus on his own, and that he'd come looking for Fisk here at Benton's rooms. And then I told the captain about the thugs trying to kidnap the man, and our belief that he might have seen something incriminating to do with the project. I said that was why we'd gotten him out of town, and that if he was returned to the tower then it was up to the Liege Guard to keep him safe there!"

"That was quick of you," I said.

"Then Captain Chaldon asked us what was so wrong with the project that we thought a man's life might be in danger because of it," Benton said gloomily. "And since the only thing that's happened is some burned papers, we didn't have a very good answer."

Fisk, usually the first to appreciate cleverness, said nothing. But he was watching Kathy intently, and color suddenly surged in her face.

"At least he didn't arrest us for taking the man out to the farm and hiding him," Kathy went on. "And he doesn't have any reason to think either of you were on the campus that night. I think he'll keep an eye on the jeweler, too. He said he'd tell Professor Dayless that the Liege had entrusted this man to the university's custody, and if anything happens to him they'll be held responsible."

"You did all you could," I said. "And we now have a better answer for the Captain about what's going on with the project."

"Or at least, an alternative sacrifice," Fisk said.

The final applicant for Benton's job still hadn't reached town, as far as they knew, and Fisk pointed out that even if Barrows did send someone to warn Lat Quicken, Captain Chaldon wasn't going to leave his bed to arrest the man over burning a few papers. This was true and we were all weary, so I agreed to go to bed—though I knew Fisk wanted to talk to Quicken himself, instead of bringing in the guard.

But when I woke next morning, to go early to the Liege Guard's office, I found Fisk awaiting me outside his door, which was closer to the stairs than mine.

We said little on that short walk. I believe in justice. I believe that most often the courts supply it. But what I was about to do would, at the least, cost a man his job, and I knew he'd only done what he had to, to save his daughter from being crippled. The taste of that was more bitter than I liked.

Capitan Chaldon was in. He asked a few pointed questions about the jeweler, but when I told him I had a better lead in the case he fell silent and heard us out.

"It sounds like I can find plenty of witnesses that Quicken was taking bribes, most probably to burn those papers," he said when I'd finished. "But what about the greater crime? Did you find any connection between him and Hotchkiss?"

"None," I said. "And none between Hotchkiss and anyone who worked on the project, thus far."

"Except for Master Benton Sevenson," Capitan Chaldon said. "Who might have kidnapped the jeweler to keep the man from informing against *him*."

I was beginning to understand why Fisk prefers to avoid the law.

"No one kidnapped the jeweler," Fisk said. "He came to Benton's rooms...well, not begging for shelter. He's not that coherent. But it seemed safer to keep him than to send him back, with everything that was going on."

"And my brother has an alibi for the time of the murder," I added. "He also spent the better part of a week reconstructing his notes for Stint, so the professor could replace his lost formulas. Benton wouldn't have done that if he was the one who burned them."

"Unless he was trying to prove his value to the project," said the captain. "Maybe even to the university, in the hopes of getting his job back."

"That's the most ridic—"

"But you plan to arrest Quicken for the papers," Fisk cut in smoothly. "So there's not much point speculating about Benton's motives. Do you mind if Michael and I go with you, and watch the arrest?"

Chaldon and I both stared at him, but the captain beat me into speech by half a breath.

"Why? You'll have a chance to confront him at his hearing—and the judicars are sitting in three days. You're now liege witnesses, you know, and required to appear."

I hadn't thought of that, and I was still too angry to respond civilly.

"I'm not required to do anything by law, Captain Chaldon—I'm unredeemed. Or had you forgotten that?"

He blinked in surprise, as if he actually had forgotten.

"Being unredeemed just means that the law doesn't owe *you* protection," he said. "Given your service to the Realm in the Rose Conspiracy, I think the judicars would agree to accept your testimony—particularly since there are other witnesses to back it up. As for requiring you to testify...you're the one who brought the charge. If you don't want Quicken convicted, why did you bother?"

There was no good answer to that, but I wasn't prepared to admit it.

"Oh, we'll testify," said Fisk, committing me without even a glance in my direction. "But before we do, I'd like to see how Master Quicken reacts to being arrested. If you don't mind."

He left hanging the implication that if we couldn't witness the arrest we might not testify—nor did he succumb to the inviting silence that Capitan Chaldon left lying for longer than I thought necessary.

"I don't see why not," the captain finally said. "But stay to the back, and keep out of my men's way."

Fisk agreed cordially and I nodded. I had little desire to see poor Quicken's arrest...but I had considerable curiosity about what Fisk was up to.

The captain rounded up three men to assist him, and 'twas late enough by then that we went to the university instead of Quicken's home. He ignored the stares of the scholars, bypassed the guard on the tower door with a wave of the hand, and found the gamekeeper in the tower's yard, pushing assorted vegetables into rabbit cages.

"Master Quicken?"

The man turned and saw us. After one brief flash of fear all expression left his face.

The captain didn't dally over it. "We've heard witness that you've been taking payments from someone dressed as a nobleman, with whom you've exchanged letters, and who paid you large sums three times now. Did this man bribe you to burn those papers?"

Most would have been startled into some hasty reply, though truth or lie might be a tossup. Quicken took the time to think it over.

"If you don't mind, sir, I'd like to talk to my employer before I go answering questions."

"I do mind," the captain said firmly. "Did you burn those papers? And what about Hotchkiss? Were you bribed to kill him, as well?"

"No!" Quicken's shocked gaze flashed from one of us to the next. "I never killed him, or anybody else. Why should I? He'd nothing to do with...with anything, far as I know."

"Then you admit to having burned the papers?" Chaldon demanded.

But Quicken was done being startled into admissions.

"I need to talk to Professor Dayless before I answer any questions about the project. When I was hired on, she made me swear not to tell anyone anything about it. If I'm going to talk I need her permission."

I didn't think Quicken felt that much loyalty to the project or anyone who worked on it, except mayhap Benton. Though he had gotten Professor Dayless' permission before he spoke to me.

He would speak to the judicars, or they'd come to their conclusion and sentence him without his own voice raised in his defense. Which is why everyone testifies to them. So Capitan Chaldon shrugged, and told his men to take Quicken off to gaol while he had a word with Professor Dayless.

I expected Fisk to follow the captain up the tower stairs, or mayhap go to visit the jeweler himself, but instead he followed Quicken and his guards.

The gamekeeper went with them meekly, his gaze downcast, his face so set all I could tell was that behind that impassive mask he was thinking furiously. 'Twas only as we neared the gates that he looked at Fisk and me.

"It's Josh told you about the money, isn't it?"

Since there was no other reason for us to be there 'twas an obvious deduction, but I confirmed it anyway.

"I'm sorry, Master Quicken," I added. "But 'tis a crime I can't let my brother be accused of. Not when another man is guilty."

He eyed me grimly, but then a sigh expanded his thin chest.

"Aye, I see that. I'm not surprised at Josh, either. All the spine of a slug, that one."

"Are you going to admit burning the papers?" Fisk asked.

All his guards were listening for the answer, so 'twas not startling when he said, "I'll answer that at my hearing. After I've talked with the professor."

We passed through the gates together, but as the others set off for the barracks and the cells Fisk fell back and let them go.

"Well?" I asked, when they were out of earshot. "Did you learn whatever you were looking for?"

Fisk turned to me, eyes blazing with determination.

"He didn't do it."

CHAPTER 25

Fisk

"What do you mean, 'He didn't do it?'" Michael demanded. "The man all but confessed to burning those papers."

"Oh, he may have done that. But he didn't kill Hotchkiss, and there are so many holes in this case you could use it for a sieve. Think about it, Michael."

I turned back toward Benton's rooms. And for once, my mind wasn't on seeing Kathy again.

Michael fell into step beside me. "I agree he'd no motive to kill Master Hotchkiss. But Hotchkiss' murder may have nothing to do with Benton's troubles."

"Then why did the killer print out that pass, to make sure Benton had an alibi? I could see Quicken doing that, except it's such a...scholarly alibi. Quicken would have had someone lure Benton to a tavern, or some other public place. And it's not just the murder," I went on. "If Quicken got the money months ago, why did he wait so long to burn those papers? Why did someone keep paying him, for months, while he did nothing?

And why didn't he just mix up the rabbits, or give them the wrong formula, or replace them with new-caught rabbits that had never been dosed? He could have sabotaged the experiment by doing any of those things, and he'd probably never have been caught. I'm not even sure he burned those papers, and I know he didn't kill Hotchkiss."

Michael trudged beside me in silence, for several long moments.

"You're right. We know Quicken took a bribe, most probably to sabotage the project—though we don't even *know* that. And there's far too much going on that we haven't a clue about. But aside from seeing what Quicken says at his hearing, what more can we do?"

One of the things I like best about Michael is that he has the courage to admit it when he's wrong. And when he doesn't know what to do next. Unfortunately...

"I don't have any answers," I admitted. "Just questions. But maybe..."

My steps were getting faster, before I'd even completed the thought.

"Maybe Kathy can think of something."

"How would I know?" Kathy said. "I've never even met Master Quicken. Though looking for someone else, who may or may not have been bribed, seems like a long shot."

"But with Quicken under arrest, whoever paid him may do something else to sabotage the project," Michael said hopefully. "That might give us another thread to pull."

"Then they'd better do it in the next few days," said Kathy. "Because once the third applicant for Benton's job arrives in town, we're out of time."

"Maybe we don't need to rely on that," I said. "We may be out of suspects, but we still have one piece of physical evidence."

I went over to one of Benton's shelves and sorted through the pile of clutter that had accumulated over the past ten days. I carried the forged lecture pass back to the table.

"We never found where this came from. We got distracted."

"You spoke to both of Slowbend's printers," Michael pointed out. "Do you want to go to Crown City, and ask among the printers there?"

"We may have to," I said. "But you don't need a print shop to own a press, particularly in a university town. The presses aren't that expensive; it's a complete set of type that costs. In fact, that's probably why they were forced to use a slightly different set, because it was the closest match they had to the one Demkin's used for the original passes—but it wasn't a perfect match."

"How are you going to find out who might have a printing press tucked away in their attic?" Kathy asked.

"By asking the helpful Peebles, of course."

Clerk Peebles looked wary as we trooped into her office, all of us but Benton, who cringed at the thought of approaching his friends, colleagues, and scholars while he was still considered a cheat. Though if they all felt like Clerk Peebles and Mistress Flynn, he might have been pleasantly surprised.

Peebles knew of two professors who owned presses, though one had taken his apart for cleaning several months ago, and she didn't know if he'd reassembled it.

"...and there's that deserted shop by the river the university picked up," she finished. "If you start asking the hobbyists, you'll be sure to hear that story. But it's been locked up for years now."

"There are ways around locks," I said. "Are you telling me the university owns a print shop? Then why does Demkin's do most of your printing?"

"It's closed," she said. "It's hard to print without a printer, not to mention half a dozen assistants. When the old printer died, his two sons thought they could make more money by printing more of the items that sold best. Why bother to print and bind some engineering book that would only sell four or five hundred copies? So they put out nothing but...scholar's fare," she finished primly.

"Bawdy ballads?" Kathy guessed. "I take it they'd forgotten that scholars are always broke."

"And less than a year later, so were they," Peebles said. "The shop went cheap. They just wanted a stake so they could go to the city, and become clothing decorators."

"You mean embroiderers?" I asked. My mother took in mending and did a bit of embroidery. It was easier than carrying bricks but it didn't pay well, and as the hours stretched it was a harder job than you might think.

"No," said Peebles. "They'd concocted a glue that would stick most things to fabric, and survive a number of washings. Glass gems, silk braid, ribbons. They planned to set up a shop selling little pots of the stuff, along with beads and so on, to those who wanted to look well-dressed without paying a seamstress to actually be well-dressed."

"It sounds cheap." Lady Katherine was wearing a cinnamon brown skirt with a soft leather vest, and a shirt whose only extravagance was the tightness of the weave and the foam of lace at her elbows. It might not have cost half the reward I'd earned for bringing down a murderous traitor, but I bet it would put a dent in it.

For a moment I despaired. But she was rich, I wasn't, and my plan was to get that small estate by way of reward, not purchase. So I'd better get on with it.

"It is cheap," said Peebles. "But Crown City's full of people who want to be courtiers and don't have money. There's a fair chance they're making a fortune."

There was an even better chance they'd gone broke, and were now carrying bricks. But what interested me was the shop they'd left behind. I smiled hopefully at Peebles.

"Since that shop belongs to the university, you've probably got a key?"

She didn't want to give it to us, but I wanted to get into the shop now, instead of waiting till the middle of the night to burgle the place. I pointed out that there wasn't much damage we could do—which was a lie, because if it was still there we could have made a decent sum by stealing the type. Kathy talked about how Benton's whole future was riding on this, and Michael added that it wasn't impossible that their father might buy the shop for Benton, if his academic career fell through. I was pretty sure this was a lie too, though I suppose it wasn't *impossible*—just unlikely.

The excuse that we might be interested in buying the place was enough for Clerk Peebles, who handed over the key with a pointed request that we get it back to her before she left work that evening.

We stopped for luncheon on the way but the shop wasn't far, midway between the university and the waterfront. Close enough to pick up deliveries from the docks, and near enough to the school that scholars wouldn't hesitate to make the trip. In fact, it was closer to the university than either of the other print shops. Across the street were a boot maker and a baker, both of whom seemed to be thriving.

The boot maker's clerk came out on his front step to watch us, and I nodded pleasantly at him. "I'm glad I've got a key."

"'Twould be hard to break in without being seen," Michael agreed. "At least, here at the front."

"We'll check the back," I said. "But meanwhile..."

I opened the door and we all went in. But before I shut it, I took a minute to try all the likely keys on the ring we'd taken from Hotchkiss' desk. None of them worked.

"So 'tis not a key the professors are likely to have," said Kathy.

"Mayhap," her brother replied. "But that still leaves anyone with access to Clerk Peebles' desk drawer, and as Fisk told the good sergeant, that's most of the university."

I closed the door and the dusty stillness settled around us. There was a lot of dust in the front room where we stood, on the shelves, small tables and bookstands. Through an archway I could see at least two presses in the workroom beyond. In its time, this place had bustled with printing and sales...now it only rustled with mice.

"Come on. Let's take a look."

It took only a glance to know we'd found what we were seeking—the smallest of the four presses was the only thing in the shop that wasn't coated with dust and spider webs.

"But we'd better make sure, anyway." I went over to the big rack of cases where type was stored. They too were locked, and Mistress Peebles hadn't given me those keys. But they were labeled with the fonts stored in them, and I'd come prepared. Kathy watched with considerable interest as I pulled out my picks. I tried to console myself with the knowledge that it had been too late to present myself as a solid, upstanding citizen before we'd even met—her brother had rescued me from the judgment scaffold.

"This is a good building," she said. "Sound. And you can see the river through that alley across the street."

It didn't sound like much, after all these years roving with Michael, but I'd grown up in a town where the smallest sliver of a sea view was treasured.

"You like dust and mice?"

"Dust can be cleaned. And I also like cats. You seem to know a lot about printing. Is it just from your father's work?"

"Some," I said. This wasn't the first time she'd asked about my past—I tried to convince myself it was more than just friendliness. But she was a friendly girl, so odds were I was conning myself. "I worked as an ink boy a time or two, when cash ran short. But... Do you know the difference between a printer and a bandit?"

"Yes," said Kathy promptly. "'Tis that blood's easier to get off your hands than ink."

Michael snickered. "You shouldn't step on his lines, Kathy. Trotting out those musty jokes is Fisk's favorite pastime."

"Well, it is hard to get ink off your hands," I said. "You can get some of it with oil, but it never really comes out of the creases, or around your nails."

"How about blood? Does that come off so easily?" Kathy's voice was flippant, but I had a feeling she was serious underneath. But serious why? Because she was considering a future with me? Or because she wanted to know more about the man who was trying to help her brother? This guessing game was driving me mad, but I knew better than to lie. Not if I wanted that future.

"I wouldn't know," I said. "Not in the moral sense. I've never killed anyone. Which isn't to say..." I turned the final pin and the lock popped open. "...that I've led a moral life."

There were several fonts that were similar to the one used on the forged pass, and we carried samples of half a dozen y's and q's out to the front room to examine them in the light from the big windows.

It was Michael, with his sharp eyes, who found the letters with the long, curly tails.

"Should we ink it?" Kathy asked. "To make sure? It looks different, backwards."

"We don't need ink."

I looked around till I found the pile of scrap wood that all workshops accumulate, and picked out a piece of smooth soft wood, and another that was harder. I set one y and one q face down on the soft one, with the harder piece on top of the type's flat back, and thumped the wood with my fist. The lower block was softer than I'd thought, and I had to wiggle the tiny type bits free. The dust around the presses was dark—from oil, not ink, which dries into a hard sticky lump. I scraped up a fingerful of dust and rubbed it into the indentation the letters had left. Even before I pulled out Benton's pass to compare, I knew we'd found them.

Which, as it turned out, didn't tell us nearly as much as I'd hoped.

"We should search the rest of the shop," Michael said. "Just in case."

So we did, but all we learned was that the windows in the family apartment above the shop had a better view of the river.

Kathy sounded a bit wistful, pointing that out. "'Tis a nice place."

It might be, if you hadn't been raised in a manor house. Was she hinting she might not care? If she was—how I hoped she was—that was unbearably sweet. But I intended to offer her more than a broken down print shop. Preferably before I took the terrible risk of asking.

"They should have been able to make money," I said. "It's closer to the university than its competitors, and two presses aren't enough for a place like this. I grant you, Crown City is close enough to take up the slack, but scholars with a book, they're like mothers with an infant. They want to keep checking on it all the time. And when printers lay type they find all kinds of small errors. Then they have to ask the author if he really meant to say that, and how he wants to fix it. You need to be in the same town."

There was only one thing left to discover, and that was if anyone had seen our killer. In a busy crowded neighborhood I had some hopes for that. But it took us the rest of the afternoon to find the baker's mother-in-law, who lived over his shop and kept an eye on things. She'd seen a plumpish man in a scholar's coat go in, late one night about two weeks ago, and stay so long she'd finally gone to bed.

"But since the university owns the shop, I didn't think anything of it. He had a key, after all."

She stared curiously at us, who also had a key, though no scholar's coat to go with it.

"The coat's no problem," I said, as we set off to return that useful key. "I lifted one from a laundry yard on my first night in town. And every professor or scholar owns one."

"She was looking down on the man," Kathy said. "So he might be thinner or plumper than he appeared."

"And as we've already established," Michael finished, "everyone at the university might lay hands on Clerk Peebles' keys. Which narrows our pool of suspects to exactly the same as 'twas before."

I had to agree. We were nowhere.

CHAPTER 26

Michael

In the days before Quicken's hearing, we did nothing. Oh, I trailed after Fisk and Kathy as they tracked down others who owned a printing press, and asked if anyone had sought to borrow it. They hoped that whoever had printed the pass might have searched elsewhere before he found the deserted shop—but none of us were surprised when their inquiries proved futile.

And worse yet, the third professor applying for Benton's job arrived in Slowbend. Fisk had gone to visit the jeweler when he learned this, and after he told us Benton became so quiet that I knew he'd dared to hope after all. Fisk hadn't learned the date of the interview, and it still might take them several days to choose among the applicants.

But our time was almost gone.

When the day of the hearing dawned, we gathered in the square before the guard barracks, where the low platform of the judgment scaffold had been set up. Benton and Kathy were relegated to stand with the rest of the crowd, but Captain Chaldon collared Fisk and me, and sent us to sit on the bench where witnesses waited to be called. Professor Dayless, already seated there, nodded in response to my greeting but said nothing. She was so nearby that Fisk and I couldn't talk without being overheard. The bench was hard, too.

I was about to start some conversation with the Professor whether she wanted it or not—but then the judicars came in, three of them, one plump, one old, one thin. Here in the Crown's fief they were clad in robes of the Liege's blue, with silver braid on their collars and the bottoms of their sleeves.

Despite the formal garb, it worked much like the village judgments I've seen. First a blacksmith whose shoddy work had lamed a horse, then a boy whose slingshot had broken a window, came up to receive judgment on the debt they owed. The last was Master Quicken, which meant the judicars considered his case the worst of the three.

After the boy's grumbling father paid the whole price of the window, even though it might have been previously cracked, as he'd claimed, Captain Chaldon climbed to the platform. He said that since I'd reported it, I should bear witness to Quicken's bribe taking. The plump judicar, who seemed to be the court's spokesman, called for me to come forward.

I didn't know what Captain Chaldon had told them, but all three judicars stared as I mounted the steps to the platform. The last time I'd stood upon a judgment scaffold it hadn't gone well for me. This warm summer day was very different from the icy wind that had once raised goose bumps on my skin, and my palms were sweating as I climbed the short stair. My heart beat uncomfortably hard.

The thin judicar cast me a knowing look, but he only directed me to tell them why I'd gone to Trowbridge, and what I'd learned there.

I had to start by explaining that I was Benton's brother, and when I gave my own name the Liege Guardsmen in the audience stared. But no one else paid much attention, and I relaxed a bit and related our conversation with Master Barrows as accurately as I could.

The judicars then asked Fisk if he could confirm what I'd said and he did so, without having to leave the anonymous security of the bench. They told me I could step down, but to hold myself in readiness in case Master Quicken wished to dispute my testimony.

I don't know where they kept Quicken—in the barracks overlooking the square, mayhap—but as I gratefully resumed my seat on the hard backless bench, two guards led him forward. The others accused hadn't even been in the guards' custody, and despite his escort Quicken wore no chains. I had to remind myself that, although to me this was a matter on which my brother's future rested, and mayhap a murder as well, the only charge before this court was vandalism.

Quicken's expression was still impassive, but his shoulders hunched like a man expecting a blow. He went up the scaffold's rickety steps with the nimbleness of a man accustomed to walking rough ground, and faced the judicars readily.

"Master Lat Quicken," the plump one said. "You've been accused by Michael Sevenson of taking a bribe from an unknown party, presumably to destroy the..." He looked down at his notes. "...the research papers of a confidential project at Pendarian University, which had employed you as a gamekeeper. Do you dispute Sevenson's testimony? It is, at this point, unsubstantiated except by his colleague," the judicar added helpfully.

Quicken considered it, in his careful way. "No. If I did, they'd just send off for Josh, and he'd tell you the same. Aye, I took their bribe."

"Whose bribe?" the old judicar asked. "And what were you asked to do?"

I found myself leaning forward, for it looked like we might finally get some answers.

"He didn't give his name," Quicken said. "Not ever. Nor signed his letters, either. Just showed up with a purse full of coin, over ten gold roundels when I counted it up, and asked if I needed it." His Adam's apple bobbed in his thin throat. "Master Sevenson, who spoke before, he told you about my Nan. What he didn't know, when that bastard turned up, the infection was on her. The fever came and went, but each time it came back stronger. The doctor was saying as how the bone might be infected, and without magica to heal it she'd lose the leg. A long course of magica," he added grimly. "More than he could spare, for charity. More than anyone was like to spare."

A murmur of sympathy rippled through the crowd behind us, and the old judicar sighed.

"He knew of your distress, this stranger?"

"He didn't say so," the gamekeeper said. "But I think he must have. 'Cause I wouldn't have taken his money without."

Having seen Quicken's attitude toward his employers, I wasn't certain of that. But it did seem the man had chosen his victim carefully.

"So you accepted the bribe," the plump judicar prompted. "What did he ask you to do in exchange?"

"At first, just report on what they were doing and if it worked." Quicken was more relaxed now, speaking freely. "To 'keep him appraised' was how he put it."

"So when you first took bribe money, it was only to spy on the project?" the thin judicar asked.

Quicken hesitated again, but he answered. "No, sir. He said up front that if they looked to be making progress, he'd want me to do something about it. But if the bone was infected... I didn't care. I didn't care about anything but my Nan."

'Twas clear from their expressions that not even the judicars blamed him for that. Only a monster could.

Fisk shifted on the bench, and I glanced aside and saw him frowning. Benton had told me of young Nan's illness, so 'twas no lie. Though as Fisk himself had taught me, a thing may be perfectly true, but still be an act.

Was Quicken acting? Why?

"Did you report on the experiment's progress, as you'd been paid to?" the plump judicar asked.

"Aye, sir. I'd pass him notes, through Josh, and he'd write back with questions. Or sometimes just send another purse."

"And when the project began to make progress, that's when you burned the papers?"

Quicken's gaze fell. "Well sir, he'd paid me all that money. I had to do something. I'd seen Professor Dayless making her rough notes, but I knew there was a finished copy so it didn't seem I'd be doing much harm. Didn't know Professor Stint hadn't copied his stuff," he added, with an apologetic glance at the crowd.

I turned and saw that Stint stood in the audience. Not a potential witness, then.

Fisk's frown had deepened to a scowl, and he jabbed an elbow into my ribs. I nodded, for I'd already realized that while Quicken hadn't denied burning the papers, he hadn't admitted to it, either.

But it seemed the judicars thought he had. The next sharp question came from the thin judicar.

"Did you have anything to do with the death of Master Hotchkiss, who was murdered in his home on campus shortly before you burned those notes?"

"No, sir. I had nothing to do with that, and I don't know anything about it." Quicken hesitated a moment, but then went on. "If that's connected to the project, I don't see how. Maybe the professors did research in the library or something, but Hotchkiss never came round to see it. And the man who paid me never mentioned him, or the library, or anything."

"But you do confess to accepting a bribe to betray your employer, to revealing information you were expected to keep confidential, and to destroying property not your own in an attempt to harm the project you were paid to assist?" the old judicar asked precisely.

"Aye, sir," Quicken said. "I did all that. I'd have done worse, if it was the only way to save my daughter."

I thought they'd pronounce his sentence then. They'd have the university's statement of damages in their notes, and there seemed to be little more they needed to establish. But they told Quicken to stand aside, that his employer wished to speak.

Professor Dayless' black skirts rustled as she brushed past us. When she climbed the short stair her gaze met that of the gamekeeper, but Quicken's stoic expression didn't change.

The judicars looked a bit impatient.

"We already have the university's accounting for the damage they suffered," the plump man said. "Do you have something to add?"

"Yes." Accustomed to speaking before a rowdy class-room, the professor was in no way intimidated. "In fact the university has appointed me, as head of the project in question, to speak for them in the matter of our debt claim."

She handed over a paper and the judicars passed it down the table. The plump man's brows rose, the old one looked resigned, and the thin one looked as if a boring case had suddenly become interesting.

"Very well," said the plump man. "Does Pendarian wish to modify their claim?"

"We do," the professor said. "As head of the project, I can confirm that Master Quicken's 'sabotage' did very little harm."

"That's easy for you to say!" Stint's voice rang from the audience. "I'm still trying to recreate—"

"No comments from the audience are allowed," the plump judicar said. "If you want to speak, sir, tell the guard and he'll carry your request to us."

Professor Stint subsided, but I thought 'twas more be-cause of Professor Dayless' withering scowl than the judicar's wishes. And having seen her fury at her own notes' destruction, I had a hard time believing she took the loss so lightly now.

"Whatever Professor Stint may say, the project will be moving forward again shortly," she went on calmly. "I'd be more concerned about the information Quicken passed on. But since he had no access to Stint's formu-las before they were burned, and has not passed them on, it seems no harm was done there either. As project supervisor, the university has left it to me to reassess our damages. Considering the threat to Master Quick-en's daughter, I've chosen to be merciful and set them at three weeks of Professor Stint's salary and one week of mine. That comes to forty-three silver roundels."

I heard a choked-off exclamation from Stint, and the crowd gasped. The judicars stared. Forty-three silver roundels was only a fraction of the first purse Quicken had taken, and we knew there'd been more.

The thin judicar leaned forward. "Professor, if the court levies their usual ten percent charge for the hearing, Master Quicken will have made a great deal of money by taking those bribes. Does the university want that? Don't you want the money left over after his daughter's treatment? If not for your project, then for the university's merit fund, or—"

"I choose to charge Master Quicken only for the damage he caused," Professor Dayless said firmly. "In compassion for his daughter's—ongoing—needs. Your decision is up to you."

Since the function of the court is to make things right between those offended, and those who owe them, the judicars were bound to take her at her word.

Quicken's tearful wife paid his fine in full, and the crowd was still buzzing with puzzled speculation when Fisk rose and dragged me away.

"I don't believe it," he said, the moment we were out from under Professor Dayless' eye. "Not for one minute. She might have let him off the worst penalty because of his daughter, but she'd never let him keep that money. Not when it could go to her precious project or the university."

"And yet, she did exactly that," I pointed out. "Unless Quicken has some power to compel her..."

We both stopped talking. The more I thought on it, the more likely it seemed.

"But 'tis ridiculous," I said. "We've already got one blackmailer, and what could a woman her age have done? She has no rich spouse to cheat on—she's married to her job. And if she did commit some academic crime—how many decades ago was her thesis written?—Quicken has no way to learn of it."

"No." Fisk's eyes blazed with sudden understanding. "It's not some old sin—it's those lying rabbits. The project, Michael! It has to be the project. She's cheating on it, somehow. And Quicken, who's not nearly as stupid as the professors think, knew about it. When he got caught, he turned it against her to get himself off. It fits!"

"It even fits with what happened to Benton," I said, in rising excitement. "They feared he'd notice whatever they were up to, so they forged that thesis to get rid of him. They were willing to destroy his life, to get him off the project."

"Not they," said Fisk. "She. If Stint was in on it, he wouldn't have been yelping protests this morning. So it has to do with the rabbits, not the formulas. I'll bet those good results they suddenly started getting... aren't. She's faking the data. She's doing something with the rabbits' results to make them look better than they are. And Quicken, who knows those rabbits well, probably knew it all along, but he didn't care. She must have... Curse it, I told her myself what the jeweler said about those rabbits! That's why she faked his escape! She may have hoped he'd wander off to some other town, or even get killed by the guard. But he's so incoherent she didn't need to worry much about him."

"Unlike Benton," I said grimly. "Who was spending more and more time with the rabbits, and would have revealed her cheating the instant he realized it. But how are we to prove this? Neither Dayless or Quicken is going to talk, and she's probably spent the last two weeks covering her tracks."

"She has," said Fisk slowly. "If those promising rabbits suddenly stop doing well, she can claim that Stint didn't recreate the formula correctly. He could pass the blame for that on to Benton, if he wants to. But if I were Master Quicken, I'd worry about being the only one alive who knows what she did. If it was me, I'd tell the professor that I'd written down everything I knew, and that my record would be revealed if anything happened to me. And then," he said, "I'd write down a record."

CHAPTER 27

Fisk

In the old days, before I set out to burgle someone's home I'd spend the better part of a week watching my target. I'd observe, not only that household's nightly routine, but their neighbors'. I'd learn how many people lived there, and which of them might react violently to a burglar. I'd scout a number of escape routes I could take in a hurry, and how many people along them owned dogs. I'd try to get into the house on the pretext of delivering something, to get an idea what might be worth stealing and what I'd be likely to trip over in the dark.

So of course, Michael and I set out to burgle Quicken's house without ever having set eyes on it.

The helpful Peebles gave us directions in exchange for an account of what had happened at the hearing, about which rumors were already flying around the campus. Michael told her that we wanted to ask Quicken a few questions, away from his employer's presence—which, he later told me, he fully intended to do, once we'd read Quicken's record and he had no reason to lie to us.

I was still reasonably sure Quicken would have written up some kind of document—with a project this crooked, in which everyone involved had more money and power than I did, I'd have made several. On the other hand, the odds that he'd left those documents with a friend, or kinsman, or even a lawyer, were high. But Michael had a "feeling" we should tackle Quicken's place tonight. "Like you get in the silence before a thunderclap," he said.

I never sensed anything before a thunderclap, but I'd been around Michael long enough to respect his Gifts.

I'd also been around him long enough to know that, though he was probably sensing something real, it didn't always mean what he thought it meant. So I was deeply grateful when he told Kathy, over her objections, that we were leaving her safely behind.

Michael didn't usually overprotect his sister, and for a moment I wondered if he was keeping her home because he suspected there was something going on between us. But since nothing was going on, I didn't see how he could suspect.

How would Michael react when he did find out? Assuming he ever had to find out, that Kathy didn't run screaming from my proposal in the first place. Or even worse, compassionately tell me that we were such good friends and she didn't want to see our relationship change.

I wasn't reassured when Kathy said that, after reading my letters for so many years, she wanted to see me burgle something. In fact, I was beginning to regret how candid my correspondence had been. But Michael put his brotherly foot down, and we saddled up and set off for Master Quicken's house about an hour before dark.

We left the dog behind too—the rasping gasps he makes trying to bark might be loud enough to matter.

According to Peebles, Quicken had a cottage an hour's walk from town, on the estate of a university board member—whose property included a stream-cut canyon that actually held enough game to keep. But the board member and his family were in the city for the summer, trying to get a daughter wed, so Quicken had been able to take a job with the project. It also meant the manor house would be "empty." Empty, except for whatever housekeeper, maids, menservants, and grooms the owner had left behind to get in our way.

The sun was setting when we arrived at the manor's gates, with a sliver of the tan Creature Moon about to follow it down. But the Green Moon was rising so there would be plenty of light...plenty of light for people to see us, that is.

Yielding to Michael's understanding of the countryside we rode past those imposing gates, beyond which lay the impressive manor. After a hundred yards the tall stone wall became shorter, and then gave way to a fence of long wooden rails, with fields of sprouting things beyond them. There was a reason Michael was in charge of this part of the expedition—half a mile down the road we found a gap in the fence, with a rutted cart track beyond.

"'Tis for produce carts, plows, and livestock to pass away from the house," he told me. "Many don't mind such things, but sooner or later a new bride will complain about the 'low' traffic on the drive, and a road like

this is made. Then folk usually find 'tis a more convenient way to reach the road from the fields, anyway."

We took the track, which soon degenerated to a pair
of ruts, toward the looming bluff. Then we rode along
the bottom of its slope back toward the manor, till we
came to Quicken's cottage.

It was easy to find, because lamplight glowed in several of the windows. There weren't any woods here
on the plain, but the bottom of the bluff was cluttered
with scrubby bushes, many as tall as small trees, so we
lurked in them. There must have been some moisture
nearby—I could smell that fresh, wet-earth scent, that's
so much cleaner in the countryside than city mud.

"We'll wait till they've been asleep at least two hours,"
I said. "Then I'll go in, and you can keep the horses quiet."

We had an excellent view of the cottage from where
we lurked, and the manor's upper floors were visible
in the distance, though all its windows were dark. With
the family gone, the staff had probably closed off the
upper rooms.

"I'll go in with you." Michael kept his voice low too,
though we were some distance from the house. "I'm
more likely to know where someone would hide things
in a country cottage."

It was a country cottage, with several large sheds
and a privy out back.

"Maybe," I said. "Assuming he didn't leave his documents with someone else, rendering this whole thing
pointless. But I told you why murders happen during
a burglary, remember? I'm a lot more worried about
someone waking up and catching you."

"I can be as quiet as you can," said Michael, stung.
"In fact, I'm quieter."

"Tramping through the woods, yes. Burgling a house, no."

There wasn't much point to it, because burgling was the part of the expedition I was in charge of and I wasn't about to let him come with me. And it wasn't only because I needed to earn that reward—if I got her brother killed, any hope I had of wooing Kathy would vanish. I couldn't say that to Michael, however, and our bickering passed the time as we waited for the lamplight to go out...and waited...and waited.

I counted four rooms on the lower floor, and two rooms with dormer windows above. I was able to count them because the lamps kept moving from one room to another.

Clearly no one was going to bed. It wasn't even much of a surprise, when Quicken went to the largest shed and emerged five minutes later leading a big placid horse, already harnessed for the cart to which Quicken hitched him.

"'Tis probably a plow horse from the manor," Michael murmured. "Too old for field work, but able to pull a small wagon like that all night."

His hand hovered over Chant's nose, ready to cover his nostrils to silence any neigh. This trick fails about half the time, in my experience. But we must have been upwind, or downwind, or whatever it is, because Chant stayed silent. Tipple did too—not because the trick worked, but because trying to bite the hand I laid over her nose distracted her from neighing.

Quicken's horse did raise its head, ears pricked in our direction. But the gamekeeper just gave its neck a friendly slap, before he led it over to the kitchen door and the loading began.

It took longer than I expected, more "moving out" than "fleeing for our lives." Pots and pans rattled their way into the wagon bed, soon to be muffled, not only by pillows and blankets, but by big feather ticks as well. The only thing they didn't pack was the furniture.

The daughter had been working inside, as her mother carried things out and her father packed them into the wagon bed. But finally the last lamp was extinguished, and Nan came limping out to be lifted up to the driving bench. She still walked with a crutch, but her leg moved easily and she was putting weight on it. I thought the doctor was probably right, that she'd heal fully in time.

The track they drove out on ran past the bushes where we stood. Michael and I held both the horse's noses again, and for once it worked. There was enough light for me to see that the tearful wife wasn't crying now; she looked angry and determined. The daughter's thin face showed excited interest as she gazed at the darkened countryside, but she cuddled close to her mother's side.

I waited till they were almost out of sight before I turned to Michael.

"Now what? If there were any documents in that house, they're in the wagon now."

"It appears that Master Quicken has decided to do more about his fears than write a note," Michael said.

"That's usually why people flee in the middle of the night. But what do we do about it?"

"I'm surprised," Michael admitted. "Except for Hotchkiss' murder, nothing about this project, even if 'tis a cheat, seems to be worth abandoning your life. And that's what Master Quicken is doing."

"I think Dayless might kill, to keep her job," I said. "She has all your brother's obsession, without his conscience or his heart. Quicken may be right to run.

Although..." The thought emerged slowly, like a monstrous fish rising from deep water. "Even if Quicken threatens her somehow, I don't think she'd do anything this fast. She'd want to wait till the hearing, and her project, aren't at the forefront of everyone's mind before she arranged any little accidents. I wonder what spooked him, to make him move this quickly."

Too quickly. The furniture that hadn't fit into that cart was probably precious to his wife.

"You're right." Michael's voice was no longer low, and he swung into Chant's saddle. "Something has frightened Master Quicken, and I don't think he's a man who frightens easily."

"So?" I mounted Tipple as I spoke.

"So let's go ask him."

There was no reason for us to gallop over a rough track by moonlight, so we didn't, though some uneasy notion I couldn't quite bring to the surface made me itch to do so. I expended my nervous energy arguing with Michael. The direct approach might have done better than subterfuge so far, but that didn't mean Quicken would tell us anything, much less the truth. If someone had gotten me hauled up before the judicars, I certainly wouldn't.

Once we'd reached the main road the flat countryside made it easy to see Quicken's wagon, even in the distance. Of course he could see us too, but with a loaded wagon and a lame child he could hardly outrun us. We chased after him at an unthreatening walk, drawing slowly nearer.

I don't know when he spotted us, or what was going through his head, but when we were a dozen yards away he pulled his horse to a stop and waited till we rode up to him. And then sat, silent, leaving us to make the first, revealing move. This man was no fool, for all his lack of higher education.

Of course, Michael made it. "Master Quicken. We hoped we might speak with you. Alone, mayhap?"

The wife clutched her daughter and started to protest, but Quicken held up a hand for silence. "You've got no call to stop me from leaving. I paid my debt. I'm as free to come and go as any man."

"Which makes the fact that you're running off in the middle of the night even more interesting," I pointed out. "What are you afraid of?"

I expected the man to think this over, and his wife put a hand on his arm to stop him, but he answered almost at once. "You're right, we ought to talk. Away from here," he added, with a glance at his daughter's wide eyes.

We dismounted and tied our horses to the wagon, like neighbors stopping for a chat, while Quicken set the wagon brake and climbed down. Then we all set off, walking up the road together.

"'Tis Professor Dayless, isn't it?" Michael asked, as soon as we were out of earshot. "She's faking her project results."

"Aye. She'd come down at night, switch the rabbits' collars and move 'em from one cage to another, so it looked like they were getting better at avoiding the magica."

I suddenly remembered the first time I'd seen the professor, descending to the yard from a tower I'd thought empty because all the lights were out. I may have been lucky she'd chosen to scream.

"But those were rabbits that were always better at avoiding it," Quicken continued. "She thinks if something's got brown fur they all look alike. It don't do to go tampering with nature, in my opinion. Not that the likes of them would ever ask me," he finished dryly.

"She forged the thesis Benton was supposed to have copied," Michael said. "Because he was spending so much time with the rabbits that she feared he'd learn to recognize them?"

Quicken snorted. "Professor Sevenson, he'd started naming 'em. And could call 'em by name without even a look at their collars. Of course she spooked. I'd seen what she was doing long ago, but till that court bastard turned up with his fat purse I'd no reason to say anything. After that, I just kept track of what rabbit she'd switched off for another and when. He paid me fine, for my notes."

"I'll bet he did." I could picture the scene that courtier had planned, Pendarian University presenting their newly "Gifted" rabbits to get more funding, and some rival stepping forward with a detailed record of exactly how those rabbits had been switched for their more Gifted kindred. But one thing still didn't make sense.

"Why tell us this now? You're talking pretty freely, for a man who blackmailed the person he owed to get his legal debt reduced."

Michael, who'd probably planned to approach this question more slowly, shot me a startled look. But if a guarded man like Quicken was being this open, he had to have a reason. I was beginning to worry about what that reason was.

"And why run now, in the middle of the night?" I went on, getting more nervous as I spoke. "Why not quit your job openly, say you're moving to join Barrows or something, and pack up all your furniture to take with you? You don't have to do this." I gestured to the dark, silent fields. "What's happening? It's tonight, isn't it, whatever you're running from? It's going to happen tonight."

Quicken looked at me in some alarm, but for the first time since I'd seen him at the hearing his shoulders straightened.

"That's what she wanted out of the bargain," he said. "That I clear out tonight. She said it's all going wrong, too many people beginning to look too close."

"'Twas not you who burned those papers," Michael said. "'Twas the professor, trying to cover her tracks. To get rid of the original notes she took. She couldn't just destroy them because too many people had seen them; Benton, Stint, all her scholar assistants."

Quicken waved this aside. "Aye, but that's not all of it. She said there's something else she has to take care of. Said she'd get me out of the debt if I'd run this very night. That way she could blame whatever she plans to do on me, but since I'd be clean away to another fiefdom it wouldn't hurt either of us. And I could keep the money. And all the evidence she'd cheated would be gone, and no one would ever suspect she did it."

"Did what?" I asked, with considerable interest.

"She didn't say. I didn't ask," Quicken admitted. "I did tell her I wouldn't be party to killing anyone, and she promised she wouldn't do that. She promised. Only..."

"You don't trust her," I said.

CHAPTER 28

Michael

We left Quicken on the deserted road, with all his world packed into the small cart that waited for him, and ran to get our horses. This main road was smooth enough to alternate between a walk and a trot, which slow as it might feel was the fastest way to cover the miles back to town.

Even though the discovery that Professor Dayless meant to act tonight sent the need for haste shivering down my nerves.

"What else do you think she needs to destroy?" I asked Fisk, on one of the stretches where we walked to let our horses recover their wind. "She got rid of the notes that incriminated her in that first fire."

"How should I know?" Fisk sounded as twitchy as I felt. "Once we've stopped her we can ask. I'm more worried about why she killed Hotchkiss."

"Do you still think 'tis his death at the core of this?"

Fisk turned a glare on me, but I waved it aside. "Not that. At the moment, I don't give a tinker's curse which of us takes charge. But we've found no connection between Hotchkiss and either Dayless or the project."

"Benton being framed connects them. The blackmailees all have alibis, and we haven't found anything else that could have gotten Hotchkiss killed."

"Yes, but she could have known where Hotchkiss was working, and planted the forged thesis there without him knowing anything about it."

"Or she could have bribed him to find it," Fisk said. "And even if she didn't, he might have figured out for himself that it was forged. Either way, he would then have turned around and tried to blackmail *her*. That fits."

It did fit. And worse... "If 'tis true, then she's already killed once."

It's all going wrong, too many people beginning to look too close, she'd told Quicken.

Fisk was already kicking Tipple into a trot, and Chant followed with no more than my tension to spur him on.

'Twas still some time before we caught sight of the sleeping town, its wide skirts no more than a jagged line on the horizon. The university's tall classrooms and bell tower stood out more clearly. And by the light of the great Green Moon, I saw a wisp of white drift up from a dark rectangle at the campus' western edge.

I pulled Chant to a stop, staring, and Fisk brought Tipple up to us.

"What is it?"

Before I could answer another hazy finger reached toward the sky, and I heard Fisk's breath catch. I put our thoughts into words.

"She's done it. She's burning the tower."

Fisk urged Tipple into a gallop before I finished speaking, but Chant and I soon caught up with them as Tipple has shorter legs.

We were near enough to run the horses all the way to town, though once we entered the narrow streets the shadows forced us to slow again. A fall, any injury to us or the horses, would have slowed us even more.

'Twas during one of those achingly slow trots down a very dark street—too dark for trotting to be safe, in truth—that Fisk spoke.

"You fought a fire with magic once before. Can you do it again?"

He had to raise his voice over clatter of the horse's hooves, but if some sleepy townsman overheard it no longer seemed the catastrophe I'd once have thought it.

"Yes," I said, with an assurance that took even me by surprise. "I think I can."

Fisk cast me an odd look, but we then turned into a moonlit lane and were able to canter once more, and the chance to talk was lost.

By the time we reached the university gates our horses were exhausted, and we could no longer see the smoke. But the bitter scent of burning lay in the air, most uncommon on a pleasant summer night.

The gatekeeper must have heard our approach. He came stumbling out of a nearby building, jogging across the grass in his nightshirt to peer at us through the bars.

The gates, of course, were closed.

"Let us in," I shouted. "The tower's on fire!"

He'd been pulling his keys from his pocket, but now he turned to stare at the dark campus, though even Fisk and I, with our sound eyes, could see nothing from here. Then he sniffed the air and his expression changed. He snatched up his whistle and began to blow, a shrill blast that tore the nerves as a cat's claw tears skin.

He dropped it only to put his key into the lock, and began to shout instead, "Fire! Fire in the tower."

"The west tower," Fisk inserted neatly, when he paused to draw breath. "Where Professor Dayless works."

"Fire," the man's voice boomed. "Fire in the west tower."

The gates opened, and he dragged one aside for Fisk and me to gallop through. As we passed I heard the whistle blow again, several times, followed by more shouts of fire in the tower.

The grassy lawns between those wide-spaced buildings were perfect for speed, and our weary horses did their courageous best. They got us to the tower just as other shouts and whistles began to sound, spreading from the distant gate. The alarm would no doubt travel quickly, but an evil orange light now glowed behind most of the fourth floor windows, and some on the third floor had begun to flicker.

The guard sat slumped in his chair, not moving when we pulled our gasping horses to a stop, dismounted, or even when I shouted and Fisk started up the steps.

Fisk didn't bother to shake the man, but went through his pockets with brisk efficiency. At least he was breathing, which relieved my worst fear.

"Drugged?"

"Who knows. Curse her, she took his keys!"

After that 'twas hardly worthwhile to try the door, but I did so—because if it was unlocked we'd no time to play the fool.

But of course 'twas locked, and Fisk brushed me aside almost before I'd released the latch.

"Can you pick it?"

"Not fast, but Hotchkiss was a trusted member of the staff, and locksmiths often use the same pin patterns."

He pulled out the librarian's keys and began trying likely ones.

I went to the guard, felt the back of his skull for lumps or blood, lifted his head gently to be sure his neck wasn't broken...and since 'twas not, I gave him a hard slap. His eyelids fluttered, which encouraged me, and I slapped him several times. He'd started to move, and reached up weakly to stop me, when I heard a click and Fisk's triumphant cry.

"Go down!" I ordered, dragging the guard to the top of the steps. "The tower's on fire."

I wasn't sure he'd obey, but even if he rolled down 'twould do him little harm and I'd no time for more.

Fisk opened the door. I expected a roar of flames and a billow of smoke. But almost more alarming, a great draft tugged at my shirt sleeves, as though the building had drawn breath. The grumbling mutter of the fire grew louder.

We need to breathe. 'Twas a prayer in the heart as much as a thought, and as I stepped into the stifling darkness of the tower's entry a bubble of fresh night air followed me in.

Since magic is visible to me I could see the bubble's skin of power, glowing softly in the dimness. 'Twas not the perfect sphere I'd shaped in my mind, but a lumpy oval that wavered and bent as drafts of hot air pushed against it. But I could also feel its connection to the magic that flowed from me, and despite its shifting shape it felt secure.

Fisk had stopped at the jeweler's door, pulling out his keys, but when I stepped up beside him and the bubble flowed over his head he yelped and dropped them.

"We'll get your friend on our way out," I promised. "First let's check the second floor. I'm worried about Stint."

Fisk's eyes were wide, and grew even wider as his hand passed out of the bubble when he picked up the keys.

"This is...this is magic?" He pulled his hand back in, then reached through the skin of the bubble once more, wiggling his fingers, trying to track its shape.

"Come on." I pulled him toward the stairs as I spoke. "You can play after we've found Stint."

Fisk hooked a hand through my belt, to keep near me as we climbed the stairs, but I think he was still experimenting with that division between hot and cold air—he stumbled several times, once tugging my belt so hard he almost pulled me over. 'Twas fascinating, I must admit. My hand on the stair's railing, outside the bubble, grew hotter and hotter as we climbed. But the air inside stayed cool and fresh, even though we both breathed it.

At the far end of the second floor hallway only moonlight lit the windows, but I still hoped we wouldn't have to go farther up. I ran down the hall to the laboratory door, and Fisk followed perforce. Thank goodness none of the other doors bore a lock.

Moonlight flowed though these windows too, glittering on glassware and picking out the limp body that lay face down on the floor.

We flung ourselves down beside Stint, Fisk rolling him over, while I wished/willed/wanted the bubble to flow over his head, for he too needed to *breathe*. But he didn't stir and dread gripped me.

"Is he dead?"

Fisk laid his hand lightly over Stint's nose and mouth. "He's breathing. Drugged like the guard, probably, which means we'll never wake him enough to walk down stairs."

Stint was a big man, with both muscle and a bit of fat. "I'll get his arms, you get his feet," I said.

We carried him down the corridor thus, but when we reached the stairs—the rather steep stairs—we decided to each take an arm and drag him. If he slid from step to step his back shouldn't suffer too badly and his head wouldn't even be bumped.

This proved harder in the doing than the planning, for Stint's limp body kept rolling down upon us, and his rump hit the steps harder than I'd intended. But 'twas not till we were nearly at the bottom that a crash shook the staircase, and the fire roared once more.

"That's the roof." Fisk had to raise his voice, to be heard above the flames. "The fourth floor's gone."

"I don't think there'd be anyone up there," I said. "She already took care of Benton, but Stint probably became suspicious after her performance at the hearing...this morning?"

It seemed more like a week had passed, but I had no time to consider the matter. The air outside our over-stretched shelter was growing hotter, and we dragged Stint swiftly down the hallway till we reached the jeweler's door, where Fisk dropped the arm he held with a thump.

"You take him the rest of the way. I'll get the jeweler out."

I hated to leave him, but he was right. The fire was so loud I didn't argue, grabbing Stint's arm and pulling his suddenly-much-heavier weight across the smooth stone floor.

The bubble seemed to cling to Fisk a moment before it let go. As I reached the entry, I looked back to see him patiently trying key after key in the lock.

'Twas only when I passed through the door that the bubble vanished, as if it had never been. But Fisk hadn't seemed to be suffocating, and as several scholars rushed to help me carry Stint down the landing stairs I was too busy to give it further heed.

I explained that the professor had been drugged, not smothered by the smoke, just as the guard had, and we carried him off to the medical scholars who were setting up a field surgery under the guidance of one of their professors.

Scholars clad in britches and untied shirts, or even their nightgowns, were running everywhere, rolling barrels of water forward and flinging buckets about. As I turned back my mind began to sort the chaos, and I realized they were flinging water on the walls of nearby buildings and the grass around the tower—but not the tower itself. Even as that thought crossed my mind, the rhythmic thwack of axes stopped, and first of the big elms on the other side of the courtyard's wall crashed down, and was hastily dragged off by a team of shouting students. The sound of axes resumed, and the next tree shivered.

The tower had been given up for lost, and I stood far enough from it to see why. Flames soared from the roof, dazzling against the darkness. With stone walls between those flames and the firefighters, 'twas clearly a hopeless cause.

Was Fisk still inside? The lower floors were untouched, but that wouldn't last much longer.

I was hurrying back to the tower when I saw the jeweler dash out, his arms full of shining bits of metal. He was coughing as he ran down the steps, but aside from that he showed no harm. Several scholars caught his arms and guided him to the medical camp. I stopped, and waited for Fisk to follow him. And waited. And waited.

Fisk didn't come.

It had likely been no more than a score of seconds since the jeweler emerged, but 'twas still too long. One of the firefighters grabbed at me as I ran back to the tower, but I shoved him off so hard he fell, and took the steps two at a time.

My bubble returned as I stepped through the door again, obedient as a dog called to heel, and I used the air inside it to shout Fisk's name as I ran.

I went first to the jeweler's room, fearing that in his madness he might have done Fisk some injury or trapped him there. But the strange room, with its hanging scarves and odd shadows, showed no sign of another person. I went back down the corridor, flinging open doors as I went. It occurred to me that he might have needed to breathe, for the air outside my bubble was scorching now, and I crossed one room to look into the yard, but there was no one there.

Why would he go upstairs again? Fisk, of all people, never took risks without good reason.

There was nowhere else he could have gone, so I dashed up the stairs to the second floor. Firelight now flickered on the stairs at the hallway's end, but 'twas far from where I stood, and I realized that a building designed to slow invaders as they climbed might also slow the fire on its way down.

I threw open doors on my way to the laboratory, finding nothing, and smoke was beginning to billow down the stairs. I burst into the laboratory and 'twas as empty as we'd left it. Panicked, baffled, beginning to despair, I bellowed Fisk's name as loud as I could—then stood and listened. And this time I was answered, not by a shout, but by the sound of footsteps on the ceiling above my head.

He was in Dayless' office! The *idiot*. But whatever the reason he'd gone up there, calling him names wouldn't change it.

My bubble was visible without magic now, a patch of clear space in the thickening smoke, as I ran for the stairs to the third floor. Looking up I could see tiny flames licking between the planks of the ceiling—which clearly might come down at any moment—so I wasted no time darting up. Beyond the stair there was no fire in sight, but the smoke was thick and I could hear Fisk's coughing though the open door of Professor Dayless' office.

Fisk was searching for something; the desk was pulled apart, its drawers tumbled on the floor, and all the books tossed from their shelves. He had rolled up the rug and was tapping the floor beneath, and didn't even notice me till my bubble swept over him. When the fresh air hit his lungs he started coughing harder.

Curses crowded my brain, but I wasted time on only two words as I dragged him to his feet. "Out. Now."

"Just...minute," Fisk coughed. "I want to look... Ceiling's still fine."

He was actually resisting me, which made him crazier than the jeweler.

"You think the ceiling is fine?"

In fairness to him, the office ceiling hadn't started to burn. So I dragged him into the hallway and pointed at the tiny tongues of light that rippled along the beams and planks above our only exit.

Fisk's reddened eyes widened. He set off for the stairwell at the best speed he could manage, but he was coughing so hard it wasn't very fast. I grabbed his arm and dragged him along at a run, despite the fact that he was doubled over and clutching his ribs.

He'd been in the smoke so long the harsh scent clung to his clothes and hair, tainting the air inside my bubble But it stayed breathable as we clattered down the stairs, down interminable hallways and more stairs—all of them now filled with smoke—and finally stumbled out into the firelit tumult outside the burning tower.

A number of people ran forward as I half-carried Fisk down the steps, but I assured them there was no one else in the building and we needed no aid. My bubble had disappeared as we emerged, and after brushing off our helpers I set off for the medical camp to see if they could do something about the coughs that shook Fisk's body every time he tried to breathe.

Once I had time to look, I saw that while there were more people present, 'twas actually more orderly. A large part of the crowd was milling about, but the town's fire brigade had arrived, and the scholars and some of the townsfolk had been organized into bucket lines.

The sodden grass squished beneath my boots, and a spike of fire nearly as tall as the tower now surged skyward, illuminating the scene for hundreds of yards around. 'Twas no wonder half the town had gathered to gawk, and get in the fire teams' way. In fairness, they may have come to take a place in the bucket line when their fellows tired. But now they just stood, staring at the flames and forcing Fisk and me to move around them.

I almost walked past her before I recognized the older woman, with her graying hair in braid down her back, clad in a dressing gown instead of professorial black. Professor Dayless didn't notice us, gazing up like the others. Her expression wavered between agony and something that looked like triumph.

"Professor! You shouldn't be alone in this commotion. Let me help you to the healers."

I gathered her into my free arm as I spoke, sweeping her along with us. Fisk was already leaning less heavily.

"I don't need a healer." She stiffened, and had she been less guilty she'd have pulled away. I could all but hear her wondering what she'd have done if innocent, and in her hesitation she was lost.

"Mayhap not," I said agreeably. "But you've suffered a terrible shock. The loss of all your work! And there's someone I think you should see."

"Who? I don't need a doctor." But she must have decided 'twas better not to make a scene, and let me carry her along. Fortunately, the healers' shelter was crowded with medical scholars, wrapping sprained wrists and examining thrown backs.

"Oh, I don't see him." The concern in my voice wasn't feigned. If they'd taken Stint away for further treatment... Then I saw him, sitting up and talking to a mediciner who waved fingers before his eyes.

Unfortunately, Dayless saw him too. She spun in my tightening grasp, and I had to let go of Fisk to hold on to her. He swayed, but kept his feet.

"Let me go, you impertinent whelp!"

For all her formidable intellect, the professor's strength was no match for mine—but she made me use it and our struggle was attracting attention. Indeed, several husky scholars were coming toward me, looking outraged and determined. It might all have gone awry, except that the people near us who weren't prepared to intervene had backed away—and fallen silent, so Professor Stint's voice was clearly audible.

"Wait a minute. I remember now...that tea... She drugged me!"

This stopped the scholars, who stared from one of their teachers to the other in confusion. A doctor, taking in the scene, said, "He was drugged. We'd best hold them both."

This decided Professor Dayless. She stamped her heel on the bridge of my foot, nearly breaking it or so it felt, ripped out of my grasp and ran...right into Captain Chaldon's arms.

"Forgive me, Professor," he said calmly. "But the doctors summoned me here because they say Professor Stint has been drugged. And since he was pulled, unconscious, from that tower, it seems there may have been a crime committed."

"Really? How did you guess?" Fisk muttered, between coughs. His breathing seemed to be settling, though he still clutched his ribs.

"That's a bit far-fetched, isn't it?" Professor Dayless had recovered her nerve. "If it's true it would be very shocking, but I—"

"You brought me tea." Stint's voice was slurred, and his eyes didn't quite track. "I got dizzy. Thought I was sick. I called, but you didn't come. I was trying to go for help...when...when..." He listed to one side and an alert scholar grabbed him and propped him upright.

"The man is clearly intoxicated," Professor Dayless said icily. "We had tea together two days ago, and he's probably confusing that memory with whatever he took. Or drank."

"He's not drunk," one of the doctors put in. "It looks like an opiate to me, though we'd have to test his urine to be sure."

The scholars looked much interested in this.

"Then he took a sleeping draught," said Dayless. "What has that to do with me? And why, as your theory seems to run, would I want to drug my colleague and set my own complex on fire? All my notes are ashes now, the rabbits dead, my work ruined. Ruined!"

"I expect you did it for the same reason you framed Professor Sevenson." I spoke clearly, in a voice meant to carry. The more people who spread this rumor the better. "You feared Benton would come to recognize the rabbits well enough to realize you were switching them out, to make it look as if your experiment was getting better results than it did. As Lat Quicken had realized, though you didn't learn that till he threatened to expose you unless you reduced his debt to the university. But when you did that, it made Stint suspicious. And he'd never agree to keep silent and vanish, as Quicken did."

Chaldon's gaze went to the flaming tower, and he may have been suspicious as well for he put it together very quickly.

"Professor Dayless, you'll be held for questioning," he said. "For attempted murder, arson, false testimony, and whatever else I need to keep you till Professor Stint sobers up, and we can get to the bottom of this. Or rather, prove it, because I think the truth is clear. The only thing I don't understand is why you killed Hotchkiss."

He'd been speaking to her, but his gaze slid to Fisk and me as he asked this. 'Twould have been quite flattering, if I'd only had the answer.

"I didn't!" Professor Dayless said. "You have to understand, we may not quite have gotten the results we needed, but we were getting close. I know we were close! All we need is a little more time and I'm sure we'll succeed. So I may have made my tea a bit strong. He said he'd been having trouble sleeping, and I thought—"

"No, I didn't," said Stint. "No trouble sleeping, and even if I had, why'd I want t' sleep in the laboratory?"

"But I didn't kill anyone," the professor went on. "I might have left a lamp burning somewhere, but that's merely an accident."

She was still explaining why she'd take a lamp up to the fourth floor, which had been filled with flammable papers, when the deputies led her away. Captain Chaldon returned to assisting the fire marshal, and I turned Fisk toward the healers' tent once more.

"Why did she kill Hotchkiss?" I asked. "And if she didn't, who did?"

"I have no idea," he said.

"She sounded like she didn't do it."

I'd had a lot of practice, listening to people denying they'd killed the librarian. Professor Dayless had sounded as innocent as the others. When she'd spoken of the fire, and drugging Professor Stint, she sounded guilty. I mentioned this to Fisk, who rolled his eyes.

"Attempted murder is a debt you can pay off, eventually," he pointed out. "Committed murder you can't. She has an excellent motive to lie about that."

"Mayhap," I admitted, though it still didn't sound right. "But 'tis out of our hands. And I don't think they've done that final interview, so Benton can get his job back. Though he'll be sorry about the rabbits."

"Why? He could probably keep them, if he wants." Fisk gestured to a dim corner of the healers' tent, which I'd not noticed. The jeweler sat on a cot, surrounded by rabbit cages. The scholars must have taken them from the yard and brought them here. A girl, mayhap one of the maids, sat beside him speaking soothingly. But the jeweler's attention was on stroking the quivering lump of fur in his lap. The rabbit evidently regarded him as shelter from the lights and noise around it, for it snuggled against him.

"He's forgiven them for lying," said Fisk, which made no more sense now than it had when he first said it.

"Then mayhap he can keep them. We'd better get you something to settle that cough."

"I'd have thought you'd have done that by now," said Kathy's voice behind me.

Fisk spun so fast he almost lost his balance. "Kath— I mean, Lady Katherine. What are you doing here? This isn't..."

"What? A proper place for a lady? With half the campus going up in flames I knew you two would be in the thick of it, so I figured I'd better come help. Or bail you out of gaol. Again."

She had been helping. She set down a pail of water, and handed Fisk a cup and a sopping wet cloth as she spoke.

"I knew there was a reason I...ah, thank you," Fisk said. He drank deeply, then pressed the cloth to his eyes.

"Your hands are burned too," Kathy observed. "How come you're such a mess and Michael looks so tidy?"

'Twas not a question I was prepared to answer, even to my sister, but it reminded me of the question I'd not had time to ask.

"Fisk, what under two moons were you doing in Professor Dayless' office? You cursed near went up with the tower!"

"Ah." Fisk's gaze darted to Kathy, then away. "I know scholars well enough that I was pretty sure she'd have another set of notes, with the true results of their experiment, tucked away somewhere. Getting rid of them, as well as Stint, was probably why she chose this way to do it. She could get rid of every threat in the same 'accident.' She'd been getting 'results,' so she might even be able to get more funding, and start over with a new partner."

His voice was still rough but he'd stopped coughing. And since I'd now had time to think about how near we'd both come to dying in that inferno, I was all the more angry.

"We'd no need of any notes to prove her guilt! Stint's testimony, and Quicken's if we needed to track him down, would provide plenty of evidence. Why take such a foolish risk?"

"Well, she seemed to think her experiment could succeed. And if there was some value in those notes, someone who turned them over to the Heir might be able to request...to get a favor in return."

This made no sense to me, but his gaze had strayed to Kathy once more. And her face lit with sudden fury.

"Fisk, you moron! Is that what you were thinking? That you had to get someone *else's* permission? You idiot!"

She threw her arms around Fisk's neck, and kissed him. 'Twas not a sisterly kiss, either. Fisk's arms went around her, gently, but in a way that made it clear he intended to hold onto this woman forever.

Kathy and Fisk? I felt as if the fire had suddenly swept over me, sucking all the air away. Why hadn't I noticed? Why hadn't they said something?

For a moment I was outraged—not so much by the thought of them together, which was beginning to feel less strange by the minute—but by the fact that either one of them would keep something so important from me.

On the other hand, from what Kathy said, it sounded like they'd been keeping their feelings secret from each other, too. So I could hardly blame them.

Still, Kathy and Fisk...?

They stopped kissing, perhaps for want of breath, but instead of pulling apart Kathy lowered her head to Fisk's shoulder. And in that moment, 'twas as clear as anything I'd ever seen that they were right for each other. Right *together.*

If anything, Fisk was holding her closer than when they'd kissed. As if he feared that, at any moment, she might be pulled from his arms.

As well he might! Father would disown Kathy, or lock her up in a tower, or marry her off to someone...

Unless he was stopped. And looking at the way my sister clung to Fisk, stopping him was a knight errant's job. Father would never forgive any of us, but if it made Fisk and Kathy happy I didn't care. I consider happiness more important in a marriage than rank or money—which was just as well, because Kathy wouldn't inherit a cracked copper if she wed Fisk.

Without letting go of my sister, Fisk opened his eyes and looked at me. "I really hope you don't have a problem with this."

"Not at all." In truth, I was pleased he didn't ask my permission—a squire would have, but a friend didn't have to. I returned the compliment, by not asking if his intentions were honorable. "But I advise you to get married now, before Father or anyone else hears about this. Kathy's old enough to consent, but until she marries or turns twenty-five she's Father's legal ward."

Fisk's shoulders sagged in sudden relief, which amused me. He knew me too well to fear that I'd object, unless love of my sister had overset his reason.

In fact, it had overset his reason so badly he'd almost gotten us both killed.

I resolved to keep a close eye on Fisk till he recovered his wits, and became more accustomed to being in love.

"Kathy's actually the Liege's ward," was Fisk's explanation for blatant insanity. "That's why I needed to earn his favor. Or at least get on the Heir's good side. But that idea's in ashes now."

His gaze went to the burning tower, still a bit wistful, and Kathy shivered.

"You really are crazy," she told him. "Even if you'd found those notes, and they were worth something, we could still have gotten married now and you could have exchanged them for something more practical. Like a small estate."

"You're worth more than any estate," Fisk told her. "There's nothing worth more than love."

This maudlin sentiment was so unlike my erstwhile squire, I almost asked what had become of the real Fisk. But it must have been the first time that word had passed between them, for they kissed again. And went on kissing, though I paid no attention, for something nagged at me. The worth of love, the price of love, no number for love... But there was a number for everything.

Motive bloomed in my mind, brighter than the flaming tower.

I gasped, but Fisk and Kathy ignored me. I glared at them, but they went on kissing. I finally had to shake Fisk's shoulder, whereupon they both glared at me.

"I know, and I'm sorry, but I know who killed Hotchkiss! And I think I can prove it."

CHAPTER 29

Fisk

Since he was babbling about Hotchkiss' murder, I wasn't too surprised when Michael led us to the library. I had requested, somewhat politely, that he either tell us who killed Hotchkiss or go away—and though I was deeply grateful to Michael for taking the news about Kathy and me so well, truthfully, I was hoping for the latter. But he said he had to check one more thing, and Kathy was beginning to be curious, so I pulled out Hotchkiss' keys and let us into the dark building.

We could probably have gone from room to room using the moonlight that poured through the windows, but Michael took down one of the lamps beside the door—he had to pull it from its stand—and then kindled it.

I noted that his new ability to keep us alive in burning buildings didn't mean he could suddenly do everything with magic, and used the darkness while he fumbled around to steal a few more kisses—a sweet theft, that could make the rest of my life joyous...if I could only figure out some way to marry the wench.

At least, thank goodness, Michael was on our side—we'd need all the help we could get! It was very well for Kathy to say we that could get married legally right now—infuriating not only her powerful father, but the *High Liege*. Kathy seemed to think that if we were wed there was nothing they could do about it, which was nonsense. Even if they weren't prepared to make her a widow—and I preferred not to bet my life on that—there were legal means to break up a marriage. It wasn't easy, but it could be done—particularly if a well-dowered maiden entered into that marriage without her guardian's consent. Mostly the guardian would just get the dowry back, but not always. I didn't care about Kathy's dowry, but the other legal possibilities went from bad to very bad in short order.

Convicting me of kidnapping, forcible marriage, and rape—no matter what either of us said—was one of the most likely.

Finding out who'd killed Hotchkiss might win us a bit of good will, from the local law, at least. So when Michael finally got the lamp lit, I followed him over to the directory with only moderate regret.

But he wasn't looking at the directory, he was reading the numbered subject list beside it.

"Emotions, Thought, the Human Mind, 000 to 009," he muttered. "That's not enough. Where are they?"

"Far end of the hallway on the right," Kathy told him, looking at the building map.

Michael set off without another word, striding briskly. With Kathy's hand in mine, we trailed him at a more leisurely pace. By the time we reached the room, which had once been some lady's parlor, Michael had already found the master sheet for that section, framed and hung on the wall beside the door.

"001," he read. "Love of a child for a parent. 001.2, love of a child for a grandparent. 001.3, love of a child for a friend. 002 starts with romantic love, between man and woman."

My heart contracted with sudden, painful understanding. Kathy had seen it too. Her grip on my hand was tight with horror and pity.

"Nothing, nothing, nothing," she whispered. "The number for love."

"Love of a parent for a child is 003," Michael said. "It goes on all through life, listing all the loves that man may know. And Hotchkiss created this system years after the death of Seymour Peebles."

"Whose mother," I said, "has access to the keys to every building the university owns. Including Hotchkiss' house. And that abandoned print shop."

Michael turned to us, his face set with distress and determination.

"I'm going back to the tower to get Captain Chaldon. You two find one of those master lists you told me about, and meet us at the gates."

He left us the lamp when he departed, and I heard him bump into something in the hallway and swear. But I had no desire to laugh.

Kathy's face was full of sorrow and I put an arm around her, just for comfort. For both our comfort, which was almost sweeter than a kiss.

"Can we stop this, Fisk? Should we?"

"Michael will be talking to the Captain in minutes. As for whether we should have tried to stop him, I honestly don't know. But your brother's not just thinking about Clerk Peebles. He's thinking about the next person who'll be suspected of this murder. Some random burglar, say, who might not have an alibi."

"Ah." I felt her sigh as much as heard it. "Then I suppose we'd better get that master list for him."

Since we knew where it was kept, that was easy. We reached the gates several minutes before Michael and Captain Chaldon came to join us.

"Good, you've got it," Michael said. "Do you recognize this, Captain?"

"Not without reading the title." The captain's voice was tart, and I deduced that Michael hadn't told him much.

People resist conclusions less if they reach them on their own, so I just handed over the thick book. To my surprise, he recognized it.

"This is the master list for the alphanumeric system. I thought they never let it out of the library."

"They would for this," I told him.

Michael had already passed through the gates, unguarded in this emergency. I took back the book and led the Captain and Kathy after him. Having walked her home after our dinner, Michael knew where Clerk Peebles lived.

It was a tall narrow house, in a row of such houses. As we approached, I couldn't help but wonder if the cobbles we walked across were the ones that had shattered Seymour Peebles' head when he jumped. And whether his mother remembered that, every time she approached her own front door.

If she'd gone to the fire I don't know what we'd have done—I could hardly have picked her door lock under Captain Chaldon's eyes. But candlelight glowed in her windows—she must have heard the alarm, and sensibly decided that a middle-aged woman wouldn't be much use fighting fires. She was ready, though. She opened the door immediately when Michael knocked, fully dressed.

"What's happening on the campus? Am I needed there? I thought..."

She took in the fact that none of us were scholar-messengers, and then the insignia on Captain Chaldon's coat, and the animation died out of her face. This was how she'd look when she was old, and Kathy darted from my side to throw an arm around her, though she stood steady and straight.

"We'd like to see your son's room," Michael said.

It was all he needed to say and her face changed again...but oddly, she looked stronger now.

"It's the second door at the top of the stairs," she said. "I locked it after Seymour's death. Couldn't bear it. But it hasn't been locked for over a month, now."

Kathy took her into a comfortable front room, off to the right, while Michael led the rest of us up the stairs. He took a lit candle from the entry with him, and collected another from a stand on the landing.

Under the dust, Seymour Peebles' room could have been that of any young scholar. Perhaps a bit tidier than most, before his death, but filled with the books and notes that were now scattered wildly over the floor, where he'd tossed them in his final despair. I understood why his mother hadn't been able to clean it out, to throw those notes away. But even if she had, he'd scribbled on the walls as well, when a thought had struck him and he'd no paper to hand.

Tree-root-wood-bark-leaves-blossom-fruit-seed appeared by the window, with a list of numbers in the 530's. Beside a chest of drawers was a sketch of a human skeleton, with a list of numbers in the 650's that ran from eye level down to the floor. A complex thing to number, human anatomy.

But Seymour Peebles had created a number for everything. And his "friend," Winton Hotchkiss, had stolen them.

Chaldon must have spent more time in the library than I'd have expected, for he got it almost at once.

"These numbers." He gestured to marked walls, the paper strewn floor. "Do they match?"

"You can check." I held out the master list that had sprung from those tumbled notes.

The captain sighed. "There's hardly any need, is there. The man I was partnered with when I first joined the guard, he'd investigated Seymour Peebles' suicide. There was no doubt he took his own life, but his mother was so insistent that he'd been betrayed by someone he trusted... Dovan looked for the man. He never found a trace."

"Hotchkiss hid their friendship," Michael said. "Mayhap at first 'twas from embarrassment, fear of mockery if he befriended someone as odd as Seymour. Or mayhap he befriended him in the first place because he recognized that this odd, awkward youth had hit on something valuable...and he didn't want anyone to suspect the truth when he stole it."

From what I knew of Hotchkiss, I'd bet on the latter. In fact, I wouldn't put it past him to have deliberately provoked the bright, unstable scholar. To have shattered that newfound trust as brutally as he could, hoping Seymour would be so traumatized, so incoherent, he'd be unable to present a convincing case that Hotchkiss had taken his work, instead of the other way around.

Though Seymour may have suspected something; Hotchkiss had clearly never been invited into this room, or seen the strange, brilliant scribbles on its walls.

As we walked back down the stairs to confront his mother, I found myself thinking that if he'd survived, Seymour Peebles might someday have acquired magic. Or maybe in time, with respect and the freedom to change the whole scholarly world with his numbers, he might have settled and become more normal.

Either way, Hotchkiss had made sure he'd never have the chance.

By the time we reached the front room, I was really hoping we'd find Nancy Peebles had run for it. I knew Kathy wouldn't stop her, and I had a feeling the captain wouldn't have pursued her very hard.

But she was waiting for us, seated on a very worn, upholstered chair. A matching chair, worn only a little, sat on the other side of a small table, and it took only a moment's thought to understand why Kathy had chosen to sit on a footstool instead. None of the rest of us took that empty chair.

"Mistress Peebles," Captain Chaldon said. "When did you first realize that Hotchkiss had stolen the alphanumeric system from your son?"

He was good. If he'd asked her if she'd killed the man, she might have lied. But that question was one she was dying—maybe literally—to answer. I wished, once again, that she'd run.

"Not for a very long time. I took that job with the university to look for the person who'd betrayed my son, you know."

She spoke calmly, but her hands kept smoothing the skirt over her knees.

"Oh, I went to them, and said I'd lost my old job because I'd missed so much time after Seymour died. That much was true, and they gave me a job out of pity. But the reason I wanted to work there was to hunt for my son's killer. Secretary to the admissions clerk, that's where I started, and it was perfect. I studied the records of every scholar who was here at the same time as Seymour, watched them when they came back to visit, kept track of their careers.

"But Hotchkiss was clever. He waited for more than three years after Seymour's death before he even began talking about the system, and he spent several more years 'developing it.' Talking to professors and department heads about how to subdivide their subjects, bringing out the numbers one discipline at a time. There was no reason to doubt he was working it all out slowly, just as he claimed. And I was looking at the mathematicians, and some of the sciences that use a lot of math, not at historians."

She gave Michael a rueful smile. "So maybe it's fitting, that it was a historian who helped me see it. I was there at your brother's hearing, taking notes of the proceedings. He was so angry, so helpless. It reminded me of Seymour, that day he came home and locked himself in his room."

Her gaze fell to her hands, clenched on her knees, and she released them self-consciously.

"I had no idea what he was going to do. What he'd done. He never let anyone into his room for fear they'd disturb his papers—that's why there was a lock on his door. I was still pounding on it, begging him to tell me what was wrong, when the neighbors came. I only glanced into his room once after the guard had inspected it. Seeing all his neat piles of paper tossed about... I said I couldn't bear to clean it, but the truth is he'd been so adamant about keeping everyone out, I felt like he'd know. Like he still cared, somehow. But after Professor Sevenson was betrayed as well, I dug out the key and went into my son's room. I'd been using that library, using the alphanumeric system, for almost fifteen years. I knew then, who'd betrayed my son. And your brother, and who knows how many other people. Years I'd spent, looking in the wrong place, while that man walked around the campus collecting fame for Seymour's genius. I searched his house, you know. I hoped there'd be some evidence that the system was Seymour's work. I thought I could leave it on his desk or a shelf, that someone would find it..."

Her voice had begun to shake, but her eyes were dry.

"Why didn't you go to Headman Portner, and the board?" Kathy asked. "Surely they'd have listened."

"They probably would," Mistress Peebles admitted. "He'd have been fired, and disgraced...and once he worked off his debt to the university, he'd have gone right on with his life. My son is dead. It wasn't enough, it wasn't *justice*. I'm glad you came tonight," she went on, to my surprise. "I did my best to give Professor Sevenson an alibi. After that hearing, I knew he'd be suspected. And I was horrified when you fell under suspicion, and did all I could to help you clear yourselves. If you'd found someone else to accuse... When I made my decision, I promised myself that if someone else was about to be convicted for my crime I'd come forward. I'm glad I won't have to take that test. I'd hate fail it."

"So you confess to killing Master Hotchkiss?" Captain Chaldon asked.

"Why deny it? I have the university's master keys, so it was easy to sneak in and mix the drug into his tea. He could barely stagger when he came down those stairs. Going for help, I suppose."

The indifference in her voice was chilling.

"But he saw me coming. He knew why he died. And the truth will come out. That's justice enough." Her hands were relaxed now.

"Mistress Peebles, I must place you under arrest for the willful murder of Winton Hotchkiss." The captain sounded regretful. "Would you like to pack some things, before you go with me?"

"I suppose I'd better." Her expression was still calm, but when she rose I saw her waver and realized her knees were shaking.

I understood, now, why she hadn't run—and her son would get the recognition he deserved. But I wished Hotchkiss hadn't been the vicious worm he was, or that her son had been stronger. I wished there was something I could say...

It was Michael who found it.

"Mistress Peebles," he said, as she turned toward the stairs. "You should know, your son, he didn't think love was nothing. He put it before everything else in the universe. Zero, zero, zero: love. And the love he put first, zero, zero, one, was the love of a child for a parent."

She knew the alphanumeric system. She knew what that meant.

When Captain Chaldon took her up to pack her bag, her face was wet with tears.

CHAPTER 30

Michael

"Twas as if he told her he loved her from beyond the grave," Kathy said. "That poor woman. I don't blame her in the least for killing that monster! Surely the judicars won't hang her. If there was ever a case for which someone should go unredeemed..."

Having gone to bed only hours before dawn, we'd all slept past noon, then slowly gathered around...could you still call it the breakfast table? But Kathy was right, cases like this were exactly what the legal status "unredeemed" had been created for.

"I think Captain Chaldon will push for it," I told her. "If the university agrees, the judicars might well choose to be lenient. Hotchkiss may not have pushed her son out that window, but he was still responsible for Seymour's death. And 'tis not as if she's likely to kill again."

"Will the university argue for leniency?" Kathy aimed the question at Benton, who'd heard our account of the previous night with shock, then pity. He'd gone to join the townsfolk on the bucket lines, been seen by some of his old students, and was quite surprised at how they welcomed him. Indeed, he'd sat up talking with Scholar Flynn—he still blushed saying her name—till nearly dawn, and reached his bed even later than the rest of us.

"I don't know." Benton looked troubled. "They might sympathize, I think. But she did choose to commit murder, when she could have gone to them for justice. And even if you put the legal aspects aside, having two senior members of the staff turn out to be homicidal villains... When you add in the things Hotchkiss did, it's going to be a huge scandal. I mean, what parent would send their child to a school where the staff are blackmailing and murdering each other? Portner may feel he has to respond with severity. I can't blame him, really."

"I can," said Fisk. "And if he's thinking along those lines, we'd better change his mind before he makes some public statement he can't back out of. Come along, Michael."

Thus we found ourselves outside Headman Portner's office a few hours after midday. We weren't the only ones who'd been up late, either. Portner's secretary declined to admit us.

"You'll understand, what with the fire and the arres— ah, the other matters, the Headman is very busy. Perhaps you could come back tomorrow?"

'Twas a reasonable request, so I understood why his brows flew up when Fisk said, "No. We need to see the Headman now. He wants to see us, too, because I have an idea that might block one of the lawsuits that are heading his way. Or rather, heading the university's way."

Ten minutes later we were admitted to Portner's office. 'Twas a room fit for his rank, with leather-padded chairs, a great maple-wood desk, and shelf after shelf of books. Portner suited the room, with a lean face and a high, intellectual forehead. But his arms were thick with muscle, and his broad hands would have looked at home wielding a pick or a shovel.

Those hands bore blisters today, and there was a reddened burn across his nose and down one cheek. He'd been fighting the fire last night, not standing back and observing—or worse, trying to supervise, and getting in the fire marshal's way. I began to see why Benton respected this man...so 'twas somewhat discouraging that he regarded Fisk and me with the look you might turn on a moldy sandwich.

"I don't know what you think you're doing here," he said. "But no lawsuit will stop me from doing what's right for this university, and the scholars in it. I'm busy today, so say what you have to, quickly, then get out of my office."

"I don't know what your subject was." Fisk took a chair as he spoke, defying the Headman's disapproval. "But I expect you have enough math to know what happens when you multiply two negative numbers?"

"Get out of my office. I don't have time for games." He looked angry, but beneath the anger I saw weariness and grief. He hadn't the heart for games either, and despite his scowl my hopes began to rise.

"All right," said Fisk. "Though I think it's an interesting analogy. But as a man of the world, I'm sure you've seen that when two scandals arise at the same time, the greater extinguishes the lesser."

Portner had started to rise, probably to throw us out, but at that he sank back into his chair.

"It's a terrible scandal," Fisk went on, "for a professor—suddenly seized with madness, say—to have corrupted the Heir's project, and then tried to destroy the evidence. But it's a much worse scandal to hang a woman, for killing the man who stole her son's work and drove him to his death. A man who used that stolen work to become a famous scholar, on the staff of your own university. If word of that tragic tale spread—if the university itself pled the woman's case, demanding that she be made unredeemed instead of hanging—I can't imagine anyone would be interested in a tedious academic project that somehow went wrong."

Portner was thinking furiously now, so I decided to give him more to chew on.

"Folk would have even less reason to think about that project, if someone who'd been wrongfully accused to keep him from suspecting what was happening was fully reinstated. Instead of having to sue the university over it."

"Oh, I'd already decided to return Professor Sevenson's degree—and his job, if he wants it," Portner said. "We haven't hired anyone else, so the only loss is that we paid for their travel, and... Well, there's no difficulty there."

"Doesn't the board have to agree to it?" Fisk asked.

I'd not thought of that, having little knowledge of how universities function.

"The board will do what I tell them to, in this," Portner said. "Or they'll find themselves looking for a new Headman. I never liked that case against Professor Sevenson. The evidence seemed uncontestable, but there was something off... I didn't suspect Monica Dayless, though. At all. Do you really think poor Peebles' tragedy, and what his mother did because of it, could make people...overlook what Dayless did?"

"Depends on how it's played," Fisk said frankly. "If the university tries to make amends for being fooled by Hotchkiss, pleading for leniency toward Clerk Peebles..."

"You could even give her her job back, if she's declared unredeemed," I put in helpfully. "'Tis hard for someone outside the law to find a job."

My voice may have been too fervent, for he looked at me oddly.

"I'll admit, this is a bad time to be without our head clerk. And if people start flocking to withdraw their children it'll get worse. But wouldn't they be appalled, to find themselves dealing with the murderess herself when they did? And she did murder a man. Are we supposed to forget that?"

"She murdered the man who killed her son," said Fisk. "They may be appalled at first, but once they meet her she can explain. I can't promise they'll leave their kid in your school, but they'll understand why she did it. And they'll be more likely to understand, and forgive, than they will if they *don't* meet her."

"And Seymour Peebles was completely innocent," Portner mused. "I could spread the word about how the university is trying to right that wrong, by officially renaming the alphanumeric system after its true creator. The Peebles system. Academics all over the Realm would be talking about that."

"All evidence of what happened with the project was destroyed in the fire," Fisk pointed out. "You can't lie about it, but Professor Dayless can pay off her debt to the university in some non-professorial job."

Being forced to work in a menial capacity for the university where she'd once taught—likely for years— would probably be more painful for the professor than going unredeemed. But *she'd* deserved it, and I found I felt little sympathy for her. Unlike Clerk Peebles, even though she'd succeeded in her murderous intent, and Dayless had failed. And if extenuating circumstances made so much difference in my consideration of these two women, should I not bring them into my consideration of how Fisk had let Jack Bannister go free?

"Simply working off a legal debt, in the usual way, will attract a lot less public attention than a mother/ murderer saved from the gallows," Fisk went on. "And while the rest of the Realm is entranced by all this drama, everybody else just goes back to work. You quietly return the Heir's money—" The headman winced, but he nodded, too. "—and the case is closed. Hardly any fuss at all."

"I take it back," Portner said. "I'm glad you came by today. Though I'll have to think more about what Nancy Peebles did before I agree. And since you've given me so much to think about, on top of everything else I have to deal with, you can save my staff some trouble and carry my letter to Professor Sevenson."

He reached into a pile of papers that had been pushed aside and extracted it. The ink was still tacky, but it had been written before we arrived—so he might do the right thing by everyone else, as well.

I wanted to get this letter to Benton as soon as I could, and Fisk was eager to brag to Kathy about what he'd arranged. He deserved the bulk of the praise, though I'd assisted him ably. Just as last night, he'd so ably assisted me.

The truth was that we worked well together. It seemed a pity to dissolve such a team, even over a matter of principle. Particularly as it seemed that my former squire might become my brother-in-law. Assuming Father didn't kill him.

Benton was overjoyed by Portner's offer; full reinstatement of his degree, his job, and the university's official apology. He promptly departed to share it with the friends he'd discovered last night.

Kathy was more concerned with the greater tragedy.

"Will he really argue for Mistress Peebles to be declared unredeemed, instead of hanging? It seems a lot to ask."

"It's to his own advantage," said Fisk. "He's an ethical man, but I don't see there's any justice to be had from hanging the helpful Peebles. And since it's in the best interest of his university not to... With compassion and selfishness both on the side of letting her off? He'll do it."

"Captain Chaldon may argue for her as well," I added. "And most of the judicars are probably parents. 'Tis no light thing, to be unredeemed," I finished soberly. "But if she gets her old job back, surrounded by people who understand why she did it... She'll be all right."

"The alphanumeric system will become the Peebles system," Fisk said. "Her son's name, his genius, will be recognized as long as there are libraries. She'll be better than all right."

"And she has you to thank for that, squi— partner."

I had hoped to catch him off guard, but of course I didn't.

"Partner? I think I'm in charge. I was the one who persuaded Portner to let Benton off the hook. And I did it using Hotchkiss' murder as my lever, which makes that the 'pivotal' crime."

Even Kathy grimaced at that pun, and he grinned at her. But...

"Portner had written that letter before we got there. And 'twas Professor Dayless' cheating that got Benton into trouble in the first place. And anyway, I'm the one who *solved* Hotchkiss' murder. So if anyone is to be placed in charge, 'tis clearly—"

"But I'm the one who figured out what was going on with the project! It's not much use for your theory to be right, if you never solve the crime. So I—"

"Men!" Kathy stamped her foot, a habit she must have picked up at court, for I'd never seen her make such a pettish gesture. Or mayhap Fisk had driven her to it.

"Can't you simply admit you're a team?" she went on. "Why does anyone have to be in charge?"

Only a woman could ask something so silly. Fisk and I both stared.

"Someone has to be in charge," Fisk said. "Suppose we disagree about where to go? Or what to do? Someone has to make the final call."

It occurred to me that I'd stopped making 'final calls' some years ago...until I'd decided to go after Jack Banister, against Fisk's wishes. And nearly gotten both of us killed, though I hadn't been wrong. But I had been wrong to expect Fisk to fall in with a decision he didn't believe in. 'Twas time to admit it.

"We could discuss such matters," I said. "We could argue for our opinions, and work out where to go and what to do. That's how partners would handle decisions. Even serious disagreements."

Finally, I had caught him off guard. Fisk stared at me so skeptically I couldn't help but smile.

"I'm not saying 'twould be easy. But being a knight errant shouldn't be easy. I accept your challenge, Kathy."

I held out my hand to my new partner—knowing that in doing so, I was also accepting the challenge *of* Kathy, and how to get the two of them wed. Fisk knew it too, and he needed my help.

Just as I needed his.

"Well," he said. "I can't let your sister think *I'm* not up to a challenge."

His hand gripped mine, strong and sincere, sealing the bargain.

"Done!" Kathy's slim fingers fell atop our grip. "We'll all face that challenge...together."

The End

About the Author

Hilari Bell

HILARI BELL writes SF and fantasy for kids and teens. She's an ex-librarian, a job she took to feed her life-long addiction to books, and she lives in Denver with a family that changes shape periodically—currently it's her mother, her adult niece and their dog, Ginger. Her hobbies are board games and camping—particularly camping, because that's the only time she can get in enough reading. Though when it comes to reading, she says, there's no such thing as "enough."

HILARI BELL

Author of THE GOBLIN WOOD and THE FARSALA·TRILOGY

Lady's Pursuit

A
Knight AND Rogue
NOVEL

CHAPTER 1

Michael

A damsel in distress—
or at least, a damsel mysteriously vanished and quite
possibly in distress—is a most fitting a task for a knight
errant. But this damsel had gone missing from the High
Liege's court, and peril lurked there. Not for me, which
I would have shrugged off, but for those I held most
dear. Which is probably why I made the mistake of saying, "She's only been gone for about twelve hours—that
could be accounted for by a lame horse or a broken
wheel. Surely she's returned by now. I say we send this
fellow back, and wait for word that all's well."

The messenger, who'd ridden all night to deliver the
letter Kathy held, looked indignantly at me, but he
spoke to my sister. "The Heir's fair worried, Mistress.
He bid me get this letter to you as fast as I could ride."

Fisk, Kathy and I stood on the landing of my brother's lodging, which he'd begun to hint he'd like us to
vacate eventually—a request that seemed reasonable

given that the knocking of the messenger had roused us shortly after dawn. Kathy was clad in a well-worn dressing gown, her mouse-brown hair in a tousled braid down her back and rosy light reflecting in her spectacles as she read. There was no reason for Fisk to look at her as if she was the source of the sunrise...which increased my apprehension about going to court.

"Meg didn't take a coach," Kathy told me, still reading. "'Tis a bit incoherent—he must be really worried—but Rupert says she left on foot. She might have rented... Why does he think she'd rent a carriage to come to me? Or come to me at all, for that matter."

This was addressed to the messenger, who shrugged. "I'm to bring back your reply, if you don't return yourself, Mistress Katherine. And escort you if you need it."

"She doesn't need an escort," said Fisk. "We'll take her."

"I don't think..." I didn't think that was a good idea, but I couldn't reveal my reasons in front of the messenger.

"I do think," said Fisk. "And so does Kathy. You're out-voted... Partner."